T0113231

LIVING WITH MUSIC

RALPH ELLISON

LIVING WITH MUSIC

RALPH ELLISON'S JAZZ WRITINGS

Edited and with an Introduction by
Robert G. O'Meally

THE MODERN LIBRARY

NEW YORK

Ellison, Ralph.
Living with music: Ralph Ellison's jazz writings/
Ralph Ellison; edited by Robert G. O'Meally.
p.   cm.
ISBN 978-0-375-76023-5
1. Jazz—History and criticism.   I. O'Meally, Robert G.
II. Title.
ML3507 .E45 2001
781.65'09—dc21   00-068698

Contents

INTRODUCTION: JAZZ SHAPES

Robert G. O'Meally

Much in Negro life remains a mystery; perhaps the zoot suit conceals profound political meaning; perhaps the symmetrical frenzy of the Lindy-hop conceals clues to great potential power—if only Negro leaders would solve this riddle.[1]

—RALPH ELLISON (1943)

Without the presence of Negro American style, our [U.S.] jokes, tall tales, even our sports would be lacking in the sudden turns, shocks and swift changes of pace (all jazz-shaped) that serve to remind us that the world is ever unexplored, and that while a complete mastery of life is mere illusion, the real secret of the game is to make life swing.[2]

—RALPH ELLISON (1970)

My basic sense of artistic form is musical.... Basically my instinctive approach to writing is through *sound*.... What is the old phrase—"the planned dislocation of the senses"? That *is* the condition of fiction, I think. Here is where sound becomes sight and sight becomes sound.[3]

—RALPH ELLISON (1974)

Ralph Ellison (1914–1994) was a promising musician when, under the spell of certain nineteenth-century novelists and twentieth-century poets, he began to transform himself into a writer. Celebrated around the world as the author of *Invisible Man* (1952), Ellison is also known by jazz scholars and aficionados as an original and incisive music critic whose specialty was jazz. This volume gathers Ellison's essays on music, the first dating from 1954, when he contributed a piece to *The Saturday Review* on flamenco, the Spanish dance music that he believed, in its deepest meanings, had affinities with the blues. This volume also includes several interviews and letters as well as fiction—including excerpts from *Invisible Man* and *Juneteenth*, and some pieces never heretofore published in book form.

Taken together, these varied musical writings are among the most eloquent works ever written about jazz. Further, they constitute an elegant and insightful statement on the purposes of art and artist, especially in the United States of the middle to late twentieth century, and of living with music (still the only alternative, as Ellison says in the title essay, to dying with noise).[4]

In assessing Ellison's theory of jazz's meanings, it is vital to consider the following formative aspects of his experience: (1) his religious family, in which the language and rituals of the church were part of everyday life; (2) his perspective as a trumpeter who had been an avid student of classical music and who was immersed, in his hometown of Oklahoma City and then in New York, in jazz "as a total way of life"; (3) his preference, as a southwesterner who came of age in the 1930s, for big-band jazz that was danceably hard-swinging and steeped in the blues; (4) his explorations, in the 1930s, of the American Communist Party, from which he later turned away significantly; (5) his dedication, as a Negro American "enlisted for life," as he once put it, in the struggle for freedom and justice (especially considering the extraordinary cultural influence of blacks in the United States); (6) his readings of modern criticism and particularly of the Cambridge Ritualist scholar/critics, tightly linked with the rise of anthropology and the conviction that art evolves from rituals that celebrate the victory of day over night, spring over winter, life over death, heroes over dragons (for Ellison, the jazz artist is a prototypical American, cut in the hero's mold); and, perhaps above all, (7) his dislike of all schematic intellectual constructs, however comprehensive their data or claims, that failed to allow for the unscheduled entrance of the individual of vision and discipline—the Charlie Christian in the tenement, the *hero*.[5]

———

In 1973, just before Ellison gave a talk at Harvard University as part of a panel on Alain Locke and the Harlem Renaissance,[6] I spoke with him at the back of Boylston Hall. I posed what he likely heard as a naïve question: "Don't you think the Harlem Renaissance failed because we failed to create institutions to preserve our gains?" (Given that I was a black student in a dashiki, he probably also took this to be blankly black-nationalistic.) He drew on his cigar and calmly told me: "No." Just before being led toward the stage, he paused to look at me with steely eyes: "We *do* have institutions," he said. "We have the Constitution and the Bill of Rights. *And we have jazz*."

At the time, I found this declaration utterly bewildering. How was jazz an institution? If it was some sort of institution-without-walls, what were its meanings? And how did it relate to U.S. cornerstone documents—which in those days were not part of the black freedom struggle as I knew it? (*"We"* have the Bill of Rights? Which "we" was he talking about?) How did this idea of music-as-institution link the multifaceted Harlem Renaissance with the Black Arts Movement of the 1960s and 1970s? What, in short, was the relation between what Ellison meant by jazz and my dashiki?

And how—speaking now from the standpoint of the new millennium, with places such as Columbia and Harvard, Lincoln Center, Carnegie Hall, and the Smithsonian formally studying and presenting the music—does jazz function as an institution today? It seems clear that we have gained much from canonizing the music, establishing it in colleges and museums, giving it grants, and so on. What have we lost? And how is this new activity political?

More than a quarter century after that stunning encounter, I am still reaching for answers to these questions and their cousins. Some of the answers are in this book. For Ellison, I think, jazz was a classic expression of U.S. vernacular music (i.e., a brash and freewheeling mélange that disdains the artistic categories of "high" and "low") that speaks eloquently to the United States's predicament as a still-forming nation, black, white, brown, and beige, that is still "in a state of relative nakedness," as he once put it. "But this nakedness allows for a great degree of personal improvisation, and with the least hindrance from traditional social forms, rituals, manners, etc."[7] Ellison's jazz celebrates the capacity to improvise in an uncharted field, an art that is hearty with African-American (that is, American) voices, stories, and values. This is potent music that, in the hands of Louis Armstrong, Duke Ellington, and others, embodies democratic communication at its finest: an artistic and implicitly political "gesture," in Ellison's ringing phrase, "toward perfection."

With its insistence on individuality of sound (something not sought in symphony players) and on the capacity to swing with and against one's fellow players; its accents on improvisation and readiness for changes; and its connections with the comedy lanced by tragedy that defines the blues, jazz is a musical language that reminds us what and where we are as U.S. citizens, dashiki or no dashiki. (I realize now that in those days such a shirt was as American as apple pie.)

Jazz is an institution in the sense of that word's Latin root, *statuere:* "to put in place" or "to stand," as in *statue* and *statute.* For Ellison, jazz stands for values and strategies of living that have served as unseen but vital sources of strength for Americans who, whether at the nation's Savoy Ballrooms, at house parties, or at breakfast barbecues, celebrate themselves as unself-conscious heirs to a democracy, which, scarred and battered as it is, remains our "home in the world, which is called love."[8]

———

In interviews and speeches, Ellison often recounted his discovery, as a music major at Tuskegee Institute, of T. S. Eliot's *The Waste Land* and the shock of recognition that charged him forever. "There was nothing to do but look up the references in the footnotes to the poem," he says, "and thus began my conscious education in literature."[9] For present purposes, it is crucial to note that Ellison repeatedly relates this epiphanic literary discovery to jazz—specifically to the "rowdy poetic flights" of Louis Armstrong. In 1962, for example, Ellison was advising: "Consider that at least as early as T. S. Eliot's creation of a new aesthetic for poetry through the artful juxtapositioning of earlier styles, Louis Armstrong, way down the river in New Orleans, was working out a similar technique for jazz."[10]

Mysterious in its "discontinuities, its changes of pace and its hidden system of organization," Eliot's poetry struck Ellison as playfully jazzlike in its uses of multiple voices and of found-object art. It recalled Armstrong's nonchalant quotations of Verdi, Broadway ballads, and "The Hoochie-Coochie Song" within the frame of a single improvised solo. For understanding Ellison's aesthetics, it is equally important to remember that *The Waste Land* evoked a landscape that was, as the poem's footnotes spelled out, readable in terms of myth, ritual, and heroic quest. Thus did that poem lead young Ellison to Jessie Weston's *From Ritual to Romance* and then to Jane Ellen Harrison, Gilbert Murray, and Sir James Frazer—prime movers in the Cambridge Ritualist school. Ellison went on to discover Joseph Campbell, Kenneth Burke, Stanley Edgar Hyman, Richard Slotkin, and other critics who have insisted that myth and ritual provide ways of understanding the underlying patterns of history and art. Some of Ellison's discoveries along these lines were encouraged by Albert Murray, his Tuskegee schoolmate and friend who in his M.A. thesis (1949) applied Kenneth Burke's "dramatistic" critical terms to T. S. Eliot's poetry.

For Ellison, then, jazz can be a complexly functional drama that serves its makers and its hearers with sustaining images and values ("statutes") by which to live. Good-time-rolling music that it often is, jazz teaches us how to confront modern life's shifting cultural terrain and thus provides what Burke calls "equipment for living." Indeed, Ellison saw the jazz artists as having a high calling and as candidates for community leadership, heroes, and heroes-in-training. (This is why, in *Invisible Man* and *Juneteenth*, both sustained studies of national leadership, blues and jazz players figure so prominently as guides.)

Jazz players were important role models for young Ellison and his friends. In a passage aimed at social scientists who might overstate the plight of fatherless black boys, Ellison describes the cultural heroism of Duke Ellington and his band:

> They were news from the great wide world, an example and a goal; and I wish that all those who write so knowledgeably of Negro boys having no masculine figures with whom to identify would consider the long national and international career of Ellington and his band, the thousands of one-night stands played in the black communities of this nation. Where in the white community, in *any* white community, could there have been found images, examples such as these? Who were so

worldly, who so elegant, who so mockingly creative?
Who so skilled at their given trade and who treated the
social limitations placed in their path with greater disdain? . . . For us, Duke was a culture hero, a musical magician who worked his powers through his mastery of
form, nuance, and style, a charismatic figure whose personality influenced even those who had no immediate
concern with the art of jazz.[11]

For Ellison, Louis Armstrong was another such larger-
than-life role model with whom to identify. Like Charlie
Christian, Armstrong, born in poverty, was proof that you
never knew where a genius was going to come from.[12] Here
was a clear case of the artist as creator of a Yeatsian persona
or "second self": "theatrical, consciously dramatic . . . wearing a mask."[13] Armstrong, the artist working behind the entertainer's smile, delighted Ellison with his subtlety and
doubleness—qualities he termed, in his first novel, "invisibility." In a letter of 1957 to Albert Murray, Ellison says,

> Here, way late, I've discovered Louis singing Mack
> the Knife. Shakespeare invented Caliban, or changed
> himself into him—Who the hell dreamed up Louie?
> Some of the bop boys consider him Caliban but if he is
> he's a mask for a lyric poet who is much greater than
> most now writing. . . . Man and mask, sophistication and
> taste hiding behind clowning and crude manners—the
> American joke, man.[14]

In 1976, Ellison spoke to interviewers about Armstrong's
trumpet playing: "If Louis Armstrong's meditations on the
'Potato Head Blues' aren't marked by elegance," he said,
"then the term is too inelegant to name the fastidious refinement, the mastery of nuance, the tasteful domination of
melody, rhythm, sounding brass and tinkling cymbal which
marked his style."[15]

In the short story "A Coupla Scalped Indians" (1956), Ellison's characters, black boys at puberty, model themselves after jazz players performing in the story's distance.[16] The youngsters interpret the jazz horns as voices of experience "trading twelves" (not only twelve-bar-blues exchanges but solos that evoke the highly competitive African-American verbal dances of derision called the dirty dozens) that offer them strategies for crossing over into manhood within the hostile territory of white America. The trombone "sounds like he's playing the dozens with the whole wide world," one boy says. And the trumpet speaks as a "soldier" who is "slipping 'em in the twelves and choosing 'em, all at the same time. Talking 'bout they mamas and offering to fight 'em. Now he ain't like that ole clarinet; clarinet so sweet-talking he just *eases* you in the dozens." Satirical, subversive, now bluntly warlike, now secretly so, jazz here suggests ways to confront chaos and also hints at the mysteries of adult sexuality and reproduction, of mamas "strictly without" drawers, as one boy hears the trombone to say. That the youngsters are on their way to a carnival connects them not just with Boy Scouts and the dozens-y blues but also with "Indians" as well as the carnival traditions of New Orleans and many other black Atlantic locales where carnival is a rite of spring.

Not a famous musician like Ellington or Armstrong (or a musical trader of twelves), Mrs. Zelia N. Breaux nonetheless also played the part of heroic role model in Ellison's life. Architect and superintendent of the extensive and rigorous music program in the black school system of Oklahoma City, the multi-instrumentalist Breaux insisted on strictly the classics by day. By night, however, she was the owner/operator of the Ira Aldridge Theater, where Duke and Louis reigned in front of the footlights, along with Bessie Smith, Ida Cox, Jimmy Rushing, and the Blue Devils as creators and perpetuators of the shouts, smears, and muted rhapsodies that characterize the blues and jazz. Thus was Breaux, whom Ellison revered as "a surrogate mother," a highly responsible and effective bearer of American culture in all its Duke-ish doubleness and Louisiana "invisibility." Just as important for Ellison, the musician who eventually wanted to write novels, Breaux and the other players he encountered as a boy taught by example that, just as it took more than a broken heart to play the blues, becoming a writer of fiction (in which, again, the European "classic" could be combined with local speech and song) is a matter of practice and more practice and *more practice.*

Indeed—again in light of Ellison's vision of the artist as hero—the very first monster blocking the path of those hoping to become musicians or writers is the stubborn, burly one of *technique,* one of the key terms in the Ellison aesthetic lexicon. Avoiding the classicist's traditional bias in favor of defining technique as *classical* training, nothing else, Ellison sees it as the artist's "very stern discipline" and concentrated study not just of an art form but also of the local and national culture, the truths of which the artist would reveal. "Perhaps the zoot suit conceals profound political meaning; perhaps the symmetrical frenzy of the Lindy-hop conceals clues to great potential power."

For Ellison, the ideal artist is not merely a recorder of deeds but a visionary, a creator of brave new worlds—one whose technical tools and weapons must be sharp and ever at the ready. In fascinatingly opposed images, Ellison describes the artist's quest for technique as a "fight to achieve reality" by holding fast to the mercurial Proteus of American experience;[17] and elsewhere, using a homelier figure of speech, Ellison likens the achievement of technique to a struggle to unstick oneself from a Tar Baby:

> Let Tar Baby, that enigmatic figure from Negro folklore, stand for the world. He leans, black and gleaming,

against the wall of life utterly noncommittal under our scrutiny, our questioning, starkly unmoving before our naïve attempts at intimidation. Then we touch him playfully and before we can say *Sonny Liston!* we find ourselves stuck. Our playful investigations become a labor, a fearful struggle, an *agon*. Slowly we perceive that our task is to learn the proper way of freeing ourselves, to develop technique.[18]

This idea of developing artistic technique as a step toward freedom is echoed in *Invisible Man*. That novel's main character, bumblingly in quest of his direction as a community leader, hears—quite significantly between the beams of Louis Armstrong's music—a woman who wails about freedom and unfreedom. He asks: "Old woman, what is this freedom you love so well?" "I done forgot, son," she says. "First I think it's one thing, then I think it's another. It gits my head to spinning. *I guess now it ain't nothing but knowing how to say what I got up in my head.*"[19] This identification of artistic know-how with aesthetic and psychic freedom has deep historical significance for blacks (and thus, again, for all of us) in America. "For the art," Ellison says in his review of LeRoi Jones's *Blues People* (1964), "the blues, the spirituals, the jazz, the dance—was what we had in place of freedom." And "technique was then, as today," he went on, "the key to creative freedom."[20] Had the narrator of *Invisible Man* only listened properly to the hard-bought words of the woman in the Prologue or to Trueblood or the blues-singing tall-tale talker who calls himself Peter Wheatstraw, he would have taken a seven-league stride toward freedom and the leadership he hoped to offer.

For the player of jazz, the quest for technical mastery has not (at least until recent years, when jazz began to be taught in grade schools and colleges) been a matter of assigned homework as such but of apprenticeships under master players and of jousting rites of passage toward (heroic) individuality and adulthood. In 1959, Ellison wrote an eloquent statement about the jam session as the jazz player's "true academy":

> Here it is more meaningful to speak not of courses of study, of grades and degrees, but of apprenticeship, ordeals, initiation ceremonies, of rebirth. For after the jazzman has learned the fundamentals of his instrument and the traditional techniques of jazz—the intonations, the mute work, manipulation of timbre, the body of traditional styles—he must then "find himself," must be reborn, must find, as it were, his soul. All this through achieving that subtle identification between his instrument and his deepest drives which will allow him to express his own unique ideas and his own unique voice. He must achieve, in short, his self-determined identity.[21]

Unlike the classical player, the jazz artist must achieve a technique that uncovers the self, that answers the question that Ellison says is *the* question of American art: who am I?[22]

Having slain the dragons (or at least the first wave of dragons) of technique and self-discovery, Ellison's hopeful jazz artist is ready to move toward the role as leader of community, or of, as Ellison repeatedly says, *communal* rites. Beyond the question of role modeling, the jazz artist leads a ritual celebration of the American self and group, a liberal and lusty extension of the American slave's will to self-assertion and freedom against a world of violent denials. As such, jazz comprises an audacious lifting of the personal and, indeed, of the group's (including, Ellison would say, the national) voice: the un-Europeanized equivalent in music to black storytelling sessions like the one invoked in a letter to Albert Murray shortly after Ellison had completed *Invisible*

Man. In rollicking off-the-record prose that characterizes many of these letters, Ellison reported that his editor was

> having a time deciding what kind of novel it is, and I can't help him. For me it's just a big fat ole Negro lie, meant to be told during cotton picking time over a water bucket full of corn [whiskey], with dipper passing back and forth at a good fast clip so that no one, not even the narrator himself, will realize how utterly preposterous the lie actually is.[23]

Such "lies" (in-group stories with a point), said Ellison in 1967,

> tell what Negro experience really is. We back away from the chaos of experience and from ourselves, and we depict the humor as well as the horror of our living. We project Negro life in a metaphysical perspective, and we have seen it with a complexity of vision that seldom gets into our writing.[24]

Unproctored by the thou-shalt-nots of the academy, jazz at its best is a twice-told freedom song that is thick with ritual repetition, with history retained, critiqued, and transferred with gusto and a dance affirming a place and a people; jazz is a bodacious trading of fours and eights and twelves, "just a big fat ole Negro lie."

Not only are jazz artists singers of the self and historians of levels of American experience not recorded otherwise, but as leaders of the Saturday-night public dance they are joy-bell ringers, good-time-rolling "stewards of our vaunted American optimism." Even on this upbeat side of Ellison's slate of jazz's deeper purposes, though, the music offers more than sunny entertainment. His jazz is a complex comedy in which (again, as in Armstrong and Eliot) gathered fragments of past art are turned, reverently and irreverently, into bluesy style and statement. In the revelry of Saturday night, jazz makers and their audience of dancers engage in a musical parody that, Ellison observes in relation to Duke Ellington's sly habits of spoken and musical expression, could be

> as mocking of our double standards, hypocrisies, and pretensions as the dancing of those slaves who, looking through the windows of a plantation manor house from the yard, imitated the steps so gravely performed by the masters within and then added to them their own special flair, burlesquing the white folks and then going on to force the steps into a choreography uniquely their own. The whites, looking out at the activity in the yard, thought they were being flattered by imitation and were amused by the incongruity of tattered blacks dancing courtly steps, while missing completely the fact that before their eyes a European cultural form was becoming Americanized, undergoing a metamorphosis through the mocking activity of a people partially sprung from Africa. So, blissfully unaware, the whites laughed while the blacks danced out their mocking reply.[25]

Here then is jazz as a rippling, subversive comic art, deflating self and others in a cakewalking communal celebration and bash.

Here, too, was black laughter, as if from the old South's tall tales of Negroes laughing with their heads stuck down in "laughing-barrels" (set up to free public spaces of black hilarity). And the Negro in the barrel, Ellison writes, "was apt to double up with a second gale of laughter . . . triggered, apparently, by his own mental image of himself laughing at himself." Whatever the cause of all this black mirth, "it was most disturbing to a white observer." If whites looking on joined in "the black merriment issuing from the laughing barrels," Ellison says, the whites' laughter "meant that somehow the Negro in the barrel had them *over* a barrel."[26]

On the comic side, too, jazz is an art of understatement, implying, as Ellison has said of the blues, "far more than they state outright."[27] In the blues's comical recitation of mishaps, part of what is implied is a warning that, like Peter Wheatstraw in *Invisible Man,* you may have run into luck that has "feet like a monkey.... Legs like a maaad bulldog."[28] Such cautionary blue notes inoculate Saturday nighters against the inevitable turns for the worse that bedevil a new country, however bright its promise. All of which, says Albert Murray in *Stomping the Blues,* connects the music to a rite of purification—ritually confronting and then swinging and jitterbugging the misery blues to the floor.[29] Murray and Ellison, for whom there can be no jazz without a blues foundation, describe these forms of music as part and parcel of ceremonial rites (comic in shape) of courtship and fertility: bringing men and women face-to-face to keep the human race alive and (as the musicians say) *kicking.*

Where Ellison and Murray part company—and this is very important for those who tend to see them in precisely the same frame—has to do with Ellison's unwavering insistence that issues of racial and national power politics are boldly stitched into the fabric of the music itself. This is especially evident in Ellison's detection of deeply destructive tragic elements in the culture out of which the music emerges. For instance, again in mythic terms, Ellison writes of Southern blacks relocated in the North as an exiled blues people whose history

> reads like the legend of some tragic people out of mythology, a people who aspired to escape from its own unhappy homeland to the apparent peace of a distant mountain, but who, in migrating, made some fatal error of judgment and fell into a great chasm of mazelike passages that promise ever to lead to the mountain but ever end against a wall.[30]

To underscore this tragic sense of black life,[31] Ellison presents, in fiction and in essays, many reflections "on being the target of racism" (the title of a late essay): lynchings in the South (as well as less direct stringings-up, northern-style), warnings to stay away from the voting booths, and other acts of race hatred and violence. Ellison's most devastating image in this vein is one he frequently evoked of Tulsa, Oklahoma, through which the Ellison family passed en route to Gary, Indiana, when he was a boy. More than fifty years later, Ellison recalled the trip:

> On our way North we stopped in Tulsa to see an older cousin who had a fine brick home in the prosperous Negro community of Greenwood. But shortly after we arrived in Gary, as luck would have it—and luck is always ambiguous and ambivalent—there was a depression in steel, so it was my fate to have been brought back through Tulsa and see that Greenwood had been devastated and all but destroyed by bomb and fire in that riot of 1921.[32]

For Ellison, jazz's radiant sense of possibility and transcendence is always set against "our awareness of limitation (dramatized so brutally in the Tulsa riot of 1921)."[33] Painful experiences, he wrote in 1958, "go into the forging of a true singer of the blues."[34] Thus are black Americans not only the stewards of optimism (for if blacks can be hopeful about the way the American wheel turns, who can dare to frown?) but also the stewards of tragic memory and of the blues. In 1966, Ellison told a group at Langston University what he meant by the blues as a frame of mind:

> I refer not simply to the song form, but to a basic and complex attitude toward experience. It is an attitude toward life which looks pretty coldly and realistically at the human predicament, and which expresses the individual's insistence upon enduring in face of his limita-

tions, and which is in itself a kind of triumph over self and circumstance.... I can only say that there is a part of my temperament which finds its expression in this crazy mixture of modes.[35]

This bluesy attitude pervades everything that Ellison writes. In *Invisible Man,* the farmer Trueblood's crime of incest sows horror and chaos and marks him as a man living a blues that only the "crazy mixture of modes" in the blues themselves can render tolerable. Singing a desperate gospel-tinged blues ("I don't know what it was," the farmer says, "some kinda church song, I guess.... I sings me some blues that night ain't never been sang before"), Trueblood finally is able to achieve sufficient perspective on his crime to go back home and continue living in the thick of the misery he has caused.[36] Trueblood gains perspective from the blues as he also learns the truth of the book's protagonist's assertion upon hearing Armstrong's "Black and Blue": "This familiar music had demanded action."[37]

True to Ellison's sense of the blues as healing music, Trueblood's victory over circumstance is temporary, conditional, and vexed. It is a product of "antagonistic cooperation," a key term for Ellison and Murray that indicates painful but productive engagement with the stubborn fact that life is a low-down dirty deal.[38] This agonizing confrontation with the hard facts of the blues is at the heart of Ellison's sense of the music as tragic and heroic. So is the will to remain optimistic enough to take productive action within the social sphere of the blues. "Trouble, trouble / I've had it all my days," proclaims Jimmy Rushing, whose voice, Ellison says, sounds with a "rock-bottom sense of reality, coupled with our sense of the possibility of rising above it."[39]

The Trueblood scene's "some kinda church song" blues is very significant in terms of comedy and tragedy, of spiritual concerns at the hard-rock core of the blues. In "Flamenco," Ellison praises the bluesy, spiritual Spanish music not for its invocation of invisible ghosts but for its acceptance of the linkage of human urges and sufferings and the hope of continuity:

> Perhaps what attracts us most to flamenco, as it does to the blues, is the note of unillusioned affirmation of humanity which it embodies. The gypsies, like the slaves, are an outcast though undefeated people who have never lost their awareness of the physical source of man's most spiritual moments; even their Christ is a man of flesh and bone who suffered and bled before his apotheosis. In its more worldly phases the flamenco voice resembles the blues voice, which mocks the despair stated explicitly in the lyric, and it expresses the great human joke directed against the universe, that joke which is the secret of all folklore and myth: that though we be dismembered daily we shall always rise up again.[40]

In *Juneteenth*, Bliss's repeated cry, "Father, Why Hast Thou Forsaken Me?!" may be heard as an exalted shouting of the down-home blues—a plea for meaning in a world that has exploded. Likewise, the "How Long Blues" (the particular blues by Leroy Carr that Ellison often mentions) echoes the "How long, O Lord" of the Bible and sounds, for all its secularity, an urgent yearning for wholeness, meaning, and inner peace. Certainly it is as if for Ellison the public dance became the ritual ground that substituted for much of what he had known as a church boy in Oklahoma City. "If there were a choir here," Ellison told a Philadelphia crowd in 1971, "I would say let us sing 'Let Us Break Bread Together.' I am not particularly religious," he went on, "but I am claimed by music."[41]

Tightly linked to the religious dimensions of the music is the emphasis, throughout the Ellison canon, on the palpable, *physical* dimensions of the blues/jazz ritual. Riding the edge of nostalgia, Ellison remembers the public jazz dance of his youth as a site where women and men played instruments that became extensions of their mouths and hands and fingers. Armstrong, for instance, "emphasizes the physicality of his music with sweat, spittle and facial contortions; he performs the magical feat of making romantic melody issue from a throat of gravel; and some few years ago was recommending to all and sundry his personal physic, 'Pluto Water,' as a purging way to health, happiness and international peace."[42] This is a music of bodies touching and sweating, bodies in motion, with "no 'squares' sitting around just to be entertained."[43]

For Ellison, the jazz dance's combination of instrumentalist, singer, and dancer formed an artistic and communal triumvirate.[44] Ellison recalls "Deep Second," Oklahoma City's most famous jazz street, and Rushing's role "as official floor manager or master-of-the-dance at Slaughter's Hall, the leader of a public rite." It was a rocking scene for dancers only, and

> Jimmy danced them all, gliding before the crowd over the polished floor, sometimes with a girl, sometimes with a huge megaphone held chest-high before him as he swayed. . . . It was when Jimmy's voice began to soar with the spirit of the blues that the dancers—and the musicians—achieved that feeling of communion which was the true meaning of the public jazz dance. The blues, the singer, the band and the dancers formed the vital whole of jazz as an institutional form, and even today neither part is quite complete without the rest. The thinness of much of so-called "modern jazz" is especially reflective of this loss of wholeness, and it is quite possible that Rushing retains his vitality simply because he has kept close to the small Negro public dance.[45]

Note here Ellison's warning that when it comes to determining whether or not jazz's magic is working, Savoy

Ballroom—seasoned dancers are more reliable than music critics. "For the jazz artist," says Ellison, "there is some insurance in continuing to play for dance audiences, for here the criticism is unspoiled by status-directed theories; Negroes simply won't accept shoddy dance music, so the artist has a vital criticism danced out in the ritual of the dance."[46]

Ellison's jazz involves the physical sensation of human bodies moving through softly lit halls and stages—the *places* of jazz. Throughout his fiction and essays, the assertions that "geography is fate" (Heraclitus' maxim) and that "scene is motive" (one of Kenneth Burke's terms in *A Rhetoric of Motives*) are frequently conjured. The dance floor and stages of Harlem's Savoy Ballroom were the sites of "one of our great cultural institutions," he told a Senate committee in 1966.[47] And in the music itself were imbedded the sounds of places associated with the history of jazz and its makers: "animal cries, train whistles, and the loneliness of night" along with juke-house noises, the husky voices of storytellers and preachers alike. Ellison remembers hearing Rushing's voice carrying from Slaughter's Hall to where, as a boy, he lay in bed, listening:

> Heard thus, across the dark blocks lined with locust trees, through the night throbbing with the natural aural imagery of the blues, with high-balling trains, departing bells, lonesome guitar chords simmering up from a shack in the alley, it was easy to imagine the voice as setting the pattern to which the instruments of the Blue Devils Orchestra and all the random sounds of night arose, affirming, as it were, some ideal native to the time and to the land.[48]

In this southwestern music, Ellison heard a scratchy but lyrical optimism not typical of the Deep South's hard grit- and gravel-textured blues. He also detected there a frontier assertiveness (associated, again, with tragic awareness): a will to investigate limits and then to push steadily against them. In connection with this blues-based southwestern jazz, Ellison often points out that key civil-rights actions were first taken in this part of the country. "I'm going to the nation / Goin' to the territor' "[49]—blues lines that gave Ellison's second collection of essays its title—suggests the Indian Nation/Oklahoma Territory as a freer place, a mythic land of promise, a country of the blues.

With all this in mind, and not forgetting that many in Ellison's generation lost interest in jazz after the big-band era, one may easily see why Ellison grew impatient with the beboppers of the 1940s. In an essay of 1948 titled "Harlem Is Nowhere," Ellison explains the cultural disintegration of Southern blacks in the cauldron of the urban North as a failure of the immigrants to transport their institutions from back home. Even the jazz of the North proves inadequate: "The lyrical ritual elements of folk jazz," he writes, "have given way to the near-themeless technical virtuosity of bebop, a further triumph of technology over humanism."[50] Where the music of sixteen and more musicians swinging behind Rushing and Bennie Moten evoked for Ellison the romance and derring-do of the frontier, bebop was to him the frantic shriek of a lost, big-citified people whose home is "nowhere."

Ellison's strong distaste for bebop—so evident in the letters to Albert Murray published as *Trading Twelves*—stems from the disconnection of the music from the public dance floor (yes, some dancers, notably rhythm tap dances, could "bop" to the new music, but still the period of the Savoy Ballrooms and Slaughter's Halls was fading quickly). This left the music without its vital physical immediacy and prey to what Ellison felt was a decadent intellectualism. Speaking of clubs like New York's Village Gate, with no dancing allowed and little singing, and of bop music played there, he said: "The world evoked by this music is a different world.... The music here is more abstract. It has become separated from the ritual form of the dance, and the vocal definitions once supplied by song are missing. More important, the response of its audience is more intellectual. Indeed, it is *mainly* intellectual and thus its participation is less immediate."[51]

And consider the metaphors of physicality (and especially of maleness) that Ellison often used to criticize the bebop players. Bop suffered from tonal "thinness"—in Charlie Parker's case, "vibratoless . . . ineffectuality, as though he could never quite make it."[52] Many of these boppers "were even of a different physical build," Ellison writes. "Often they were quiet and of a reserve which contrasted sharply with the exuberant and outgoing lyricism of the older men."[53] Such players were "academic" reciters of dry exercises, with little to do with the robust world of Saturday night. It is telling that when (in "Golden Age, Time Past") Ellison goes in search of bebop, all he finds is a relic and a rumor nearly faded away.[54]

Against this pattern of decline, certain heroic players continue on. If bebop was a false direction of the music, for Ellison it came and then it faded. (Though now, ironically, bop is canonized as the standard by those who find the subsequent wave of jazz to be "overly technical," "disconnected," and "decadent.") Through it all, from the Ellisonian perspective Ellington keeps swinging, and so does Armstrong. With southwesterners Jimmy Rushing, Charlie Christian, and Hot Lips Page, those two reign as the major heroes of this collection.

Indeed, Armstrong, whose name appears more than any other in these pages, may be regarded as the supreme hero, both of *Invisible Man* and of the essays. Ellison, the former trumpet player, defends that great trumpeter/singer against charges of Uncle Tomming and of trivializing the music by excessive clowning. With his sense of jazz as ritual drama—the sound of continuity, transcendent communication, and superior democracy—he defends Armstrong's determination to keep the music deeply meaningful and swinging. Ellison also realizes that Armstrong's clowning was no more a case of selling out than were Dizzy Gillespie's stage antics or even Miles Davis's performances of indifference.[55] All were part of the show and fraught, Ellison reminds us, with the double and triple entendres of Negro-American humor.

It remains to be added that Ellison did not merely write *about* music and musicians as models for heroic adulthood and artistic commitment; music itself became a model for him as a writer. As one used to the discipline of practicing scales and holding long notes to develop tone and control, he studied the styles of his favorite writers and even copied certain stories by Hemingway by hand, to grasp the feeling of literary creation. In 1955, his wife, Fanny, whispered to a group of students: "When he can't find the words at the typewriter, he goes upstairs and plays the trumpet."[56]

In "A Coupla Scalped Indians," not only does this music translate into verbal messages; formally, too, the descriptions of the characters, their talk, and thoughts are all rendered in language that is highly rhythmical and otherwise full of music. One kid's voice "grumbled on like a trombone with a big, fat, pot-shaped mute stuck in it." As the narrator recalls the dreaded Mackie, he, too, slips into a hornlike voice, as if trying to conjure and then ward off her troubling spirit:

> *Ho' Aunt Mackie, talker-with-spirits* [the narrator says to himself], *prophetess-of-disaster, odd-dweller-alone in a riverside shack surrounded by sunflowers, morning-glories, and strange magical weeds* (Yao, as Buster, during our Indian phase, would have put it, Yao!); *Old Aunt Mackie, wizen-faced walker-with-a-stick, shrill-voiced ranter in the night,*

*round-eyed malicious one, given to dramatic trances and fiery
flights of rage; Aunt Mackie, preacher of wild sermons on the
busy streets of the town, hot-voiced chaser of children, snuff-
dipper, visionary; wearer of greasy headrags, wrinkled gingham
aprons, and old men's shoes; Aunt Mackie, nobody's sister but still
Aunt Mackie to us all* (Ho, Yao!); *teller of fortunes, concocter of
powerful, body-rending spells* (Yah, Yao!); *Aunt Mackie, the remote one though always seen about us; night-consulted adviser to
farmers on crops and cattle* (Yao!); *herb-healer, root-doctor, and
town-confounding oracle to wildcat drillers seeking oil in the
earth*—(Yaaaah-Ho!).[57]

"Cadillac Flambé" (1973)[58] presents a jazz bassist who,
near Washington, D.C., decides on the mock sacrifice of a
convertible god-car in an outrageous act that also wards off
those who "put the *Indian* sign on this town a long time ago."
The story dwells in the realm of ritual but also seems to
refer to the black urban riots of its era and perhaps to the
revolutionary blasting and burning of new music performed
by such players as Ornette Coleman and Cecil Taylor. Both
stories evoke the cadences of jazz in their language.

So does their forerunner, *Invisible Man,* as its protagonist
recalls his days as a student speaker in the college chapel:
"Directing my voice at the highest beams and farthest
rafters, ringing them, the accents staccato upon the ridge-
pole and echoing back with a tinkling." He remembers his
jazzlike thoughts as he stood at the podium, improvising his
speech: *"Ha! to the gray-haired matron in the final row. Ha! Miss
Susie, Miss Susie Gresham, back there looking at that co-ed smiling at
that he-ed—listen to me, the bungling bugler of words, imitating the
trumpet and the trombone's timbre, playing thematic variations like a
baritone horn."*[59] Later, the young man delivers a funeral sermon that pours out as an improvised solo, one which, in its
rhythmical riffing, seems scored for Louis Armstrong–style
trumpet.

The work collected in *Living with Music* makes the point that just as music can influence a writer's training and aesthetic sensibilities (see "Richard Wright's Blues" for Ellison's famous description of *Black Boy* as a book based on the blues), it can have an impact on other arts as well. Like the narrator of *Invisible Man*, visual artists not only hear the music; they *see* it as well. The painter Romare Bearden, says Ellison, works out of a palette of blues and jazz. In his paintings,

> . . . the poetry of the blues is projected through synthetic forms which visually are in themselves tragicomic and eloquently poetic. A harsh poetry this, but poetry nevertheless, with the nostalgic imagery of the blues conceived as visual form, image, pattern and symbol— including the familiar trains (evoking partings and reconciliations) and the conjure women (who appear in these works with the ubiquity of the witches who haunt the drawing of Goya) who evoke the abiding mystery of the enigmatic women who people the blues. Here too are renderings of those rituals of rebirth and dying, of baptism and sorcery which give ceremonial continuity to the Negro American community.[60]

As a novelist, Ellison sees the tragicomic storyline in the music; as a former musician, he hears the blues sounding through fiction and other forms of expression. Most emphatically, he detects a blues-based jazz element at the core of twentieth-century American culture, in which styles of dancing, speaking, dressing, and playing sports may be termed, in Ellison's phrase, "jazz-shaped." These shapes suggest a tragicomic life-pulse that Ellison believes to be definitively American: a Deep Second dance that knows that the black night of the blues may yet yield, if not a resurrection, then at least an institution on which we all may depend.

1. "Editorial Comment," *Negro Quarterly,* winter 1943, p. 300.

2. *The Collected Essays of Ralph Ellison,* ed. John F. Callahan (New York: Random House, 1995), pp. 797–98.

3. Ibid.

4. From "Living with Music," pp. 3–14, below.

5. For more on Ellison's life and art, see Robert G. O'Meally, *Craft of Ralph Ellison* (Cambridge, Mass.: Harvard University Press, 1980).

6. For the fullest account of this panel, see "The Alain L. Locke Symposium," *Harvard Advocate,* spring 1974, pp. 9–29.

7. "A Conversation with Ralph Ellison," transcript of a talk given at Langston University, Oklahoma, 1966.

8. *Collected Essays,* p. 154.

9. Ibid., p. 203.

10. From "On Bird, Bird-Watching and Jazz," p. 65, below.

11. From "Homage to Duke Ellington on His Birthday," p. 77, below.

12. See "What These Children Are Like" (1963), in *Collected Essays,* pp. 542–51.

13. Directly and indirectly, in essays and in fiction, Ellison refers frequently to W. B. Yeats's *Per Amica Silentia Lunae* (London: Macmillan, 1918), esp. pp. 25–28.

14. From *Trading Twelves: The Selected Letters of Ralph Ellison and Albert Murray,* ed. Albert Murray and John F. Callahan (New York: Modern Library, 2000), pp. 166–67.

15. *Conversations with Ralph Ellison,* ed. Maryemma Graham and Amrijit Singh (Jackson: University of Mississippi Press, 1995), p. 329.

16. See p. 179, below.

17. *Collected Essays,* pp. 153–54.

18. Ibid., pp. 191–92.

19. From an excerpt of *Invisible Man,* p. 139, below.

20. From "Blues People," p. 120, below.

21. From "The Golden Age, Time Past," p. 50, below.

22. See *Collected Essays,* p. 219.

23. *Trading Twelves,* p. 21.

24. *Collected Essays,* p. 733.

25. From "Homage to Duke Ellington on His Birthday," p. 77, below.

26 See *Collected Essays,* pp. 652, 653.

27. From "Remembering Jimmy," p. 43, below.

28. From an excerpt of *Invisible Man,* p. 172, below.

29. *Stomping on the Blues* (New York: McGraw-Hill, 1976).

30. *Collected Essays,* p. 323.

31. In the 1930s, as his letters show, Ellison was reading Miguel de Unamuno's *The Tragic Sense of Life* (London: Macmillan, 1921), to which he would allude throughout his writing career.
32. *Collected Essays,* p. 451.
33. From "Remembering Jimmy," p. 43, below.
34. From "As the Spirit Moves Mahalia," p. 87, below.
35. Unpublished transcript of a talk at Langston University, 1966, p. 5.
36. This episode from *Invisible Man* is included below, p. 148.
37. From an episode from *Invisible Man* is included below, p. 139.
38. Perhaps both Ellison and Murray—who was the first to use the term to describe the creative tensions in jazz—came across it initially in William Graham Sumner's *Folkways* (Boston: Ginn and Co., 1906), a standard textbook during their college years. Sumner used the expression to describe competition and cooperation among animals as well as humans: "It consists in the combination of two persons or groups to satisfy a great common interest while minor antagonisms of interest which exist between them are suppressed" (17–18).
39. From "Remembering Jimmy," p. 43, below.
40. From "Flamenco," p. 95, below.
41. From "Homage to William L. Dawson," p. 133, below.
42. *Collected Essays,* pp. 106–7.
43. From "Flamenco," p. 95, below.
44. In an unpublished script written circa 1958 for a PBS television program called *USA Arts,* which aired in 1966 as "Bop! Goes Intellectual," Ellison includes drinking as a fourth ingredient in the jazz dance's ritual. "Here," he writes, "each element was as important as the other. The musicians moved the dancers, the liquor released the dancers, the dancers inspired the musicians, the singers evoked, with their songs and passions, a common culture and a common attitude towards life."
45. From "Remembering Jimmy," p. 43, below.
46. *Collected Essays,* p. 298.
47. Ellison, "Harlem's America," *New Leader* 49 (September 26, 1966): 23.
48. From "Remembering Jimmy," p. 43, below.
49. Bessie Smith sings these traditional lyrics in the "Work House Blues," Columbia Record 14032, July 23, 1924; the lines also turn up on blues by Skip James ("Hard Luck Child," 1931), Sam Collins ("I'm Sitting on Top of the World," 1931), and Jessie James ("Lonesome Day Blues," 1936).
50. *Collected Essays,* p. 325.
51. Unpublished television script.
52. From "On Bird, Bird-Watching and Jazz," p. 65, below.
53. Ibid., p. 74.

54. For new research on "The Golden Age, Time Past," I am indebted to Maxine Gordon.

55. It is intriguing, however, that in a letter to Murray, Ellison complains of Armstrong's performance at Newport: "Louis was wearing his ass instead of his genius" (*Trading Twelves*, p. 175).

56. Vigot Sjoman, "En Val Synlig Man," *Dagens Nyeter* 3 (January 1955): 4.

57. See p. 184, below.

58. See p. 213, below.

59. *Invisible Man*, pp. 110–11.

60. *Collected Essays*, p. 691.

LIVING WITH MUSIC

LIVING WITH MUSIC

This piece exemplifies how Ellison used his masterful storytelling gifts in his nonfiction. (Paule Marshall has said that Ellison's true second novel was his 1964 collection of essays and interviews, Shadow and Act.*) Using his own story of being a musician who has become a writer, Ellison offers acute definitions of jazz and of the jazz artist's motives and modes of training. He also makes the key point that in the modern United States, with its high-tech communication, cultures blend rapidly and contend with one another: "The step from the spirituality of the spirituals to that of the Beethoven of the symphonies or the Bach of the chorales is not as vast as it seems," writes Ellison. "Nor is the romanticism of a Brahms or Chopin completely unrelated to that of Louis Armstrong." Note, too, the idea of music as defense against chaos and as Proustian madeleine (sweet catalyst of remembrance), reaching "the unconscious levels of the mind" and working "its magic with mood and memory." Considering the essay's background narrative, concerning the building of high-quality audio systems, a practice at which Ellison was extremely skillful, it is fitting that this piece first appeared—as part of a series by audiophiles who were not working musicians—in* High Fidelity *in December 1955.*

In those days it was either live with music or die with noise, and we chose rather desperately to live. In the process our apartment—what with its booby-trappings of audio equipment, wires, discs and tapes—came to resemble the Collyer mansion, but that was later. First there was the neighborhood, assorted drunks and a singer.

We were living at the time in a tiny ground-floor-rear apartment in which I was trying to write. I say "trying" advisedly. To our right, separated by a thin wall, was a small restaurant with a juke box the size of the Roxy. To our left, a night-employed swing enthusiast who took his lullaby music so loud that every morning promptly at nine Basie's brasses started blasting my typewriter off its stand. Our living room looked out across a small backyard to a rough stone wall to an apartment building which, towering above, caught every passing thoroughfare sound and rifled it straight down to me. There were also howling cats and barking dogs, none capable of music worth living with, so we'll pass them by.

But the court behind the wall, which on the far side came knee-high to a short Iroquois, was a forum for various singing and/or preaching drunks who wandered back from the corner bar. From these you sometimes heard a fair barbershop style "Bill Bailey," free-wheeling versions of "The Bastard King of England," the saga of Uncle Bud, or a deeply felt rendition of Leroy Carr's "How Long Blues." The preaching drunks took on any topic that came to mind: current events, the fate of the long-sunk *Titanic,* or the relative merits of the Giants and the Dodgers. Naturally there was great argument and occasional fighting—none of it fatal but all of it loud.

I shouldn't complain, however, for these were rather entertaining drunks, who, like the birds, appeared in the spring and left with the first fall cold. A more dedicated fellow was there all the time, day and night, come rain, come shine. Up on the corner lived a drunk of legend, a true phenomenon, who could surely have qualified as the king of all the world's winos, not excluding the French. He was neither poetic like the others nor ambitious like the singer (to whom we'll presently come), but his drinking bouts were truly awe-inspiring and he was not without his sensitivity. In the throes of his passion he would shout to the whole wide world one concise command, "Shut up!" Which was disconcerting enough to all who heard (except, perhaps, the singer), but such were the labyrinthine acoustics of court-yards and areaways that he seemed to direct his command at me. The writer's block which this produced is indescrib-able. On one heroic occasion he yelled his obsessive com-mand without one interruption longer than necessary to take another drink (and with no appreciable loss of volume, penetration or authority) for three long summer days and nights, and shortly afterwards he died. Just how many lines of agitated prose he cost me I'll never know, but in all that chaos of sound I sympathized with his obsession, for I, too, hungered and thirsted for quiet. Nor did he inspire me to a painful identification, and for that I was thankful. Identifi-cation, after all, involves feelings of guilt and responsibil-ity, and since I could hardly hear my own typewriter keys I felt in no way accountable for his condition. We were sim-ply fellow victims of the madding crowd. May he rest in peace.

No, these more involved feelings were aroused by a more intimate source of noise, one that got beneath the skin and worked into the very structure of one's consciousness—like the "fate" motif in Beethoven's Fifth or the knocking-at-the-gates scene in *Macbeth*. For at the top of our pyramid of noise there was a singer who lived directly above us; you might say we had a singer on our ceiling.

Now, I had learned from the jazz musicians I had known as a boy in Oklahoma City something of the discipline and devotion to his art required of the artist. Hence I knew something of what the singer faced. These jazzmen, many of them now world-famous, lived for and with music intensely. Their driving motivation was neither money nor fame, but the will to achieve the most eloquent expression of idea-emotions through the technical mastery of their instruments (which, incidentally, some of them wore as a priest wears the cross) and the give and take, the subtle rhythmical shaping and blending of idea, tone and imagination demanded of group improvisation. The delicate balance struck between strong individual personality and the group during those early jam sessions was a marvel of social organization. I had learned too that the end of all this discipline and technical mastery was the desire to express an affirmative way of life through its musical tradition, and that this tradition insisted that each artist achieve his creativity within its frame. He must learn the best of the past, and add to it his personal vision. Life could be harsh, loud and wrong if it wished, but they lived it fully, and when they expressed their attitude toward the world it was with a fluid style that reduced the chaos of living to form.

The objectives of these jazzmen were not at all those of the singer on our ceiling, but though a purist committed to the mastery of the *bel canto* style, German *lieder,* modern French art songs and a few American slave songs sung as if *bel canto,* she was intensely devoted to her art. From morning to night she vocalized, regardless of the condition of her voice, the weather or my screaming nerves. There were times when her notes, sifting through her floor and my ceiling, bouncing down the walls and ricocheting off the building in the rear, whistled like tenpenny nails, buzzed like a saw, wheezed like the asthma of a Hercules, trumpeted like an enraged African elephant, and the squeaky pedal of her piano rested plumb center above my typing chair. After a year of non-cooperation from the neighbor on my left I became desperate enough to cool down the hot blast of his phonograph by calling the cops, but the singer presented a serious ethical problem: could I, an aspiring artist, complain against the hard work and devotion to craft of another aspiring artist?

———

Then there was my sense of guilt. Each time I prepared to shatter the ceiling in protest I was restrained by the knowledge that I, too, during my boyhood, had tried to master a musical instrument and to the great distress of my neighbors—perhaps even greater than that which I now suffered. For while our singer was concerned basically with a single tradition and style, I had been caught actively between two: that of Negro folk music, both sacred and profane, slave song and jazz, and that of Western classical music. It was most confusing; the folk tradition demanded that I play what I heard and felt around me, while those who were seeking to teach the classical tradition in the schools insisted that I play strictly according to the book and express that which I was *supposed* to feel. This sometimes led to heated clashes of wills. Once during a third-grade music appreciation class a friend of mine insisted that it was a large green snake he saw swimming down a quiet brook instead of the snowy bird the teacher felt that Saint-Saëns's *Carnival of the Animals* should evoke. The rest of us sat there and lied like little black, brown and yellow Trojans about that swan, but our stalwart classmate held firm to his snake. In the end he got himself spanked and reduced the teacher to tears, but truth, reality and our environment were redeemed. For we were all familiar with snakes, while a swan was simply something the Ugly Duckling of the story grew up to be. Fortunately some of us grew up with a genuine appreciation of classical music *despite* such teaching methods. But as an aspiring trumpeter I was to wallow in sin for years before being awakened to guilt by our singer.

Caught mid-range between my two traditions, where one attitude often clashed with the other and one technique of playing was by the other opposed, I caused whole blocks of people to suffer.

Indeed, I terrorized a good part of an entire city section.

During summer vacation I blew sustained tones out of the window for hours, usually starting—especially on Sunday mornings—before breakfast. I sputtered whole days through M. Arban's (he's the great authority on the instrument) double- and triple-tonguing exercises, with an effect like that of a jackass hiccupping off a big meal of briars. During school-term mornings I practiced a truly exhibitionist "Reveille" before leaving for school, and in the evening I generously gave the ever-listening world a long, slow version of "Taps," ineptly played but throbbing with what I in my adolescent vagueness felt was a romantic sadness. For it was farewell to day and a love song to life and a peace-be-with-you to all the dead and dying.

On hot summer afternoons I tormented the ears of all not blessedly deaf with imitations of the latest hot solos of Hot Lips Page (then a local hero), the leaping right hand of Earl "Fatha" Hines, or the rowdy poetic flights of Louis Armstrong. Naturally I rehearsed also such school-band standbys as the *Light Cavalry* Overture, Sousa's "Stars and Stripes Forever," the *William Tell* Overture, and "Tiger Rag." (Not even an after-school job as office boy to a dentist could stop my efforts. Frequently, by way of encouraging my development in the proper cultural direction, the dentist asked me proudly to render Schubert's *Serenade* for some poor devil with his jaw propped open in the dental chair. When the drill got going, or the forceps bit deep, I blew real strong.)

Sometimes, inspired by the even then considerable virtuosity of the late Charlie Christian (who during our school days played marvelous riffs on a cigar-box banjo), I'd give whole summer afternoons and the evening hours after heavy suppers of black-eyed peas and turnip greens, cracklin' bread and buttermilk, lemonade and sweet potato cobbler, to practicing hard-driving blues. Such food oversupplied me with bursting energy, and from listening to Ma Rainey, Ida Cox and Clara Smith, who made regular appearances in our town, I knew exactly how I wanted my horn to sound. But in the effort to make it do so (I was no embryo Joe Smith or Tricky Sam Nanton), I sustained the curses of both Christian and infidel—along with the encouragement of those more sympathetic citizens who understood the profound satisfaction to be found in expressing oneself in the blues.

Despite those who complained and cried to heaven for Gabriel to blow a chorus so heavenly sweet and so hellishly hot that I'd forever put down my horn, there were more tolerant ones who were willing to pay in present pain for future pride.

For who knew what skinny kid with his chops wrapped around a trumpet mouthpiece and a faraway look in his eyes might become the next Armstrong? Yes, and send you, at some big dance a few years hence, into an ecstasy of rhythm and memory and brassy affirmation of the goodness of being alive and part of the community? Someone had to, for it was part of the group tradition, though that was not how they said it.

"Let that boy blow," they'd say to the protesting ones. "He's got to talk baby talk on that thing before he can preach on it. Next thing you know he's liable to be up there with Duke Ellington. Sure, plenty Oklahoma boys are up there with the big bands. Son, let's hear you try those 'Trouble in Mind Blues.' Now try and make it sound like ole Ida Cox sings it."

And I'd draw in my breath and do Miss Cox great violence.

———

Thus the crimes and aspirations of my youth. It had been years since I had played the trumpet or irritated a single ear with other than the spoken or written word, but as far as my singing neighbor was concerned I had to hold my peace. I was forced to listen, and in listening I soon became involved to the point of identification. If she sang badly I'd hear my own futility in the windy sound; if well, I'd stare at my typewriter and despair that I would ever make my prose so sing. She left me neither night nor day, this singer on our ceiling, and as my writing languished I became more and more upset. Thus one desperate morning I decided that since I seemed doomed to live within a shrieking chaos I might as well contribute my share; perhaps if I fought noise with noise I'd attain some small peace. Then a miracle: I turned on my radio (an old Philco AM set connected to a small Pilot FM tuner) and heard the words

> Art thou troubled?
> Music will calm thee . . .

I stopped as though struck by the voice of an angel. It was Kathleen Ferrier, that loveliest of singers, giving voice to the aria from Handel's *Rodelinda*. The voice was so completely expressive of words and music that I accepted it without question; what lover of the vocal art could resist her?

Yet it was ironic, for after giving up my trumpet for the typewriter I had avoided too close a contact with the very art which she recommended as balm. For I had started music early and lived with it daily, and when I broke I tried to break clean. Now in this magical moment all the old love, the old fascination with music superbly rendered, flooded back. When she finished I realized that with such music in my own apartment, the chaotic sounds from without and above had sunk, if not into silence, then well below the level where they mattered. Here was a way out. If I was to live and write in that apartment, it would be only through the grace of music. I had tuned in a Ferrier recital, and when it ended I rushed out for several of her records, certain that now deliverance was mine.

But not yet. Between the hi-fi record and the ear, I learned, there was a new electronic world. In that realization our apartment was well on its way toward becoming an audio booby trap. It was 1949, and I rushed to the Audio Fair.

I have, I confess, as much gadget resistance as the next American of my age, weight and slight income, but little did I dream of the test to which it would be put. I had hardly entered the fair before I heard David Sarser's and Mel Sprinkle's Musician's Amplifier, took a look at its schematic and, recalling a boyhood acquaintance with such matters, decided that I could build one. I did—several times—before it measured within specifications. And still our system was lacking. Fortunately my wife shared my passion for music, so we went on to buy, piece by piece, a fine speaker system, a first-rate AM-FM tuner, a transcription turntable and a speaker cabinet. I built half a dozen or more preamplifiers and record compensators before finding a commercial one that satisfied my ear, and finally we acquired an arm, a magnetic cartridge and—glory of the house—a tape recorder. All this plunge into electronics, mind you, had as its simple end the enjoyment of recorded music as it was intended to be heard. I was obsessed with the idea of reproducing sound with such fidelity that even when using music as a defense behind which I could write, it would reach the unconscious levels of the mind with the least distortion. But it didn't come easily. There were wires and pieces of equipment all over the tiny apartment (I became a compulsive experimenter), and it was worth your life to move about without first taking careful bearings. Once we were almost crushed in our sleep by the tape machine, for which there was space only on a shelf at the head of our bed.

But it was worth it. For now when we played a recording on our system even the drunks on the wall could recognize its quality. I'm ashamed to admit, however, that I did not always restrict its use to the demands of pleasure or defense. Indeed, with such marvels of science at my control I lost my humility. My ethical consideration for the singer up above shriveled like a plant in too much sunlight. For instead of soothing, music seemed to release the beast in me. Now when jarred from my writer's reveries by some especially enthusiastic flourish of our singer, I'd rush to my music system with blood in my eyes and burst a few decibels in her direction. If she defied me with a few more pounds of pressure against her diaphragm, then a war of decibels was declared.

If, let us say, she were singing "Depuis le Jour" from *Louise*, I'd put on a tape of Bidu Sayão performing the same aria, and let the rafters ring. If it was some song by Mahler, I'd match her spitefully with Marian Anderson or Kathleen Ferrier; if she offended with something from *Der Rosenkavalier*, I'd attack her flank with Lotte Lehmann. If she brought me up from my desk with art songs by Ravel or Rachmaninoff, I'd defend myself with Maggie Teyte or Jennie Tourel. If she polished a spiritual to a meaningless artiness I'd play Bessie Smith to remind her of the earth out of which we came. Once in a while I'd forget completely that I was supposed to be a gentleman and blast her with Strauss's *Zarathustra*, Bartók's *Concerto for Orchestra*, Ellington's "Flaming Sword," the famous crescendo from *The Pines of Rome*, or Satchmo scatting "I'll be Glad When You're Dead" (you rascal you!). Oh, I was living with music with a sweet vengeance.

One might think that all this would have made me her most hated enemy, but not at all. When I met her on the stoop a few weeks after my rebellion, expecting her fully to slap my face, she astonished me by complimenting our music system. She even questioned me concerning the artists I had used against her. After that, on days when the acoustics were right, she'd stop singing until the piece was finished and then applaud—not always, I guessed, without a justifiable touch of sarcasm. And although I was now getting on with my writing, the unfairness of this business bore in upon me. Aware that I could not have withstood a similar comparison with literary artists of like caliber, I grew remorseful. I also came to admire the singer's courage and control, for she was neither intimidated into silence nor goaded into undisciplined screaming; she persevered, she marked the phrasing of the great singers I sent her way, she improved her style.

Better still, she vocalized more softly, and I, in turn, used music less and less as a weapon and more for its magic with mood and memory. After a while a simple twirl of the volume control up a few decibels and down again would bring a live-and-let-live reduction of her volume.

We have long since moved from that apartment and that most interesting neighborhood, and now the floors and walls of our present apartment are adequately thick, and there is even a closet large enough to house the audio system; the only wire visible is that leading from the closet to the corner speaker system. Still, we are indebted to the singer and the old environment for forcing us to discover one of the most deeply satisfying aspects of our living. Perhaps the enjoyment of music is always suffused with past experience; for me, at least, this is true.

It seems a long way and a long time from the glorious days of Oklahoma jazz dances, the jam sessions at Halley Richardson's place on Deep Second, from the phonographs shouting the blues in the back alleys I knew as a delivery boy, and from the days when watermelon men with voices like mellow bugles shouted their wares in time with the rhythm of their horses' hoofs, and farther still from the washerwomen singing slave songs as they stirred sooty tubs in sunny yards; and a long time, too, from those intense, conflicting days when the school music program of Oklahoma City was tuning our earthy young ears to classical accents, with music appreciation classes and free musical instruments and basic instruction for any child who cared to learn, and uniforms for all who made the band. There was a mistaken notion on the part of some of the teachers that classical music had nothing to do with the rhythms, relaxed or hectic, of daily living, and that one should crook the little finger when listening to such refined strains. And the blues, the spirituals and jazz? They would have destroyed them and scattered the pieces. Nevertheless, we learned some of it all, for in the United States when traditions are juxtaposed they tend, regardless of what we do to prevent it, irresistibly to merge. Thus, musically at least, each child in our town was an heir of all the ages. One learns by moving from the familiar to the unfamiliar, and while it might sound incongruous at first, the step from the spirituality of the spirituals to that of the Beethoven of the symphonies or the Bach of the chorales is not as vast as it seems. Nor is the romanticism of a Brahms or Chopin completely unrelated to that of Louis Armstrong. Those who know their native culture and love it unchauvinistically are never lost when encountering the unfamiliar.

Living with music today we find Mozart and Ellington, Kirsten Flagstad and Chippie Hill, William L. Dawson and Carl Orff all forming part of our regular fare. For all exalt life in rhythm and melody; all add to its significance. Perhaps in the swift change of American society in which the meanings of one's origin are so quickly lost, one of the chief values of living with music lies in its power to give us an orientation in time. In doing so, it gives significance to all those indefinable aspects of experience which nevertheless help to make us what we are. In the swift whirl of time music is a constant, reminding us of what we were and of that toward which we aspire. Art thou troubled? Music will not only calm, it will ennoble thee.

Ralph Ellison's Territorial

Vantage

This interview was conducted in 1976 by Ron Welburn, a writer and literary scholar who had been Ellison's student at New York University, for The Grackle: Improvised Music in Transition, *a periodical that kept its small circulation going from 1976 until 1979. True to his usual practice, Ellison collected Welburn's transcription of the conversation (along with the audiotape), and returned the manuscript expanded but edited to retain a sense of improvised conversation. "Territorial Vantage" is important for its emphasis on the vibrant music scene of early Oklahoma City, and especially for its insistence on the significance of lesser-known "territorial" jazz bands, representatives of jazz's invisible but potent history. Ellison also fills out the picture of music at Tuskegee Institute of the 1930s, and of New York of the late thirties and forties. Along the way, he offers compelling statements about race and music: "Jazz is Afro-American in origin, but it's more American than some folks want to admit. . . . When a black musician says he was influenced by white musicians I believe him"; and about the perils of institutionalizing jazz music instruction: "Today I think it fortunate that jazz wasn't taught [at Tuskegee] because it has developed its own unique body of techniques through its free-swinging, improvisational, irreverent attitude. Teaching it formally might well have imposed too many thou-shalt-nots and imposed stability upon a developing form. Dance halls and jam sessions along with recordings are the true academy for jazz."* (The Grackle, 1977–78)

As a boy when did you become conscious of "improvised music"? What characterized it and what of it could you call "Jazz"?

There was so much of it around me that I suppose I was born with a consciousness of it. There were several bands sponsored by such lodges as the Elks. These were military and concert bands, but the musicians also played in jazz orchestras and gig combos. Territorial orchestras were constantly in and out of Oklahoma City. Moten, George E. Lee, T. Holder, Andy Kirk were among them. And there were people who amused themselves by playing guitars, Jew's harps, kazoos, yukes, mandolins, C Melody saxophones, or performed on combs by vibrating a piece of tissue paper placed against the comb's teeth. Much of this was improvised music, including blues and jazz riffs. The bandmen played standard marches, such as those of Sousa, arrangements of the classics, and novelty numbers, such as "Laughing Trombone," which contained elements of ragtime and jazz. There were string orchestras which played everything from the light classics to the blues. There was not too definite a line drawn between the types of music, at least not in my kid's consciousness. This happened later, after I began to study music in school. Negro culture was music-centered, and in grade school I became aware of the standard ways of playing repertory, whether for single groups or for the school band and orchestra. Those of us who tried to play jazz listened to whatever was around, whether played by local or visiting jazzmen or on records. Incidently, the first song taught to me as a two-year-old was "Dark Brown, Chocolate to the Bone." To this I was taught to dance the Eagle Rock. I had older cousins who were in tune with jazz and the blues while their mother was a great one for singing hymns to the accompaniment of their player piano. I can still see the image of Liszt on one of the boxes which held the piano rolls, just as I can still hear one of my cousins picking out the early version of "Squeeze Me" on the piano keys. So, in such homes, and it was more or less typical, you had a general openness to music of various styles. King Oliver came and went regularly and was very popular. But there was another side. In our AME church the choir director was one of the local physicians who disdained the spirituals. He preferred the more formal religious music. The church had an organ, and orchestra, and a fair sized choir which performed the music of Handel. I have a vague memory of going to an orchestral rehearsal with my father and seeing him play the drums.

What kind of music education did the Oklahoma school system provide?

Thanks to Mrs. Zelia N. Breaux, who was a very influential educator, it was quite extraordinary. The kids were taught music from the early grades, including sight-reading. There was a music appreciation course with phonographs and recordings taught city-wide in the black schools, and rare for most schools even today, we were taught four years of harmony and two of musical form. There was a marching and concert band, which I entered at the age of eight, two glee clubs, an orchestra and chorus, and each year Mrs. Breaux produced and directed an operetta. The leads and the chorus were students. I participated in several, both as a musician and as an actor. In my first I played one of the children in "The Gypsy Rover." Later, when I was older, I was taught a tap dance routine for a role in an operetta whose title I've forgotten. Interestingly enough, Mrs. Breaux, who was an all-around musician, playing trumpet, violin and piano, did not encourage us to play jazz. And yet as one of the owners of the local theater she brought all kinds of jazz musicians before the public. King Oliver, Ma Rainey, and Ida Cox were frequently on the bill, and Bessie Smith and quite a number of T.O.B.A. circuit offerings came to her

Aldridge Theater.* Before sound movies were common she employed a pit orchestra and such members of the original Blue Devils orchestra as Walter Page, Icky Lawrence, and Willie Lewis were employed there. A number of the local jazz musicians, such as Page, were conservatory-trained and were capable of reading at sight the scores that were issued with the motion pictures. Icky Lawrence was a trumpeter who played with the Ideal Orchestra, the first sustained group in our community. Icky Lawrence was their trumpeter, Crackshot McNeal was its elegant drummer—get hold of musicians from the early Basie period and they'll tell you what an excellent drummer he was. There was Willie Lewis, a jolly rotund fellow who did the arranging and played the piano, and Gut Bucket Coleman on trombone. These were versatile musicians and gifted jazzmen. Later, the band that was to stay the longest and become the most famous was the Blue Devils. Among its members were Walter Page, Hot Lips Page, Icky Lawrence, Buster Smith, and sometimes Edward Christian, Charlie Christian's gifted older brother.

Did bands like Sam Wooding's get out there?

I don't recall Sam Wooding's, but it's quite possible. Alphonso Trent was in and out of Oklahoma City; I think he was based principally in Dallas. George E. Lee was a famous Kansas City band; he called it a novelty singing orchestra and featured musicians who were versatile on several instruments. His sister, Julia, performed with them and gave the group quite a bit of glamour with her fine clothes and fine looks. Frequently, they played battles of music against Bennie Moten, and often won.

Oklahoma City was home base for the Blue Devils while Bennie Moten, Andy Kirk's Twelve Clouds of Joy, and

---

* T.O.B.A. was the acronym for the Theater Owners Booking Association, a network of theater owners bringing a variety of shows—church music, blues, jazz, plays, vaudeville, and minstrel acts—to black audiences from the early 1910s to the end of the 1920s.

George E. Lee were Kansas City based. Of course, they sometimes spent months in Oklahoma City, which like Kansas City was a good town for dance bands. There were dressing towns and dancing towns; a good dancing town was one in which bands could find employment both among Negroes and whites.

Who were some of the better-known local musicians, and which of them went on to greater things?

Edward Christian, Charlie's older brother, was an arranger and band leader. He played violin, tuba, string bass and piano. Charlie Christian and Jimmy Rushing were the most famous jazz musicians produced by Oklahoma City, but there were also Harry Youngblood, Harold Canon, and Frank Mead. During the forties Lem Johnson was very active around New York. Oscar Pettiford, Al Hibbler, Sammy Price, Ben Webster, and Lester Young were on the scene from time to time. I remember Lester Young being there in 1929.

So much of it is a matter of packaging a style for the white public. A variety of art, music or dance, will have existed among Afro-Americans for years, during which time it reaches a level of perfection, as did the style known as Stomp. By the time it was introduced to white audiences it had been changed to "Swing." But in those days there wasn't that kind of distinction made between rhythm and blues; the Southwestern bands played both. During public dances blues numbers were played as a matter of course. When the band was swinging the dancers and the dancers were swinging the musicians—usually around midnight—*that's* when the blues were evoked. Earlier in the evening blues were played up-tempo.

The term "Blue Devils" is English and referred to a state of psychic depression, but during the range wars in cattle country those who were given to cutting barbwire fences were called "Blue Devils." Perhaps Walter Page chose the name because of its outlaw connotations. Incidentally, that orchestra merged with Bennie Moten's after Moten died, and later became Basie's. Moten was undergoing a tonsilectomy when a slip of the doctor's scalpel severed his jugular vein; Moten's fans wanted to lynch that Negro doctor.

Didn't James Reese Europe die similarly? Did you ever encounter him or Will Marion Cook?

No, Europe was knifed to death in 1919 by a drummer, so all I ever saw of him was a photograph of him directing a band. I knew of Cook because the boy's glee club sang several of his compositions. I did know Cook's wife, Abbie Mitchell, when she was on the faculty of the Tuskegee school of music. Cook's music was widely popular.

What of the Oklahoma City school music scene overall? And what others besides blacks were involved in the blues and jazz scene?

Oklahoma City had a number of school bands, most of them white. Our instruments were supplied by the Board of Education but our uniforms were bought with funds raised by the citizens, black and white, throughout the city. Usually our travel expenses were raised by public subscription. Our band accompanied the football team to such cities as Tulsa or Muskogee. I played varsity football, so on certain trips I traveled as a member of the team. We also traveled to Wichita and Topeka, and one year the Elks lodge took us out to Denver for a convention which featured an oratorical contest. Many whites supported our travels.

I don't recall members of other racial groups participating in jam sessions, although there might have been whites and others playing in the white dance halls that were unavailable to a kid like myself. But I don't remember any coming over to the East side, and this despite the relative friendliness between the races. Incidently, I'm told that a local white man copyrighted a blues as early as 1913. Yes, and there was an Indian-looking guy who played trombone in one of the Kansas City orchestras. He was called Big Chief Moore.

In what shape was ragtime in Oklahoma in your youth?

The craze had given way to jazz, but people still played it. The custodian of the Slaughter's building, where the most important dance hall was located, would sit down at the piano and play a very intricate rag; but he was such an evil bastard that I was afraid to ask him what it was or where he'd learned to play. There were musicians who worked as barbers or as packing plant workers who played ragtime. And the spirit of ragtime was in many of the military marches and you found it on piano rolls that had been cut by Scott Joplin and James P. Johnson and others. I can't remember a time when I wasn't familiar with the "Maple Leaf Rag." It was played by small orchestras and you found it in band books. There were also a number of comic numbers designed to show off the trombone sections of concert bands, like "Laughing Trombone" and "Papa Charlie Trombone." Ask any old military or side show musician or look into old band books and you'll find that the ragtime influence was widespread.

What was "Papa Charlie" style?

A lot of smears, imitations of preachers preaching, laughing. These passages were written in. After a chorus there'd come a break and the trombone would take over. Played by a good improvisor it became real jazz.

What Ellington used with Tricky Sam and Bubber Miley?

Yes, the style was in the air. Listen to the trombone accompaniment on old blues recordings and you'll hear some of it.

What of your own musical experiences?

After I developed enough skill I played in pick-up groups— gig bands—under Edward Christian. My first instrument in the school band was the mellophone. I'd loan mine to Hot Lips Page and the other Blue Devils trumpeters would borrow the mellophones from the other members of the mellophone section in order to play special choruses. In exchange I'd insist upon being allowed to sit in on trumpet during a Blue Devils rehearsal. I could read better than some of the jazzmen so very often I'd be asked to arbitrate when they got into arguments over interpretation. I also played solos with the band and at weddings. I also held first chair in the school orchestra. I wasn't able to do much about jazz gigs because I was still an adolescent and my widowed mother kept a tight rein on me.

At Tuskegee, where I majored in music, we were not encouraged to play jazz. But the summer I arrived there I played in a band under Shorty Hall. Shorty had been trained by Captain Drye, an old 10th Cavalry bandmaster who directed the Tuskegee band and taught me trumpet. Shorty, by the way, taught Dizzy Gillespie in North Carolina. That summer we played dances for teachers, for students and for the physicians who staffed the Veterans Hospital. We also played dances in nearby towns, such as Columbus, Georgia, and Montgomery, Alabama. During my time at Tuskegee I played with one of the student orchestras. There were two, both big bands. Jazz was discouraged because it was thought to degrade the instrumental techniques which were being taught. Trumpeters were taught the methods of Arban and St. Jacombe and it was felt that jazz techniques would interfere. I went out for the football team and was told to forget it. I was told: "We're not spending all this time and money training you to develop your embouchure and have you go out there and get your mouth stepped on or your fingers mashed."

It's true that black colleges have historically discouraged blues and jazz. Orrin Clayton Suthern, who taught at my alma mater, Lincoln University in Pennsylvania, was no exception in the sixties.

Suthern? He taught me at Tuskegee, in the thirties. But my feelings about that matter are mixed. To an extent it was fortunate that not everyone tried to teach the blues because they were not of its spirit, and it was not part of their background. We have to recognize that there are various cultural backgrounds and levels in our group. Some people knew nothing of the blues or even of the spirituals while others knew nothing of classical music. Others knew both. Musicians like Walter Page had studied in conservatories but played jazz, blues and anything else. Other jazzmen were more limited. At Tuskegee there were faculty members who had studied in Europe: Andrew Fletcher Roseman, Hazel Harrison, Portia Pittman and Abbie Mitchell. William L. Dawson, the director of the music school, had played in everything from jazz orchestras to the Chicago Civic Symphony, but he was the only faculty member with that broad a range. Today I think it fortunate that jazz wasn't taught because it has developed its own unique body of techniques through its free-swinging, improvisational, irreverent attitude. Teaching it formally might well have imposed too many thou-shalt-nots and imposed stability upon a developing form. Dance halls and jam sessions along with recordings are the true academy for jazz. However, one of the good things about the division of musical culture in Afro-America is that there have always been musicians trained in European styles and techniques, who pass it on to youngsters who opt for jazz. Shorty Hall, who I mentioned earlier, was hardly four feet tall, but he could blow the hell off of a big-bore symphonic trumpet. And I mean that he played all the difficult variations and triple tonguing. He had the facility of Al Hirt. So there is a direct line leading from Captain Drye, the ex-cavalry bandmaster, through Shorty Hall to Dizzy. Mrs. Breaux never played jazz herself but she taught the fundamentals to many students who did.

Did Alain Locke's "The Negro and His Music" of 1936 stir any interest among black intellectuals then?

I don't know to what extent. It was part of the *Bronze Booklet* series and I read them all. I remember Sterling Brown's was the best and I found them all useful, but generally the series struck me as inadequate. In Locke's there seemed to be so much which wasn't adequately handled and I got more information from James Weldon Johnson's *Black Manhattan* and *Along This Way*. He had been involved in so much of our musical experience and some of the musicians he mentioned had been out to Oklahoma City. The role of blacks on Broadway was exciting and gave me a broader sense of possibility. I really didn't need someone to tell me about the spirituals because I grew up around them. In school we sang them and every type of Afro-American music . . . except [chuckle] the blues.

I'm sure some of the newspapers in the area covered music.

Oklahoma had and still has one of our most famous papers, the *Black Dispatch*. It was published and edited by Roscoe Dungee and was widely read for its editorials. But I'm afraid that the music commentary we got usually came from the *Chicago Defender* or the *Pittsburgh Courier,* papers which emphasized entertainment and brought the excitement of the big cities to the provinces.

But were there no write-ups of a concert, or talk about the nuts and bolts of what bands like Basie and Hines were doing?

Not unless written elsewhere by columnists who covered entertainment. Local dances would be announced and reported, but there was little music criticism.

On more than one occasion you have stated that certain black jazzmen, like Coleman Hawkins and Pres, were influenced by white jazzmen such as Frankie Trumbauer: their biographies have verified that; but isn't the impetus for this "jazz" improvisory style something that sprang from the Afro-American imaginative genius?

This argument about who did what and who influenced whom imposes racial considerations which don't belong to discussions of culture. In those days when a musician was learning his instrument and trying to develop his own style he listened to any musician who had something to offer, who excited him; they weren't fighting the race problem but assimilating styles and techniques. The Ellington sidemen interviewed by Stanley Dance mention a number of white jazzmen who influenced their styles. It was the music, the style, the ability to execute that was important. If a white musician sounded good; if he had the facility with his instrument you took what you could use—just as they took what they could use from us. Jazz is Afro-American in origin, but it's more American than some folks want to admit. When I got to New York I was amazed to find white trumpeters working at developing what they called a "dirty" tone. These were men who could produce the brilliant tone associated with the classical trumpet style, and I came to realize that they were trying to develop the Negro blues voice as it sounds on the trumpet and trombone. In other words, they were studying the voicing and technique of jazz, techniques that were already well-rounded and complex but which hadn't been codified in textbooks. Having grown up around musicians who couldn't produce anything *but* a "dirty tone" I found this ironic. Especially in light of the fact that at Tuskegee we were made to spend hours every day learning to make the trumpet speak as a trumpet. That was a basic goal. You strove for a militant, brilliant tone. If you played cornet your tone would be mellower, but it had to be vibrant and you had to learn to control your vibrato and make it speak in a number of voices, from the lyrical to the militant. The blues timbre, the sound of the Negro voice, was already in you, and if you didn't produce it instinctively you could listen to those who used it; on the stage or on recordings, or from hucksters selling watermelons and so on. I heard Louis Armstrong in person for the first time in 1929, but I had been listening to his recordings and admiring the sound of his trumpet for years. When a black musician says he was influenced by white musicians I believe him and see no reason to doubt him. It's most American. This is a pluralistic society and culturally the melting pot really melts. Trumbauer must have learned from black musicians. Here, there's a long history of interchanging musical styles between the races.

You worked on the Works Progress Administration interviewing people for the purpose of folklore research. Did the W.P.A. have any disposition toward jazz? There were projects for collecting memoirs; did any of that involve, in an official capacity, collecting songs and recording blues musicians?

Working with folklore was only a minor phase of my work on the writers project. Most of my time there was spent doing research for a history of Negroes in New York, but I had no contact with what was happening on music projects. The music project was a world within itself. I know that much attention was given to producing musicals and giving concerts, and that free musical instruction was provided the public. I took a few trumpet lessons from a man who held the first trumpet chair with the Metropolitan Opera Orchestra. I seem to recall that the people who "discovered" Leadbelly were employed by the W.P.A., and that collectors were sent into the field with recording machines. I'm unfamiliar with what their official attitude toward jazz and the blues might have been.

Minton's was becoming active in the late thirties, early forties. How did you respond to the nascent music there and were people dancing to it, that you know of?

Few people were capable of dancing to it; it was more a listener's music. I did a piece for *Esquire* on Minton's (viz *Shadow & Act*). You encountered the new style not only at Minton's but at the Apollo as well. There you heard Earl Hines with Sarah Vaughan and Eckstine, and you heard bebop flourishes at the Savoy Ballroom. I danced a lot and used to be there once or twice a week. I went to the Apollo twice a week usually on Wednesdays and Sundays, often with Langston Hughes. There was music all over the district. The Renaissance Ballroom and Smalls Paradise, with both local and nationally known bands, Lucky Millinder's and the Savoy Sultans, etc. I was very interested in Erskine Hawkins's group because when I went to Tuskegee they were still at Alabama State down in Montgomery. The state of Alabama didn't support the college adequately so the orchestra would go out and raise money. Erskine was the composer of "Tuxedo Junction," which was popular with white bands at the time; but I always preferred the way the Collegians played it—they put the real feeling into it. The band was so successful in the North that they decided to go professional—which led to real contention between them and the president of Alabama State. He forced them to give up the name "Alabama State Collegians" and they took the name of the leader, Erskine Hawkins. Billy Daniels was their singer. I'm speaking of a period which included part of the Depression, but there was quite a ferment in entertainment. Perhaps all the more so because there were so many good musicians out of work. Nevertheless there was a great deal of dancing and experimentation. As a musician I became discouraged. There was so much competition and having no money I couldn't afford to join the union. However, I did hang around the Rhythm Club so as to keep in touch with the pros. I began trying to write in 1937 and finally gave up all hope of becoming a professional musician. By 1940 I was living next door to Teddy Wilson. He was playing at Cafe Society DownTown and my wife and I often went there and frequently joined him and his wife at various after hours hangouts where musicians met after work to jam.

What was the reaction of New Yorkers to Gillespie and Parker?

It was mixed because most people couldn't dance to bop. Very often Dizzy and Bird were so engrossed with their experiments that they didn't provide enough music for the supportive rite of dancing. That bothered me. And the political stance they took was annoying because I thought it irrelevant. By political I mean the idea they projected of inventing a music that whites couldn't play—I touch on this in the article I did on Minton's—and their studied ignoring of the audience I found a drag. I didn't need it. I could write and express my political attitudes through other forms of action. When I wanted to hear music I wanted to hear music, not to be politicized. But the things they were doing with chords and the melodic line were fascinating. But it didn't really develop; it became much too quickly a series of clichés, and I was sorry for that. With any new development there's that danger, especially when younger musicians grab it as their thing. The lyrical phase of bop was truly promising. Numbers like Tadd Dameron's "If You Could See Me Now" sung by Sarah Vaughan fascinated me to no end. Dameron and Fats Navarro were gifted musicians. There were a number of brilliant trumpeters, one or two more brilliant than Gillespie, who is part clown and part musician. As an ex-trumpeter I wasn't nearly as excited by his work as I was by Clark Terry. Just personal taste. Anyway, you didn't have to listen to the boppers because there were always good bands playing somewhere in Harlem. And when you ran into the boppers at the Savoy they usually played numbers that anyone could dance to. Although I had given up music by the time bop began to flourish I still went to jam sessions. There was a place on St. Nicholas Avenue that was owned by Sidney Bechet, a shell-like place somewhere in the 130s near Seventh Avenue where Art Tatum and Teddy Wilson used to jam. And there was Clark Monroe's Uptown House, another bopper joint. At 136th Street and Lenox there was a joint where the singing waiters sang dirty songs and improvised lyrics as they dashed back and forth serving drinks. Around the corner on 137th there was the Red Rooster, and down on 116th Street Jimmy Daniels ran a club that was frequented by the international set. A very sophisticated place.

When did you recognize the role that blues and jazz played in shaping not only the national music consciousness but in having an effect on the image that Americans had of themselves? You have reiterated that idea several times in lectures and writings.

Here's a dramatic instance: In 1929 Louis Armstrong had been playing in Kansas City and when he came down to Oklahoma City the bandstand in our segregated dance hall was suddenly filled with white women. They were wild for his music and nothing like that had ever happened in our town before. His music was our music but they saw it as theirs too, and were willing to break the law to get to it. So you could see that Armstrong's music was affecting attitudes and values that had no immediate relationship to it. Then there was the popularity of Earl Hines's radio broadcasts and that of the Mills Brothers. Back in '28 and '29, when we were still in short pants we were pretending to be asleep and staying up late just to hear them imitate instruments with their voices. White kids were doing the same thing. Somehow music was transcending the racial divisions. Listening to songs such as "I'm Just Wild About Harry" and knowing that it was the work of Negroes didn't change all our attitudes but it helped all kinds of people identify with Americanness or American music. Among all the allusions to earlier poetry that you find in Eliot's *The Waste Land* he still found a place to quote from "Under the Bamboo Tree," a lyric from a song by James Weldon Johnson, Bob Cole, and Rosamond Johnson. During the twenties when *The Waste Land* was published many readers made the connection. Johnson was secretary of the NAACP and that was another connection which provided some sense of the complexity of the American identity. A similar process was going on in our segregated schools. We were being made aware in the early grades that the poetry of Countee Cullen and Langston Hughes had a connection with the larger body of American poetry. Our teachers were excited over this and passed their excitement to their students. Given the racial stereotypes Negroes must learn to recognize the elements of their own cultural contribution as they appear in elements of the larger American culture. If we saw a new dance style we could recognize the black elements, the steps and gestures, in it. If you watched Fred Astaire and admired his work you knew nevertheless that you saw more exciting—and authentic—dancing on the stage of the Aldridge Theater.

Henry Cowell's American Composers on American Music *(1933) reveals how unprepared its commentators were for blues and jazz.*

When you consider the facts that Irene and Vernon Castle learned much from James Reese Europe and the influence of jazz in the work of Copland and Gershwin, I'm not so sure of that. I'm told that a white man copyrighted a blues in Oklahoma City in 1913; and the man who backed Scott Joplin was a Kansas publisher. Perhaps the geographical location has a lot to do with it. Even back in slavery times whites were fascinated by Afro-American music and certainly the minstrel show, for many years our most popular musical entertainment, owed its form, its content, and music to Afro-American music and dance. I'd say that white American composers were mixed in their attitudes. The music was infectious, they accepted its resources but when it came to identifying it as a viable part of American music they were hindered by racial considerations. Nevertheless anyone writing music in the United States was influenced by it; thus the spate of "Ethiopian Airs" written by whites; Dvořák made use of Afro-American tonalities and rhythms—as did Delius.

When I was growing up what is currently identified as Country music was sold by 5 & 10 cent stores in the form of recordings and we recognized Negro influences, just as we recognized Irish, French and Spanish influences in Afro-American music. In Oklahoma there were blacks who danced square-dances—not in imitation of white people but because square-dancing was part of their culture.

Have you detected any so-called "Southwestern" styled elements in later music at large, or in expressive culture at large, like the "Texas sax" projection of Louis Jordan that has been in part incorporated into much media commercial playing?

Well, if you come up with anything musically new in this country it gets watered down as it enters the mainstream. Singers and instrumentalists imitate that which is original in other singers and instrumentalists. The Southwestern rhythm and that great freedom within discipline that you first heard in Count Basie's band was swiftly incorporated into Benny Goodman and most of the white big bands.

When a style is definitive, when it expresses the time of day, that's what happens. But we know that "swing" was generated in the Southwest and quickly took over. Back when it was called stomp or jump it created an effect quite different from what you got on the East coast, say with Ellington; the orchestration and the spirit was different. In it the presence of the blues was more obvious, as were the kinds of improvisation. There was the percussive of the brass section that you get in "Going to Chicago," and the lyricism of the Basie band. Being definitive, the feeling generated was attractive to any number of musicians outside the Southwest. If they're exciting, musical styles tend to be nationalized. They enter the mainstream.

Where do we go from the point of the dissemination of style in the commercialized cultural forms?

Cultural forms, especially forms of popular music, become trivialized through the efforts of promoters to package novelty. This has a negative effect on art. The jazz of the thirties and forties was not exhausted artistically; they were supplanted by promoters who were more interested in making money than in art. The big bands were broken up by agents who convinced sidemen that they would make more money by going on the road as members or leaders of small combos. We can't overlook the economic conditions that made it difficult to maintain a big band, nor the war, but the agents were largely responsible. In this country the direction of culture is always being tampered with by people who have little concern for art, and yet their manipulations have consequences in other areas of the society, often leading to chaos in our lifestyles and moral disorientation. As with the Beatles, who with their Liverpool-accented rebellion and Afro-American influenced music hit this country and its young like a ton of bricks. I think that some of the attitudes promoted by the boppers, their discouragement of the dancers, the legend of Parker's drug habit—such things helped make the Beatles phenomenon possible. The artistic quality of the Beatles' music was masked by their irreverent behavior. It sounded easier than it actually was and this was helped by the use of electrified instruments and their costumes. Such details made many white kids believe that they could create a do-it-yourself type of music. As I indicated in the Minton's piece so many who didn't grasp the agony of Parker or the music he created imitated his drug-taking and irresponsibility. Suddenly you couldn't visit friends who had adolescent children without having to listen to them bang on guitars and little electric pianos. And yet for all its tastelessness, at a time when Johnny Hodges was hardly making a living, such noise became the source of great wealth and facile celebrity.

Willie "the Lion" Smith mentioned in his autobiography that music was more fun before the promoters got into it.

Jazz was part of a total culture, at least among Afro-Americans. People saved their nickels and dimes in order to participate in it. Hell, we used to work like the dickens to get the admission fee when a dance was being played by someone we admired. Jazzmen were heroes . . . I guess they still are.

Some of the musicians who've come along since 1960 have had their music susceptible to its being qualitatively diminished.

It might be their artistic good luck. You always have an ambivalence toward this sort of thing because you feel that it is artistic quality that should be promoted. It happens with classical music but it isn't so susceptible to manipulation. But on the level of vernacular music there's always this group of promoters who stand between the audience and the musician. It suggests that today jazz still demands sacrifice just as it did when I was growing up. Dedicated musicians accepted the fact that it would often be necessary to be out of work for weeks or even months. Such difficulties went with the art. Duke Ellington never gave up his one-night stands, perhaps because he realized that traveling around the country involved a process that was musically fertilizing.

It placed him in contact with newer styles and undiscovered musicians of talent. He was like a football scout, covering the fields and listening to what was going on. It would seem to me that today's musician might adopt such an attitude. Perhaps they'd do better if they went back to playing for dances, went back to the communal situation in which there's a closer identification between their artistic goals and their prospective audience's desire to participate in the creation of the jazz spell.

Dancers today seem programmed. For example, disco. But if you were to take a Gillespie or Moody or some of the younger acoustically in-clined musicians, and have a music you could dance to without the disco sound, it might be beautiful.

I assume that audiences haven't been exposed to the kind of music you suggest. I suspect that the discotheque is itself the product of economic rather than artistic developments. It's just easier to get records and loudspeakers than to hire a good band and pay union wages.

THE CHARLIE CHRISTIAN STORY

Taking its title from an album of reissued recordings by the great jazz guitarist who translated to his instrument the good news of Lester Young's coolly inventive tenor-saxophone lines, this review/essay, like several pieces in this volume, calls for a more search-ing history of jazz. "For while there is now a rather extensive history of discography and recording sessions," Ellison writes here, "there is but the bare beginnings of a historiography of jazz. We know much of jazz as entertainment, but a mere handful of clichés constitutes our knowledge of jazz as experience." An improved jazz history will know about the music's Charlie Christians: their complex racial and class backgrounds, their formal and informal schooling (even in the "territorial" spaces and bands under the radar of most jazz histo-ries, even as it involves the media and informal apprenticeships as well as the awareness of musical traditions not directly associated with jazz). This revamped history will be more subtly aware of the evolving forms of the art itself and of the variety of scenes from which the artists sprang. And it will ponder the work of these musi-cians prior to their arrival in New York or "discovery." For more on this question of fateful geography, see also Ellison's essay called "What These Children Are Like" (1963, included in The Col-lected Essays of Ralph Ellison*) where again Ellison's fellow-*

*Oklahoman Charlie Christian is celebrated along with the depressed area of Oklahoma City they both knew: "This was an alive commu-nity in which the harshness of slum life was inescapable, but in which the strength and imagination of these people was much in ev-idence . . . . But how many geniuses do you get anywhere? And where do you find a first-class imagination? Who really knows? Imagination is where you find it; thus we must search the whole scene." (*Satur-day Review, *May 17, 1958)*

———

Jazz, like the country which gave it birth, is fecund in its in-ventiveness, swift and traumatic in its developments and ter-ribly wasteful of its resources. It is an orgiastic art which demands great physical stamina of its practitioners, and many of its most talented creators die young. More often than not (and this is especially true of its Negro exponents) its heroes remain local figures known only to small-town dance halls, and whose reputations are limited to the radius of a few hundred miles.

A case in point, and a compelling argument for closer study of roots and causes, is a recording devoted to the art of Charlie Christian, probably the greatest of jazz guitarists. He died in 1942 after a brief, spectacular career with the Benny Goodman Sextet. Had he not come from Oklahoma City in 1939 at the instigation of John Hammond, he might have shared the fate of many we knew in the period when Christian was growing up (and I doubt that it has changed very much today).

Some of the most brilliant of jazzmen made no records; their names appeared in print only in announcements of some local dance or remote "battles of music" against equally uncelebrated bands. Being devoted to an art which traditionally thrives on improvisation, these unrecorded artists very often have their most original ideas enter the public domain almost as rapidly as they are conceived, to be quickly absorbed into the thought and technique of their fellows. Thus the riffs which swung the dancers and the band on some transcendent evening, and which inspired others to competitive flights of invention, become all too swiftly a part of the general style, leaving the originator as anonymous as the creators of the architecture called Gothic.

There is in this a cruel contradiction implicit in the art form itself, for true jazz is an art of individual assertion within and against the group. Each true jazz moment (as distinct from the uninspired commercial performance) springs from a contest in which each artist challenges all the rest; each solo flight, or improvisation, represents (like the successive canvases of a painter) a definition of his identity as individual, as member of the collectivity and as a link in the chain of tradition. Thus, because jazz finds its very life in an endless improvisation upon traditional materials, the jazzman must lose his identity even as he finds it; how often do we see even the most famous of jazz artists being devoured alive by their imitators, and, shamelessly, in the public spotlight?

So at best the musical contributions of these local, unrecorded heroes of jazz are enjoyed by a few fellow musicians and by a few dancers who admire them and afford them the meager economic return which allows them to keep playing. But often they live beyond the period of youthful dedication, hoping in vain that some visiting big-band leader will provide the opportunity to break through to the wider spheres of jazz. Indeed, to escape these fates the artists must be very talented, very individual, as restlessly inventive as Picasso, and very lucky.

Charles Christian, when Hammond brought him to the attention of Goodman, had been for most of his life just such a local jazz hero. Nor do I use the term loosely, for having known him since 1923, when he and my younger brother were members of the same first-grade class, I can recall no time when he was not admired for his skillful playing of stringed instruments. Indeed, a great part of his time in the manual-training department of Douglass School was spent constructing guitars from cigar boxes, instruments upon which both he and his older brother Clarence were dazzlingly adept. Incidentally, in their excellent notes to the album, Al Avakian and Bob Prince are mistaken when they assume that Christian was innocent of contact with musical forms more sophisticated than the blues, and it would be well that here I offer a correction. Before Charlie was big enough to handle a guitar himself he served as a guide for his father, a blind guitarist and singer. Later he joined with his father, his brothers Clarence and Edward (an arranger, pianist, violinist and performer on the string bass and tuba), and made his contribution to the family income by strolling with them through the white middle-class sections of Oklahoma City, where they played serenades on request. Their repertory included the light classics as well as the blues, and there was no doubt in the minds of those who heard them that the musical value they gave was worth far more than the money they received. Later on Edward, who took leading roles in the standard operettas performed by members of the high-school chorus, led his own band and played gigs from time to time with such musicians as "Hot Lips" Page, Walter Page, Sammy Price and Lem C. Johnson (to mention a few), all members at some point of the Blue Devils Orchestra, which later merged with the Benny Moten group to become the famous Count Basie Band. I need only mention that Oklahoma City was a regular stopping point for Kansas City–based orchestras, or that a number of the local musicians were conservatory-trained and were capable of sight-reading the hodgepodge scores which during the "million-dollar production" stage of the silent movies were furnished to the stands of pit orchestras.

The facts in these matters are always more intriguing than the legends. In the school which we attended, harmony was taught from the ninth through the twelfth grades; there was an extensive and compulsory music-appreciation program, and, though Charles was never a member, a concert band and orchestra and several vocal organizations. In brief, both in his home and in the community Charles Christian was subjected to many diverse musical influences. It was the era of radio, and for a while a local newspaper gave away cheap plastic recordings of such orchestras as Jean Goldkette's, along with subscriptions. The big media of communication were active for better or worse even then, and the Negro community was never completely isolated from their influence.

However, perhaps the most stimulating influence upon Christian, and one with whom he was later to be identified, was that of a tall, intense young musician who arrived in Oklahoma City sometime in 1929 and who, with his heavy white sweater, blue stocking cap and up-and-outthrust silver saxophone, left absolutely no reed player and few young players of any instrument unstirred by the wild, excitingly original flights of his imagination. Who else but Lester Young, who with his battered horn upset the entire Negro section of the town? One of our friends gave up his valved instrument for the tenor saxophone and soon ran away from home to carry the new message to Baltimore, while a good part of the efforts of the rest was spent trying to absorb and transform the Youngian style. Indeed, only one other young musician created anything like the excitement attending Young's stay in the town. This was Carlton George, who had played with Earl Hines and whose trumpet style was shaped after the excursions of Hines's right hand. He, however, was a minor influence, having arrived during the national ascendancy of Louis Armstrong and during the local reign of Oran ("Hot Lips") Page.

When we consider the stylistic development of Charles Christian we are reminded how little we actually know of the origins of even the most recent of jazz styles, or of when and where they actually started, or of the tensions, personal, sociological or technical, out of which such an original artist achieves his stylistic identity. For while there is now a rather extensive history of discography and recording sessions, there is but the bare beginnings of a historiography of jazz. We know much of jazz as entertainment, but a mere handful of clichés constitutes our knowledge of jazz as experience. Worse, it is this which is frequently taken for all there is, and we get the impression that jazz styles are created in some club on some particular occasion, and there and then codified according to the preconceptions of the jazz publicists in an atmosphere as grave and traditional, say, as that attending the deliberations of the Academie Française. It is this which leads to the notion that jazz was invented in a particular house of ill fame by "Jelly Roll" Morton, who admitted the crime himself; that swing was invented by Goodman in about 1935; and that T. Monk, K. Clarke and J. B. "D." Gillespie invented "progressive" jazz at Minton's Playhouse in Harlem about 1941.

This is, of course, convenient but only relatively true, and the effort to let the history of jazz as entertainment stand for the whole of jazz ignores the most fundamental knowledge of the dynamics of stylistic growth which has been acquired from studies in other branches of music and from our knowledge of the growth of other art forms. The jazz artist who becomes nationally known is written about as though he came into existence only upon his arrival in New York. His career in the big cities, where jazz is more of a commercial entertainment than part of a total way of life, is stressed at the expense of his life in the South, the Southwest and the Midwest, where most Negro musicians found their early development. Thus we are left with an impression of mysterious rootlessness, and the true and often annoying complexity of American cultural experience is over-simplified.

With jazz this has made for the phenomena of an art form existing in a curious state of history and pre-history simultaneously. Not that it isn't recognized that it is an art with deep roots in the past, but that the nature of its deep connection with social conditions here and now is slighted. Charlie Christian is a case in point. He flowered from a background with roots not only in a tradition of music, but in a deep division in the Negro community as well. He spent much of his life in a slum in which all the forms of disintegration attending the urbanization of rural Negroes ran riot. Although he himself was from a respectable family, the wooden tenement in which he grew up was full of poverty, crime and sickness. It was also alive and exciting, and I enjoyed visiting there, for the people both lived and sang the blues. Nonetheless, it was doubtless here that he developed the tuberculosis from which he died.

More important, jazz was regarded by most of the respectable Negroes of the town as a backward, low-class form of expression, and there was a marked difference between those who accepted and lived close to their folk experience and those whose status strivings led them to reject and deny it. Charlie rejected this attitude in turn, along with those who held it, even to the point of not participating in the musical activities of the school. Like Jimmy Rushing, whose father was a businessman and whose mother was active in church affairs, he had heard the voice of jazz and would hear no other. Ironically, what was perhaps his greatest social triumph came in death, when the respectable Negro middle class not only joined in the public mourning, but acclaimed him as a hero and took credit for his development. The attention which the sheer quality of his music should have secured him was won only by his big-town success.

Fortunately for us, Charles concentrated on the guitar and left the school band to his brother Edward, and his decision was a major part of his luck. For although it is seldom recognized, there is a conflict between what the Negro American musician feels in the community around him and the given (or classical) techniques of his instrument. He feels a tension between his desire to master the classical style of playing and his compulsion to express those sounds which form a musical definition of Negro American experience. In early jazz these sounds found their fullest expression in the timbre of the blues voice, and the use of mutes, water glasses and derbies on the bells of their horns arose out of an attempt to imitate this sound. Among the younger musicians of the thirties, especially those who contributed to the growth of bop, this desire to master the classical technique was linked with the struggle for recognition in the larger society, and with a desire to throw off those nonmusical features which came into jazz from the minstrel tradition. Actually, it was for this reason that Louis Armstrong (who is not only a great performing artist but a clown in the Elizabethan sense of the word) became their scapegoat. What was not always understood was that there were actually two separate bodies of instrumental technique: the one classic, widely recognized and "correct"; and the other eclectic, partly unconscious and "jazzy." And it was the tension between these two bodies of technique which led to many of the technical discoveries of jazz. Further, we are now aware of the existence of a fully developed and endlessly flexible technique of jazz expression, which has become quite independent of the social environment in which it developed, if not of its spirit.

Interestingly enough, the guitar (long regarded as a traditional instrument of Southern Negroes) was subjected to little of this conflict between techniques and ways of experiencing the world. Its role in the jazz orchestra was important but unobtrusive, and before Christian little had been done to explore its full potentialities for jazz. Thus Christian was able to experiment with the least influence from either traditional or contemporary sources. Starting long before he was aware of his mission—as would seem to be the way with important innovators in the arts—he taught himself to voice the guitar as a solo instrument, a development made possible through the perfecting of the electronically amplified instrument, and the rest is history.

With Christian the guitar found its jazz voice. With his entry into jazz circles his musical intelligence was able to exert its influence upon his peers and to affect the course of the future development of jazz. This album of his work—so irresistible and danceable in its swing, so intellectually stimulating in its ideas—is important not only for its contribution to our knowledge of the evolution of contemporary jazz style; it also offers one of the best arguments for bringing more serious critical intelligence to this branch of our national culture.

REMEMBERING JIMMY

This extraordinary essay, like the piece on Charlie Christian, is a review of recent recordings by an artist Ellison had known since his earliest days in Oklahoma City. It offers indispensable definitions of jazz and blues and the settings where the writer first heard them performed. Here Ellison also presents lush, firsthand accounts of Rushing's "steel-bright" yet "silky smooth" voice "jetting from the dance hall like a blue flame in the dark . . . skimming the froth of reeds and rhythm as it called some woman's anguished name." More than anyplace else, "Remembering Jimmy" is where Ellison answers the question of jazz as local and national institution: the earthy but nonetheless metaphysical poetry of its lyrics, its capacity to provide perspective and a sense of wholeness while reminding Americans "who and where we are." Some of the mystery of the scene depicted here is suggested by the fact that Rushing's music first flowed from "what seemed to be the least desirable side of the city (but which some years later was found to contain one of the state's richest pools of oil)." In the introduction to Shadow and Act, *where this essay first appeared between hard covers, Ellison gives thanks "to Jimmy Rushing, who through his friendship and through our many hour-long telephone conversations has helped to keep my sense of my Oklahoma background—especially the jazz—so vividly alive."* (Saturday Review, *July 12, 1958)*

———

In the old days the voice was high and clear and poignantly lyrical. Steel-bright in its upper range and, at its best, silky smooth, it was possessed of a purity somehow impervious to both the stress of singing above a twelve-piece band and the urgency of Rushing's own blazing fervor. On dance nights, when you stood on the rise of the school grounds two blocks to the east, you could hear it jetting from the dance hall like a blue flame in the dark, now soaring high above the trumpets and trombones, now skimming the froth of reeds and rhythm as it called some woman's anguished name— or demanded in a high, thin, passionately lyrical line, "Baaaaay-bay, Bay-aaaay-bay! Tell me what's the matter now!"—above the shouting of the swinging band.

Nor was there need for the by now famous signature line: "If anybody asks you who sang this song / Tell 'em / it was little Jimmy Rushing / he's been here and gone," for everyone on Oklahoma City's "East Side" knew that sweet, high-floating sound. "Deep Second" was our fond nickname for the block in which Rushing worked and lived, and where most Negro businesses and entertainments were found, and before he went on to cheer a wider world his voice evoked the festive spirit of the place. Indeed, he was the natural herald of its blues-romance, his song the singing essence of its joy. For Jimmy Rushing was not simply a local entertainer; he expressed a value, an attitude about the world for which our lives afforded no other definition. We had a Negro church and a segregated school, a few lodges and fraternal organizations, and beyond these there was all the great white world. We were pushed off to what seemed to be the least desirable side of the city (but which some years later was found to contain one of the state's richest pools of oil), and our system of justice was based upon Texas law; yet there was an optimism within the Negro community and a sense of possibility which, despite our awareness of limitation (dramatized so brutally in the Tulsa riot of 1921), transcended all of this, and it was this rock-bottom sense of reality, coupled with our sense of the possibility of rising above it, which sounded in Rushing's voice.

And how it carried! In those days I lived near the Rock Island roundhouse, where, with a steady clanging of bells and a great groaning of wheels along the rails, switch engines made up trains of freight unceasingly. Yet often in the late-spring night I could hear Rushing as I lay four blocks away in bed, carrying to me as clear as a full-bored riff on "Hot Lips" Page's horn. Heard thus, across the dark blocks lined with locust trees, through the night throbbing with the natural aural imagery of the blues, with high-balling trains, departing bells, lonesome guitar chords simmering up from a shack in the alley, it was easy to imagine the voice as setting the pattern to which the instruments of the Blue Devils Orchestra and all the random sounds of night arose, affirming, as it were, some ideal native to the time and to the land. When we were still too young to attend night dances, but yet old enough to gather beneath the corner streetlamp on summer evenings, anyone might halt the conversation to exclaim, "Listen, they're raising hell down at Slaughter's Hall," and we'd turn our heads westward to hear Jimmy's voice soar up the hill and down, as pure and as miraculously unhindered by distance and earthbound things as is the body in youthful dreams of flying.

"Now, that's the Right Reverend Jimmy Rushing preaching now, man," someone would say. And rising to the cue another would answer, "Yeah, and that's old Elder 'Hot Lips' signifying along with him, urging him on, man." And, keeping it building, "Huh, but though you can't hear him out this far, Ole Deacon Big-un [the late Walter Page] is up there patting his foot and slapping on his big belly [the bass viol] to keep those fools in line." And we might go on to name all the members of the band as though they were the Biblical four-and-twenty elders, while laughing at the impious wit of applying church titles to a form of music which all the preachers assured us was the devil's potent tool.

Our wit was true, for Jimmy Rushing, along with the other jazz musicians whom we knew, had made a choice, had dedicated himself to a mode of expression and a way of life no less "righteously" than others dedicated themselves to the church. Jazz and the blues did not fit into the scheme of things as spelled out by our two main institutions, the church and the school, but they gave expression to attitudes which found no place in these and helped to give our lives some semblance of wholeness. Jazz and the public jazz dance was a third institution in our lives, and a vital one, and though Jimmy was far from being a preacher, he was, as official floor manager or master-of-the-dance at Slaughter's Hall, the leader of a public rite.

He was no Mr. Five-by-five in those days, but a compact, debonair young man who dressed with an easy elegance. Much later, during theater appearances with Basie's famous band, he sometimes cut an old step from slavery days called "falling off the log" for the sheer humor provided by the rapid and apparently precarious shifting of his great bulk, but in the Oklahoma days he was capable of an amazing grace of movement. A nineteenth-century formality still clung to public dances at the time, and there was quite a variety of steps. Jimmy danced them all, gliding before the crowd over the polished floor, sometimes with a girl, sometimes with a huge megaphone held chest-high before him as he swayed. The evenings began with the more formal steps, to popular and semi-classical music, and proceeded to become more expressive as the spirit of jazz and the blues became dominant. It was when Jimmy's voice began to soar with the spirit of the blues that the dancers—and the musicians—achieved that feeling of communion which was the true meaning of the public jazz dance. The blues, the singer, the band and the dancers formed the vital whole of jazz as an institutional form, and even today neither part is quite complete without the rest. The thinness of much of so-called "modern jazz" is especially reflective of this loss of wholeness, and it is quite possible that Rushing retains his vitality simply because he has kept close to the small Negro public dance.

The occasion for this shamelessly nostalgic outburst is provided by a series of Rushing recordings issued over the past few years: Vanguard's *Jazz Showcase;* Columbia's *Goin' to Chicago, Listen to the Blues with Jimmy Rushing, If This Ain't the Blues, The Jazz Odyssey of James Rushing, Esq.,* and *Little Jimmy Rushing and the Big Brass.* An older recording, Decca's *Kansas City Jazz,* contains Rushing's best version of his classic "Good Morning, Blues," and offers a vivid idea of the styles and combinations of musicians which made up the milieu in which Rushing found his early development. These discs form a valuable introduction to the art of Jimmy Rushing in all its fervor and variety.

Rushing is known today primarily as a blues singer, but not so in those days. He began as a singer of ballads, bringing to them a sincerity and a feeling for dramatizing the lyrics in the musical phrase which charged the banal lines with the mysterious potentiality of meaning which haunts the blues. And it was, perhaps, Rushing's beginning as a ballad singer which gives his blues interpretations their special quality. For one of the significant aspects of his art is the imposition of a romantic lyricism upon the blues tradition (compare his version of "See See Rider" with that of Ma Rainey), a lyricism which is not of the Deep South, but of the Southwest: a romanticism native to the frontier, imposed upon the violent rawness of a part of the nation which only thirteen years before Rushing's birth was still Indian territory. Thus there is an optimism in it which echoes the spirit of those Negroes who, like Rushing's father, had come to Oklahoma in search of a more human way of life.

Rushing is one of the first singers to sing the blues before a big band, and even today he seldom comes across as a blues "shouter," but maintains the lyricism which has always been his way with the blues. Indeed, when we listen to his handling of lyrics we become aware of that quality which makes for the mysteriousness of the blues: their ability to imply far more than they state outright, and their capacity to make the details of sex convey meanings which touch upon the metaphysical. For, indeed, they always find poetry in the limits of the Negro vocabulary. Perhaps because he is more educated and came from a family already well on its rise into what is called the "Negro middle class," Jimmy has always shown a concern for the correctness of language, and out of the tension between the traditional folk pronunciation and his training in school, he has worked out a flexibility of enunciation and a rhythmical agility with words which make us constantly aware of the meanings which shimmer just beyond the limits of the lyrics. The blues is an art of ambiguity, an assertion of the irrepressibly human over all circumstance, whether created by others or by one's own human failings. They are the only consistent art in the United States which constantly remind us of our limitations while encouraging us to see how far we can actually go. When understood in their more profound implication, they are a corrective, an attempt to draw a line upon man's own limitless assertion.

Significantly, Jimmy Rushing was able to spread the appeal of the blues to a wider American audience after the Depression had made us a bit more circumspect about the human cost of living our "American way of life." It seems especially fitting now, when circumstance and its own position of leadership has forced the nation once more to examine its actions and its intentions, that the blues are once more becoming popular. There is great demand for Rushing in Europe, from which he has just returned with the Goodman band. And I think we need him more here at home. Certainly this collection of discs will make us aware that there is emotional continuity in American life, and that the abiding moods expressed in our most vital popular art form are not simply a matter of entertainment; they also tell us who and where we are.

THE GOLDEN AGE, TIME PAST

First called "The Rumpus at Minton's" and later, simply "Minton's" (in memory of the Harlem club made famous by its policy of encouraging the new brand of jazz eventually called bebop), this eloquent essay was written for a special issue of Esquire *magazine devoted to the legacy of jazz in America. (For Ellison's comments on writing the piece, see his letter to Albert Murray, September 28, 1958.) This was the introductory section of* Esquire's *three-part survey of "The Golden Age of Jazz," the other essays being "The Golden Age of Jazz, Time Present" and "The Golden Age of Jazz, Time Future." For his part, Ellison chooses to focus on bebop and its roots in the traditional jam session, "the jazzman's true academy." Acknowledging the new music's connections with dance halls and their celebrations of shared culture; with the Rhythm Club and its various supports for working musicians; and with the boldness of the new jazz generation's self-patrolled and relentless search for artistic excellence in a modern idiom—Ellison also offers here a stinging critique of bebop, which he associates less with jazz's legacy of fecund creation than, alas, with overintellectuality and despair. Thus for him the imposed title is an ironic comment on those who remember only the creativity of the bop period without recalling what, for Ellison, was a much more golden age of jazz: the earlier years of the mythic players at*

*Minton's. Thus, this essay is also a critique of American forgetful-
ness, selective memory, and cultural waste. Also interesting to note
here are Ellison's own efforts as a writer to jam with other writers as
he attempted to create a modern artistic language, one that "made it
new" without committing bebop's sins of fragmentation and disten-
tion from the local community's vital rituals. Two years after this
"Golden Age" piece was published, a fascinating coda appeared in a
University of Chicago magazine. "In music," the interviewers said to
Ellison, "nothing new is happening, with the possible exception of
Ornette Coleman." To which Ellison replied dryly that he was "more
apt to be caught up by Ray Charles than Ornette Coleman—or the
Modern Jazz Quartet. So much is happening in Charles, so many
levels of tradition are operating, and there's such an exuberance. . . .
The other day I heard him playing something that sounded like rock
and roll, but I'm sure that if you started peeling those layers back
you'd find something much richer and something which would bear a
lot of analysis. Much of what pretends to be new in jazz seems
merely pretentious." Faced with a choice involving the boppers or the
avant-garde players of the next decade, Ellison would take the hard-
driving, true Golden Age blues players and singers every time.*

*As a postscript for those wondering about Ellison's politics of this
period, note that in 1961 the writer donated the manuscript of this
essay to the Congress of Racial Equality for an auction to raise
money for the Negro student sit-in movement.* (Esquire, *January
1959*)

———

> That which we do is what we are. That which we re-
> member is, more often than not, that which we would
> like to have been, or that which we hope to be. Thus
> our memory and our identity are ever at odds, our
> history ever a tall tale told by inattentive idealists.

It has been a long time now, and not many remember how it
was in the old days, not really. Not even those who were
there to see and hear as it happened, who were pressed in
the crowds beneath the dim rosy lights of the bar in the

smoke-veiled room, and who shared, night after night, the mysterious spell created by the talk, the laughter, grease paint, powder, perfume, sweat, alcohol and food—all blended and simmering, like a stew on the restaurant range, and brought to a sustained moment of elusive meaning by the timbres and accents of musical instruments locked in passionate recitative. It has been too long now, some seventeen years.

Above the bandstand there later appeared a mural depicting a group of jazzmen holding a jam session in a narrow Harlem bedroom. While an exhausted girl with shapely legs sleeps on her stomach in a big brass bed, they bend to their music in a quiet concatenation of unheard sound: a trumpeter, a guitarist, a clarinetist, a drummer, their only audience a small, cock-eared dog. The clarinetist is white. The guitarist strums with an enigmatic smile. The trumpet is muted. The barefooted drummer, beating a folded newspaper with whisk-brooms in lieu of a drum, stirs the eye's ear like a blast of brasses in a midnight street. A bottle of port rests on a dresser, but like the girl it is ignored. The artist, Charles Graham, adds mystery to, as well as illumination within, the scene by having them play by the light of a kerosene lamp. The painting, executed in a harsh documentary style reminiscent of W.P.A. art, conveys a feeling of musical effort caught in timeless and unrhetorical suspension, the sad remoteness of a scene observed through a wall of crystal.

Except for the lamp, the room might well have been one in the Hotel Cecil, the building on 118th Street in which Minton's Playhouse is located, and although painted in 1946, some time after the revolutionary doings there had begun, the mural should help recall the old days vividly. But the décor of the place has been changed, and now it is covered most of the time by draperies. These require a tricky skill of those who would draw them aside. And even then there will still only be the girl who must sleep forever unhearing, and the men who must forever gesture the same soundless tune. Besides, the time it celebrates is dead and gone, and perhaps not even those who came when it was still fresh and new remember those days as they were. Neither would they remember Henry Minton, who gave the place his name, nor those who shared in the noisy lostness of New York: the rediscovered community of the feasts, evocative of home, of the South, of good times, the best and most unself-conscious of times, created by the generous portions of Negro American cuisine—the hash, grits, fried chicken, the ham-seasoned vegetables, the hot biscuits and rolls and the free whiskey—with which, each Monday night, Teddy Hill honored the entire cast of current Apollo Theatre shows. They were gathered here from all parts of America, and they broke bread together, and there was a sense of good feeling and promise, but what shape the fulfilled promise would take they did not know, and few except the more rest-less of the younger musicians even questioned. Yet it was an exceptional moment and the world was swinging with change.

Most of them, black and white alike, were hardly aware of where they were or what time it was; nor did they wish to be. They thought of Minton's as a sanctuary, where in an atmosphere blended of nostalgia and a music-and-drink-lulled suspension of time they could retreat from the wartime tensions of the town. The meaning of time-present was not their concern; thus when they try to tell it now the meaning escapes them. For they were caught up in events which made that time exceptionally and uniquely *then,* and which brought, among the other changes which have re-shaped the world, a momentous modulation into a new key of musical sensibility—in brief, a revolution in culture.

So how *can* they remember? Even in swiftly changing America there are few such moments, and at best Americans give but a limited attention to history. Too much happens too rapidly, and before we can evaluate it, or exhaust its meaning or pleasure, there is something new to concern us.

Ours is the tempo of the motion picture, not that of the still camera, and we waste experience as we wasted the forest. During the time it was happening the sociologists were concerned with riots, unemployment, and industrial tensions, the historians with the onsweep of the war, and the critics and most serious students of culture found this area of our national life of little interest. So it was left to those who came to Minton's out of the needs of feeling, and when the moment was past no one retained more than a fragment of its happening. Afterward the very effort to put the fragments together transformed them, so that in place of true memory they now summon to mind pieces of legend. They retell the stories as they have been told and written, glamorized, inflated, made neat and smooth, with all incomprehensible details vanished along with most of the wonder—not how it was as they themselves knew it.

When asked how it was back then, back in the forties, they will smile; then, frowning with the puzzlement of one attempting to recall the details of a pleasant but elusive dream, they'll say: "Oh, man, it was a hell of a time! A wailing time! Things were jumping, you couldn't get in here for the people. The place was packed with celebrities. Park Avenue, man! Big people in show business, college professors along with the pimps and their women. And college boys and girls. Everybody came. You know how the old words to the 'Basin Street Blues' used to go before Sinatra got hold of it? *Basin Street is the street where the dark and the light folks meet*—that's what I'm talking about. That was Minton's, man. It was a place where everybody could come to be entertained because it was a place that was jumping with good times."

Or some will tell you that it was here that Dizzy Gillespie found his own trumpet voice; that here Kenny Clarke worked out the patterns of his drumming style; where Charlie Christian played out the last creative and truly satisfying moments of his brief life, his New York home; where Charlie Parker built the monument of his art; where Thelonious Monk formulated his contribution to the chordal progressions and the hide-and-seek melodic methods of modern jazz. And they'll call such famous names as Lester Young, Ben Webster and Coleman Hawkins; or Fats Waller, who came here in the after-hours stillness of the early morning to compose. They'll tell you that Benny Goodman, Art Tatum, Count Basie and Lena Horne would drop in to join in the fun; that it was here that George Shearing played on his first night in the United States; or of Tony Scott's great love of the place; and they'll repeat all the stories of how, when and by whom the word "bebop" was coined here—but, withal, few actually remember, and these leave much unresolved.

Usually music gives resonance to memory (and Minton's was a hotbed of jazz), but not the music in the making here then. It was itself a texture of fragments, repetitive, nervous, not fully formed; its melodic lines underground, secret and taunting; its riffs jeering—"Salt peanuts! Salt peanuts!"—its timbres flat or shrill, with a minimum of thrilling vibrato. Its rhythms were out of stride and seemingly arbitrary, its drummers frozen-faced introverts dedicated to chaos. And in it the steady flow of memory, desire and defined experience summed up by the traditional jazz beat and blues mood seemed swept like a great river from its old, deep bed. We know better now, and recognize the old moods in the new sounds, but what we know is that which was then becoming. For most of those who gathered here, the enduring meaning of the great moment at Minton's took place off to the side, beyond the range of attention, like a death blow glimpsed from the corner of the eye, the revolutionary rumpus sounding like a series of flubbed notes blasting the talk with discord. So that the events which made Minton's *Minton's* arrived in conflict and ran their course; then the heat was gone and all that is left to mark its passage is the controlled fury of the music itself, sealed pure and irrevocable, banalities and excellencies alike, in the early recordings, or swept along by our restless quest for the new, to be diluted in more recent styles, the best of it absorbed like drops of fully distilled technique, mood and emotions into the great stream of jazz.

Left also to confuse our sense of what happened is the word "bop," hardly more than a nonsense syllable, by which the music synthesized at Minton's came to be known. A most inadequate word which does little, really, to help us remember. A word which throws up its hands in clownish self-deprecation before all the complexity of sound and rhythm and self-assertive passion which it pretends to name, a mask-word for the charged ambiguities of the new sound, hiding the serious face of art.

Nor does it help that so much has come to pass in the meantime. There have been two hot wars and that which continues, called "cold." And the unknown young men who brought a new edge to the sound of jazz and who scrambled the rhythms of those who used the small clear space at Minton's for dancing are no longer so young or unknown; indeed, they are referred to now by nickname in even the remotest of places. And in Paris and Munich and Tokyo they'll tell you the details of how, after years of trying, "Dizzy" (meaning John Birks Gillespie) vanquished "Roy" (meaning Roy Eldridge) during a jam session at Minton's, to become thereby the new king of trumpeters. Or how, later, while jetting over the world on the blasts of his special tilt-belled horn, he jammed with a snake charmer in Pakistan. "Sent the bloody cobra, man," they'll tell you in London's Soho. So their subsequent fame has blurred the sharp, ugly lines of their rebellion even in the memories of those who found them most strange and distasteful.

What's more, our memory of some of the more brilliant young men has been touched by the aura of death, and we feel guilt that the fury of their passing was the price paid for the art they left us to enjoy unscathed: Charlie Christian, burned out by tuberculosis like a guitar consumed in a tenement fire; Fats Navarro, wrecked by the tensions and needling temptations of his orgiastic trade, a big man physically as well as musically, shrunken to nothingness; and, most notably of all, Charlie Parker, called "Bird," now deified, worshiped and studied and, like any fertility god, mangled by his admirers and imitators, who coughed up his life and died—as incredibly as the leopard which Hemingway tells us was found "dried and frozen" near the summit of Mount Kilimanjaro—in the hotel suite of a baroness. (Nor has anyone explained what a "yardbird" was seeking at that social altitude, though we know that ideally anything is possible within a democracy, and we know quite well that upper-class Europeans were seriously interested in jazz long before Newport became hospitable.) All this is too much for memory; the dry facts are too easily lost in legend and glamour. (With jazz we are yet not in the age of history, but linger in that of folklore.) We know for certain only that the strange sounds which they and their fellows threw against the hum and buzz of vague signification that seethed in the drinking crowd at Minton's, and which, like disgruntled conspirators meeting fatefully to assemble the random parts of a bomb, they joined here and beat and blew into a new jazz style these sounds we know now to have become the clichés, the technical exercises and the standard of achievement not only for fledgling musicians all over the United States, but for Dutchmen and Swedes, Italians and Frenchmen, Germans and Belgians, and even Japanese. All these, in places which came to mind during the Minton days only as points where the war was in progress and where one might soon be sent to fight and die, are now spotted with young men who study the discs on which the revolution hatched in Minton's is preserved with all the intensity that young American painters bring to the works, say, of Kandinsky, Picasso and Klee. Surely this is an odd swing of the cultural tide. Yet Stravinsky, Webern and Berg notwithstanding, or, more recently, Boulez or Stockhausen, such young men (many of them excellent musicians in the highest European tradition) find in the music made articulate at Minton's some key to a fuller freedom of self-realization. Indeed, for many young Europeans the developments which took place here and the careers of those who brought it about have become the latest episodes in the great American epic. They collect the recordings and thrive on the legends as eagerly, perhaps, as young Americans.

Today the bartenders at Minton's will tell you how customers come fresh off the ships or planes, bringing their brightly expectant and—in this Harlem atmosphere—startlingly innocent European faces, to buy drinks and stand looking about for the source of the mystery. They try to reconcile the quiet reality of the place with the events which fired, at such long range, their imaginations. They come as to a shrine—as we to the Louvre, Notre Dame or St. Peter's; as young Americans hurry to the Café Flore, the Deux Magots, the Rotonde or the Café du Dôme in Paris. For some years now they have been coming to ask, with all the solemnity of pilgrims inquiring of a sacred relic, to see the nicotine-stained amplifier which Teddy Hill provided for Charlie Christian's guitar. And this is quite proper, for every shrine should have its relic.

Perhaps Minton's has more meaning for European jazz fans than for Americans, even for those who regularly went there. Certainly it has a *different* meaning. For them it is associated with those continental cafés in which great changes, political and artistic, have been plotted; it is to modern jazz what the Café Voltaire in Zurich is to the Dadaist phase of modern literature and painting. Few of those who visited Harlem during the forties would associate it so, but there is a context of meaning in which Minton's and the musical activities which took place there can be meaningfully placed.

Jazz, for all the insistence of the legends, has been far more closely associated with cabarets and dance halls than with brothels, and it was these which provided both the employment for the musicians and an audience initiated and aware of the overtones of the music; which knew the language of riffs, the unstated meanings of the blues idiom, and the dance steps developed from, and complementary to, its rhythms. And in the beginning it was in the Negro dance hall and night club that jazz was most completely a part of a total cultural expression, and in which it was freest and most satisfying, both for the musicians and for those in whose lives it played a major role. As a night club in a Negro community, then, Minton's was part of a national pattern.

But in the old days Minton's was far more than this; it was also a rendezvous for musicians. As such, and although it was not formally organized, it goes back historically to the first New York center of Negro musicians, the Clef Club. Organized in 1910, during the start of the great migration of Negroes northward, by James Reese Europe, the director whom Irene Castle credits with having invented the fox trot, the Clef Club was set up on West 53rd Street to serve as a meeting place and booking office for Negro musicians and entertainers. Here wage scales were regulated, musical styles and techniques worked out, and entertainment was supplied for such establishments as Rector's and Delmonico's, and for such producers as Florenz Ziegfeld and Oscar Hammerstein. Later, when Harlem evolved into a Negro section, a similar function was served by the Rhythm Club, located then in the old Lafayette Theatre building on 132nd Street and Seventh Avenue. Henry Minton, a former saxophonist and officer of the Rhythm Club, became the first Negro delegate to Local 802 of the American Federation of Musicians, and was thus doubly aware of the needs, artistic as well as economic, of jazzmen. He was generous with loans, was fond of food himself and, as an old acquaintance recalled, "loved to put a pot on the range" to share with unemployed friends. Naturally when he opened Minton's Playhouse many musicians made it their own.

Henry Minton also provided, as did the Clef and Rhythm

clubs, a necessity more important to jazz musicians than food: a place in which to hold their interminable jam sessions. And it is here that Minton's becomes most important to the development of modern jazz. It is here, too, that it joins up with all the countless rooms, private and public, in which jazzmen have worked out the secrets of their craft. Today jam sessions are offered as entertainment by night clubs and on radio and television, and some are quite exciting, but what is seen and heard is only one aspect of the true jam session: the "cutting session," or contest of improvisational skill and physical endurance between two or more musicians. But the jam session is far more than this, and when carried out by musicians in the privacy of small rooms (as in the mural at Minton's), or in such places as Halley Richardson's shoeshine parlor in Oklahoma City (where I first heard Lester Young jamming in a shine chair, his head thrown back, his horn even then outthrust, his feet working on the footrests, as he played with and against Lem Johnson, Ben Webster, and other members of the old Blue Devils Orchestra (this was 1929) or during the after hours in Piney Brown's old Sunset Club in Kansas City; in such places as these, with only musicians and jazzmen present, then the jam session is revealed as the jazzman's true academy.

It is here that he learns tradition, group techniques and style. For although since the twenties many jazzmen have had conservatory training and are well grounded in formal theory and instrumental technique, when we approach jazz we are entering quite a different sphere of training. Here it is more meaningful to speak not of courses of study, of grades and degrees, but of apprenticeship, ordeals, initiation ceremonies, of rebirth. For after the jazzman has learned the fundamentals of his instrument and the traditional techniques of jazz—the intonations, the mute work, manipulation of timbre, the body of traditional styles—he must then "find himself," must be reborn, must find, as it were, his soul. All this through achieving that subtle identification between his instrument and his deepest drives which will allow him to express his own unique ideas and his own unique voice. He must achieve, in short, his self-determined identity.

In this his instructors are his fellow musicians, especially the acknowledged masters, and his recognition of manhood depends upon their acceptance of his ability as having reached a standard which is all the more difficult for not having been rigidly codified. This does not depend upon his ability to simply hold a job, but upon his power to express an individuality in tone. Nor is his status ever unquestioned, for the health of jazz and the unceasing attraction which it holds for the musicians themselves lies in the ceaseless warfare for mastery and recognition—not among the general public, though commercial success is not spurned, but among their artistic peers. And even the greatest can never rest on past accomplishments, for, as with the fast guns of the Old West, there is always someone waiting in a jam session to blow him literally, not only down, but into shame and discouragement.

By making his club hospitable to jam sessions even to the point that customers who were not musicians were crowded out, Henry Minton provided a retreat, a homogeneous community where a collectivity of common experience could find continuity and meaningful expression. Thus the stage was set for the birth of bop.

In 1941 Mr. Minton handed over the management to Teddy Hill, the saxophonist and former band leader, and Hill turned the Playhouse into a musical dueling ground. Not only did he continue Minton's policies, he expanded them. It was Hill who established the Monday Celebrity Nights, the house band which included such members from his own disbanded orchestra as Kenny Clarke, Dizzy Gillespie, Thelonious Monk, sometimes Joe Guy, and later Charlie Christian and Charlie Parker, and it was Hill who allowed the musicians free rein to play whatever they liked. Perhaps no other club except Clarke Monroe's Uptown House was so permissive, and with the hospitality extended to musicians of all schools the news spread swiftly. Minton's became the focal point for musicians all over the country.

Herman Pritchard, who presided over the bar in the old days, tells us that every time they came, "Lester Young and Ben Webster used to tie up in battle like dogs in the road. They'd fight on those saxophones until they were tired out; then they'd put in long-distance calls to their mothers, both of whom lived in Kansas City, and tell them about it."

And most of the masters of jazz came either to observe or to participate and be influenced and listen to their own discoveries transformed, and the aspiring stars sought to win their approval, as the younger tenor men tried to win the esteem of Coleman Hawkins. Or they tried to vanquish them in jamming contests as Gillespie is said to have outblown his idol, Roy Eldridge. It was during this period that Eddie "Lockjaw" Davis underwent an ordeal of jeering rejection until finally he came through as an admired tenor man.

In the perspective of time we now see that what was happening at Minton's was a continuing symposium of jazz, a summation of all the styles, personal and traditional, of jazz. Here it was possible to hear its resources of technique, ideas, harmonic structure, melodic phrasing and rhythmical possibilities explored more thoroughly than was ever possible before. It was also possible to hear the first attempts toward a conscious statement of the sensibility of the younger generation of musicians as they worked out the techniques, structures and rhythmical patterns with which to express themselves. Part of this was arbitrary, a revolt of the younger against the established stylists; part of it was inevitable. For jazz had reached a crisis, and new paths were certain to be searched for and found. An increasing number of the younger men were formally trained, and the post-Depression developments in the country had made for quite a break between their experience and that of the older men. Many were even of a different physical build. Often they were quiet and of a reserve which contrasted sharply with the exuberant and outgoing lyricism of the older men, and they were intensely concerned that their identity as Negroes place no restriction upon the music they played or the manner in which they used their talent. They were concerned, they said, with art, not entertainment. Especially were they resentful of Louis Armstrong, whom (confusing the spirit of his music with his clowning) they considered an Uncle Tom.

But they too, some of them, had their own myths and misconceptions: that theirs was the only generation of Negro musicians who listened to or enjoyed the classics; that to be truly free they must act exactly the opposite of what white people might believe, rightly or wrongly, a Negro to be; that the performing artist can be completely and absolutely free of the obligations of the entertainer, and that they could play jazz with dignity only by frowning and treating the audience with aggressive contempt; and that to be in control, artistically and personally, one must be so cool as to quench one's own human fire.

Nor should we overlook the despair which must have swept Minton's before the technical mastery, the tonal authenticity, the authority and the fecundity of imagination of such men as Hawkins, Young, Goodman, Tatum, Teagarden, Ellington and Waller. Despair, after all, is ever an important force in revolutions.

They were also responding to the nonmusical pressures affecting jazz. It was a time of big bands, and the greatest prestige and economic returns were falling outside the Negro community—often to leaders whose popularity grew from the compositions and arrangements of Negroes—to white instrumentalists whose only originality lay in the enterprise with which they rushed to market with some Negro musician's hard-won style. Still there was no policy of racial discrimination at Minton's. Indeed, it was very much like those Negro cabarets of the twenties and thirties in which a megaphone was placed on the piano so that anyone with the urge could sing a blues. Nevertheless, the inside-dopesters will tell you that the "changes" or chord progressions and melodic inversions worked out by the creators of bop sprang partially from their desire to create a jazz which could not be so easily imitated and exploited by white musicians to whom the market was more open simply *because* of their whiteness. They wished to receive credit for what they created; besides, it was easier to "get rid of the trash" who crowded the bandstand with inept playing and thus make room for the real musicians, whether white or black. Nevertheless, white musicians like Tony Scott, Remo Palmieri and Al Haig who were part of the development at Minton's became so by passing a test of musicianship, sincerity and temperament. Later, it is said, the boppers became engrossed in solving the musical problems which they set themselves. Except for a few sympathetic older musicians, it was they who best knew the promise of the Minton moment, and it was they, caught like the rest in all the complex forces of American life which comes to focus in jazz, who made the most of it. Now the tall tales told as history must feed on the results of their efforts.

On Bird, Bird-Watching,

and Jazz

Here is the last of Ellison's celebrated pieces written for the Saturday Review. *Like the "close-reading" New Critics of the literary academy of that era, Ellison offers careful, critical descriptions of Parker's style, which he finds, at its best, full of invention and subversive mockery. And true to the myth-and-ritual school of New Critics, Ellison sees Parker's life and art as well as his audience responses to them as part of an ancient pattern that uncovers the inner workings of present culture. Note the appearances, in the background, of Ellison's real hero Louis Armstrong, whose big-toned lyricism and ability to manipulate the entertainer's mask without descending into racialized "funereal posturing" make him the truer exemplar of the artist's powers to affirm life, not just to reveal the psychology of a disturbed audience. "Symbolic birds, myth and ritual—what strange metaphors to arise during the discussion of a book about a jazz musician!" Ellison expounds. "And yet who knows very much of what jazz is really about? Or how shall we ever know until we are willing to confront anything and everything which it sweeps across our path?" (*Saturday Review, *July 28, 1962)*

Bird: The Legend of Charlie Parker, a collection of anecdotes, testimonies and descriptions of the life of the famous jazz saxophonist, may be described as an attempt to define just what species of bird Bird really was. Introduced by Robert Reisner's description of his own turbulent friendship and business relations with Parker, it presents contributions by some eighty-three fellow Bird watchers, including a wife and his mother, Mrs. Addie Parker. There are also poems, photographs, descriptions of his funeral, memorial and estate, a chronology of his life, and an extensive discography by Erik Wiedemann.

One of the founders of postwar jazz, Parker had, as an improviser, as marked an influence upon jazz as Louis Armstrong, Coleman Hawkins or Johnny Hodges. He was also famous for his riotous living, which, heightened by alcohol and drugs, led many of his admirers to consider him a latter-day François Villon. Between the beginning of his fame in about 1945 and his death in 1955, he became the central figure of a cult which glorified in his escapades no less than in his music. The present volume is mainly concerned with the escapades, the circumstances behind them and their effect upon Bird's friends and family.

Oddly enough, while several explanations are advanced as to how Charles Parker, Jr., became known as "Bird" ("Yardbird," in an earlier metamorphosis), none is conclusive. There is, however, overpowering internal evidence that whatever the true circumstance of his ornithological designation, it had little to do with the chicken yard. Randy roosters and operatic hens are familiars to fans of the animated cartoons, but for all the pathetic comedy of his living—and despite the crabbed and constricted character of his style—Parker was a most inventive melodist, in bird-watcher's terminology, a true songster.

This failure in the exposition of Bird's legend is intriguing, for nicknames are indicative of a change from a given to an achieved identity, whether by rise or fall, and they tell us something of the nicknamed individual's interaction with his fellows. Thus, since we suspect that more of legend is involved in his renaming than Mr. Reisner's title indicates, let us at least consult Roger Tory Peterson's *Field Guide to the Birds* for a hint as to why, during a period when most jazzmen were labeled "cats," someone hung the bird on Charlie. Let us note too that "legend" originally meant "the story of a saint," and that saints were often identified with symbolic animals.

Two species won our immediate attention, the goldfinch and the mockingbird—the goldfinch because the beatnik phrase "Bird lives," which, following Parker's death, has been chalked endlessly on Village buildings and subway walls, reminds us that during the thirteenth and fourteenth centuries a symbolic goldfinch frequently appeared in European devotional paintings. An apocryphal story has it that upon being given a clay bird for a toy, the infant Jesus brought it miraculously to life as a goldfinch. Thus the small, tawny-brown bird with a bright red patch about the base of its bill and a broad yellow band across its wings became a representative of the soul, the Passion and the Sacrifice. In more worldly late-Renaissance art, the little bird became the ambiguous symbol of death and the soul's immortality. For our own purposes, however, its song poses a major problem: it is like that of a canary—which, soul or no soul, rules the goldfinch out.

The mockingbird, *Mimus polyglottos,* is more promising. Peterson informs us that its song consists of "long successions of notes and phrases of great variety, with each phrase repeated a half-dozen times before going on to the next," that mockingbirds are "excellent mimics" who "adeptly imitate a score or more species found in the neighborhood," and that they frequently sing at night—a description which not only comes close to Parker's way with a saxophone but even hints at a trait of his character. For although he *usually* sang at night, his playing was characterized by velocity, by long-continued successions of notes and phrases, by swoops, bleats, echoes, rapidly repeated bebops—I mean rebopped bebops—by mocking mimicry of other jazzmen's styles, and by interpolations of motifs from extraneous melodies, all of which added up to a dazzling display of wit, satire, burlesque and pathos. Further, he was as expert at issuing his improvisations from the dense brush as from the extreme treetops of the harmonic landscape, and there was, without doubt, as irrepressible a mockery in his personal conduct as in his music.

Mimic thrushes, which include the catbird and brown thrasher, along with the mockingbird, are not only great virtuosi, they are the tricksters and con men of the bird world. Like Parker, who is described as a confidence man and a practical joker by several of the commentators, they take off on the songs of other birds, inflating, inverting and turning them wrong side out, and are capable of driving a prowling ("square") cat wild. Utterly irreverent and romantic, they are not beyond bugging human beings. Indeed, on summer nights in the South, when the moon hangs low, mockingbirds sing as though determined to heat every drop of romance in the sleeping adolescent's heart to fever pitch. Their song thrills and swings the entire moon-struck night to arouse one's sense of the mystery, promise and frustration of being human, alive and hot in the blood. They are as delightful to eye as to ear, but sometimes a similarity of voice and appearance makes for a confusion with the shrike, a species given to impaling insects and smaller songbirds on the points of thorns, and they are destroyed. They are fond of fruit, especially mulberries, and if there is a tree in your yard, there will be, along with the wonderful music, much chalky, blue-tinted evidence of their presence. Under such conditions, be careful and heed Parker's warning to his friends—who sometimes were subjected to a shrikelike treatment—"you must pay your dues to Bird."

Though notes of bitterness sound through Mr. Reisner's book, he and his friends paid willingly for the delight and frustration which Parker brought into their lives. Thus their comments—which are quite unreliable as history—constitute less a collective biography than a celebration of his living and a lamentation of his dying, and are, in the ritual sense, his apotheosis or epiphany into the glory of those who have been reborn in legend.

Symbolic birds, myth and ritual—what strange metaphors to arise during the discussion of a book about a jazz musician! And yet who knows very much of what jazz is really about? Or how shall we ever know until we are willing to confront anything and everything which it sweeps across our path? Consider that at least as early as T. S. Eliot's creation of a new aesthetic for poetry through the artful juxtapositioning of earlier styles, Louis Armstrong, way down the river in New Orleans, was working out a similar technique for jazz. This is not a matter of giving the music fine airs—it doesn't need them—but of saying that whatever touches our highly conscious creators of culture is apt to be reflected here.

The thrust toward respectability exhibited by the Negro jazzmen of Parker's generation drew much of its immediate fire from their understandable rejection of the traditional entertainer's role—a heritage from the minstrel tradition—exemplified by such an outstanding creative musician as Louis Armstrong. But when they fastened the epithet "Uncle Tom" upon Armstrong's music they confused artistic quality with questions of personal conduct, a confusion which would ultimately reduce their own music to the mere matter of race. By rejecting Armstrong they thought to rid themselves of the entertainer's role. And by way of getting rid of the role, they demanded, in the name of their racial identity, a purity of status which by definition is impossible for the performing artist.

The result was a grim comedy of racial manners, with the musicians employing a calculated surliness and rudeness, treating the audience very much as many white merchants in poor Negro neighborhoods treat their customers, and the white audiences were shocked at first but learned quickly to accept such treatment as evidence of "artistic" temperament. Then comes a comic reversal. Today the white audience expects the rudeness as part of the entertainment. If it fails to appear, the audience is disappointed. For the jazzmen it has become a proposition of the more you win, the more you lose. Certain older jazzmen possessed a clearer idea of the division between their identities as performers and as private individuals. Offstage and while playing in ensemble, they carried themselves like college professors or high church deacons; when soloing they donned the comic mask and went into frenzied pantomimes of hotness—even when playing "cool"—and when done, dropped the mask and returned to their chairs with dignity. Perhaps they realized that whatever his style, the performing artist remains an entertainer, even as Heifetz, Rubinstein or young Glenn Gould.

For all the revolutionary ardor of his style, Dizzy Gillespie, a cofounder with Parker of modern jazz and a man with a savage eye for the incongruous, is no less a clown than Louis, and his wide reputation rests as much upon his entertaining personality as upon his gifted musicianship. There is even a morbid entertainment value in watching the funereal posturing of the Modern Jazz Quartet, and doubtless part of the tension created in their listeners arises from the anticipation that during some unguarded moment, the grinning visage of the traditional delight-maker (inferior because performing at the audience's command, superior because he can perform effectively through the magic of his art) will emerge from behind those bearded masks. In the United States, where each of us is a member of some minority group and where political power and entertainment alike are derived from viewing and manipulating the human predicaments of others, the maintenance of dignity is never a simple matter, even for those with highest credentials. Gossip is one of our largest industries, the president is fair

game for caricaturists, and there is always someone around
to set a symbolic midget upon J. P. Morgan's unwilling knee.

———

No jazzman, not even Miles Davis, struggled harder to escape the entertainer's role than Charlie Parker. The pathos
of his life lies in the ironic reversal through which his struggles to escape what in Armstrong is basically a *make-believe*
role of clown—which the irreverent poetry and triumphant
sound of his trumpet makes even the squarest of squares
aware of—resulted in Parker's becoming something far
more "primitive": a sacrificial figure whose struggles against
personal chaos, onstage and off, served as entertainment for
a ravenous, sensation-starved, culturally disoriented public
which had only the slightest notion of its real significance.
While he slowly died (like a man dismembering himself
with a dull razor on a spotlighted stage) from the ceaseless
conflict from which issued both his art and his destruction,
his public reacted as though he were doing much the same
thing as those saxophonists who hoot and honk and roll on
the floor. In the end he had no private life and his most tragic
moments were drained of human significance.

Here, perhaps, is an explanation, beyond all questions of
reason, drugs or whiskey, of the violent contradictions de-
tailed in Mr. Reisner's book of Parker's public conduct. In
attempting to escape the role, at once sub- and superhuman, in which he found himself, he sought to outrage his
public into an awareness of his most human pain. Instead, he
made himself notorious, and in the end became unsure
whether his fans came to enjoy his art or to be entertained
by the "world's greatest junkie," the "supreme hipster." Sensitive and thoroughly aware of the terrifying cost of his art
and his public image, he had to bear not only the dismem-
berment occasioned by rival musicians who imitated every
nuance of his style—often with far greater financial return—but the imitation of his every self-destructive excess
of personal conduct by those who had in no sense earned

the right of such license. Worse, it was these who formed his cult.

Parker operated in the underworld of American culture, on that turbulent level where human instincts conflict with social institutions, where contemporary civilized values and hypocrisies are challenged by the Dionysian urges of a between-wars youth born to prosperity, conditioned by the threat of world destruction, and inspired—when not seeking total anarchy—by a need to bring social reality and our social pretensions into a more meaningful balance. Significantly enough, race is an active factor here, though not in the usual sense. When the jazz drummer Art Blakey was asked about Parker's meaning for Negroes, he replied, "They never heard of him." Parker's artistic success and highly publicized death have changed all that today, but interestingly enough, Bird was indeed a "white" hero. His greatest significance was for the educated white middle-class youth whose reaction to the inconsistencies of American life was the stance of casting off its education, language, dress, manners and moral standards: a revolt, apolitical in nature, which finds its most dramatic instance in the figure of the so-called white hipster. And whatever its justification, it was, and is, a reaction to the chaos which many youth sense at the center of our society.

For the postwar jazznik, Parker was Bird, a suffering, psychically wounded, law-breaking, life-affirming hero. For them he possessed something of the aura of that figure common to certain contemporary novels which R.W.B. Lewis describes as the "picaresque saint." He was an obsessed outsider—and Bird was thrice alienated: as Negro, as addict, as exponent of a new and disturbing development in jazz—whose tortured and in many ways criminal striving for personal and moral integration invokes a sense of tragic fellowship in those who saw in his agony a ritualization of their own fears, rebellions and hunger for creativity. One of the most significant features of Reisner's book lies, then, in his subtitle, even though he prefers to participate in the recreation of Bird's legend rather than perform the critical function of analyzing it.

Reisner, a former art historian who chooses to write in the barely articulate jargon of the hipster, no more than hints at this (though Ted Joans spins it out in a wild surrealist poem). But when we read through the gossip of the accounts we recognize the presence of a modern American version of the ancient myth of the birth and death of the hero. We are told of his birth, his early discovery of his vocation, his dedication to his art, of his wanderings and early defeats; we are told of his initiation into the mysteries revealed by his drug and the regions of terror to which it conveyed him; we are told of his obsessive identification with his art and his moment of revelation and metamorphosis. Here is Parker's own version:

> I remember one night I was jamming in a chili house (Dan Wall's) on Seventh Avenue between 139th and 140th. It was December, 1939 . . . I'd been getting bored with the stereotyped changes that were being used all the time, all the time, and I kept thinking there's bound to be something else. I could hear it sometimes but I couldn't play it. Well, that night, I was working over "Cherokee," and, as I did, I found that by using the higher intervals of a chord as a melody line and backing them with appropriately related changes, I could play the thing I'd been hearing. I came alive.

From then on he reigns as a recognized master, creating, recording, inspiring others, finding fame, beginning a family. Then comes his waning, suffering, disintegration and death.

Many of the bare facts of Parker's life are presented in the useful chronology, but it is the individual commentator's embellishments on the facts which create the mythic dimension. Bird was a most gifted innovator and evidently a most ingratiating and difficult man—one whose friends had no need for an enemy, and whose enemies had no difficulty in justifying their hate. According to his witnesses, he stretched the limits of human contradiction beyond belief. He was lovable and hateful, considerate and callous; he stole from friends and benefactors and borrowed without conscience, often without repaying, and yet was generous to absurdity. He could be most kind to younger musicians or utterly crushing in his contempt for their ineptitude. He was passive and yet quick to pull a knife and pick a fight. He knew the difficulties which are often the lot of jazz musicians, but as a leader he tried to con his sidemen out of their wages. He evidently loved the idea of having a family and being a good father and provider, but found it as difficult as being a good son to his devoted mother. He was given to extremes of sadism and masochism, capable of the most staggering excesses and the most exacting physical discipline and assertion of will. Indeed, one gets the image of such a character as Stavrogin in Dostoevsky's *The Possessed,* who while many things to many people seemed essentially devoid of a human center—except, and an important exception indeed, Parker was an artist who found his moments of sustained and meaningful integration through the reed and keys of the alto saxophone. It is the recordings of his flights of music which remain, and it is these which form the true substance of his myth.

Which brings us, finally, to a few words about Parker's style. For all its velocity, brilliance and imagination there is in it a great deal of loneliness, self-depreciation and self-pity. With this there is a quality which seems to issue from its vibratoless tone: a sound of amateurish ineffectuality, as though he could never quite make it. It is this amateurish-sounding aspect which promises so much to the members of a do-it-yourself culture; it sounds with an assurance that you too can create your own do-it-yourself jazz. Dream stuff, of course, but there is a relationship between the

Parker *sound* and the impossible genre of teen-age music which has developed since his death. Nevertheless he captured something of the discordancies, the yearning, romance and cunning of the age and ordered it into a haunting art. He was not the god they see in him, but for once the beatniks are correct: Bird lives, perhaps because his tradition and his art blew him to the meaningful center of things.

But what kind of bird was Parker? Back during the thirties members of the old Blue Devils Orchestra celebrated a certain robin by playing a lugubrious little tune called "They Picked Poor Robin." It was a jazz-community joke, musically an extended "signifying riff" or melodic naming of a recurring human situation, and was played to satirize some betrayal of faith or loss of love observed from the bandstand. Sometimes it was played as the purple-fezzed musicians returned from the burial of an Elk, whereupon reaching the Negro business and entertainment district the late Walter Page would announce the melody dolefully on his tuba; then poor robin would transport the mourners from their somber mood to the spirit-lifting beat of "Oh, Didn't He Ramble" or some other happy tune. Parker, who studied with Buster Smith and jammed with other members of the disbanded Devils in Kansas City, might well have known the verse which Walter Page supplied to the tune:

> Oh, they picked poor robin clean
>   (repeat)
> They tied poor robin to a stump
> Lord, they picked all the feathers
> Round from robin's rump
> Oh, they picked poor robin clean.

Poor robin was picked again and again, and his pluckers were ever unnamed and mysterious. Yet the tune was inevitably productive of laughter even when we ourselves were its object. For each of us recognized that his fate was somehow our own. Our defeats and failures, even our final defeat by death, were loaded upon his back and given ironic significance and thus made more bearable. Perhaps Charlie was poor robin come to New York and here to be sacrificed to the need for entertainment and for the creation of a new jazz style, and awaits even now in death a meaning-making plucking by perceptive critics. The effectiveness of any sacrifice depends upon our identification with the agony of the hero-victim; to those who would still insist that Charlie was a mere yardbird, our reply can only be, "Ain't nobody *here* but us chickens, boss!"

HOMAGE TO DUKE ELLINGTON
ON HIS BIRTHDAY

This major essay, fascinating on many levels, considers Ellington "America's greatest composer" and an elusive but alluring artist and model for behavior. Throughout the piece we are aware of Ellison's sense of Duke operating behind his characteristic "aura of mockery," his "enigmatic smile." In part what we witness is the great, good humor of the dance-bandmaster as a bringer of joy and herald of possibility, leader of a good-time public rite that is underscored with the timbres of the blues. But Duke's more sly and secret joke is related to the American humor famously described by Henry James as a mysterious but definitive cultural gift. The Ellingtonian smile continues the creatively subversive American process of imitating and parodying (and then mocking the misunderstood imitation of an imitation) evoked in the slave's highly ironic versions of big-house dances done by white masters before whose eyes "a European cultural form was becoming Americanized, undergoing a metamorphosis through the mocking activity of a people partially sprung from Africa." Further, Ellington wore a protective mask ("we wear the mask," Ellison writes elsewhere, "for purposes of aggression as well as for defense"), behind which he got his work done in spite of America's incapacity to see him for the genius that he was: "Ellington's is a creative mockery," Ellison writes, "in that it rises above itself to offer us something better, more creative and hopeful, than we've attained while seeking other stan-dards." In other words, while we came to party or to relax at the bandstand, Ellington came, smiling, to offer everything we came for and then something more, "something better." (Washington, D.C., Sunday Star, *April 27, 1969)*

———

It is to marvel: the ageless and irrepressible Duke Ellington is seventy, and another piano player of note, President Richard M. Nixon, has ordered in his honor a state dinner to be served in the house where, years ago, Duke's father, then a butler, once instructed white guests from the provinces in the gentle art and manners proper to such places of elegance and power. It is good news in these times of general social upheaval that traces of the old American success story remain valid, for now where the parent labored the son is to be honored for his achievements. And perhaps it is inevitable that Duke Ellington should be shown the highest hospitality of the nation's First Family in its greatest house, and that through the courtesy of the chief of state all Americans may pay, symbolically, their respects to our greatest composer.

Perhaps it is also inevitable (and if not inevitable, certainly it is proper) that that which a Pulitzer Prize jury of a few years ago was too insecure, or shortsighted, to do, and that which our institutions dedicated to the recognition of artistic achievement have been too prejudiced, negligent, or concerned with European models and styles to do, is finally being done by presidents. For it would seem that Ellington's greatness has been recognized by everyone except those charged with recognizing musical excellence at the highest levels—and even some of these have praised him privately while failing to grant him public honor.

Nevertheless, he is far from being a stranger to the White House, for during the occupancy of President and Mrs. Lyndon B. Johnson, Ellington became something of a regular guest there, and indeed, it was President Johnson who appointed him to the National Council on the Arts, thereby giving recognition to our most important indigenous art form in the person of its most outstanding creator. Certainly there is no better indication that those on the highest levels of governmental power have at last begun to recognize our arts and their creators as national treasures. Perhaps in Ellington's special case this is a proper and most fitting path to official national recognition, since for more than forty years his music has been not only superb entertainment but an important function of national morale. During the Depression whenever his theme song "East St. Louis Toodle-oo" came on the air, our morale was lifted by something inescapably hopeful in the sound. Its style was so triumphant and the moody melody so successful in capturing the times yet so expressive of the faith which would see us through them. And when the "Black and Tan Fantasy" was played we were reminded not only of how fleeting *all* human life must be, but with its blues-based tension between content and manner, it warned us not only to look at the darker side of life but also to remember the enduring necessity for humor, technical mastery, and creative excellence. It was immensely danceable and listenable music and ever so evocative of other troubled times and other triumphs over disaster. It was also most Negro American in its mocking interpolations from Chopin's B-flat minor piano concerto to which, as Barry Ulanov has reminded us, it was once popular to sing the gallows-humored words: "Where shall we all / be / a hundred years / from now?"

And how many generations of Americans, white and black, wooed their wives and had the ceremonial moments of their high school and college days memorialized by Ellington's tunes? And to how many thousands has he brought definitions of what it should mean to be young and alive and American? Yes, and to how many has he given a sense of personal elegance and personal style? A sense of possibility? And who, seeing and hearing Ellington and his marvelous band, hasn't been moved to wonder at the mysterious, unanalyzed character of the Negro American—and at the white American's inescapable Negro-ness?

Even though few recognized it, such artists as Ellington and Louis Armstrong were the stewards of our vaunted American optimism and guardians against the creeping irrationality which ever plagues our form of society. They created great entertainment, but for them (ironically) and for us (unconsciously) their music was a rejection of that chaos and license which characterized the so-called Jazz Age associated with F. Scott Fitzgerald, and which has returned once more to haunt the nation. Place Ellington with Hemingway, they are both larger than life, both masters of that which is most enduring in the human enterprise: the power of man to define himself against the ravages of time through artistic style.

———

I remember Ellington from my high school days in Oklahoma City, first as a strangely familiar timbre of orchestral sounds issuing from phonograph records and radio. Familiar because beneath the stylized jungle sounds (the like of which no African jungle had ever heard) there sounded the blues, and strange because the mutes, toilet plungers, and derby hats with which I was acquainted as a musician had been given a stylized elegance and extension of effect unheard of even in the music of Louis Armstrong. It was as though Ellington had taken the traditional instruments of Negro American music and modified them, extended their range, enriched their tonal possibilities. We were studying the classics then, working at harmony and the forms of symphonic music. And while we affirmed the voice of jazz and the blues despite all criticism from our teachers because they spoke to a large extent of what we felt of the life we lived most intimately, it was not until the discovery of Ellington that we had any hint that jazz possessed possibilities of a range of expressiveness comparable to that of classical European music.

And then Ellington and the great orchestra came to town; came with their uniforms, their sophistication, their skills; their golden horns, their flights of controlled and disciplined fantasy; came with their art, their special sound; came with Ivy Anderson and Ethel Waters singing and dazzling the eye with their high-brown beauty and with the richness and bright feminine flair of their costumes, their promising manners. They were news from the great wide world, an example and a goal; and I wish that all those who write so knowledgeably of Negro boys having no masculine figures with whom to identify would consider the long national and international career of Ellington and his band, the thousands of one-night stands played in the black communities of this nation. Where in the white community, in *any* white community, could there have been found images, examples such as these? Who were so worldly, who so elegant, who so mockingly creative? Who so skilled at their given trade and who treated the social limitations placed in their paths with greater disdain?

Friends of mine were already collecting Ellington records, and the more mature jazzmen were studying, without benefit of formal institutions of learning, his enigmatic style. Indeed, during the thirties and forties, when most aspiring writers of fiction were learning from the style and example of Hemingway, many jazz composers, orchestrators, and arrangers were following the example of Ellington, attempting to make something new and uniquely their own out of the traditional elements of the blues and jazz. For us, Duke was a culture hero, a musical magician who worked his powers through his mastery of form, nuance, and style, a charismatic figure whose personality influenced even those who had no immediate concern with the art of jazz.

My mother, an Afro-American Methodist Episcopalian

who shouted in church but who allowed me nevertheless to leave sunrise Christmas services to attend breakfast dances, once expressed the hope that when I'd completed my musical studies I'd have a band like Ellington's. I was pleased and puzzled at the time, but now I suspect that she recognized a certain religious element in Ellington's music—an element which has now blossomed forth in compositions of his own form of liturgical music. Either that, or she accepted the sound of dedication wherever she heard it and thus was willing to see Duke as an example of the mysterious way in which God showed His face in music.

I didn't meet Ellington at the time. I was but a young boy in the crowd that stood entranced around the bandstand at Slaughter's Hall. But a few years later, when I was a student in the music department at Tuskegee, I shook his hand, talked briefly with him of my studies and of my dreams. He was kind and generous even though harassed (there had been some trouble in travel and the band had arrived hours late, with the instruments misplaced and the musicians evil as only tired, black, Northern-based musicians could be in the absurdly segregated South of the 1930s), and those of us who talked with him were renewed in our determination to make our names in music.

A few years later, a stranger in Harlem, I lived at the YMCA and spent many a homesick afternoon playing Duke's records on the jukebox in Small's Paradise Bar, asking myself why I was in New York and finding reassurance in the music that although the way seemed cloudy (I had little money and would soon find it necessary to sleep in the park below City College), I should remain there and take my chances.

Later, I met Langston Hughes, who took me up to Sugar Hill to visit the Duke in his apartment. Much to my delight, the great musician remembered me, was still apologetic because of the lateness of the band's arrival at Tuskegee, and asked me what he could do to aid the music department. I suggested that we were sadly deficient in our library of classical scores and recordings, and he offered to make the school a gift of as extensive a library of recordings as was needed. It was an offer which I passed on to Tuskegee with great enthusiasm, but which, for some reason, perhaps because it had not come directly from Ellington himself or perhaps because several people in the department regarded jazz as an inferior form of music, was rejected. That his was a genuine gesture, I had no doubt, for at the time I was to see a further example of his generosity when Jimmie Lunceford's orchestra, then considered an Ellington rival, came on the radio. The other musicians present kidded Ellington about the challenge of Lunceford's group, to which he responded by listening intently until the number was finished and then commenting "Those boys are interesting. They are trying, they are really trying," without a trace of condescension but with that enigmatic Ellington smile. The brief comment and the smile were enough, the kidding stopped, for we had all been listening—and not for the first time— and we knew that Duke had little to fear from the challenge of Lunceford or anyone else.

———

Somewhere during his childhood a friend had nicknamed Edward Kennedy Ellington "Duke," and he had proceeded to create for himself a kingdom of sound and rhythm that has remained impregnable to the fluctuations of fad and novelty, even the passing on of key members of his band.

Jazz styles have come and gone and other composer-conductors have been given the title "King of Jazz" and Duke knew the reason why, as did the world—just as he knew the value of his own creation. But he never complained, he simply smiled and made music. Now the other kings have departed, while his work endures and his creativity continues.

When the Pulitzer Prize committee refused to give him a special award for music (a decision which led certain members of that committee to resign), Ellington remarked, "Fate is being kind to me. Fate doesn't want me to be too famous too young," a quip as mocking of our double standards, hypocrisies, and pretensions as the dancing of those slaves who, looking through the windows of a plantation manor house from the yard, imitated the steps so gravely performed by the masters within and then added to them their own special flair, burlesquing the white folks and then going on to force the steps into a choreography uniquely their own. The whites, looking out at the activity in the yard, thought that they were being flattered by imitation and were amused by the incongruity of tattered blacks dancing courtly steps, while missing completely the fact that before their eyes a European cultural form was becoming Americanized, undergoing a metamorphosis through the mocking activity of a people partially sprung from Africa. So, blissfully unaware, the whites laughed while the blacks danced out their mocking reply.

In a country which began demanding the projection of its own unique experience in literature as early as the 1820s, it was ironic that American composers were expected to master the traditions, conventions, and subtleties of European music and to force their own American musical sense of life into the forms created by Europe's greatest composers. Thus the history of American classical music has been marked by a struggle to force American experience into European forms.

In other words, our most highly regarded musical standards remained those of the Europe from which the majority of Americans derived. Fortunately, however, not all Americans spring from Europe (or not only from Europe), and while these standards obtained, Negro American composers were not really held to them, since it seemed obvious that blacks had nothing to do with Europe—even though during slavery Negroes had made up comic verses about a dance to which "Miss Rose come in her mistress's clothes / But how she got them nobody knows / And long before the ball did meet / She was dancing Taglioni at the corner of the street" (Taglioni being a dancer who was the rage of Europe during the 1850s).

Be that as it may, the dominance of European standards did work a hardship on the Negro American composer because it meant that no matter how inventive he might become, his music would not be considered important—or even American—(1) because of his race and (2) because of the form, if he was a jazzman, in which he worked. Therefore, such a composer as Ellington was at odds with European music and its American representatives, just as he was at odds with the racial attitudes of the majority of the American population, and while primarily a creative composer, he was seen mainly in his role as entertainer. Doubtless this explains the withholding from Ellington of the nation's highest honors.

It isn't a matter of being protected, as he suggests, from being too famous too young—he is one of the world's most famous composers and recognized by the likes of Stravinsky, Stokowski, and Milhaud as one of the greatest moderns—but the fact that his creations are far too *American.* Then there is also the fact of Ellington's aura of mockery. Mockery speaks through his work and through his bearing. He is one of the most handsome of men, and to many his stage manners are so suave and gracious as to appear a put-on—which quite often they are. And his manner, like his work, serves to remind us of the inadequacies of our myths, our legends, our conduct, and our standards. However, Ellington's is a creative mockery in that it rises above itself to offer us something better, more creative and hopeful, than we've attained while seeking other standards.

———

During a period when groups of young English entertainers who based their creations upon the Negro American musical tradition have effected a questionable revolution of manners among American youths, perhaps it is time we paid our respects to a man who has spent his life reducing the violence and chaos of American life to artistic order. I have no idea where we shall all be a hundred years from now, but if there is a classical music in which the American experience has finally discovered the voice of its own complexity, it will owe much of its direction to the achievements of Edward Kennedy Ellington. For many years he has been telling us how marvelous, mad, violent, hopeful, nostalgic, and (perhaps) decent we are. He is one of the musical fathers of our country, and throughout all these years he has, as he tells us so mockingly, loved us madly. We are privileged to have lived during his time and to have known so great a man, so great a musician.

AS THE SPIRIT MOVES MAHALIA

This review of recordings by Mahalia Jackson offers brilliantly sus-
tained, poetic paragraphs in which the gospel singer's art is compared
not only with flamenco and a variety of world musics, but also most
emphatically with the blues and jazz. One of her songs contains "a
riff straight out of early Ellington." Jackson glories in a church-
song tradition which, says Ellison (continuing his critique of bebop
jazz musicians), "could teach the jazz modernists quite a bit about
polyrhythmics and polytonality." Elsewhere he observes that Jackson
and her piano accompanist, Mildred Falls, "create a rhythmical drive
such as is expected of the entire Basie band." (Here perhaps Ellison
takes a shot at Count Basie's band of the fifties, generally so much less
spontaneous and weaker, he felt, than that band's earlier incarna-
tions.) This essay's main point, however, is that Mahalia Jackson is
not primarily a popular concert entertainer but an "interpretive
artist" and a "high priestess in the religious ceremony of her church"
who is able (in a phrase Ellison also uses to praise jazz and blues
artists) "to evoke a shared community of experience." Decidedly not
a jazz or blues singer—a position the former church boy Ellison un-
derstands and respects—she nonetheless performs one of the funda-
mental services of the public jazz dance: in a world of denials, she
affirms the African-American, and therefore American, culture and

*its traditions in all their kaleidoscopic multiethnic variety. Not only
are there significant "common singing techniques of the spirituals
and the blues," but sometimes the function of the music of early Sunday morning and late Saturday night is virtually the same. (*Saturday Review, *September 27, 1958)*

———

There are certain women singers who possess, beyond all
the boundaries of our admiration for their art, an uncanny
power to evoke our love. We warm with pleasure at mere
mention of their names; their simplest songs sing in our
hearts like the remembered voices of old dear friends, and
when we are lost within the listening anonymity of dark-
ened concert halls, they seem to seek us out unerringly.
Standing regal within the bright isolation of the stage, their
subtlest effects seem meant for us and us alone: privately, as
across the intimate space of our own living rooms. And
when we encounter the simple dignity of their immediate
presence, we suddenly ponder the mystery of human greatness.

Perhaps this power springs from their dedication, their
having subjected themselves successfully to the demanding
discipline necessary to the mastery of their chosen art. Or
perhaps it is a quality with which they are born, as some are
born with bright orange hair. Perhaps, though we think not,
it is acquired, a technique of "presence." But whatever its
source, it touches us as a rich abundance of human warmth
and sympathy. Indeed, we feel that if the idea of aristocracy
is more than mere class conceit, then these surely are our
natural queens. For they enchant the eye as they caress the
ear, and in their presence we sense the full, moony glory of
womanhood in all its mystery—maid, matron and matri-
arch. They are the sincere ones whose humanity dominates
the artifices of the art with which they stir us, and when they
sing we have some notion of our better selves.

Lotte Lehmann is one of these, and Marian Anderson.
Both Madame Ernestine Schumann-Heink and Kathleen

Ferrier possessed it. Nor is it limited to these mistresses of high art. Pastora Pavon, *La Niña de los Peines,* the great flamenco singer, is another, and so is Mahalia Jackson, the subject of this piece, who reminds us that while not all great singers possess this quality, those who do, no matter how obscure their origin, are soon claimed by the world as its own.

———

Mahalia Jackson, a large, handsome brown-skinned woman in her middle forties, who began singing in her father's church at the age of five, is a Negro of the *American* Negroes, and is, as the Spanish say, a woman of much quality. Her early experience was typical of Negro women of a certain class in the South. Born in New Orleans, she left school in the eighth grade and went to work as a nursemaid. Later she worked in the cotton fields of Louisiana and as a domestic. Her main social life was centered in the Baptist church. She grew up with the sound of jazz in her ears, and, being an admirer of Bessie Smith, was aware of the prizes and acclaim awaiting any mistress of the blues, but in her religious views the blues and jazz are profane forms and a temptation to be resisted. She also knew something of the painful experiences which go into the forging of a true singer of the blues.

In 1927, following the classical pattern of Negro migration, Mahalia went to Chicago, where she worked as a laundress and studied beauty culture. Here, too, her social and artistic life was in the Negro community, centered in the Greater Salem Baptist Church. Here she became a member of the choir and a soloist with a quintet which toured the churches affiliated with the National Baptist Convention. Up until the forties she operated within a world of music which was confined, for the most part, to Negro communities, and it was by her ability to move such audiences as are found here that her reputation grew. It was also such audiences which, by purchasing over two million copies of her famous "Move On Up a Little Higher," brought her to national attention.

When listening to such recordings as *Sweet Little Jesus Boy, Bless This House, Mahalia Jackson,* or *In the Upper Room,* it is impossible to escape the fact that Mahalia Jackson is possessed of a profound religious conviction. Nor can we escape the awareness that no singer living has a greater ability to move us, regardless of our own religious attitudes, with the projected emotion of a song. Perhaps with the interpretive artist the distinction so often made between popular and serious art is not so great as it seems. Perhaps what counts is the personal quality of the individual artist, the depth of his experience and his sense of life. Certainly Miss Jackson possesses a quality of dignity and the ability to project a sincerity of purpose which is characteristic of only the greatest of interpretive artists.

Nor should it be assumed that her singing is simply the expression of the Negro's "natural" ability as is held by the stereotype (would that it were only true!). For although its techniques are not taught formally, Miss Jackson is the master of an art of singing which is as complex and of an even older origin than that of jazz.

It is an art which was acquired during those years when she sang in the comparative obscurity of the Negro community, and which, with the inevitable dilutions, comes into our national song style usually through the singers of jazz and the blues. It is an art which depends upon the employment of the full expressive resources of the human voice— from the rough growls employed by blues singers, the intermediate sounds, half-cry, half-recitative, which are common to Eastern music, the shouts and hollers of American Negro folk cries, the rough-edged tones and broad vibratos, the high, shrill and grating tones which rasp one's ears like the agonized flourishes of flamenco, to the gut tones, which remind us of where the jazz trombone found its human source. It is an art which employs a broad rhythmic freedom and accents the lyric line to reinforce the emotional impact. It utilizes half-tones, glissandi, blue notes, humming and moaning. Or again, it calls upon the most lyrical, floating tones of which the voice is capable. Its diction ranges from the most precise to the near liquidation of word-meaning in the sound: a pronunciation which is almost of the academy one instant and of the broadest cotton-field dialect the next. And it is most eclectic in its use of other musical idiom; indeed, it borrows any effect which will aid in the arousing and control of emotion. Especially is it free in its use of the effects of jazz; its tempos (with the characteristic economy of Negro expression, it shares a common rhythmic and harmonic base with jazz) are taken along with its intonations, and, in ensemble singing, its orchestral voicing. In Mahalia's own "Move On Up a Little Higher" there is a riff straight out of early Ellington. Most of all it is an art which swings, and in the South there are many crudely trained groups who use it naturally for the expression of religious feeling who could teach the jazz modernists quite a bit about polyrhythmics and polytonality.

Since the forties this type of vocal music, known loosely as "gospel singing," has become a big business, both within the Negro community and without. Negro producers have found it highly profitable to hold contests in which groups of gospel singers are pitted against one another, and the radio stations which cater to the Negro market give many hours of their air time to this music. Today there are groups who follow regular circuits just as the old Negro jazzmen, blues singers and vaudeville acts followed the old T.O.B.A. circuit through the Negro communities of the nation. Some form the troupes of traveling evangelists and move about the country with their organs, tambourines, bones and drums. Some are led by ex-jazzmen who have put on the cloth, either sincerely or in response to the steady employment and growing market. So popular has the music become that there is a growing tendency to exploit its generic relationship to jazz and so-called rock-and-roll.

Indeed, many who come upon it outside the context of

the Negro community tend to think of it as just another form of jazz, and the same confusion is carried over to the art of Mahalia Jackson. There is a widely held belief that she is really a blues singer who refuses, out of religious superstitions, perhaps, to sing the blues, a jazz singer who coyly rejects her rightful place before a swinging band. And it *is* ironically true that just as a visitor who comes to Harlem seeking out many of the theaters and movie houses of the twenties will find them converted into churches, those who seek today for a living idea of the rich and moving art of Bessie Smith must go not to the night clubs and variety houses where those who call themselves blues singers find their existence, but must seek out Mahalia Jackson in a Negro church. And I insist upon the church and not the concert hall, because for all her concert appearances about the world she is not primarily a concert singer but a high priestess in the religious ceremony of her church. As such she is as far from the secular existentialism of the blues as St. John of the Cross is from Sartre. And it is in the setting of the church that the full timbre of her sincerity sounds most distinctly.

Certainly there was good evidence of this last July at the Newport Jazz Festival, where one of the most widely anticipated events was Miss Jackson's appearance with the Ellington Orchestra. Ellington had supplied the "Come Sunday" movement of his *Black, Brown and Beige Suite* (which with its organlike close had contained one of Johnny Hodges's most serenely moving solos, a superb evocation of Sunday peace) with lyrics for Mahalia to sing. To make way for her, three of the original movements were abandoned, along with the Hodges solo, but in their place she was given words of such banality that for all the fervor of her singing and the band's excellent performance, that Sunday sun simply would not arise. Nor does the recorded version change our opinion that this was a most unfortunate marriage and an error of taste, and the rather unformed setting of the Twenty-third

Psalm which completes the side does nothing to improve things. In fact, only the sound and certain of the transitions between movements are an improvement over the old version of the suite. Originally "Come Sunday" was Ellington's moving *impression* of Sunday peace and religious quiet, but he got little of this into the words. So little, in fact, that it was impossible for Mahalia to release that vast fund of emotion with which Southern Negroes have charged the scenes and symbols of the Gospels.

Only the fortunate few who braved the Sunday-morning rain to attend the Afro-American Episcopal Church services heard Mahalia at her best at Newport. Many had doubtless been absent from church or synagogue for years, but here they saw her in her proper setting and the venture into the strangeness of the Negro church was worth the visit. Here they could see, to the extent we can visualize such a thing, the world which Mahalia summons up with her voice, the spiritual reality which infuses her song. Here it could be seen that the true function of her singing is not simply to entertain, but to prepare the congregation for the minister's message, to make it receptive to the spirit, and with effects of voice and rhythm to evoke a shared community of experience.

As she herself put it while complaining of the length of the time allowed her during a recording session, "I'm used to singing in church, where they don't stop me until the Lord comes." By which she meant, not until she had created the spiritual and emotional climate in which the Word is made manifest; not until, and as the spirit moves her, the song of Mahalia the high priestess sings within the heart of the congregation as its own voice of faith.

When in possession of the words which embody her religious convictions, Mahalia can dominate even the strongest jazz beat and instill it with her own fervor. *Bless This House* contains songs set to rumba, waltz and two-step, but what she does to them provides a triumphal blending of popular dance movements with religious passion. In *Sweet Little Jesus Boy*, the song "The Holy Babe" is a Negro version of an old English count-rhyme, and while enumerating the gifts of the Christian God to man, Mahalia and Mildred Falls, her pianist, create a rhythmical drive such as is expected of the entire Basie band. It is all joy and exultation and swing, but it is nonetheless religious music. Many who are moved by Mahalia and her spirit have been so impressed by the emotional release of her music that they fail to see the frame within which she moves. But even *In the Upper Room* and *Mahalia Jackson*—in which she reminds us most poignantly of Bessie Smith, and in which the common singing techniques of the spirituals and the blues are most clearly to be heard—are directed toward the afterlife and thus are intensely religious. For those who cannot, or will not, visit Mahalia in her proper setting, these records are the next best thing.

FLAMENCO

"Flamenco," Ellison's first published music essay, evokes his debt to Ernest Hemingway: the sweat-on-wine-bottle detail, the strings of independent clauses, the deadpan tone that is nonetheless full of passion. Like Hemingway, Ellison uses the occasion of the journalistic piece, in this case a review of new recordings of flamenco music, to make his own statement about life and art. Here the concern for spiritual values within the context of secular art and the conviction that art's power derives significantly from its connection with ritual define Ellison's perspective as a music writer here and throughout his career. Note particularly his sense of flamenco as an attractively hybrid music of Spain, "which is neither Europe nor Africa," he writes, "but a blend of both": flamenco, a form that rhymes with other world musics, particularly the blues. Note, too, Ellison's emphasis on the inextinguishable power of the artist-as-hero. In an interview contemporaneous with this piece, Ellison said of the Spanish dancer/musician Vicente Escudero (celebrated here) that he "could recapitulate the history and spirit of the Spanish dance with a simple arabesque of his fingers." In an intensely charged scene in Invisible Man, Ellison presents an old Negro woman who sings "a spiritual as full of weltschmerz as flamenco." First published as "Introduction to Flamenco," this piece was written for the Saturday Review, December 11, 1954.

———

Recently in Paris in Leroy Haynes's restaurant in the Rue de Martyrs, where American Negro fliers and jazz musicians bend over their barbecue and red beans and rice in an attitude as pious as that of any worshiper in Sacre Coeur, which dominates Montmartre above, a gypsy woman entered and told my fortune. She was a handsome woman, dressed in the mysterious, many-skirted costume of the gypsies, and she said that I was soon to take a journey, and that I was to find good fortune. I said jokingly that I had had good fortune, for after dreaming of it for many years I had been to Madrid.

"You went when you should have gone," she said, peering at my hand. "Had you gone earlier you might have found death. But that is of the past. I speak of good fortune in the future."

"There I heard real flamenco," I said, "and that is a good fortune I shall never forget."

"Flamenco," she said. "You understand flamenco? Then you must go see Escudero. You must hear Pepe el del Matrona and Rafael Romero."

"I've heard of Escudero," I said, "but who are these others?"

"You will see," she said. "You will see and hear also."

"This is real good fortune," I said. "I thought Escudero was dead."

"Not dead," she said, holding my hand over a damp spot on the tablecloth, "only old. But to see *him* is a little more than to take a walk. The fortune of your hand comes after a journey over water."

She then offered, for a further consideration, to tell me other things, but this was enough. I was amused (for sure enough we were flying home two days hence), my wife and friends were laughing that I had submitted to having my palm read, and the knowledge that the legendary Vicente Escudero was dancing again after so many years of retirement was enough good fortune for any one day.

So that evening we saw the old master in the full glory of his resurrection. Dry, now, and birdlike in his grace, Escudero is no longer capable of floor-resounding vigor, but conveys even the stamping fury of the Spanish dance with the gentlest, most delicate, precise, and potent of gestures and movement—reasserting in terms of his own medium a truth which Schumann-Heink, Roland Hayes, and Povla Frijsh have demonstrated in terms of the art of song: that with the great performer it is his style, so tortuously achieved, so carefully cultivated, which is the last to go down before age. And so with the singer Pepe el del Matrona, who at seventy-four is able to dominate the space of even the largest theater with his most pianissimo arabesques of sound.

But more important here than the inspiring triumph of artistic style over time was the triumph, in this most sophisticated of Western cities, of Cante Flamenco, a folk art which has retained its integrity and vitality through two centuries during which the West assumed that it had, through enlightenment, science, and progress, dispensed with those tragic, metaphysical elements of human life which the art of flamenco celebrates. Certainly Escudero and Matrona draw a great deal of their vitality from this tradition that contains many elements which the West has dismissed as "primitive," that epithet so facile for demolishing all things cultural which Westerners do not understand or wish to contemplate. Perhaps Spain (which is neither Europe nor Africa but a blend of both) was once more challenging to our Western optimism. If so, it was not with pessimism but with an affirmative art, which draws its strength and endurance from a willingness to deal with the whole man (Unamuno's man of flesh and blood who must die) in a world which is viewed as basically impersonal and violent; if so, through her singers and dancers and her flamenco music she was making the West a most useful and needed gift.

I haven't yet discovered the specific nature of the gift of fortune which my gypsy promised me, but until something better appears I'll accept Westminster's new three-volume *Anthology of Cante Flamenco*, which has just won the Grand Prix de Disque, as the answer. Escudero isn't in it, but members of his entourage are: Pepe el del Matrona, Rafael Romero, and the great flamenco guitarist Perico el del Lunar, who along with eight other artists present thirty-three excellently recorded examples of flamenco song style.

Cante Flamenco is the very ancient folk music of the Andalusian gypsies of southern Spain. Its origins are as mysterious as those of the gypsies themselves, but in it are heard Byzantine, Arabic, Hebraic, and Moorish elements fused and given the violent, rhythmical expressiveness of the gypsies. Cante Flamenco, or *cante hondo* (deep song, as the purer, less florid form is called), is a unique blending of Eastern and Western modes and as such it often baffles when it most intrigues the Western ear. In our own culture the closest music to it in feeling is the Negro blues, early jazz, and the slave songs (now euphemistically termed "spirituals"). Even a casual acquaintance with Westminster's anthology reveals certain parallels, and jazz fans will receive here a pleasant shock of recognition. Soon to be released free to those who purchase the *Anthology* is a forty-page booklet containing the text of the songs and a historical survey of flamenco literature written by Professor Tomas Andrade de Silva of the Royal Conservatory at Madrid.

Like Negro folk music, Cante Flamenco (which recognizes no complete separation between dance and song, the basic mood, the guitar and castanets, hold all together) is a communal art. In the small rooms in which it is performed there are no "squares" sitting around just to be entertained, everyone participates very much as during a noncommercial jam session or a Southern jazz dance. It can be just as noisy and sweaty and drunken as a Birmingham "breakdown"; while one singer "riffs" (improvises) or the dancers "go to town" the others assist by clapping their hands in the intricate percussive manner called *palmada* and by stamping out the rhythms with their feet. When a singer, guitarist, or dancer has negotiated a particularly subtle passage (and this is an art of great refinements) the shouts of *¡Olé!* arise to express appreciation of his art, to agree with the sentiments expressed, and to encourage him on to even greater eloquence. Very often the *Anthology* side containing the *cantes con baile* (dance songs) sounds like a revivalists' congregation saying "Amen!" to the preacher.

Flamenco, while traditional in theme and choreography, allows a maximum of individual expression, and a democratic rivalry such as is typical of a jam session; for, like the blues and jazz, it is an art of improvisation, and like them it can be quite graphic. Even one who doesn't understand the lyrics will note the uncanny ability of the singers presented here to produce pictorial effects with their voices. Great space, echoes, rolling slopes, the charging of bulls, and the prancing and galloping of horses flow in this sound much as animal cries, train whistles, and the loneliness of night sound through the blues.

The nasal, harsh, anguished tones heard on these sides are not the results of ineptitude or "primitivism"; like the "dirty tone" of the jazz instrumentalist, they are the result of an esthetic which rejects the beautiful sound sought by classical Western music.

Not that flamenco is simply a music of despair; this is true mainly of the *seguidillas,* the *soleares,* and the *saetas* (arrows of song) which are sung when the holy images are paraded during Holy Week, and which Rafael Romero sings with a pitch of religious fervor that reminds one of the great Pastora Pavon (*La Niña de los Peines*). But along with these darker songs the *Anthology* offers all the contrasts, the gay *alegrías, bulerías, sevillanas,* the passionate *peteneras,* lullabies (*nana*), prison songs, mountain songs, and laments. Love, loneliness, disappointment, pride—all these are themes for Cante Flamenco. Perhaps what attracts us most to flamenco, as it does to the blues, is the note of unillusioned affirmation of humanity which it embodies. The gypsies, like the slaves, are an outcast though undefeated people who have never lost their awareness of the physical source of man's most spiritual moments; even their Christ is a man of flesh and bone who suffered and bled before his apotheosis. In its more worldly phases the flamenco voice resembles the blues voice, which mocks the despair stated explicitly in the lyric, and it expresses the great human joke directed against the universe, that joke which is the secret of all folklore and myth: that though we be dismembered daily we shall always rise up again. Americans have long found in Spanish culture a clarifying perspective on their own. Now in this anthology of Spanish folklore we have a most inviting challenge to listen more attentively to the deeper voice of our own.

RICHARD WRIGHT'S BLUES

This early essay, written about the time Ellison was starting Invisible Man, *offers an important assertion of the compass of Richard Wright's cultural inheritances, including his international modernist reading and his debt to the local language and perspectives of the blues. It is also a seminal statement of Ellison's philosophy of the music—defined in terms of existentialist endurance as well as tragicomic wisdom—and about how the blues can influence the forms and strategies of writers and other artists who are not musicians. At the time of this essay's publication, Ellison and his literary mentor Wright were very close friends, as their correspondence (much of it available in the library at Yale University) testifies. For a fuller picture of Ellison's complicated, changing views of Wright, see also Ellison's "Richard Wright and Recent Negro Fiction" (*Direction, Summer 1941*) as well as "The World and the Jug" and "Remembering Richard Wright" (both in* The Collected Essays of Ralph Ellison*). "Richard Wright's Blues" first appeared in* The Antioch Review *in the summer of 1945.*

————

If anybody ask you
who sing this song,

> Say it was ole [Black Boy]
> done been here and gone.*

As a writer, Richard Wright has outlined for himself a dual role: to discover and depict the meaning of Negro experience, and to reveal to both Negroes and whites those problems of a psychological and emotional nature which arise between them when they strive for mutual understanding.

Now, in *Black Boy,* he has used his own life to probe what qualities of will, imagination and intellect are required of a Southern Negro in order to possess the meaning of his life in the United States. Wright is an important writer, perhaps the most articulate Negro American, and what he has to say is highly perceptive. Imagine Bigger Thomas projecting his own life in lucid prose guided, say, by the insights of Marx and Freud, and you have an idea of this autobiography.

Published at a time when any sharply critical approach to Negro life has been dropped as a wartime expendable, it should do much to redefine the problem of the Negro and American democracy. Its power can be observed in the shrill manner with which some professional "friends of the Negro people" have attempted to strangle the work in a noose of newsprint.

What in the tradition of literary autobiography is it like, this work described as a "great American autobiography"? As a non-white intellectual's statement of his relationship to Western culture, *Black Boy* recalls the conflicting pattern of identification and rejection found in Nehru's *Toward Freedom.* In its use of fictional techniques, its concern with criminality (sin) and the artistic sensibility, and in its author's judgment and rejection of the narrow world of his origin, it recalls Joyce's rejection of Dublin in *A Portrait of the Artist.* And as a psychological document of life under oppressive

---

* Signature formula used by blues singers at conclusion of song.

conditions, it recalls *The House of the Dead,* Dostoyevsky's profound study of the humanity of Russian criminals.

Such works were perhaps Wright's literary guides, aiding him to endow his life's incidents with communicable significance, providing him with ways of seeing, feeling and describing his environment. These influences, however, were encountered only after these first years of Wright's life were past, and were not part of the immediate folk culture into which he was born. In that culture the specific folk-art form which helped shape the writer's attitude toward his life and which embodied the impulse that contributes much to the quality and tone of his autobiography was the Negro blues.

This would bear a word of explanation. The blues is an impulse to keep the painful details and episodes of a brutal experience alive in one's aching consciousness, to finger its jagged grain, and to transcend it, not by the consolation of philosophy but by squeezing from it a near-tragic, near-comic lyricism. As a form, the blues is an autobiographical chronicle of personal catastrophe expressed lyrically. And certainly Wright's early childhood was crammed with catastrophic incidents. In a few short years his father deserted his mother, he knew intense hunger, he became a drunkard begging drinks from black stevedores in Memphis saloons; he had to flee Arkansas, where an uncle was lynched; he was forced to live with a fanatically religious grandmother in an atmosphere of constant bickering; he was lodged in an orphan asylum; he observed the suffering of his mother, who became a permanent invalid, while fighting off the blows of the poverty-stricken relatives with whom he had to live; he was cheated, beaten and kicked off jobs by white employees who disliked his eagerness to learn a trade; and to these objective circumstances must be added the subjective fact that Wright, with his sensitivity, extreme shyness and intelligence, was a problem child who rejected his family and was by them rejected.

Thus, along with the themes, equivalent descriptions of milieu and the perspectives to be found in Joyce, Nehru, Dostoyevsky, George Moore and Rousseau, *Black Boy* is filled with blues-tempered echoes of railroad trains, the names of Southern towns and cities, estrangements, fights and flights, deaths and disappointments, charged with physical and spiritual hungers and pain. And like a blues sung by such an artist as Bessie Smith, its lyrical prose evokes the paradoxical, almost surreal image of a black boy singing lustily as he probes his own grievous wound.

In *Black Boy* two worlds have fused, two cultures merged, two impulses of Western man become coalesced. By discussing some of its cultural sources I hope to answer those critics who would make of the book a miracle and of its author a mystery. And while making no attempt to probe the mystery of the artist (who Hemingway says is "forged in injustice as a sword is forged"), I do hold that basically the prerequisites to the writing of *Black Boy* were, on the one hand, the microscopic degree of cultural freedom which Wright found in the South's stony injustice, and, on the other, the existence of a personality agitated to a state of almost manic restlessness. There were, of course, other factors, chiefly ideological, but these came later.

Wright speaks of his journey north as

> taking a part of the South to transplant in alien soil, to see if it could grow differently, if it could drink of new and cool rains, bend in strange winds, respond to the warmth of other suns, and perhaps, to bloom.

And just as Wright, the man, represents the blooming of the delinquent child of the autobiography, just so does *Black Boy* represent the flowering—cross-fertilized by pollen blown by the winds of strange cultures—of the humble blues lyric. There is, as in all acts of creation, a world of mystery in this, but there is also enough that is comprehensible for Americans to create the social atmosphere in which other black boys might freely bloom.

For certainly in the historical sense Wright is no exception. Born on a Mississippi plantation, he was subjected to all those blasting pressures which in a scant eighty years have sent the Negro people hurtling, without clearly defined trajectory, from slavery to emancipation, from log cabin to city tenement, from the white folks' fields and kitchens to factory assembly lines, and which, between two wars, have shattered the wholeness of its folk consciousness into a thousand writhing pieces.

Black Boy describes this process in the personal terms of *one* Negro childhood. Nevertheless, several critics have complained that it does not "explain" Richard Wright. Which, aside from the notion of art involved, serves to remind us that the prevailing mood of American criticism has so thoroughly excluded the Negro that it fails to recognize some of the most basic tenets of Western democratic thought when encountering them in a black skin. They forget that human life possesses an innate dignity and mankind an innate sense of nobility; that all men possess the tendency to dream and the compulsion to make their dreams reality; that the need to be ever dissatisfied and the urge ever to seek satisfaction is implicit in the human organism; and that all men are the victims and the beneficiaries of the goading, tormenting, commanding and informing activity of that imperious process known as the Mind—the Mind, as Valéry describes it, "armed with its inexhaustible questions."

Perhaps all this (in which lies the very essence of the human, and which Wright takes for granted) has been forgotten because the critics recognize neither Negro humanity nor the full extent to which the Southern community renders the fulfillment of human destiny impossible. And while it is true that *Black Boy* presents an almost unrelieved picture of a personality corrupted by brutal environment, it also presents those fresh, human responses brought to its world by the sensitive child:

> There was the *wonder* I felt when I first saw a brace of mountainlike, spotted, black-and-white horses clopping down a dusty road . . . the *delight* I caught in seeing long straight rows of red and green vegetables stretching away in the sun . . . the faint, cool kiss of *sensuality* when dew came on to my cheeks . . . the vague *sense of the infinite* as I looked down upon the yellow, dreaming waters of the Mississippi . . . the echoes of *nostalgia* I heard in the crying strings of wild geese . . . the *love* I had for the mute regality of tall, moss-clad oaks . . . the hint of *cosmic cruelty* that I *felt* when I saw the curved timbers of a wooden shack that had been warped in the summer sun . . . and there was the *quiet terror* that suffused my senses when vast hazes of gold washed earthward from star-heavy skies on silent nights. [italics mine]

And a bit later, his reactions to religion:

> Many of the religious symbols appealed to my sensibilities and I responded to the dramatic vision of life held by the church, feeling that to live day by day with death as one's sole thought was to be so compassionately sensitive toward all life as to view all men as slowly dying, and the trembling sense of fate that welled up, sweet and melancholy, from the hymns blended with the sense of fate that I had already caught from life.

There was also the influence of his mother—so closely linked to his hysteria and sense of suffering—who (though he only implies it here) taught him, in the words of the dedication prefacing *Native Son,* "to revere the fanciful and the imaginative." There were also those white men—the one who allowed Wright to use his library privileges and the other who advised him to leave the South, and still others whose offers of friendship he was too frightened to accept.

Wright assumed that the nucleus of plastic sensibility is a human heritage: the right and the opportunity to dilate, deepen and enrich sensibility—democracy. Thus the drama of *Black Boy* lies in its depiction of what occurs when Negro sensibility attempts to fulfill itself in the undemocratic South. Here it is not the individual that is the immediate focus, as in Joyce's *Stephen Hero*, but that upon which his sensibility was nourished.

Those critics who complain that Wright has omitted the development of his own sensibility hold that the work thus fails as art. Others, because it presents too little of what they consider attractive in Negro life, charge that it distorts reality. Both groups miss a very obvious point: that whatever else the environment contained, it had as little chance of prevailing against the overwhelming weight of the child's unpleasant experiences as Beethoven's quartets would have of destroying the stench of a Nazi prison.

We come, then, to the question of art. The function, the psychology, of artistic selectivity is to eliminate from an art form all those elements of experience which contain no compelling significance. Life is as the sea, art a ship in which man conquers life's crushing formlessness, reducing it to a course, a series of swells, tides and wind currents inscribed on a chart. Though drawn from the world, "the organized significance of art," writes Malraux, "is stronger than all the multiplicity of the world; . . . that significance alone enables man to conquer chaos and to master destiny."

Wright saw his destiny—that combination of forces before which man feels powerless—in terms of a quick and casual violence inflicted upon him by both family and community. His response was likewise violent, and it has been his need to give that violence significance which has shaped his writings.

———

What were the ways by which other Negroes confronted their destiny?

In the South of Wright's childhood there were three general ways: they could accept the role created for them by the whites and perpetually resolve the resulting conflicts through the hope and emotional cartharsis of Negro religion; they could repress their dislike of Jim Crow social relations while striving for a middle way of respectability, becoming—consciously or unconsciously—the accomplices of the whites in oppressing their brothers; or they could reject the situation, adopt a criminal attitude, and carry on an unceasing psychological scrimmage with the whites, which often flared forth into physical violence.

Wright's attitude was nearest the last. Yet in it there was an all-important qualitative difference: it represented a groping for *individual* values, in a black community whose values were what the young Negro critic Edward Bland has defined as "pre-individual." And herein lay the setting for the extreme conflict set off, both within his family and in the community, by Wright's assertion of individuality. The clash was sharpest on the psychological level, for, to quote Bland,

> In the pre-individualistic thinking of the Negro the stress is on the group. Instead of seeing in terms of the individual, the Negro sees in terms of "races," masses of peoples separated from other masses according to color. Hence, an act rarely bears intent against him as a Negro individual. He is singled out not as a person but as a specimen of an ostracized group. He knows that he never exists in his own right but only to the extent that others hope to make the race suffer vicariously through him.

This pre-individual state is induced artificially, like the regression to primitive states noted among cultured inmates of Nazi prisons. The primary technique in its enforcement is to impress the Negro child with the omniscience and omnipotence of the whites to the point that whites appear as ahuman as Jehovah, and as relentless as a Mississippi flood. Socially it is effected through an elaborate scheme of taboos supported by a ruthless physical violence, which strikes not only the offender but the entire black community. To wander from the paths of behavior laid down for the group is to become the agent of communal disaster.

In such a society the development of individuality depends upon a series of accidents, which often arise, as in Wright's case, from conditions within the Negro family. In Wright's life there was the accident that as a small child he could not distinguish between his fair-skinned grandmother and the white women of the town, thus developing skepticism as to their special status. To this was linked the accident of his having no close contacts with whites until after the child's normal formative period.

But these objective accidents not only link forward to these qualities of rebellion, criminality and intellectual questioning expressed in Wright's work today. They also link backward into the shadow of infancy where environment and consciousness are so darkly intertwined as to require the skill of a psychoanalyst to define their point of juncture. Nevertheless, at the age of four, Wright set the house afire and was beaten near to death by his frightened mother. This beating, followed soon by his father's desertion of the family, seems to be the initial psychological motivation of his quest for a new identification. While delirious from this beating, Wright was haunted "by huge wobbly white bags like the full udders of a cow, suspended from the ceiling above me [and] I was gripped by the fear that they were going to fall and drench me with some horrible liquid."

It was as though the mother's milk had turned acid, and with it the whole pattern of life that had produced the ignorance, cruelty and fear that had fused with mother love and exploded in the beating. It is significant that the bags were of the hostile color white, and the female symbol that of the cow, the most stupid (and, to the small child, the most frightening) of domestic animals. Here in dream symbolism is expressed an attitude worthy of an Orestes. And the significance of the crisis is increased by virtue of the historical fact that the lower-class Negro family is matriarchal; the child turns not to the father to compensate if he feels mother-rejection, but to the grandmother, or to an aunt—and Wright rejected both of these. Such rejection leaves the child open to psychological insecurity, distrust and all of those hostile environmental forces from which the family functions to protect it.

One of the Southern Negro family's methods of protecting the child is the severe beating—a homeopathic dose of the violence generated by black and white relationships. Such beatings as Wright's were administered for the child's own good—a good which the child resisted, thus giving family relationships an undercurrent of fear and hostility, which differs qualitatively from that found in patriarchal middle-class families, because here the severe beating is administered by the mother, leaving the child no parental sanctuary. He must ever embrace violence along with maternal tenderness, or else reject in his helpless way the mother.

The division between the Negro parents of Wright's mother's generation, whose sensibilities were often bound by their proximity to the slave experience, and their children, who historically and through the rapidity of American change stand emotionally and psychologically much farther away, is quite deep. Indeed, sometimes as deep as the cultural distance between Yeats's *Autobiographies* and a Bessie Smith blues. This is the historical background to those incidents of family strife in *Black Boy* which have caused reviewers to question Wright's judgment of Negro emotional relationships.

We have here a problem in the sociology of sensibility that is obscured by certain psychological attitudes brought to Negro life by whites. The first is the attitude which compels whites to impute to Negroes sentiments, attitudes and insights which, as a group living under certain definite social conditions, Negroes could not humanly possess. It is the identical mechanism which William Empson identifies in literature as "pastoral." It implies that since Negroes possess the richly human virtues credited to them, then their social position is advantageous and should not be bettered, and, continuing syllogistically, the white individual need feel no guilt over his participation in Negro oppression.

The second attitude leads whites to misjudge Negro passion, looking upon it as they do out of the turgidity of their own frustrated yearning for emotional warmth, their capacity for sensation having been constricted by the impersonal mechanized relationships typical of bourgeois society. The Negro is idealized into a symbol of sensation, of unhampered social and sexual relationships. And when *Black Boy* questions whites' illusion, they are thwarted much in the manner of the Occidental who, after observing the erotic character of a primitive dance, "shacks up" with a native woman, only to discover that far from possessing the hair-trigger sexual responses of a Stork Club "babe," she is relatively phlegmatic.

The point is not that American Negroes are primitives, but that as a group their social situation does not provide for the type of emotional relationships attributed to them. For how could the South, recognized as a major part of the backward third of the nation, nurture in the black, most brutalized section of its population, those forms of human relationships achievable only in the most highly developed areas of civilization?

Champions of this "Aren't-Negroes-Wonderful?" school of thinking often bring Paul Robeson and Marian Anderson forward as examples of highly developed sensibility, but actually they are only its *promise.* Both received their development from an extensive personal contact with European culture, free from the influences which shape Southern Negro personality. In the United States, Wright, who is the only Negro literary artist of equal caliber, had to wait years, and escape to another environment before discovering the moral and ideological equivalents of his childhood attitudes.

Man cannot express that which does not exist—either in the form of dreams, ideas or realities—in his environment. Neither his thoughts nor his feelings, his sensibility nor his intellect are fixed, innate qualities. They are processes which arise out of the interpenetration of human instinct with environment, through the process called experience, each changing and being changed by the other. Negroes cannot possess many of the sentiments attributed to them because the same changes in environment which, through experience, enlarge man's intellect (and thus his capacity for still greater change) also modify his feelings—which in turn increase his sensibility, i.e., his sensitivity to refinements of impression and subtleties of emotion. The extent of these changes depends upon the quality of political and cultural freedom in the environment.

Intelligence tests have measured the quick rise in intellect which takes place in Southern Negroes after moving north, but little attention has been paid to the mutations effected in their sensibilities. However, the two go hand in hand. Intellectual complexity is accompanied by emotional complexity, refinement of thought, and refinement of feeling. The movement north affects more than the Negro's wage scale; it affects his entire psychosomatic structure.

The rapidity of Negro intellectual growth in the North is due partially to objective factors present in the environment, to influences of the industrial city and to a greater political freedom. But there are also changes within the "inner world." In the North energies are released and given *intellec-*

tual channelization—energies which in most Negroes in the South have been forced to take either a *physical* form or, as with potentially intellectual types like Wright, to be expressed as nervous tension, anxiety and hysteria. Which is nothing mysterious. The human organism responds to environmental stimuli by converting them into either physical and/or intellectual energy. And what is called hysteria is suppressed intellectual energy expressed physically.

The "physical" character of their expression makes for much of the difficulty in understanding American Negroes. Negro music and dances are frenziedly erotic, Negro religious ceremonies violently ecstatic, Negro speech strongly rhythmical and weighted with image and gesture. But there is more in this sensuousness than the unrestraint and insensitivity found in primitive cultures; nor is it simply the relatively spontaneous and undifferentiated responses of a people living in close contact with the soil. For despite Jim Crow, Negro life does not exist in a vacuum, but in the seething vortex of those tensions generated by the most highly industrialized of Western nations. The welfare of the most humble black Mississippi sharecropper is affected less by the flow of the seasons and the rhythm of natural events than by the fluctuations of the stock market, even though, as Wright states of his father, the sharecropper's memories, actions and emotions are shaped by his immediate contact with nature and the crude social relations of the South.

All of this makes the American Negro far different from the "simple" specimen for which he is taken. And the "physical" quality offered as evidence of his primitive simplicity is actually the form of his complexity. The American Negro is a Western type whose social condition creates a state which is almost the reverse of the cataleptic trance: instead of his consciousness being lucid to the reality around it while the body is rigid, here it is the body which is alert, reacting to pressures which the constricting forces of Jim Crow block off from the transforming, concept-creating activity of the brain. The "eroticism" of Negro expression springs from much the same conflict as that displayed in the violent gesturing of a man who attempts to express a complicated concept with a limited vocabulary; thwarted ideational energy is converted into unsatisfactory pantomime, and his words are burdened with meanings they cannot convey. Here lies the source of the basic ambiguity of *Native Son,* wherein in order to translate Bigger's complicated feelings into universal ideas, Wright had to force into Bigger's consciousness concepts and ideas which his intellect could not formulate. Between Wright's skill and knowledge and the potentials of Bigger's mute feelings lay a thousand years of conscious culture.

In the South the sensibilities of both blacks and whites are inhibited by the rigidly defined environment. For the Negro there is relative safety as long as the impulse toward individuality is suppressed. (Lynchings have occurred because Negroes painted their homes.) And it is the task of the Negro family to adjust the child to the Southern milieu; through it the currents, tensions and impulses generated within the human organism by the flux and flow of events are given their distribution. This also gives the group its distinctive character, which, because of Negroes' suppressed minority position, is very much in the nature of an elaborate but limited defense mechanism. Its function is dual: to protect the Negro from whirling away from the undifferentiated mass of his people into the unknown, symbolized in its most abstract form by insanity, and most concretely by lynching; and to protect him from those unknown forces *within himself* which might urge him to reach out for that social and human equality which the white South says he cannot have. Rather than throw himself against the charged wires of his prison, he annihilates the impulses within him.

The pre-individualistic black community discourages individuality out of self-defense. Having learned through experience that the whole group is punished for the actions of the single member, it has worked out efficient techniques of behavior control. For in many Southern communities everyone knows everyone else and is vulnerable to his opinions. In some communities everyone is "related," regardless of blood ties. The regard shown by the group for its members, its general communal character and its cohesion are often mentioned, for by comparison with the coldly impersonal relationships of the urban industrial community, its relationships are personal and warm.

Black Boy, however, illustrates that this personal quality, shaped by outer violence and inner fear, is ambivalent. Personal warmth is accompanied by an equally personal coldness, kindliness by cruelty, regard by malice. And these opposites are as quickly set off against the member who gestures toward individuality as a lynch mob forms at the cry of rape. Negro leaders have often been exasperated by this phenomenon, and Booker T. Washington (who demanded far less of Negro humanity than Richard Wright) described the Negro community as a basket of crabs, wherein should one attempt to climb out, the others immediately pull him back.

The member who breaks away is apt to be more impressed by its negative than by its positive character. He becomes a stranger even to his relatives and he interprets gestures of protection as blows of oppression—from which there is no hiding place, because every area of Negro life is affected. Even parental love is given a qualitative balance akin to "sadism," and the extent of beatings and psychological maimings meted out by Southern Negro parents rivals those described by the nineteenth-century Russian writers as characteristic of peasant life under the Czars. The horrible thing is that the cruelty is also an expression of concern, of love.

In discussing the inadequacies for democratic living typical of the education provided Negroes by the South, a Negro educator has coined the term *mis-education.* Within the ambit of the black family this takes the form of training the child away from curiosity and adventure, against reaching out for those activities lying beyond the borders of the black community. And when the child resists, the parent discourages him, first with the formula, "That there's for white folks. Colored can't have it," and finally with a beating.

It is not, then, the family and communal violence described by *Black Boy* that is unusual, but that Wright *recognized* and made no peace with its essential cruelty—even when, like a babe freshly emerged from the womb, he could not discern where his own personality ended and it began. Ordinarily both parent and child are protected against this cruelty, seeing it as love and finding subjective sanction for it in the spiritual authority of the Fifth Commandment, and on the secular level in the legal and extralegal structure of the Jim Crow system. The child who did not rebel, or who was unsuccessful in his rebellion, learned a masochistic submissiveness and a denial of the impulse toward Western culture when it stirred within him.

———

Why then have Southern whites, who claim to "know" the Negro, missed all this? Simply because they, too, are armored against the horror and the cruelty. Either they deny the Negro's humanity and feel no cause to measure his actions against civilized norms; or they protect themselves from their guilt in the Negro's condition—and from their fear that their cooks might poison them, or that their nursemaids might strangle their infant charges, or that their field hands might do them violence—by attributing to them a superhuman capacity for love, kindliness and forgiveness. Nor does this in any way contradict their stereotyped conviction that all Negroes (meaning those with whom they have no contact) are given to the most animal behavior.

It is only when the individual, whether white or black, *rejects* the pattern that he awakens to the nightmare of his life. Perhaps much of the South's regressive character springs from the fact that many, jarred by some casual crisis into wakefulness, flee hysterically into the sleep of violence or the coma of apathy again. For the penalty of wakefulness is to encounter ever more violence and horror than the sensibilities can sustain unless translated into some form of social action. Perhaps the impassioned character so noticeable among those white Southern liberals so active in the Negro's cause is due to their sense of accumulated horror; their passion, like the violence in Faulkner's novels, is evidence of a profound spiritual vomiting.

This compulsion is even more active in Wright and the increasing number of Negroes who have said an irrevocable "no" to the Southern pattern. Wright learned that it is not enough merely to reject the white South, but that he had also to reject that part of the South which lay within him. As a rebel he formulated that rejection negatively, because it was the negative face of the Negro community upon which he looked most often as a child. It is this he is contemplating when he writes:

> Whenever I thought of the essential bleakness of black life in America, I knew that Negroes had never been allowed to catch the full spirit of Western civilization, that they lived somehow in it but not of it. And when I brooded upon the cultural barrenness of black life, I wondered if clean, positive tenderness, love, honor, loyalty and the capacity to remember were native to man. I asked myself if these human qualities were not fostered, won, struggled and suffered for, preserved in ritual from one generation to another.

But far from implying that Negroes have no capacity for culture, as one critic interprets it, this is the strongest affirmation that they have. Wright is pointing out what should be obvious (especially to his Marxist critics): that Negro sensibility is socially and historically conditioned; that Western culture must be won, confronted like the animal in a Spanish bullfight, dominated by the red shawl of codified experience and brought heaving to its knees.

Wright knows perfectly well that Negro life is a by-product of Western civilization, and that in it, if only one possesses the humanity and humility to see, are to be discovered all those impulses, tendencies, life and cultural forms found elsewhere in Western society.

The problem arises because the special condition of Negroes in the United States, including the defensive character of Negro life itself (the "will toward organization" noted in the Western capitalist appears in the Negro as a will to camouflage, to dissimulate), so distorts these forms as to render their recognition as difficult as finding a wounded quail against the brown and yellow leaves of a Mississippi thicket; even the spilled blood blends with the background. Having himself been in the position of the quail—to expand the metaphor—Wright's wounds have told him both the question and the answer which every successful hunter must discover for himself: "Where would I hide if *I* were a wounded quail?" But perhaps that requires more sympathy with one's quarry than most hunters possess. Certainly it requires such a sensitivity to the shifting guises of humanity under pressure as to allow them to identify themselves with the human content, whatever its outer form, and even with those Southern Negroes to whom Paul Robeson's name is only a rolling sound in the fear-charged air.

Let us close with one final word about the blues: their attraction lies in this, that they at once express both the agony of life and the possibility of conquering it through sheer toughness of spirit. They fall short of tragedy only in that they provide no solution, offer no scapegoat but the self. Nowhere in America today is there social or political action based upon the solid realities of Negro life depicted in *Black Boy*; perhaps that is why, with its refusal to offer solutions, it is like the blues. Yet in it thousands of Negroes will for the first time see their destiny in public print. Freed here of fear and the threat of violence, their lives have at last been organized, scaled down to possessable proportions. And in this lies Wright's most important achievement: he has converted the American Negro impulse toward self-annihilation and "going-under-ground" into a will to confront the world, to evaluate his experience honestly and throw his findings unashamedly into the guilty conscience of America.

BLUES PEOPLE

This volume's only strongly dissenting review is this one: of Blues People, *Amiri Baraka's (then LeRoi Jones's) history of black music in the United States. Dissension brings out an unrelentingly aggressive side of Ellison, one encountered in two of the essays begun as letters to editors and ultimately placed in* Shadow *and* Act *(and then in* The Collected Essays*), "The World and the Jug" and "Change the Joke and Slip the Yoke." In language that takes no prisoners, Ellison tells Jones that his approach to the music "is enough to give even the blues the blues." For Ellison,* Blues People's *major flaws are overinvesting in totalizing ideology—for which Ellison, the former fellow-traveler of the American Communist Party, had little or no patience, given what he perceived as the party's betrayal of blacks in the early 1940s—and in social science, from which, given the sociologists' impulse to label blacks as "pathological" or "imitative" or "culturally deprived," Ellison also was permanently disaffected. What's missing, in this view, is the sustained study of blues and poetry as part of African-American (American) history, with all its tangle of motives and strategies for survival, including musical ones invented by blacks. In the face of Jones's claims of authenticity based on class and color, Ellison asks: "But what are we to say of a* *white-skinned Negro with brown freckles who owns sixteen oil wells sunk in a piece of Texas land once farmed by his ex-slave parents who were a blue-eyed, white-skinned, redheaded (kinky) Negro woman from Virginia and a blue-gummed, black-skinned, curly-haired Negro male from Mississippi, and who not only sang bass in a Holy Roller church, played the market and voted Republican, but collected blues recordings and was a walking depository of blues tradition?"* Nor does Ellison accept the idea of a white American musical *"mainstream"* that exists apart from the music of American blacks: *"It is my theory that it would be impossible to pinpoint the time when they [Negroes] were not shaping what Jones calls the mainstream of American music. . . . The most authoritative rendering of America in music is that of American Negroes."* Taken together, Blues People *and this counter-punching review comprise quite a useful dialogue—another instance, Ellison might say, of "antagonistic cooperation."* (The New York Review, *February 6, 1964)*

———

In his introduction to *Blues People* LeRoi Jones advises us to approach the work as

> a strictly theoretical endeavor. Theoretical, in that none of the questions it poses can be said to have been answered definitely or for all time (sic!), etc. In fact, the whole book proposes more questions than it will answer. The only questions it will properly move to answer have, I think, been answered already within the patterns of American life. We need only give these patterns serious scrutiny and draw certain permissible conclusions.

It is a useful warning and one hopes that it will be regarded by those jazz publicists who have the quite irresponsible habit of sweeping up any novel pronouncement written about jazz and slapping it upon the first available record liner as the latest insight into the mysteries of American Negro expression.

Jones would take his subject seriously—as the best of jazz critics have always done—and he himself should be so taken. He has attempted to place the blues within the context of a total culture and to see this native art form through the disciplines of sociology, anthropology and (though he seriously underrates its importance in the creating of a viable theory) history, and he spells out explicitly his assumptions concerning the relation between the blues, the people who created them and the larger American culture. Although I find several of his assumptions questionable, this is valuable in itself. It would be well if all jazz critics did likewise; not only would it expose those who have no business in the field, but it would sharpen the thinking of the few who have something enlightening to contribute.

Blues People, like much that is written by Negro Americans at the present moment, takes on an inevitable resonance from the Freedom Movement, but it is in itself characterized by a straining for a note of militancy which is, to say the least, distracting. Its introductory mood of scholarly analysis frequently shatters into a dissonance of accusation, and one gets the impression that while Jones wants to perform a crucial task which he feels *someone* should take on—as indeed someone should—he is frustrated by the restraint demanded of the critical pen and would like to pick up a club.

Perhaps this explains why Jones, who is also a poet and editor of a poetry magazine, gives little attention to the blues as lyric, as a form of poetry. He appears to be attracted to the blues for what he believes they tell us of the sociology of Negro American identity and attitude. Thus, after beginning with the circumstances in which he sees their origin, he considers the ultimate values of American society:

> The Negro as slave is one thing. The Negro as American is quite another. But the *path* the slave took to "citi-

zenship" is what I want to look at. And I make my analogy through the slave citizen's music—through the music that is most closely associated with him: blues and a later, but parallel, development, jazz. And it seems to me that if the Negro represents, or is symbolic of, something in and about the nature of American culture, this certainly should be revealed by his characteristic music. . . . I am saying that if the music of the Negro in America, in all its permutations, is subjected to a socioanthropological as well as musical scrutiny, something about the essential nature of the Negro's existence in this country ought to be revealed, as well as something about the essential nature of this country, i.e., society as a whole.

The tremendous burden of sociology which Jones would place upon this body of music is enough to give even the blues the blues. At one point he tells us that "the one peculiar reference to the drastic change in the Negro from slavery to 'citizenship' is in his music." And later, with more precision, he states:

The point I want to make most evident here is that I cite the beginning of the blues as one beginning of American Negroes. Or, let me say, the reaction and subsequent relation of the Negro's experience in this country in *his* English is one beginning of the Negro's conscious appearance on the American scene.

No one could quarrel with Mr. Jones's stress upon beginnings. In 1833, two hundred and fourteen years after the first Africans were brought to these shores as slaves, a certain Mrs. Lydia Maria Child, a leading member of the American Anti-Slavery Society, published a paper entitled: *An Appeal in Favor of that Class of Americans Called Africans.* I am uncertain to what extent it actually reveals Mrs. Child's ideas concerning the complex relationship between time, place, cultural and/or national identity and race, but her title sounds like a fine bit of contemporary ironic *signifying*—"signifying" here meaning, in the unwritten dictionary of American Negro usage, "rhetorical understatements." It tells us much of the thinking of her opposition, and it reminds us that as late as the 1890s, a time when Negro composers, singers, dancers and comedians dominated the American musical stage, popular Negro songs (including James Weldon Johnson's "Under the Bamboo Tree," now immortalized by T. S. Eliot) were commonly referred to as "Ethiopian Airs."

Perhaps more than any other people, Americans have been locked in a deadly struggle with time, with history. We've fled the past and trained ourselves to suppress, if not forget, troublesome details of the national memory, and a great part of our optimism, like our progress, has been bought at the cost of ignoring the processes through which we've arrived at any given moment in our national existence. We've fought continuously with one another over who and what we are, and, with the exception of the Negro, over who and what is American. Jones is aware of this and, although he embarrasses his own argument, his emphasis is to the point.

For it would seem that while Negroes have been undergoing a process of "Americanization" from a time preceding the birth of this nation—including the fusing of their bloodlines with other non-African strains—there has persisted a stubborn confusion as to their American identity. Somehow it was assumed that the Negroes, of all the diverse American peoples, would remain unaffected by the climate, the weather, the political circumstances—from which not even slaves were exempt—the social structures, the national manners, the modes of production and the tides of the market, the national ideals, the conflicts of values, the rising and falling of national morale, or the complex give and take of acculturalization which was undergone by all others who found their existence within American democracy. This confusion still persists, and it is Mr. Jones's concern with it which gives *Blues People* a claim upon our attention.

Mr. Jones sees the American Negro as the product of a series of transformations, starting with the enslaved African, who became Afro-American slave, who became the American slave, who became, in turn, the highly qualified "citizen" whom we know today. The slave began by regarding himself as enslaved African during the time when he still spoke his native language or remembered it, practiced such aspects of his native religion as were possible and expressed himself musically in modes which were essentially African. These cultural traits became transmuted as the African lost consciousness of his African background, and his music, religion, language and speech gradually became that of the American Negro. His sacred music became the spirituals, his work songs and dance music became the blues and primitive jazz, and his religion became a form of Afro-American Christianity. With the end of slavery Jones sees the development of jazz and the blues as results of the more varied forms of experience made available to the freedman. By the twentieth century the blues divided and became, on the one hand, a professionalized form of entertainment, while remaining, on the other, a form of folklore.

By which I suppose he means that some Negroes remained in the country and sang a crude form of the blues, while others went to the city, became more sophisticated, and paid to hear Ma Rainey, Bessie or some of the other Smith girls sing them in night clubs or theaters. Jones gets this mixed up with ideas of social class—middle-class Negroes, whatever that term actually means, and light-skinned Negroes, or those Negroes corrupted by what Jones calls "White" culture—preferring the "classic" blues, and black, uncorrupted, country Negroes preferring "country blues."

For as with his music, so with the Negro. As Negroes

became "middle class" they rejected their tradition and themselves; "they wanted any self which the mainstream dictated, and the mainstream *always* dictated. And this black middle class, in turn, tried always to dictate that self, or this image of a whiter Negro, to the poorer, blacker Negroes."

One would get the impression that there was a rigid correlation between color, education, income and the Negro's preference in music. But what are we to say of a white-skinned Negro with brown freckles who owns sixteen oil wells sunk in a piece of Texas land once farmed by his ex-slave parents who were a blue-eyed, white-skinned, redheaded (kinky) Negro woman from Virginia and a blue-gummed, black-skinned, curly-haired Negro male from Mississippi, and who not only sang bass in a Holy Roller church, played the market and voted Republican, but collected blues recordings and was a walking depository of blues tradition? Jones's theory no more allows for the existence of such a Negro than it allows for himself, but that "concord of sensibilities" which has been defined as the meaning of culture allows for much more variety than Jones would admit.

Much the same could be said of Jones's treatment of the jazz during the thirties, when he claims its broader acceptance (i.e., its economic success as entertainment) led to a dilution, to the loss of much of its "black" character which caused a certain group of rebellious Negro musicians to create the "anti-mainstream" jazz style called bebop.

Jones sees bop as a conscious gesture of separatism, ignoring the fact that the creators of the style were seeking, whatever their musical intentions—and they were the least political of men—a fresh form of entertainment which would allow them their fair share of the entertainment market, which had been dominated by whites during the swing era. And although the boppers were reacting, at least in part, to the high artistic achievement of Armstrong, Hawkins, Basie and Ellington (all Negroes, all masters of the blues-jazz tradition), Jones sees their music as a recognition of his contention "that when you are black in a society where black is an extreme liability [it] is one thing, but to understand that it is the society which is lacking and is impossibly deformed because of this lack, and not *yourself,* isolates you even more from that society."

Perhaps. But today nothing succeeds like rebellion (which Jones as a "beat" poet should know), and while a few boppers went to Europe to escape, or became Muslims, others took the usual tours for the State Department. Whether this makes *them* "middle class" in Jones's eyes I can't say, but his assertions—which are fine as personal statement—are not in keeping with the facts; his theory flounders before that complex of human motives which makes human history, and which is so characteristic of the American Negro.

Read as a record of an earnest young man's attempt to come to grips with his predicament as Negro American during a most turbulent period of our history, *Blues People* may be worth the reader's time. Taken as a theory of American Negro culture, it can only contribute more confusion than clarity. For Jones has stumbled over that ironic obstacle which lies in the path of any who would fashion a theory of American Negro culture while ignoring the intricate network of connections which binds Negroes to the larger society. To do so is to attempt delicate brain surgery with a switchblade. And it is possible that any viable theory of Negro American culture obligates us to fashion a more adequate theory of American culture as a whole. The heel bone is, after all, connected through its various linkages to the head bone. Attempt a serious evaluation of our national morality, and up jumps the so-called Negro problem. Attempt to discuss jazz as a hermetic expression of Negro sensibility, and immediately we must consider what the "mainstream" of American music really is.

Here political categories are apt to confuse, for while Negro slaves were socially, politically and economically separate (but only in a special sense even here), they were, in a cultural sense, much closer than Jones's theory allows him to admit.

"A slave," writes Jones, "cannot be a man." But what, one might ask, of those moments when he feels his metabolism aroused by the rising of the sap in spring? What of his identity among other slaves? With his wife? And isn't it closer to the truth that far from considering themselves only in terms of that abstraction, "a slave," the enslaved really thought of themselves as *men* who had been unjustly enslaved? And isn't the true answer to Mr. Jones's question, "What are you going to be when you grow up?" not, as he gives it, "a slave" but most probably a coachman, a teamster, a cook, the best damned steward on the Mississippi, the best jockey in Kentucky, a butler, a farmer, a stud, or, hopefully, a free man! Slavery was a most vicious system, and those who endured and survived it a tough people, but it was *not* (and this is important for Negroes to remember for the sake of their own sense of who and what their grandparents were) a state of absolute repression.

A slave was, to the extent that he was a *musician,* one who expressed himself in music, a man who realized himself in the world of sound. Thus, while he might stand in awe before the superior technical ability of a white musician, and while he was forced to recognize a superior social status, he would never feel awed before the music which the technique of the white musician made available. His attitude as "musician" would lead him to seek to possess the music expressed through the technique, but until he could do so he would hum, whistle, sing or play the tunes to the best of his ability on any available instrument. And it was, indeed, out of the tension between desire and ability that the techniques of jazz emerged. This was likewise true of American Negro choral singing. For this, no literary explanation, no cultural analyses, no political slogans—indeed, not even a high degree of social or political freedom—was required. For the art—the blues, the spirituals, the jazz, the dance—was what we had in place of freedom.

Technique was then, as today, the key to creative freedom, but before this came a will toward expression. Thus, Jones's theory to the contrary, Negro musicians have never, as a group, felt alienated from any music sounded within their hearing, and it is my theory that it would be impossible to pinpoint the time when they were not shaping what Jones calls the mainstream of American music. Indeed, what group of musicians has made more of the sound of the American experience? Nor am I confining my statement to the sound of the slave experience, but am saying that the most authoritative rendering of America in music is that of American Negroes.

For as I see it, from the days of their introduction into the colonies, Negroes have taken, with the ruthlessness of those without articulate investments in cultural styles, whatever they could of European music, making of it that which would, when blended with the cultural tendencies inherited from Africa, express their own sense of life, while rejecting the rest. Perhaps this is only another way of saying that whatever the degree of injustice and inequality sustained by the slaves, American culture was, even before the official founding of the nation, pluralistic, and it was the African's origin in cultures in which art was highly functional which gave him an edge in shaping the music and dance of this nation.

The question of social and cultural snobbery is important here. The effectiveness of Negro music and dance is first recorded in the journals and letters of travelers but it is important to remember that they saw and understood only that which they were prepared to accept. Thus a Negro dancing a courtly dance appeared comic from the outside simply because the dancer was a slave. But to the Negro dancing it—and there is ample evidence that he danced it well—burlesque or satire might have been the point, which might have been difficult for a white observer to even imagine. During the 1870s Lafcadio Hearn reports that the best singers of Irish songs, in Irish dialect, were Negro dockworkers in Cincinnati, and advertisements from slavery days described escaped slaves who spoke in Scottish dialect. The master artisans of the South were slaves, and white Americans have been walking Negro walks, talking Negro-flavored talk (and prizing it when spoken by Southern belles), dancing Negro dances and singing Negro melodies far too long to talk of a "mainstream" of American culture to which they're alien.

Jones attempts to impose an ideology upon this cultural complexity, and this might be useful if he knew enough of the related subjects to make it interesting. But his version of the blues lacks a sense of the excitement and surprise of men living in the world—of enslaved and politically weak men successfully imposing their values upon a powerful society through song and dance.

The blues speak to us simultaneously of the tragic and comic aspects of the human condition, and they express a profound sense of life shared by many Negro Americans precisely because their lives have combined these modes. This has been the heritage of a people who for hundreds of years could not celebrate birth or dignify death, and whose need to live despite the dehumanizing pressures of slavery developed an endless capacity for laughing at their painful experiences. This is a group experience shared by many Negroes, and any effective study of the blues would treat them first as poetry and as ritual. Jones makes a distinction between classic and country blues, the one being entertainment and the other folklore. But the distinction is false.

Classic blues were both entertainment *and* a form of folk-lore. When they were sung professionally in theaters, they were entertainment; when danced to in the form of record-ings or used as a means of transmitting the traditional verses and their wisdom, they were folklore. There are levels of time and function involved here, and the blues which might be used in one place as entertainment (as gospel music is now being used in night clubs and on theater stages) might be put to a ritual use in another. Bessie Smith might have been a "blues queen" to society at large, but within the tighter Negro community where the blues were part of a total way of life, and a major expression of an attitude toward life, she was a priestess, a celebrant who affirmed the values of the group and man's ability to deal with chaos.

It is unfortunate that Jones thought it necessary to ignore the aesthetic nature of the blues in order to make his ideo-logical point, for he might have come much closer had he considered the blues not as politics but as art. This would have still required the disciplines of anthropology and soci-ology, but as practiced by Constance Rourke, who was well aware of how much of American cultural expression is Negro. And he could learn much from the Cambridge School's discoveries of the connection between poetry, drama and ritual as a means of analyzing how the blues function in their proper environment. Simple taste should have led Jones to Stanley Edgar Hyman's work on the blues instead of Paul Oliver's sadly misdirected effort.

For the blues are not primarily concerned with civil rights or obvious political protest; they are an art form and thus a transcendence of those conditions created within the Negro community by the denial of social justice. As such they are one of the techniques through which Negroes have survived and kept their courage during that long period when many whites assumed, as some still assume, that they were afraid.

Much has been made of the fact that *Blues People* is one of the few books by a Negro to treat the subject. Unfortunately for those who expect that Negroes would have a special insight into this mysterious art, this is not enough. Here, too, the critical intelligence must perform the difficult task which only it can perform.

Homage to William L. Dawson

Ellison gave this speech in 1971 at the fiftieth anniversary of the Philadelphia Tuskegee Club, which was honoring composer William L. Dawson, Ellison's main professor when he was a student at Tuskegee Institute in Alabama, 1933–1936. "I rode freight trains to Macon County, Alabama, during the Scottsboro trial," Ellison wrote in 1964, "because I desired to study with the Negro conductor/composer William L. Dawson, who was, and probably still is, the greatest classical musician in that part of the country." Best known as the composer of the Negro Folk Symphony *and as one of the most subtle arrangers of Negro spirituals for choir, Dawson set up Tuskegee's School of Music, which he directed from 1931 until 1955. This unretouched transcribed speech (not printed in Ellison's lifetime) is a remarkable example of Ellison's style as an improvisational speaker, working as usual without notes, or "from the head," as he liked to put it. Note his practice of repeating and riffing (and then elaborating) on certain phrases: "It was there. . . . It was also there as a deep tradition . . . It was there . . . It was an assertion of our own sense of life" and "So we came to Tuskegee . . . so we played . . . so we studied" and "I'm not talking about politics. I'm talking about living examples. I'm talking about musical traditions." (Compare this with* Invisible Man's *improvised funeral oration for Tod Clifton.) Also fascinating here are Ellison's efforts, throughout the talk, to define in words the transcendent significance of music for a black school whose central mission involved not art but industry and agriculture: "If you can't spell it out—and some of these things cannot be spelled out in words," Ellison told the group, "they can be felt, can be grasped, can enter you, can animate your body and thus animate your mind." This undefinable artistic treasure is, Ellison said, Dawson's "great gift."*

———

Fellow Tuskegeans: I hope it isn't lost on you that something natural is happening which is at the same time a little unexpected if we consider the reputation of Tuskegee. Here a very great composer, a master of choral music, is being honored by a fellow who studied under him, who went to Tuskegee because there was a man named Dawson there, who—since this seems to be a part of the tradition, and it actually happens—rode freight trains (it was too far to walk) to get to a place where there was musical excellence and a tradition of musical creativity. Most people didn't think about it in these terms, and yet it was there. It was there, I suspect, before Mr. Dawson graduated and returned to work his wonders on the scene. But it was also there as a deep tradition, one which bathed each and every thing that was done at Tuskegee with the overtones and undertones of a sense of life which perhaps could not have been expressed except through art. It was there perhaps out of the sheer desperate need to assert our hopes and dreams against the complications of living in the South—or for that matter of living in America. For we were up against definitions of our humanity which we could not accept, and we were too busy trying to go where *we* wanted to go, and to become what *we* wanted to become, to stop and spend much time arguing about it. It was an assertion of our own sense of life, the insistent drive to define human hope in the United States, not through avoiding those aspects of reality, and especially of our condition, which were brutal and dehumanizing, but taking that too as part of the given scene, and then determining to go beyond it. Not to ignore it, not to pretend that it didn't exist, but to humanize it, to take it in, to make it connect with other aspects of living—with the dream, with the sounds of the future and the sounds of hope. We did this through music. It was the tradition far back in the slave past which enhances the activities of Tuskegee. Underneath the desire for education or the possession of more technology, underneath the drive for intellectual competency is that other thing which can only be expressed through art.

As I said, it is rather odd that a fellow who didn't make it as a musician should be here trying to say something about William L. Dawson. But I think just as he reached out through his choir, through his ability to make people who were not really musicians give voice to sublime music, he was doing something else: acting as a cultural hero, acting as a living symbol of what was possible. So we came to Tuskegee, so we played in the band and in the orchestra, so we studied. (He once threw a piece of crayon at me!) You learned that even here life was real, life was honest, life was ambiguous. But you got certain messages which you weren't quite aware that you were getting.

When Mr. Dawson stood before a choir or the band or the orchestra, you had the sense that you were dealing with realities beyond yourself—that you were being asked to give yourself to meanings which were undefinable except in terms of music and musical style. But you also had the sense that with his elegance and severity, with his grasp of the meaning of verse, the value that he could draw out of a word and make you *draw* out of it, the way he could make you phrase, could teach you to grasp the meaning of a line of verse which sometimes he had set to music—sometimes Handel—all this gave you a sense that through this activity and dedication to the arts, you were going beyond and were getting insight into your other activities.

As I have said, Tuskegee has been a place of music, and it is ironic that through all of the years of its identity as a place of agriculture and industry, it has had this other dimension, that dimension of art which went beyond the simple matter of our singing and playing instruments. During the thirties Tuskegee was one of the major musical centers of the South. It was to Tuskegee that the Metropolitan Opera groups came; it was to Tuskegee that the great string quartets and the Philharmonic came. It was not to the University of Alabama; it was not to white schools in this area, but to Tuskegee. It was here that the tradition was. I will tell you something else: it wasn't a new thing when the Tuskegee choir opened Radio City during the thirties. It was only the event through which the broader America, the broader United States became aware of what had been going on there for many, many years. We live in ourselves; we grow from what went before. What comes after us depends on what we do in preserving that which we share, and which has been handed over into our keeping.

I think it important during the fiftieth anniversary of the Philadelphia Tuskegee Club that you honor Mr. Dawson and impress upon the nation at large that something very crucial to the cultural life of the United States—and perhaps to the political life of the United States—will be lost if we allow the tradition of Tuskegee to go down. I'm not talking now about politics. I'm talking about living examples; I'm talking about musical traditions. Because what is frequently overlooked—usually overlooked—in these days when we talk of discovering our identities, is that there was an identity here all along. And when you see a choir like this—two choirs: one improvised, I understand, and one which has been together—when you hear the articulation, when you hear the blending of the voices that grew out of an *identity,* you are aware of an identity based upon struggle with basic realities. A tradition which has been extended, broadened, and enriched by William L. Dawson, a tradition which is made up of music which our forefathers heard and created out of what was around them and what they brought with them from Africa. But the magical thing about it is that it is not simply an in-group music. This tradition is an artistic definition of what the American experience *is* when faced with grace and a willingness to give oneself to the tragic dimensions of the American experience. It is very precious, and the entire nation depends upon it because there is not enough of it.

We are very lucky that an artist of Mr. Dawson's stature found his way to Tuskegee at the age of thirteen. (He must have been a little criminal, because he ran away from home.) But he spent many years there, and received the basis of his musical training at Tuskegee. Some years ago, in speaking with a group of my white colleagues along with another Tuskegeean, we were talking about the writings of Joyce and Eliot and Pound, and all of a sudden Albert Murray said, "Well, Ralph, aren't you glad that we discovered these people at Tuskegee for ourselves?" And yes, I was glad, because now I can never read the poetry of those poets without associating it with Tuskegee; without seeing the magenta skies at dusk and sunup; without seeing the clock in White Hall. I must say that I was the fellow who used to wake Dr. Bryce up when I was there, because I was a trumpeter. I used to stand out there early in the morning and blow first call, and most of the time I put you to bed, too.

Through tradition, the place, the association, the sense of discovering that which is ever new in the old and the continuing, the abiding—in this way the artist fulfills his role. If you can't spell it out—and some of these things cannot be spelled out in words—they can be felt, can be grasped, can enter you, can animate your body and thus animate your mind. This is a great gift. We are very fortunate that such a man as Mr. Dawson has touched so many of our lives. Through his dedication to art he has made it possible for me, for instance, to be as dedicated and disciplined about literature. I'm sure that the same is true for most of you who have been taught by him and touched by him. This is a secret of education which goes beyond grades, which goes beyond even brilliance of mind. This is a secret of the place, the people, the times, and that deep art of music which is far more important to us than such poor critics as I have been able to spell out.

If there were a choir here, I would say let us sing "Let Us Break Bread Together." I am not particularly religious, but I am claimed by music, and I was claimed by William L. Dawson.

THIS MUSIC DEMANDED ACTION

This excerpt from the celebrated opening movement of Invisible Man *may be seen anew in this context of Ellison the music writer. No wonder Louis Armstrong figures so prominently in the novel's prologue and also makes an important appearance in its final section: Ellison's solo-song of a novel is as full of quotation, parody, innuendo, and the blues as one of Armstrong's trumpet flights. Listening under the spell of a "reefer" to a recording by Armstrong, "What Did I Do (to Be So Black and Blue)?" the unnamed narrator hears a whole tradition—secular, sacred, full of ambiguities and paradoxes—sounding there. It is an African-American tradition, but the point is that, since the African-American is such an important representative of America ("Who is more American than Mose?" Ellison says in one interview), the discovery of a black self applies to us all. Further, the "black self" is inevitably part white, just as "the American public at large," he told an audience at Harvard, is "a little Southern in their talk and a little colored in their walk." Hence the prologue's references not only to Armstrong, the spirituals, and the blues but also to Poe, Dostoyevsky, and Melville, as well as to flamenco and perhaps (as Ellison says in one interview) to the form of the symphony or sonata. The protagonist's challenge to uncover and create an identity* *for himself is underscored by the complexity of Armstrong's workings with this particular song, "Black and Blue." Armstrong has "made poetry out of his invisibility," as Invisible Man says. He made the most of having a freer hand in the creation of his art precisely be-cause white institutional powers failed to recognize him as an artist. Armstrong's "poetry" is surely a matter of rhythm, too—suggested by the anecdote where a yokel steps inside the scientific fighter's sense of time and knocks fancy science to the floor. Armstrong's magic is also a matter of stylishly spinning these lyrics. Though they were written originally for a musical theater piece's dark-skinned female charac-ter who complained with comic melodrama that "Browns and yellers / All have fellers," the trumpeter/poet refashions the lyrics to offer a deep, tragic questioning of the bruising ("black and blue") quality of human fate, an assessment that goes beyond gender and race. In defense of Armstrong, who at that time was widely criticized as an entertainer too eager to please white audiences, Ellison makes him a kind of Elizabethan trickster and tragicomic artist, one of the book's most powerful survivors. Somehow Louis knew, in Ellison's fine phrase (in "Flamenco"), "that the real secret of the game is to make life swing." (*Invisible Man, 1952)

————

Now I have one radio-phonograph; I plan to have five. There is a certain acoustical deadness in my hole, and when I have music I want to *feel* its vibration, not only with my ear but with my whole body. I'd like to hear five recordings of Louis Armstrong playing and singing "What Did I Do to Be so Black and Blue"—all at the same time. Sometimes now I listen to Louis while I have my favorite dessert of vanilla ice cream and sloe gin. I pour the red liquid over the white mound, watching it glisten and the vapor rising as Louis bends that military instrument into a beam of lyrical sound. Perhaps I like Louis Armstrong because he's made poetry out of being invisible. I think it must be because he's un-aware that he *is* invisible. And my own grasp of invisibility aids me to understand his music. Once when I asked for a cigarette, some jokers gave me a reefer, which I lighted when I got home and sat listening to my phonograph. It was a strange evening. Invisibility, let me explain, gives one a slightly different sense of time, you're never quite on the beat. Sometimes you're ahead and sometimes behind. Instead of the swift and imperceptible flowing of time, you are aware of its nodes, those points where time stands still or from which it leaps ahead. And you slip into the breaks and look around. That's what you hear vaguely in Louis' music.

Once I saw a prizefighter boxing a yokel. The fighter was swift and amazingly scientific. His body was one violent flow of rapid rhythmic action. He hit the yokel a hundred times while the yokel held up his arms in stunned surprise. But suddenly the yokel, rolling about in the gale of boxing gloves, struck one blow and knocked science, speed and footwork as cold as a well-digger's posterior. The smart money hit the canvas. The long shot got the nod. The yokel had simply stepped inside of his opponent's sense of time. So under the spell of the reefer I discovered a new analytical way of listening to music. The unheard sounds came through, and each melodic line existed of itself, stood out clearly from all the rest, said its piece, and waited patiently for the other voices to speak. That night I found myself hearing not only in time, but in space as well. I not only entered the music but descended, like Dante, into its depths. And *beneath the swiftness of the hot tempo there was a slower tempo and a cave and I entered it and looked around and heard an old woman singing a spiritual as full of Weltschmerz as flamenco, and beneath that lay a still lower level on which I saw a beautiful girl the color of ivory pleading in a voice like my mother's as she stood before a group of slaveowners who bid for her naked body, and below that I found a lower level and a more rapid tempo and I heard someone shout:*

"Brothers and sisters, my text this morning is the 'Blackness of Blackness.' "

And a congregation of voices answered: "That blackness is most black, brother, most black . . ."

"In the beginning . . ."

"At the very start," they cried.

". . . there was blackness . . ."

"Preach it . . ."

". . . and the sun . . ."

"The sun, Lawd . . ."

". . . was bloody red . . ."

"Red . . ."

"Now black is . . ." the preacher shouted.

"Bloody . . ."

"I said black is . . ."

"Preach it, brother . . ."

". . . an' black ain't . . ."

"Red, Lawd, red: He said it's red!"

"Amen, brother . . ."

"Black will git you . . ."

"Yes, it will . . ."

". . . an' black won't . . ."

"Naw, it won't!"

"It do . . ."

"It do, Lawd . . ."

". . . an' it don't."

"Halleluiah . . ."

". . . It'll put you, glory, glory, Oh my Lawd, in the WHALE'S BELLY."

"Preach it, dear brother . . ."

". . . an' make you tempt . . ."

"Good God a-mighty!"

"Old Aunt Nelly!"

"Black will make you . . ."

"Black . . ."

". . . or black will un-make you."

"Ain't it the truth, Lawd?"

And at that point a voice of trombone timbre screamed at me, "Git out of here, you fool! Is you ready to commit treason?"

And I tore myself away, hearing the old singer of spirituals moaning, "Go curse your God, boy, and die."

I stopped and questioned her, asked her what was wrong.

"I dearly loved my master, son," she said.

"You should have hated him," I said.

"He gave me several sons," she said, "and because I loved my sons I learned to love their father though I hated him too."

"I too have become acquainted with ambivalence," I said. "That's why I'm here."

"What's that?"

"Nothing, a word that doesn't explain it. Why do you moan?"

"I moan this way 'cause he's dead," she said.

"Then tell me, who is that laughing upstairs?"

"Them's my sons. They glad."

"Yes, I can understand that too," I said.

"I laughs too, but I moans too. He promised to set us free but he never could bring hisself to do it. Still I loved him . . ."

"Loved him? You mean . . . ?"

"Oh yes, but I loved something else even more."

"What more?"

"Freedom."

"Freedom," I said. "Maybe freedom lies in hating."

"Naw, son, it's in loving. I loved him and give him the poison and he withered away like a frost-bit apple. Them boys woulda tore him to pieces with they homemade knives."

"A mistake was made somewhere," I said, "I'm confused." And I wished to say other things, but the laughter upstairs became too loud and moan-like for me and I tried to break out of it, but I couldn't. Just as I was leaving I felt an urgent desire to ask her what freedom was and went back. She sat with her head in her hands, moaning softly; her leather-brown face was filled with sadness.

"Old woman, what is this freedom you love so well?" I asked around a corner of my mind.

She looked surprised, then thoughtful, then baffled. "I done forgot, son. It's all mixed up. First I think it's one thing, then I think it's another. It gits my head to spinning. I guess now it ain't nothing but knowing how to say what I got up in my head. But it's a hard job, son. Too much is done happen to me in too short a time. Hit's like I have a fever. Ever' time I starts to walk my head gits to swirling and I falls down. Or if it ain't that, it's the boys; they gits to laughing and wants to kill up the white folks. They's bitter, that's what they is . . ."

"But what about freedom?"

"Leave me 'lone, boy; my head aches!"

I left her, feeling dizzy myself. I didn't get far.

Suddenly one of the sons, a big fellow six feet tall, appeared out of nowhere and struck me with his fist.

"What's the matter, man?" I cried.

"You made Ma cry!"

"But how?" I said, dodging a blow.

"Askin' her them questions, that's how. Git outa here and stay, and next time you got questions like that, ask yourself!"

He held me in a grip like cold stone, his fingers fastening upon my windpipe until I thought I would suffocate before he finally allowed me to go. I stumbled about dazed, the music beating hysterically in my ears. It was dark. My head cleared and I wandered down a dark narrow passage, thinking I heard his footsteps hurrying behind me. I was sore, and into my being had come a profound craving for tranquillity, for peace and quiet, a state I felt I could never achieve. For one thing, the trumpet was blaring and the rhythm was too hectic. A tom-tom beating like heart-thuds began drowning out the trumpet, filling my ears. I longed for water and I heard it rushing through the cold mains my fingers touched as I felt my way, but I couldn't stop to search because of the footsteps behind me.

"Hey, Ras," I called. "Is it you, Destroyer? Rinehart?"

No answer, only the rhythmic footsteps behind me. Once I tried crossing the road, but a speeding machine struck me, scraping the skin from my leg as it roared past.

Then somehow I came out of it, ascending hastily from

this underworld of sound to hear Louis Armstrong inno-
cently asking,

> What did I do
> To be so black
> And blue?

At first I was afraid; this familiar music had demanded
action, the kind of which I was incapable, and yet had I lin-
gered there beneath the surface I might have attempted to
act. Nevertheless, I know now that few really listen to this
music. I sat on the chair's edge in a soaking sweat, as though
each of my 1,369 bulbs had everyone become a klieg light
in an individual setting for a third degree with Ras and
Rinehart in charge. It was exhausting—as though I had
held my breath continuously for an hour under the terrifying serenity that comes from days of intense hunger. And
yet, it was a strangely satisfying experience for an invisible
man to hear the silence of sound. I had discovered unrec-
ognized compulsions of my being—even though I could
not answer "yes" to their promptings. I haven't smoked a
reefer since, however; not because they're illegal, but because to *see* around corners is enough (that is not unusual
when you are invisible). But to hear around them is too
much; it inhibits action. And despite Brother Jack and all
that sad, lost period of the Brotherhood, I believe in nothing if not in action.

Please, a definition: A hibernation is a covert preparation
for a more overt action.

Besides, the drug destroys one's sense of time completely. If that happened, I might forget to dodge some
bright morning and some cluck would run me down with an
orange and yellow street car, or a bilious bus! Or I might forget to leave my hole when the moment for action presents
itself.

Meanwhile I enjoy my life with the compliments of

Monopolated Light & Power. Since you never recognize me even when in closest contact with me, and since, no doubt, you'll hardly believe that I exist, it won't matter if you know that I tapped a power line leading into the building and ran it into my hole in the ground. Before that I lived in the darkness into which I was chased, but now I see. I've illuminated the blackness of my invisibility—and vice versa. And so I play the invisible music of my isolation. The last statement doesn't seem just right, does it? But it is; you hear this music simply because music is heard and seldom seen, except by musicians. Could this compulsion to put invisibility down in black and white be thus an urge to make music of invisibility? But I am an orator, a rabble rouser—Am? I *was*, and perhaps shall be again. Who knows? All sickness is not unto death, neither is invisibility.

I can hear you say, "What a horrible, irresponsible bastard!" And you're right. I leap to agree with you. I am one of the most irresponsible beings that ever lived. Irresponsibility is part of my invisibility; any way you face it, it is a denial. But to whom can I be responsible, and why should I be, when you refuse to see me? And wait until I reveal how truly irresponsible I am. Responsibility rests upon recognition, and recognition is a form of agreement. Take the man whom I almost killed: Who was responsible for that near murder—I? I don't think so, and I refuse it. I won't buy it. You can't give it to me. *He* bumped *me, he* insulted *me*. Shouldn't he, for his own personal safety, have recognized my hysteria, my "danger potential"? He, let us say, was lost in a dream world. But didn't *he* control that dream world—which, alas, is only too real!—and didn't *he* rule me out of it? And if he had yelled for a policeman, wouldn't *I* have been taken for the offending one? Yes, yes, yes! Let me agree with you, I was the irresponsible one; for I should have used my knife to protect the higher interests of society. Some day that kind of foolishness will cause us tragic trouble. All dreamers and sleepwalkers must pay the price, and even the invisible victim is responsible for the fate of all. But I shirked that responsibility; I became too snarled in the incompatible notions that buzzed within my brain. I was a coward . . .

But what did *I* do to be so blue? Bear with me.

Trueblood's Song

In this episode from Invisible Man, *we meet Jim Trueblood (is he true to the stereotype of black "blood" as beastly, or is he true to the American black legacy of manipulating that image?), who has nothing if not the blues. His crime of incest, linked through his dream with transgressions of racial as well as family taboos, threatens to undermine his family, to spread chaos at the root of the community. In this "autobiographical chronicle of personal catastrophe expressed lyrically" (Ellison's definition of the blues in "Richard Wright's Blues"), Trueblood is a wounded man whose singing of the blues and powerful blues narration lends him the power to endure. Trueblood's blues drive the blues away. It is also fascinating to consider the* economics *of this episode. The officials of Invisible Man's college, who formerly had invited the black farmer to campus to perform spirituals for visiting white big-shots, offer Trueblood $100 to leave the county when they first hear his story. Invisible Man, that would-be black spokesman, was hoping Trustee Norton might reward his performance as an eager chauffeur and flattering tour guide; maybe he would win "a large tip, or a suit, or a scholarship." But Trueblood is the one who gets Norton's hundred-dollar bill. What is the meaning of Norton's payment for Trueblood's blues? What does it buy? How do* *the blues function for Invisible Man? For listeners and readers of* Invisible Man *today? (*Invisible Man, *1952)*

———

Half-consciously I followed the white line as I drove, thinking about what he had said. Then as we took a hill we were swept by a wave of scorching air and it was as though we were approaching a desert. It almost took my breath away and I leaned over and switched on the fan, hearing its sudden whirr.

"Thank you," he said as a slight breeze filled the car.

We were passing a collection of shacks and log cabins now, bleached white and warped by the weather. Sun-tortured shingles lay on the roofs like decks of water-soaked cards spread out to dry. The houses consisted of two square rooms joined together by a common floor and roof with a porch in between. As we passed we could look through to the fields beyond. I stopped the car at his excited command in front of a house set off from the rest.

"Is that a *log* cabin?"

It was an old cabin with its chinks filled with chalk-white clay, with bright new shingles patching its roof. Suddenly I was sorry that I had blundered down this road. I recognized the place as soon as I saw the group of children in stiff new overalls who played near a rickety fence.

"Yes, sir. It is a log cabin," I said.

It was the cabin of Jim Trueblood, a sharecropper who had brought disgrace upon the black community. Several months before he had caused quite a bit of outrage up at the school, and now his name was never mentioned above a whisper. Even before that he had seldom come near the campus but had been well liked as a hard worker who took good care of his family's needs, and as one who told the old stories with a sense of humor and a magic that made them come alive. He was also a good tenor singer, and sometimes when special white guests visited the school he was brought up along with the members of a country quartet to sing what the officials called "their primitive spirituals" when we assembled in the chapel on Sunday evenings. We were embarrassed by the earthy harmonies they sang, but since the visitors were awed we dared not laugh at the crude, high, plaintively animal sounds Jim Trueblood made as he led the quartet. That had all passed now with his disgrace, and what on the part of the school officials had been an attitude of contempt blunted by tolerance, had now become a contempt sharpened by hate. I didn't understand in those pre-invisible days that their hate, and mine too, was charged with fear. How all of us at the college hated the black-belt people, the "peasants," during those days! We were trying to lift them up and they, like Trueblood, did everything it seemed to pull us down.

"It appears quite old," Mr. Norton said, looking across the bare, hard stretch of yard where two women dressed in new blue-and-white checked ginghams were washing clothes in an iron pot. The pot was soot-black and the feeble flames that licked its sides showed pale pink and bordered with black, like flames in mourning. Both women moved with the weary, full-fronted motions of far-gone pregnancy.

"It is, sir," I said. "That one and the other two like it were built during slavery times."

"You don't say! I would never have believed that they were so enduring. Since slavery times!"

"That's true, sir. And the white family that owned the land when it was a big plantation still lives in town."

"Yes," he said, "I know that many of the old families still survive. And individuals too, the human stock goes on, even though it degenerates. But these cabins!" He seemed surprised and confounded.

"Do you suppose those women know anything about the age and history of the place? The older one looks as though she might."

"I doubt it, sir. They—they don't seem very bright."

"Bright?" he said, removing his cigar. "You mean that they wouldn't talk with me?" he asked suspiciously.

"Yes, sir. That's it."

"Why not?"

I didn't want to explain. It made me feel ashamed, but he sensed that I knew something and pressed me.

"It's not very nice, sir. But I don't think those women would talk to us."

"We can explain that we're from the school. Surely they'll talk then. You may tell them who I am."

"Yes, sir," I said, "but they hate us up at the school. They never come there . . ."

"What!"

"No, sir."

"And those children along the fence down there?"

"They don't either, sir."

"But why?"

"I don't really know, sir. Quite a few folks out this way don't, though. I guess they're too ignorant. They're not interested."

"But I can't believe it."

The children had stopped playing and now looked silently at the car, their arms behind their backs and their new over-sized overalls pulled tight over their little pot bellies as though they too were pregnant.

"What about their men folk?"

I hesitated. Why did he find this so strange?

"He hates us, sir," I said.

"You say *he;* aren't both the women married?"

I caught my breath. I'd made a mistake. "The old one is, sir," I said reluctantly.

"What happened to the young woman's husband?"

"She doesn't have any—That is . . . I—"

"What is it, young man? Do you know these people?"

"Only a little, sir. There was some talk about them up on the campus a while back."

"What talk?"

"Well, the young woman is the old woman's daughter..."

"And?"

"Well, sir, they say ... you see ... I mean they say the daughter doesn't have a husband."

"Oh, I see. But that shouldn't be so strange. I understand that your people—Never mind! Is that all?"

"Well, sir..."

"Yes, what else?"

"They say that her father did it."

"What!"

"Yes, sir ... that he gave her the baby."

I heard the sharp intake of breath, like a toy balloon suddenly deflated. His face reddened. I was confused, feeling shame for the two women and fear that I had talked too much and offended his sensibilities.

"And did anyone from the school investigate this matter?" he asked at last.

"Yes, sir," I said.

"What was discovered?"

"That it was true—they say."

"But how does he explain his doing such a—a—such a monstrous thing?"

He sat back in the seat, his hands grasping his knees, his knuckles bloodless. I looked away, down the heat-dazzling concrete of the highway. I wished we were back on the other side of the white line, heading back to the quiet green stretch of the campus.

"It is said that the man took both his wife and his daughter?"

"Yes, sir."

"And that he is the father of *both* their children?"

"Yes, sir."

"No, no, no!"

He sounded as though he were in great pain. I looked at him anxiously. What had happened? What had I said?

"Not that! No . . ." he said, with something like horror.

I saw the sun blaze upon the new blue overalls as the man appeared around the cabin. His shoes were tan and new and he moved easily over the hot earth. He was a small man and he covered the yard with a familiarity that would have allowed him to walk in the blackest darkness with the same certainty. He came and said something to the women as he fanned himself with a blue bandanna handkerchief. But they appeared to regard him sullenly, barely speaking, and hardly looking in his direction.

"Would that be the man?" Mr. Norton asked.

"Yes, sir. I think so."

"Get out!" he cried. "I must talk with him."

I was unable to move. I felt surprise and a dread and resentment of what he might say to Trueblood and his women, the questions he might ask. Why couldn't he leave them alone!

"Hurry!"

I climbed from the car and opened the rear door. He clambered out and almost ran across the road to the yard, as though compelled by some pressing urgency which I could not understand. Then suddenly I saw the two women turn and run frantically behind the house, their movements heavy and flatfooted. I hurried behind him, seeing him stop when he reached the man and the children. They became silent, their faces clouding over, their features becoming soft and negative, their eyes bland and deceptive. They were crouching behind their eyes waiting for him to speak—just as I recognized that I was trembling behind my own. Up close I saw what I had not seen from the car: The man had a scar on his right cheek, as though he had been hit in the face with a sledge. The wound was raw and moist and from time to time he lifted his handkerchief to fan away the gnats.

"I, I—" Mr. Norton stammered, "I must talk with you!"

"All right, suh," Jim Trueblood said without surprise and waited.

"Is it true . . . I mean did you?"

"Suh?" Trueblood asked, as I looked away.

"You have survived," he blurted. "But is it true . . . ?"

"Suh?" the farmer said, his brow wrinkling with bewilderment.

"I'm sorry, sir," I said, "but I don't think he understands you."

He ignored me, staring into Trueblood's face as though reading a message there which I could not perceive.

"You did and are unharmed!" he shouted, his blue eyes blazing into the black face with something like envy and indignation. Trueblood looked helplessly at me. I looked away. I understood no more than he.

"You have looked upon chaos and are not destroyed!"

"No suh! I feels all right."

"You do? You feel no inner turmoil, no need to cast out the offending eye?"

"Suh?"

"Answer me!"

"I'm all right, suh," Trueblood said uneasily. "My eyes is all right too. And when I feels po'ly in my gut I takes a little soda and it goes away."

"No, no, no! Let us go where there is shade," he said, looking about excitedly and going swiftly to where the porch cast a swath of shade. We followed him. The farmer placed his hand on my shoulder, but I shook it off, knowing that I could explain nothing. We sat on the porch in a semicircle in camp chairs, me between the sharecropper and the millionaire. The earth around the porch was hard and white from where wash water had long been thrown.

"How are you faring now?" Mr. Norton asked. "Perhaps I could help."

"We ain't doing so bad, suh. 'Fore they heard 'bout what happen to us out here I couldn't git no help from nobody. Now lotta folks is curious and goes outta they way to help.

Even the biggity school folks up on the hill, only there was a catch to it! They offered to send us clean outta the county, pay our way and everything and give me a hundred dollars to git settled with. But we likes it here so I told 'em No. Then they sent a fellow out here, a big fellow too, and he said if I didn't leave they was going to turn the white folks loose on me. It made me mad and it made me scared. Them folks up there to the school is in strong with the white folks and that scared me. But I thought when they first come out here that they was different from when I went up there a long time ago looking for some book learning and some points on how to handle my crops. That was when I had my own place. I thought they was trying to he'p me, on accounta I got two women due to birth 'bout the same time.

"But I got mad when I found they was tryin' to git rid of us 'cause they said we was a disgrace. Yessuh, I got real mad. So I went down to see Mr. Buchanan, the boss man, and I tole him 'bout it and he give me a note to the sheriff and tole me to take it to him. I did that, jus' like he tole me. I went to the jailhouse and give Sheriff Barbour the note and he ask me to tell him what happen, and I tole him and he called in some more men and they made me tell it again. They wanted to hear about the gal lots of times and they gimme somethin' to eat and drink and some tobacco. Surprised me, 'cause I was scared and spectin' somethin' different. Why, I guess there ain't a colored man in the county who ever got to take so much of the white folkses' time as I did. So finally they tell me not to worry, that they was going to send word up to the school that I was to stay right where I am. Them big nigguhs didn't bother me, neither. It just goes to show yuh that no matter how biggity a nigguh gits, the white folks can always cut him down. The white folks took up for me. And the white folks took to coming out here to see us and talk with us. Some of 'em was big white folks, too, from the big school way cross the State. Asked me lots 'bout what I thought 'bout things, and 'bout my folks and the kids, and wrote it all down in a book. But best of all, suh, I got more work now than I ever did have before . . ."

He talked willingly now, with a kind of satisfaction and no trace of hesitancy or shame. The old man listened with a puzzled expression as he held an unlit cigar in his delicate fingers.

"Things is pretty good now," the farmer said. "Ever time I think of how cold it was and what a hard time we was having I gits the shakes."

I saw him bite into a plug of chewing tobacco. Something tinkled against the porch and I picked it up, gazing at it from time to time. It was a hard red apple stamped out of tin.

"You see, suh, it was cold and us didn't have much fire. Nothin' but wood, no coal. I tried to git help but wouldn't nobody help us and I couldn't find no work or nothin'. It was so cold all of us had to sleep together; me, the ole lady and the gal. That's how it started, suh."

He cleared his throat, his eyes gleaming and his voice taking on a deep, incantatory quality, as though he had told the story many, many times. Flies and fine white gnats swarmed about his wound.

"That's the way it was," he said. "Me on one side and the ole lady on the other and the gal in the middle. It was dark, plum black. Black as the middle of a bucket of tar. The kids was sleeping all together in they bed over in the corner. I must have been the last one to go to sleep, 'cause I was thinking 'bout how to git some grub for the next day and 'bout the gal and the young boy what was startin' to hang 'round her. I didn't like him and he kept comin' through my thoughts and I made up my mind to warn him away from the gal. It was black dark and I heard one of the kids whimper in his sleep and the last few sticks of kindlin' crackin' and settlin' in the stove and the smell of the fat meat seemed to git cold and still in the air just like meat grease when it gits set in a cold plate of molasses. And I was thinkin' 'bout the gal and this boy and feelin' her arms besides me and hearing the ole lady snorin' with a kinda moanin' and a-groanin' on the other side. I was worryin' 'bout my family, how they was goin' to eat and all, and I thought 'bout when the gal was little like the younguns sleepin' over in the corner and how I was her favorite over the ole lady. There we was, breathin' together in the dark. Only I could see 'em in my mind, knowin' 'em like I do. In my mind I looked at all of 'em, one by one. The gal looks just like the ole lady did when she was young and I first met her, only better lookin'. You know, we gittin' to be a better-lookin' race of people . . .

"Anyway, I could hear 'em breathin' and though I hadn't been it made me sleepy. Then I heard the gal say, 'Daddy,' soft and low in her sleep and I looked, tryin' to see if she was still awake. But all I can do is smell her and feel her breath on my hand when I go to touch her. She said it so soft I couldn't be sure I had heard anything, so I just laid there listenin'. Seems like I heard a whippoorwill callin', and I thought to myself, Go on away from here, we'll whip ole Will when we find him. Then I heard the clock up there at the school strikin' four times, lonesome like.

"Then I got to thinkin' 'bout way back when I left the farm and went to live in Mobile and 'bout a gal I had me then. I was young then—like this young fellow here. Us lived in a two-story house 'longside the river, and at night in the summertime we used to lay in bed and talk, and after she'd gone off to sleep I'd be awake lookin' out at the lights comin' up from the water and listenin' to the sounds of the boats movin' along. They used to have musicianers on them boats, and sometimes I used to wake her up to hear the music when they come up the river. I'd be layin' there and it would be quiet and I could hear it comin' from way, way off. Like when you quail huntin' and it's getting dark and you can hear the boss bird whistlin' tryin' to get the covey to-gether again, and he's coming toward you slow and whistlin' soft, cause he knows you somewhere around with your gun.

Still he got to round them up, so he keeps on comin'. Them boss quails is like a good man, what he got to do he *do*.

"Well, that's the way the boats used to sound. Comin' close to you from far away. First one would be comin' to you when you almost sleep and it sounded like somebody hittin' at you slow with a big shiny pick. You see the pick-point comin' straight at you, comin' slow too, and you can't dodge; only when it goes to hit you it ain't no pick a'tall but somebody far away breakin' little bottles of all kindsa colored glass. It's still comin' at you though. Still comin'. Then you hear it close up, like when you up in the second-story window and look down on a wagonful of watermelons, and you see one of them young juicy melons split wide open a-layin' all spread out and cool and sweet on top of all the striped green ones like it's waitin' just for you, so you can see how red and ripe and juicy it is and all the shiny black seeds it's got and all. And you could hear the sidewheels splashin' like they don't want to wake nobody up; and us, me and the gal, would lay there feelin' like we was rich folks and them boys on the boats would be playin' sweet as good peach brandy wine. Then the boats would be past and the lights would be gone from the window and the music would be goin' too. Kinda like when you watch a gal in a red dress and a wide straw hat goin' past you down a lane with the trees on both sides, and she's plump and juicy and kinda switchin' her tail 'cause she knows you watchin' and you *know* she know, and you just stands there and watches 'til you can't see nothin' but the top of her red hat and then that goes and you know she done dropped behind a hill—I seen me a gal like that once. All I could hear then would be that Mobile gal—name of Margaret—she be breathin' beside me, and maybe 'bout that time she'd say, 'Daddy, you still 'wake?' and then I'd grunt, 'Uhhuh' and drop on off—Gent'mens," Jim Trueblood said, "I likes to recall them Mobile days.

"Well, it was like that when I heard Matty Lou say, 'Daddy,' and I knowed she musta been dreamin' 'bout somebody from the way she said it and I gits mad wonderin' if it's that boy. I listen to her mumblin' for a while tryin' to hear if she calls his name, but she don't, and I remember that they say if you put the hand of a person who's talkin' in his sleep in warm water he'll say it all, but the water is too cold and I wouldn't have done it anyway. But I'm realizin' that she's a woman now, when I feels her turn and squirm against me and throw her arm across my neck, up where the cover didn't reach and I was cold. She said somethin' I couldn't understand, like a woman says when she wants to tease and please a man. I knowed then she was grown and I wondered how many times it'd done happened and was it that doggone boy. I moved her arm and it was soft, but it didn't wake her, so I called her, but that didn't wake her neither. Then I turned my back and tried to move away, though there wasn't much room and I could still feel her touchin' me, movin' close to me. Then I musta dropped into the dream. I have to tell you 'bout that dream."

I looked at Mr. Norton and stood up, thinking that now was a good time to leave; but he was listening to Trueblood so intensely he didn't see me, and I sat down again, cursing the farmer silently. To hell with his dream!

"I don't quite remember it all, but I remember that I was lookin' for some fat meat. I went to the white folks downtown and they said go see Mr. Broadnax, that he'd give it to me. Well, he lives up on a hill and I was climbin' up there to see him. Seems like that was the highest hill in the world. The more I climbed the farther away Mr. Broadnax's house seems to git. But finally I do reach there. And I'm so tired and restless to git to the man, I goes through the front door! I knows it's wrong, but I can't help it. I goes in and I'm standin' in a big room full of lighted candles and shiny furniture and pictures on the walls, and soft stuff on the floor. But I don't see a livin' soul. So I calls his name, but still don't nobody come and don't nobody answer. So I sees a door and goes through that door and I'm in a big white bedroom, like

I seen one time when I was a little ole boy and went to the big house with my Ma. Everything in the room was white and I'm standin' there knowin' I got no business in there, but there anyhow. It's a woman's room too. I tries to git out, but I don't find the door; and all around me I can smell woman, can smell it gittin' stronger all the time. Then I looks over in a corner and sees one of them tall grandfather clocks and I hears it strikin' and the glass door is openin' and a white lady is steppin' out of it. She got on a nightgown of soft white silky stuff and nothin' else, and she looks straight at me. I don't know what to do. I wants to run, but the only door I see is the one in the clock she's standin' in—and anyway, I can't move and this here clock is keepin' up a heapa racket. It's gittin' faster and faster all the time. I tries to say somethin', but I caint. Then she starts to screamin' and I thinks I done gone deaf, 'cause though I can see her mouth working, I don't *hear* nothin'. Yit I can still hear the clock and I tries to tell her I'm just lookin' for Mr. Broadnax but she don't hear me. Instead she runs up and grabs me around the neck and holds tight, tryin' to keep me out of the clock. I don't know what to do then, sho 'nough. I tries to talk to her, and I tries to git away. But she's holdin' me and I'm scared to touch her cause she's white. Then I gits so scared that I throws her on the bed and tries to break her holt. That woman just seemed to sink outta sight, that there bed was so soft. It's sinkin' down so far I think it's going to smother both of us. Then swoosh! all of a sudden a flock of little white geese flies out of the bed like they say you see when you go to dig for buried money. Lawd! they hadn't no more'n disappeared than I heard a door open and Mr. Broadnax's voice said, 'They just nigguhs, leave 'em do it.' "

How can he tell this to white men, I thought, when he knows they'll say that all Negroes do such things? I looked at the floor, a red mist of anguish before my eyes.

"And I caint stop—although I got a feelin' somethin' is wrong. I git aloose from the woman now and I'm runnin' for the clock. At first I couldn't git the door open, it had some kinda crinkly stuff like steel wool on the facing. But I gits it open and gits inside and it's hot and dark in there. I goes up a dark tunnel, up near where the machinery is making all that noise and heat. It's like the power plant they got up to the school. It's burnin' hot as iffen the house was caught on fire, and I starts to runnin', tryin' to git out. I runs and runs till I should be tired but ain't tired but feelin' more rested as I runs, and runnin' so good it's like flyin' and I'm flyin' and sailin' and floatin' right up over the town. Only I'm still in the *tunnel*. Then way up ahead I sees a bright light like a jack-o-lantern over a graveyard. It gits brighter and brighter and I know I got to catch up with it or else. Then all at once I was right up with it and it burst like a great big electric light in my eyes and scalded me all over. Only it wasn't a scald, but like I was drownin' in a lake where the water was hot on the top and had cold numbin' currents down under it. Then all at once I'm through it and I'm relieved to be out and in the cool daylight agin.

"I wakes up intendin' to tell the ole lady 'bout my crazy dream. Morning done come, and it's gettin' almost light. And there I am, lookin' straight in Matty Lou's face and she's beatin' me and scratchin' and tremblin' and shakin' and cryin' all at the same time like she's havin' a fit. I'm too sur-prised to move. She's cryin', 'Daddy, Daddy, oh Daddy,' just like that. And all at once I remember the ole lady. She's right beside us snorin' and I can't move 'cause I figgers if I moved it would be a sin. And I figgers too, that if I don't move it maybe ain't no sin, 'cause it happened when I was asleep— although maybe sometimes a man can look at a little ole pigtail gal and see him a whore—you'all know that? Any-way, I realizes that if I don't move the ole lady will see me. I don't want that to happen. That would be *worse* than sin. I'm whisperin' to Matty Lou, tryin' to keep her quiet and I'm figurin' how to git myself out of the fix I'm in without sin-nin'. I almost chokes her.

"But once a man gits hisself in a tight spot like that there ain't much he can do. It ain't up to him no longer. There I was, tryin' to git away with all my might, yet having to move *without* movin'. I flew in but I had to walk out. I had to move without movin'. I done thought 'bout it since a heap, and when you think right hard you see that that's the way things is always been with me. That's just about been my life. There was only one way I can figger that I could git out: that was with a knife. But I didn't have no knife, and if you'all ever seen them geld them young boar pigs in the fall, you know I knowed that that was too much to pay to keep from sinnin'. Everything was happenin' inside of me like a fight was goin' on. Then just the very thought of the fix I'm in puts the iron back in me.

"Then if that ain't bad enough, Matty Lou can't hold out no longer and gits to movin' herself. First she was tryin' to push me away and I'm tryin' to hold her down to keep from sinnin'. Then I'm pullin' away and shushin' her to be quiet so's not to wake her Ma, when she grabs holt to me and holds tight. She didn't want me to go then—and to tell the honest-to-God truth I found out that I didn't want to go neither. I guess I felt then, at that time—and although I been sorry since—just 'bout like that fellow did down in Birmingham. That one what locked hisself in his house and shot at them police until they set fire to the house and burned him up. I was lost. The more wringlin' and twistin' we done tryin' to git away, the more we wanted to stay. So like that fellow, I stayed, I had to fight it on out to the end. He mighta died, but I suspects now that he got a heapa satisfaction before he went. I *know* there ain't nothin' like what I went through, I caint tell how it was. It's like when a real drinkin' man gits drunk, or like when a real sanctified religious woman gits so worked up she jumps outta her clothes, or when a real gamblin' man keeps on gamblin' when he's losin'. You got holt to it and you caint let go even though you want to."

"Mr. Norton, sir," I said in a choked voice, "it's time we were getting back to the campus. You'll miss your appointments..."

He didn't even look at me. *"Please,"* he said, waving his hand in annoyance.

Trueblood seemed to smile at me behind his eyes as he looked from the white man to me and continued.

"I couldn't even let go when I heard Kate scream. It was a scream to make your blood run cold. It sounds like a woman who was watchin' a team of wild horses run down her baby chile and she caint move. Kate's hair is standin' up like she done seen a ghost, her gown is hanging open and the veins in her neck is 'bout to bust. And her eyes! Lawd, them eyes. I'm lookin' up at her from where I'm layin' on the pallet with Matty Lou, and I'm too weak to move. She screams and starts to pickin' up the first thing that comes to her hand and throwin' it. Some of them misses me and some of them hits me. Little things and big things. Somethin' cold and strong-stinkin' hits me and wets me and bangs against my head. Somethin' hits the wall—boom-a-loom-a-loom!—like a cannon ball, and I tries to cover up my head. Kate's talkin' the unknown tongue, like a wild woman.

" 'Wait a minit, Kate,' I says. 'Stop it!'

"Then I hears her stop a second and I hears her runnin' across the floor, and I twists and looks and Lawd, she done got my double-barrel shotgun!

"And while she's foamin' at the mouth and cockin' the gun, she gits her speech.

" 'Git up! Git up!' she says.

" 'HEY! NAW! KATE!' I says.

" 'Goddam yo' soul to hell! Git up offa my chile!'

" 'But woman, Kate, lissen ...'

" 'Don't talk, MOVE!'

" 'Down that thing, Kate!'

" 'No down, UP!'

" 'That there's buckshot, woman, BUCKshot!'

" 'Yes, it is!'

" 'Down it, I say!'

" 'I'm gon blast your soul to hell!'

" 'You gon hit Matty Lou!'

" 'Not Matty Lou—YOU!'

" 'It spreads, Kate. Matty Lou!'

"She moves around, aimin' at me.

" 'I done warn you, Jim . . .'

" 'Kate, it was a dream. Lissen to me . . .'

" 'You the one who lissen—UP FROM THERE!'

"She jerks the gun and I shuts my eyes. But insteada thunder and lightin' bustin' me, I hears Matty Lou scream in my ear,

" 'Mamma! Oooooo, MAMA!'

"I rolls almost over then and Kate hesitates. She looks at the gun, and she looks at us, and she shivers a minit like she got the fever. Then all at once she drops the gun, and ZIP! quick as a cat, she turns and grabs somethin' off the stove. It catches me like somebody diggin' into my side with a sharp spade. I caint breathe. She's throwin' and talkin' all at the same time.

"And when I looks up, Maan, Maaan! she's got a iron in her hand!

"I hollers, 'No blood, Kate. Don't spill no blood!'

" 'You low-down dog,' she says, 'it's better to spill than to foul!'

" 'Naw, Kate. Things ain't what they 'pear! Don't make no blood-sin on accounta no dream-sin!'

" 'Shut up, nigguh. You done *fouled!*'

"But I sees there ain't no use reasonin' with her then. I makes up my mind that I'm goin' to take whatever she gimme. It seems to me that all I can do is take my punishment. I tell myself, Maybe if you suffer for it, it will be best. Maybe you owe it to Kate to let her beat you. You ain't guilty, but she thinks you is. You don't want her to beat you, but she think she got to beat you. You want to git up, but you too weak to move.

"I was too. I was frozen to where I was like a younggun what done stuck his lip to a pump handle in the wintertime. I was just like a jaybird that the yellow jackets done stung 'til he's paralyzed—but still alive in his eyes and he's watchin' 'em sting his body to death.

"It made me seem to go way back a distance in my head, behind my eyes, like I was standin' behind a windbreak durin' a storm. I looks out and sees Kate runnin' toward me draggin' something behind her. I tries to see what it is 'cause I'm curious 'bout it and sees her gown catch on the stove and her hand comin' in sight with somethin' in it. I thinks to myself, It's a handle. What she got the handle to? Then I sees her right up on me, big. She's swingin' her arms like a man swingin' a ten-pound sledge and I sees the knuckles of her hand is bruised and bleedin', and I sees it catch in her gown and I sees her gown go up so I can see her thighs and I sees how rusty and gray the cold done made her skin, and I sees her bend and straightenin' up and I hears her grunt and I sees her swing and I smells her sweat and I knows by the shape of the shinin' wood what she's got to put on me. Lawd, yes! I sees it catch on a quilt this time and raise that quilt up and drop it on the floor. Then I sees that ax come free! It's shinin', shinin' from the sharpenin' I'd give it a few days before, and man, way back in myself, behind that windbreak, I says,

" 'NAAW! KATE—Lawd, Kate, NAW!!!' "

Suddenly his voice was so strident that I looked up startled. Trueblood seemed to look straight through Mr. Norton, his eyes glassy. The children paused guiltily at their play, looking toward their father.

"I might as well been pleadin' with a switch engine," he went on. "I sees it comin' down. I sees the light catchin' on it, I sees Kate's face all mean and I tightens my shoulders and stiffens my neck and I waits—ten million back-breakin' years, it seems to me like I waits. I waits so long I remembers all the wrong things I ever done; I waits so long I opens my eyes and closes 'em and opens my eyes agin, and I sees it fallin'. It's fallin' fast as flops from a six-foot ox, and while I'm waitin' I feels somethin' wind up inside of me and turn to water. I sees it, Lawd, yes! I sees it and seein' it I twists my head aside. Couldn't help it; Kate has a good aim, but for that. I moves. Though I meant to keep still, I moves! Anybody but Jesus Christ hisself woulda moved. I feel like the whole side of my face is smashed clear off. It hits me like hot lead so hot that insteada burnin' me it numbs me. I'm layin' there on the floor, but inside me I'm runnin' round in circles like a dog with his back broke, and back into that numbness with my tail tucked between my legs. I feels like I don't have no skin on my face no more, only the naked bone. But this is the part I don't understand: more'n the pain and numbness I feels relief. Yes, and to git some more of that relief I seems to run out from behind the windbreak again and up to where Kate's standin' with the ax, and I opens my eyes and waits. That's the truth. I wants some more and I waits. I sees her swing it, lookin' down on me, and I sees it in the air and I holds my breath, then all of a sudden I sees it stop like somebody done reached down through the roof and caught it, and I sees her face have a spasm and I sees the ax fall, back of her this time, and hit the floor, and Kate spews out some puke and I close my eyes and waits. I can hear her moanin' and stumblin' out of the door and fallin' off the porch into the yard. Then I hears her pukin' like all her guts is coming up by the roots. Then I looks down and seen blood runnin' all over Matty Lou. It's my blood, my face is bleedin'. That gits me to movin'. I gits up and stumbles out to find Kate, and there she is under the cottonwood tree out there, on her knees, and she's moanin'.

" 'What have I done, Lawd! What have I done!'

"She's droolin' green stuff and gits to pukin' agin, and when I goes to touch her it gits worse. I stands there holdin' my face and tryin' to keep the blood from flowin' and wonders what on earth is gonna happen. I looks up at the mornin' sun and expects somehow for it to thunder. But it's already bright and clear and the sun comin' up and the birds is chirpin' and I gits more afraid then than if a bolt of lightnin' had struck me. I yells, 'Have mercy, Lawd! Lawd, have mercy!' and waits. And there's nothin' but the clear bright mornin' sun.

"But don't nothin' happen and I knows then that somethin' worse than anything I ever heard 'bout is in store for me. I musta stood there stark stone still for half an hour. I was still standin' there when Kate got off her knees and went back into the house. The blood was runnin' all over my clothes and the flies was after me, and I went back inside to try and stop it.

"When I see Matty Lou stretched out there I think she's dead. Ain't no color in her face and she ain't hardly breathin'. She gray in the face. I tries to help her but I can't do no good and Kate won't speak to me nor look at me even; and I thinks maybe she plans to try to kill me agin, but she don't. I'm in such a daze I just sits there the whole time while she bundles up the younguns and takes 'em down the road to Will Nichols'. I can see but I caint do nothin'.

"And I'm still settin' there when she comes back with some women to see 'bout Matty Lou. Won't nobody speak to me, though they looks at me like I'm some new kinda cotton-pickin' machine. I feels bad. I tells them how it happened in a dream, but they scorns me. I gits plum out of the house then. I goes to see the preacher and even he don't believe me. He tells me to git out of his house, that I'm the most wicked man he's ever seen and that I better go confess my sin and make my peace with God. I leaves tryin' to pray, but I caint. I thinks and thinks, until I thinks my brain go'n bust, 'bout how I'm guilty and how I ain't guilty. I don't eat nothin' and I don't drink nothin' and caint sleep at night. Finally, one night, way early in the mornin', I looks up and sees the stars and I starts singin'. I don't mean to, I didn't think 'bout it, just start singin'. I don't know what it was, some kinda church song, I guess. All I know is I *ends up* singin' the blues. I sings me some blues that night ain't never been sang before, and while I'm singin' them blues I makes up my mind that I ain't nobody but myself and ain't nothin' I can do but let whatever is gonna happen, happen. I made up my mind that I was goin' back home and face Kate; yeah, and face Matty Lou too.

"When I gits here everybody thinks I done run off. There's a heap of women here with Kate and I runs 'em out. And when I runs 'em out I sends the younguns out to play and locks the door and tells Kate and Matty Lou 'bout the dream and how I'm sorry, but that what done happen is done happen.

" 'How come you don't go on 'way and leave us?' is the first words Kate says to me. 'Ain't you done enough to me and this chile?'

" 'I caint leave you,' I says. 'I'm a man and man don't leave his family.'

"She says, 'Naw, you ain't no man. No man'd do what you did.'

" 'I'm still a man,' I says.

" 'But what you gon do after it happens?' says Kate.

" 'After *what* happens?' I says.

" 'When yo black 'bomination is birthed to bawl yo wicked sin befo the eyes of God!' (She musta learned them words from the preacher.)

" 'Birth?' I says. '*Who* birth?'

" 'Both of us. Me birth and Matty Lou birth. Both of us birth, you dirty lowdown wicked dog!'

"That liketa killed me. I can understand then why Matty Lou won't look at me and won't speak a word to nobody.

" 'If you stay I'm goin' over an' git Aunt Cloe for both of us,' Kate says. She says, 'I don't aim to birth no sin for folks to look at all the rest of my life, and I don't aim for Matty Lou to neither.'

"You see, Aunt Cloe is a midwife, and even weak as I am from this news I knows I don't want her foolin' with my womenfolks. That woulda been pilin' sin up on toppa sin. So I told Kate, naw, that if Aunt Cloe come near this house I'd kill her, old as she is. I'da done it too. That settles it. I walks out of the house and leaves 'em here to cry it out between 'em. I wanted to go off by myself agin, but it don't do no good tryin' to run off from somethin' like that. It follows you wherever you go. Besides, to git right down to the facts, there wasn't nowhere I could go. I didn't have a cryin' dime!

"Things got to happenin' right off. The nigguhs up at the school come down to chase me off and that made me mad. I went to see the white folks then and they gave me help. That's what I don't understand. I done the worse thing a man could ever do in his family and instead of chasin' me out of the county, they gimme more help than they ever give any other colored man, no matter how good a nigguh he was. Except that my wife an' daughter won't speak to me, I'm better off than I ever been before. And even if Kate won't speak to me she took the new clothes I brought her from up in town and now she's gettin' some eyeglasses made what she been needin' for so long. But what I don't understand is how I done the worse thing a man can do in his own family and 'stead of things gittin' bad, they got better. The nigguhs up at the school don't like me, but the white folks treats me fine."

———

He was some farmer. As I listened I had been so torn between humiliation and fascination that to lessen my sense of shame I had kept my attention riveted upon his intense face. That way I did not have to look at Mr. Norton. But now as the voice ended I sat looking down at Mr. Norton's feet. Out in the yard a woman's hoarse contralto intoned a hymn.

Children's voices were raised in playful chatter. I sat bent over, smelling the sharp dry odor of wood burning in the hot sunlight. I stared at the two pairs of shoes before me. Mr. Norton's were white, trimmed with black. They were custom made and there beside the cheap tan brogues of the farmer they had the elegantly slender well-bred appearance of fine gloves. Finally someone cleared his throat and I looked up to see Mr. Norton staring silently into Jim Trueblood's eyes. I was startled. His face had drained of color. With his bright eyes burning into Trueblood's black face, he looked ghostly. Trueblood looked at me questioningly.

"Lissen to the younguns," he said in embarrassment. "Playin' 'London Bridge's Fallin' Down.' "

Something was going on which I didn't get. I had to get Mr. Norton away.

"Are you all right, sir?" I asked.

He looked at me with unseeing eyes. "All right?" he said.

"Yes, sir. I mean that I think it's time for the afternoon session," I hurried on.

He stared at me blankly.

I went to him. "Are you sure you're all right, sir?"

"Maybe it's the heat," Trueblood said. "You got to be born down here to stand this kind of heat."

"Perhaps," Mr. Norton said, "it is the heat. We'd better go."

He stood shakily, still staring intently at Trueblood. Then I saw him removing a red Moroccan-leather wallet from his coat pocket. The platinum-framed miniature came with it, but he did not look at it this time.

"Here," he said, extending a banknote. "Please take this and buy the children some toys for me."

Trueblood's mouth fell agape, his eyes widened and filled with moisture as he took the bill between trembling fingers. It was a hundred-dollar bill.

"I'm ready, young man," Mr. Norton said, his voice a whisper.

I went before him to the car and opened the door. He stumbled a bit climbing in and I gave him my arm. His face was still chalk white.

"Drive me away from here," he said in a sudden frenzy. "Away!"

"Yes, sir."

I saw Jim Trueblood wave as I threw the car into gear. "You bastard," I said under my breath. "You no-good bastard! *You* get a hundred-dollar bill!"

When I had turned the car and started back I saw him still standing in the same place.

Suddenly Mr. Norton touched me on the shoulder. "I must have a stimulant, young man. A little whiskey."

"Yes, sir. Are you all right, sir?"

"A little faint, but a stimulant . . ."

His voice trailed off. Something cold formed within my chest. If anything happened to him Dr. Bledsoe would blame me. I stepped on the gas, wondering where I could get him some whiskey. Not in the town, that would take too long. There was only one place, the Golden Day.

"I'll have you some in a few minutes, sir," I said.

"As soon as you can," he said.

PETER WHEATSTRAW,
THE DEVIL'S SON-IN-LAW

In this selection from Invisible Man, *the greenhorn encounters a savvy black man in Harlem, who, through ritualized verbal patter and a song, cautions the youngster not to forget his Southern black roots in the big city. In a letter to me, Ellison said that he remembered the name Peter Wheatstraw from Oklahoma City, where, in "a belligerent roar," it was often taken as an alias by pool players specializing in braggadocio. The novel's northern-citified Wheatstraw struts his stuff as a "piano player and a rounder, a whiskey drinker and a pavement pounder." Ellison made these additions to the "folkmyth" as he knew it, "to urbanize and fill out the vernacular frame." Of the Wheatstraw boasting he remembered from his youth, Ellison said: "I 'novelized' it, and you'll note that it appears at a point when the narrator is being challenged to draw upon his folk-based background for orientation and survival." Much the same may be said of Wheatstraw's blues of this episode: They caution the young man against luck with "feet like a monkey," they offer tools for survival in the bear's den of Upper Manhattan. And the traditional lyrics, heard, for instance, in Jimmy Rushing's "Boogie Woogie" (with Count Basie, 1937), suggest some of life's doubleness and trouble also represented by Aunt Mackie of "A Coupla Scalped Indians": both Mackie and "my* *baabay" of the present episode evoke what Ellison has termed "the abiding mystery of the enigmatic women who people the blues." Here again, the blues offer more than humorous entertainment (as rare and as good as that may be); they offer cautionary notes as they teach their listeners what it means to live. (*Invisible Man, 1952)

It was a clear, bright day when I went out, and the sun burned warm upon my eyes. Only a few flecks of snowy cloud hung high in the morning-blue sky, and already a woman was hanging wash on a roof. I felt better walking along. A feeling of confidence grew. Far down the island the skyscrapers rose tall and mysterious in the thin, pastel haze. A milk truck went past. I thought of the school. What were they doing now on the campus? Had the moon sunk low and the sun climbed clear? Had the breakfast bugle blown? Did the bellow of the big seed bull awaken the girls in the dorms this morning as on most spring mornings when I was there—sounding clear and full above bells and bugles and early workaday sounds? I hurried along, encouraged by the memories, and suddenly I was seized with a certainty that today was the day. Something would happen. I patted my briefcase, thinking of the letter inside. The last had been first—a good sign.

Close to the curb ahead I saw a man pushing a cart piled high with rolls of blue paper and heard him singing in a clear ringing voice. It was a blues, and I walked along behind him remembering the times that I had heard such singing at home. It seemed that here some memories slipped around my life at the campus and went far back to things I had long ago shut out of my mind. There was no escaping such reminders.

> "She's got feet like a monkey
> Legs like a frog—Lawd, Lawd!
> But when she starts to loving me

I holler Whoooo, God-dog!
Cause I loves my baabay,
Better than I do myself . . ."

And as I drew alongside I was startled to hear him call to me:

"Looka-year, buddy . . ."

"Yes," I said, pausing to look into his reddish eyes.

"Tell me just one thing this very fine morning—Hey! Wait a minute, daddy-o, I'm going your way!"

"What is it?" I said.

"What I want to know is," he said, "is you got the *dog?*"

"Dog? What dog?"

"Sho," he said, stopping his cart and resting it on its support. "That's it. *Who*—" he halted to crouch with one foot on the curb like a country preacher about to pound his Bible— *"got . . . the . . . dog,"* his head snapping with each word like an angry rooster's.

I laughed nervously and stepped back. He watched me out of shrewd eyes. "Oh goddog, daddy-o," he said with a sudden bluster, "who got the damn dog? Now I know you from down home, how come you trying to act like you never heard that before! Hell, ain't nobody out here this morning but us colored—Why you trying to deny me?"

Suddenly I was embarrassed and angry. "Deny you? What do you mean?"

"Just answer the question. Is you got him, or ain't you?"

"A *dog?*"

"Yeah, *the* dog."

I was exasperated. "No, not this morning," I said and saw a grin spread over his face.

"Wait a minute, daddy. Now don't go get mad. Damn, man! I thought sho *you* had him," he said, pretending to disbelieve me. I started away and he pushed the cart beside me. And suddenly I felt uncomfortable. Somehow he was like one of the vets from the Golden Day . . .

"Well, maybe it's the other way round," he said. "Maybe he got holt to you."

"Maybe," I said.

"If he is, you lucky it's just a dog—'cause, man, I tell you I believe it's a bear that's got holt to me . . ."

"A bear?"

"Hell, yes! *The* bear. Caint you see these patches where he's been clawing at my behind?"

Pulling the seat of his Charlie Chaplin pants to the side, he broke into deep laughter.

"Man, this Harlem ain't nothing but a bear's den. But I tell you one thing," he said with swiftly sobering face, "it's the best place in the world for you and me, and if times don't get better soon I'm going to grab that bear and turn him every way but loose!"

"Don't let him get you down," I said.

"No, daddy-o, I'm going to start with one my own size!"

I tried to think of some saying about bears to reply, but remembered only Jack the Rabbit, Jack the Bear . . . who were both long forgotten and now brought a wave of homesickness. I wanted to leave him, and yet I found a certain comfort in walking along beside him, as though we'd walked this way before through other mornings, in other places . . .

"What is all that you have there?" I said, pointing to the rolls of blue paper stacked in the cart.

"Blueprints, man. Here I got 'bout a hundred pounds of blueprints and I couldn't build nothing!"

"What are they blueprints for?" I said.

"Damn if I know—everything. Cities, towns, country clubs. Some just buildings and houses. I got damn near enough to build me a house if I could live in a paper house like they do in Japan. I guess somebody done changed their plans," he added with a laugh. "I asked the man why they getting rid of all this stuff and he said they get in the way so every once in a while they have to throw 'em out to make place for the new plans. Plenty of these ain't never been used, you know."

"You have quite a lot," I said.

"Yeah, this ain't all neither. I got a coupla loads. There's a day's work right here in this stuff. Folks is always making plans and changing 'em."

"Yes, that's right," I said, thinking of my letters, "but that's a mistake. You have to stick to the plan."

He looked at me, suddenly grave. "You kinda young, daddy-o," he said.

I did not answer. We came to a corner at the top of a hill.

"Well, daddy-o, it's been good talking with a youngster from the old country but I got to leave you now. This here's one of them good ole downhill streets. I can coast a while and won't be worn out at the end of the day. Damn if I'm-a let 'em run *me* into my grave. I be seeing you again some-time—And you know something?"

"What's that?"

"I thought you was trying to deny me at first, but now I be pretty glad to see you . . ."

"I hope so," I said. "And you take it easy."

"Oh, I'll do that. All it takes to get along in this here man's town is a little shit, grit and mother-wit. And man, I was bawn with all three. In fact, I'maseventhsonofaseventhson bawnwithacauloverbotheyesandraisedonblackcatbones-highjohntheconquerorandgreasygreens—" he spieled with twinkling eyes, his lips working rapidly. "You dig me, daddy?"

"You're going too fast," I said, beginning to laugh.

"Okay, I'm slowing down. I'll verse you but I won't curse you—My name is Peter Wheatstraw, I'm the Devil's only son-in-law, so roll 'em! You a southern boy, ain't you?" he said, his head to one side like a bear's.

"Yes," I said.

"Well, git with it! My name's Blue and I'm coming at you

with a pitchfork. Fe Fi Fo Fum. Who wants to shoot the Devil one, Lord God Stingeroy!"

He had me grinning despite myself. I liked his words though I didn't know the answer. I'd known the stuff from childhood, but had forgotten it; had learned it back of school . . .

"You digging me, daddy?" he laughed. "Haw, but look me up sometimes, I'm a piano player and a rounder, a whiskey drinker and a pavement pounder. I'll teach you some good bad habits. You'll need 'em. Good luck," he said.

"So long," I said and watched him going. I watched him push around the corner to the top of the hill, leaning sharp against the cart handle, and heard his voice arise, muffled now, as he started down.

> She's got feet like a monkeeee
> Legs
> Legs, Legs like a maaad
> Bulldog . . .

What does it mean, I thought. I'd heard it all my life but suddenly the strangeness of it came through to me. Was it about a woman or about some strange sphinxlike animal? Certainly his woman, *no* woman, fitted that description. And why describe anyone in such contradictory words? Was it a sphinx? Did old Chaplin-pants, old dusty-butt, love her or hate her; or was he merely singing? What kind of woman could love a dirty fellow like that, anyway? And how could even *he* love her if she were as repulsive as the song described? I moved ahead. Perhaps everyone loved someone; I didn't know. I couldn't give much thought to love; in order to travel far you had to be detached, and I had the long road back to the campus before me. I strode along, hearing the cartman's song become a lonesome, broad-toned whistle now that flowered at the end of each phrase into a tremulous, blue-toned chord. And in its flutter and swoop I heard the sound of a railroad train highballing it, lonely across the lonely night. He was the Devil's son-in-law, all right, and he was a man who could whistle a three-toned chord . . . God damn, I thought, they're a hell of a people! And I didn't know whether it was pride or disgust that suddenly flashed over me.

A COUPLA SCALPED INDIANS

This short story first appeared in 1956 with a headnote announcing it as "an off-shoot of his novel-in-progress"—evidently as part of the big second novel that Ellison was to struggle with for the rest of his life. Cut from the sections of that novel published posthumously in 1999 as Juneteenth, *"A Coupla Scalped Indians" connects with Ellison's cluster of Buster/Riley stories of the 1940s, tales (published in* Flying Home and Other Stories, *1996) centering on the exploits of a pair of black boys, close kin to Mark Twain's Huckleberry and Tom. This particular coming-of-age story is of special interest in this music volume because the boys, Buster and friend (nameless here in this story centering on the problem of his identity), are improvising manhood tests for themselves—using an old handbook of the Boy Scouts at a time when that organization officially forbade black membership. Winding up a day of tests made harder by their just having been circumcised, they hear carnival horns blowing in the distance. The black boys' own hornlike exchanges of words, and their translations of what the jazz horns are saying ("Clarinet so sweet-talking he just eases you in the dozens"), both indicate jazz-oriented styles for confronting "them white boys" and—beyond any question of race—the chaotic, mysterious, painful ordeal of growing into adulthood. If the boys' makeshift identities as "Indians" and "Boy Scouts"*

suggest frontier randiness and readiness, their identity as inheritors
of black styles (both of sweet-talk or subversive coolness under attack
and the will to go to war) and of jazz as an institution indicates that
they may be ready to take on the challenges of adult sexuality and
*black manhood in America. (*New World Writing, *1956)*

———

They had a small, loud-playing band and as we moved
through the trees I could hear the notes of the horns bursting like bright metallic bubbles against the sky. It was a
faraway and sparklike sound, shooting through the late afternoon quiet of the hill; very clear now and definitely
music, band music. I was relieved. I had been hearing it for
several minutes as we moved through the woods, but the
pain down there had made all my senses so deceptively
sharp that I had decided that the sound was simply a musical ringing in my ears. But now I was doubly sure, for Buster
stopped and looked at me, squinching up his eyes with his
head cocked to one side. He was wearing a blue cloth head-
band with a turkey feather stuck over his ear, and I could see
it flutter in the breeze.

"You hear what I hear, man?" he said.

"I *been* hearing it," I said.

"Damn! We better haul it outa these woods so we can see
something. Why didn't you say something to a man?"

We moved again, hurrying along until suddenly we were
out of the woods, standing at a point of the hill where the
path dropped down to the town, our eyes searching. It was
close to sundown and below me I could see the red clay of
the path cutting through the woods and moving past a white
lightning-blasted tree to join the river road, and the narrow
road shifting past Aunt Mackie's old shack, and on, beyond
the road and the shack, I could see the dull mysterious
movement of the river. The horns were blasting brighter
now, though still far away, sounding like somebody flipping
bright handfuls of new small change against the sky. I lis-

tened and followed the river swiftly with my eyes as it wound through the trees and on past the buildings and houses of the town—until there, there at the farther edge of the town, past the tall smokestack and the great silver sphere of the gas storage tower, floated the tent, spread white and cloudlike with its bright ropes of fluttering flags.

That's when we started running. It was a dogtrotting Indian run, because we were both wearing packs and were tired from the tests we had been taking in the woods and in Indian Lake. But now the bright blare of the horns made us forget our tiredness and pain and we bounded down the path like young goats in the twilight; our army-surplus mess kits and canteens rattling against us.

"We late, man," Buster said. "I told you we was gon fool around and be late. But naw, you had to cook that damn sage hen with mud on him just like it says in the book. We coulda barbecued a damn elephant while we was waiting for a tough sucker like that to get done . . ."

His voice grumbled on like a trombone with a big, fat pot-shaped mute stuck in it and I ran on without answering. We had tried to take the cooking test by using a sage hen instead of a chicken because Buster said Indians didn't eat chicken. So we'd taken time to flush a sage hen and kill him with a slingshot. Besides, he was the one who insisted that we try the running endurance test, the swimming test, *and* the cooking test all in one day. Sure it had taken time. I knew it would take time, especially with our having no scoutmaster. We didn't even have a troop, only the *Boy Scout's Handbook* that Buster had found, and—as we'd figured—our hardest problem had been working out the tests for ourselves. He had no right to argue anyway, since he'd beaten me in all the tests—although I'd passed them too. And he was the one who insisted that we start taking them today, even though we were both still sore and wearing our bandages, and I was still carrying some of the catgut stitches around in me. I had wanted to wait a few days until I was healed, but Mister Know-it-all Buster challenged me by saying that a real stud Indian could take the tests even right after the doctor had just finished sewing on him. So, since we were more interested in being *Indian* scouts than simply *Boy* Scouts, here I was running toward the spring carnival instead of being already there. I wondered how Buster knew so much about what an Indian would do, anyway. We certainly hadn't read anything about what the doctor had done to us. He'd probably made it up, and I had let him urge me into going to the woods even though I had to slip out of the house. The doctor had told Miss Janey (she's the lady who takes care of me) to keep me quiet for a few days and she dead-aimed to do it. You would've thought from the way she carried on that she was the one who had the operation— only that's one kind of operation no woman ever gets to brag about.

Anyway, Buster and me had been in the woods and now we were plunging down the hill through the fast-falling dark to the carnival. I had begun to throb and the bandage was chafing, but as we rounded a curve I could see the tent and the flares and the gathering crowd. There was a breeze coming up the hill against us now and I could almost smell that cotton candy, the hamburgers, and the kerosene smell of the flares. We stopped to rest and Buster stood very straight and pointed down below, making a big sweep with his arm like an Indian chief in the movies when he's up on a hill telling his braves and the Great Spirit that he's getting ready to attack a wagon train.

"Heap big . . . teepee . . . down yonder," he said in Indian talk. "Smoke signal say . . . Blackfeet . . . make . . . heap much . . . stink, buck-dancing in tennis shoes!"

"Ugh," I said, bowing my suddenly war-bonneted head. "Ugh!"

Buster swept his arm from east to west, his face impassive. "Smoke medicine say . . . heap . . . *big* stink! Hot toe jam!" He struck his palm with his fist, and I looked at his puffed-out cheeks and giggled.

"Smoke medicine say you tell heap big lie," I said. "Let's get on down there."

We ran past some trees, Buster's canteen jangling. Around us it was quiet except for the roosting birds.

"Man," I said, "you making as much noise as a team of mules in full harness. Don't no Indian scout make all that racket when he runs."

"No scout-um now," he said. "Me go make heap much pow-wow at stinky-dog carnival!"

"Yeah, but you'll get yourself scalped, making all that noise in the woods," I said. "Those other Indians don't give a damn 'bout no carnival—what does a carnival mean to them? They'll scalp the hell outa you!"

"Scalp?" he said, talking colored now. "Hell, man—that damn doctor scalped me last week. Damn near took my whole head off!"

I almost fell with laughing. "Have mercy, Lord," I laughed. "We're just a couple poor scalped Indians!"

Buster stumbled about, grabbing a tree for support. The doctor had said that it would make us men and Buster had said, hell, he was a man already—what he wanted was to be an Indian. We hadn't thought about it making us scalped ones.

"You right, man," Buster said. "Since he done scalped so much of my head away, I must be crazy as a fool. That's why I'm in such a hurry to get down yonder with the other crazy folks. I want to be right in the middle of 'em when they really start raising hell."

"Oh, you'll be there, Chief Baldhead," I said.

He looked at me blankly. "What you think ole Doc done with our scalps?"

"Made him a tripe stew, man."

"You nuts," Buster said. "He probably used 'em for fish bait."

"He did, I'm going to sue him for one trillion, zillion dollars, cash," I said.

"Maybe he gave 'em to ole Aunt Mackie, man. I bet with them she could work up some out*rageous* spells!"

"Man," I said, suddenly shivering, "don't talk about that old woman, she's evil."

"Hell, everybody's so scared of her. I just wish she'd mess with me or my daddy, I'd fix her."

I said nothing—I was afraid. For though I had seen the old woman about town all my life, she remained to me like the moon, mysterious in her very familiarity; and in the sound of her name there was terror.

Ho' Aunt Mackie, talker-with-spirits, prophetess-of-disaster, odd-dweller-alone in a riverside shack surrounded by sunflowers, morning-glories, and strange magical weeds (Yao, as Buster, during our Indian phase, would have put it, Yao!); *Old Aunt Mackie, wizen-faced walker-with-a-stick, shrill-voiced ranter in the night, round-eyed malicious one, given to dramatic trances and fiery flights of rage; Aunt Mackie, preacher of wild sermons on the busy streets of the town, hot-voiced chaser of children, snuff-dipper, visionary; wearer of greasy headrags, wrinkled gingham aprons, and old men's shoes; Aunt Mackie, nobody's sister but still Aunt Mackie to us all* (Ho, Yao!); *teller of fortunes, concocter of powerful, body-rending spells* (Yah, Yao!); *Aunt Mackie, the remote one though always seen about us; night-consulted adviser to farmers on crops and cattle* (Yao!); *herb-healer, root-doctor, and town-confounding oracle to wildcat drillers seeking oil in the earth*—(Yaaaah-Ho!). It was all there in her name and before her name I shivered. Once uttered, for me the palaver was finished; I resigned it to Buster, the tough one.

Even some of the grown folks, both black and white, were afraid of Aunt Mackie, and all the kids except Buster. Buster lived on the outskirts of the town and was as unimpressed by Aunt Mackie as by the truant officer and others whom the rest of us regarded with awe. And because I was his buddy I was ashamed of my fear.

Usually I had extra courage when I was with him. Like the time two years before when we had gone into the woods with only our slingshots, a piece of fatback, and a skillet and had lived three days on the rabbits we killed and the wild berries we picked and the ears of corn we raided from farmers' fields. We slept each rolled in his quilt, and in the night Buster had told bright stories of the world we'd find when we were grown-up and gone from hometown and family. I had no family, only Miss Janey, who took me after my mother died (I didn't know my father), so that getting away always appealed to me, and the coming time of which Buster liked to talk loomed in the darkness around me, rich with pastel promise. And although we heard a bear go lumbering through the woods nearby and the eerie howling of a coyote in the dark, yes, and had been swept by the soft swift flight of an owl, Buster was unafraid and I had grown brave in the grace of his courage.

But to me Aunt Mackie was a threat of a different order, and I paid her the respect of fear.

"Listen to those horns," Buster said. And now the sound came through the trees like colored marbles glinting in the summer sun.

We ran again. And now keeping pace with Buster I felt good; for I meant to be there too, at the carnival; right in the middle of all that confusion and sweating and laughing and all the strange sights to see.

"Listen to 'em, now, man," Buster said. "Those fools is starting to shout 'Amazing Grace' on those horns. Let's step on the gas!"

The scene danced below us as we ran. Suddenly there was a towering Ferris wheel revolving slowly out of the dark, its red and blue lights glowing like drops of dew dazzling a big spider web when you see it in the early morning. And we heard the beckoning blare of the band now shot through with the small, insistent, buckshot voices of the barkers.

"Listen to that trombone, man," I said.

"Sounds like he's playing the dozens with the whole wide world."

"What's he saying, Buster?"

"He's saying. 'Ya'll's mamas don't wear 'em. Is strictly without 'em. Don't know nothing 'bout 'em . . .'"

"Don't know about what, man?"

"Draw's, fool; he's talking 'bout draw's!"

"How you know, man?"

"I hear him talking, don't I?"

"Sure, but you been scalped, remember? You crazy. How he know about those people's mamas?" I said.

"Says he saw 'em with his great big ole eye."

"Damn! He must be a Peeping Tom. How about those other horns?"

"Now that there tuba's saying:

> They don't play 'em, I know they don't.
> They don't play 'em, I know they won't.
> They just don't play no nasty dirty twelves . . ."

"Man, you *are* a scalped-headed fool. How about that trumpet?"

"Him? That fool's a soldier, he's really signifying. Saying,

> So ya'll don't play 'em, hey?
> So ya'll won't play 'em, hey?
> Well pat your feet and clap your hands,
> 'Cause I'm going to play 'em to the promised land . . .

"Man, the white folks know what that fool is signifying on that horn they'd run him clear on out the world. Trumpet's got a real *nasty* mouth."

"Why you call him a soldier, man?" I said.

" 'Cause he's slipping 'em in the twelves and choosing

'em, all at the same time. Talking 'bout they mamas and offering to fight 'em. Now he ain't like that ole clarinet; clarinet so sweet-talking he just *eases* you in the dozens."

"Say, Buster," I said, seriously now. "You know, we gotta
stop cussing and playing the dozens if we're going to be Boy
Scouts. Those white boys don't play that mess."

"You doggone right they don't," he said, the turkey
feather vibrating above his ear. "Those guys can't take it,
man. Besides, who wants to be just like them? Me, *I'm* gon be
a scout and play the twelves too! You have to, with some of
these old jokers we know. You don't know what to say when
they start teasing you, you never have no peace. You have to
outtalk 'em, outrun 'em, or outfight 'em and I don't aim to be
running and fighting all the time. N'mind those white boys."

We moved on through the growing dark. Already I could
see a few stars and suddenly there was the moon. It emerged
bladelike from behind a thin veil of cloud, just as I heard a
new sound and looked about me with quick uneasiness. Off
to our left I heard a dog, a big one. I slowed, seeing the outlines of a picket fence and the odd-shaped shadows that
lurked in Aunt Mackie's yard.

"What's the matter, man?" Buster said.

"Listen," I said. "That's Aunt Mackie's dog. Last year I
was passing here and he sneaked up and bit me through the
fence when I wasn't even thinking about him . . ."

"Hush, man," Buster whispered, "I hear the son-of-a-
bitch back in there now. You leave him to me."

We moved by inches now, hearing the dog barking in the
dark. Then we were going past and he was throwing his
heavy body against the fence, straining at his chain. We hesitated, Buster's hand on my arm. I undid my heavy canteen
belt and held it, suddenly light in my fingers. In my right I
gripped the hatchet which I'd brought along.

"We'd better go back and take the other path," I whispered.

"Just stand still, man," Buster said.

The dog hit the fence again, barking hoarsely; and in the interval following the echoing crash I could hear the distant music of the band.

"Come on," I said. "Let's go round."

"Hell, no! We're going straight! I ain't letting no damn dog scare me, Aunt Mackie or no Aunt Mackie. Come on!"

Trembling, I moved with him toward the roaring dog, then felt him stop again, and I could hear him removing his pack and taking out something wrapped in paper.

"Here," he said. "You take my stuff and come on."

I took his gear and went behind him, hearing his voice suddenly hot with fear and anger saying, "Here, you 'gator-mouthed egg-sucker, see how you like this sage hen," just as I tripped over the straps of his pack and went down. Then I was crawling frantically, trying to untangle myself and hearing the dog growling as he crunched something in his jaws. "Eat it, you buzzard," Buster was saying, "see if you tough as he is," as I tried to stand, stumbling and sending an old cooking range crashing in the dark. Part of the fence was gone and in my panic I had crawled into the yard. Now I could hear the dog bark threateningly and leap the length of his chain toward me, then back to the sage hen; toward me, a swift leaping form snatched backward by the heavy chain, turning to mouth savagely on the mangled bird. Moving away, I floundered over the stove and pieces of crating, against giant sunflower stalks, trying to get back to Buster, when I saw the lighted window and realized that I had crawled to the very shack itself. That's when I pressed against the weathered-satin side of the shack and came erect. And there, framed by the window in the lamp-lit room, I saw the woman.

A brown naked woman, whose black hair hung beneath her shoulders. I could see the long graceful curve of her back as she moved in some sort of slow dance, bending forward and back, her arms and body moving as though gathering in something which I couldn't see but which she drew to her with pleasure; a young, girlish body with slender, well-rounded hips. *But who?* flashed through my mind as I heard Buster's *Hey, man; where'd you go? You done run out on me?* from back in the dark. And I willed to move, to hurry away—but in that instant she chose to pick up a glass from a wobbly old round white table and to drink, turning slowly as she stood with backward-tilted head, slowly turning in the lamplight and drinking slowly as she turned, slowly; until I could see the full-faced glowing of her feminine form.

And I was frozen there, watching the uneven movement of her breasts beneath the glistening course of the liquid, spilling down her body in twin streams drawn by the easy tiding of her breathing. Then the glass came down and my knees flowed beneath me like water. The air seemed to explode soundlessly. I shook my head but she, the image, would not go away and I wanted suddenly to laugh wildly and to scream. For above the smooth shoulders of the girlish form I saw the wrinkled face of old Aunt Mackie.

Now, I had never seen a naked woman before, only very little girls or once or twice a skinny one my own age, who looked like a boy with the boy part missing. And even though I'd seen a few calendar drawings they were not alive like this, nor images of someone you'd thought familiar through having seen them passing through the streets of the town; nor like this inconsistent, with wrinkled face mismatched with glowing form. So that mixed with my fear of punishment for peeping there was added the terror of her mystery. And yet I could not move away. I was fascinated, hearing the growling dog and feeling a warm pain grow beneath my bandage—along with the newly risen terror that this deceptive old woman could cause me to feel this way, that she could be so young beneath her old baggy clothes.

She was dancing again now, still unaware of my eyes, the

lamplight playing on her body as she swayed and enfolded the air or invisible ghosts or whatever it was within her arms. Each time she moved, her hair, which was black as night now that it was no longer hidden beneath a greasy headrag, swung heavily about her shoulders. And as she moved to the side I could see the gentle tossing of her breasts beneath her upraised arms. *It just can't be,* I thought, *it just can't,* and moved closer, determined to see and to know. But I had forgotten the hatchet in my hand until it struck the side of the house and I saw her turn quickly toward the window, her face evil as she swayed. I was rigid as stone, hearing the growling dog mangling the bird and knowing that I should run even as she moved toward the window, her shadow flying before her, her hair now wild as snakes writhing on a dead tree during a springtime flood. Then I could hear Buster's hoarse-voiced *Hey, man! Where in hell are you?* even as she pointed at me and screamed, sending me moving backward, and I was aware of the sickle-shaped moon flying like a lightning flash as I fell, still gripping my hatchet, and struck my head in the dark.

When I started out of it someone was holding me and I lay in light and looked up to see her face above me. Then it all flooded swiftly back and I was aware again of the contrast between smooth body and wrinkled face and experienced a sudden warm yet painful thrill. She held me close. Her breath came to me, sweetly alcoholic as she mumbled something about "Little devil, lips that touch wine shall never touch mine! That's what I told him, understand me? Never," she said loudly. "You understand?"

"Yes, ma'm . . ."

"Never, never, NEVER!"

"No, ma'm," I said, seeing her study me with narrowed eyes.

"You young but you younguns understand, devilish as you is. What you doing messing round in my yard?"

"I got lost," I said. "I was coming from taking some Boy Scout tests and I was trying to get by your dog."

"So that's what I heard," she said. "He bite you?"

"No, ma'm."

"Corse not, he don't bite on the new moon. No, I think you come in my yard to spy on me."

"No, ma'm, I didn't," I said. "I just happened to see the light when I was stumbling around trying to find my way."

"You got a pretty big hatchet there," she said, looking down at my hand. "What you plan to do with it?"

"It's a kind of Boy Scout ax," I said. "I used it to come through the woods . . ."

She looked at me dubiously. "So," she said, "you're a heavy hatchet man and you stopped to peep. Well, what I want to know is, is you a drinking man? Have your lips ever touched wine?"

"Wine? No, ma'm."

"So you ain't a drinking man, but do you belong to church?"

"Yes, ma'm."

"And have you been saved and ain't no backslider?"

"Yessum."

"Well," she said, pursing her lips, "I guess you can kiss me."

"MA'M?"

"That's what I said. You passed all the tests and you was peeping in my window . . ."

She was holding me there on a cot, her arms around me as though I were a three-year-old, smiling like a girl. I could see her fine white teeth and the long hairs on her chin and it was like a bad dream. "You peeped," she said, "now you got to do the rest. I said kiss me, or I'll fix you . . ."

I saw her face come close and felt her warm breath and closed my eyes, trying to force myself. *It's just like kissing some sweaty woman at church,* I told myself, *some friend of Miss Janey's.* But it didn't help and I could feel her drawing me and I found her lips with mine. It was dry and firm and winey and I could hear her sigh. "Again," she said, and once more my lips found hers. And suddenly she drew me to her and I could feel her breasts soft against me as once more she sighed.

"That was a nice boy," she said, her voice kind, and I opened my eyes. "That's enough now, you're both too young and too old, but you're brave. A regular li'l chocolate hero."

And now she moved and I realized for the first time that my hand had found its way to her breast. I moved it guiltily, my face flaming as she stood.

"You're a good brave boy," she said, looking at me from deep in her eyes, "but you forget what happened here tonight."

I sat up as she stood looking down upon me with a mysterious smile. And I could see her body up close now, in the dim yellow light; see the surprising silkiness of black hair mixed here and there with gray, and suddenly I was crying and hating myself for the compelling need. I looked at my hatchet lying on the floor now and wondered how she'd gotten me into the shack as the tears blurred my eyes.

"What's the matter, boy?" she said. And I had no words to answer.

"What's the matter, I say!"

"I'm hurting in my operation," I said desperately, knowing that my tears were too complicated to put into any words I knew.

"Operation? Where?"

I looked away.

"Where you hurting, boy?" she demanded.

I looked into her eyes and they seemed to flood through me, until reluctantly I pointed toward my pain.

"Open it, so's I can see," she said. "You know I'm a healer, don't you?"

I bowed my head, still hesitating.

"Well open it then. How'm I going to see with all those clothes on you?"

My face burned like fire now and the pain seemed to ease as a dampness grew beneath the bandage. But she would not be denied and I undid myself and saw a red stain on the gauze. I lay there ashamed to raise my eyes.

"Hmmmmmmm," she said. "A fishing worm with a headache!" And I couldn't believe my ears. Then she was looking into my eyes and grinning.

"Pruned," she cackled in her high, old woman's voice, "pruned. Boy, you have been pruned. I'm a doctor but no tree surgeon—no, lay still a second."

She paused and I saw her hand come forward, three claw-like fingers taking me gently as she examined the bandage.

And I was both ashamed and angry and now I stared at her out of a quick resentment and a defiant pride. *I'm a man,* I said within myself. *Just the same I am a man!* But I could only stare at her face briefly as she looked at me with a gleam in her eyes. Then my eyes fell and I forced myself to look boldly at her now, very brown in the lamplight, with all the complicated apparatus within the globular curvatures of flesh and vessel exposed to my eyes. I was filled then with a deeper sense of the mystery of it too, for now it was as though the nakedness was nothing more than another veil; much like the old baggy dresses she always wore. Then across the curvature of her stomach I saw a long, puckered crescent-shaped scar.

"How old are you, boy?" she said, her eyes suddenly round.

"Eleven," I said. And it was as though I had fired a shot.

"Eleven! Git out of here," she screamed, stumbling backward, her eyes wide upon me as she felt for the glass on the table to drink. Then she snatched an old gray robe from a chair, fumbling for the tie cord which wasn't there. I moved, my eyes upon her as I knelt for my hatchet, and felt the pain come sharp. Then I straightened, trying to arrange my knickers.

"You go now, you little rascal," she said. "Hurry and git out of here. And if I ever hear of you saying anything about me I'll fix your daddy and your mammy too. I'll fix 'em, you hear?"

"Yes, ma'm," I said, feeling that I had suddenly lost the courage of my manhood, now that my bandage was hidden and her secret body gone behind her old gray robe. But how could she fix my father when I didn't have one? Or my mother, when she was dead?

I moved, backing out of the door into the dark. Then she slammed the door and I saw the light grow intense in the window and there was her face looking out at me and I could not tell if she frowned or smiled, but in the glow of the lamp the wrinkles were not there. I stumbled over the packs now and gathered them up, leaving.

This time the dog raised up, huge in the dark, his green eyes glowing as he gave me a low disinterested growl. *Buster really must have fixed you,* I thought. *But where'd he go?* Then I was past the fence into the road.

I wanted to run but was afraid of starting the pain again, and as I moved I kept seeing her as she'd appeared with her back turned toward me, the sweet undrunken movements that she made. It had been like someone dancing by herself and yet like praying without kneeling down. Then she had turned, exposing her familiar face. I moved faster now and suddenly all my senses seemed to sing alive. I heard a night bird's song; the lucid call of a quail arose. And from off to my right in the river there came the leap of a moon-mad fish and I could see the spray arch up and away. There was wisteria in the air and the scent of moonflowers. And now moving through the dark I recalled the warm, intriguing smell of her body and suddenly, with the shout of the carnival coming to me again, the whole thing became thin and dreamlike. The images flowed in my mind, became shadowy; no part was left to fit another. But still there was my pain and here was I, running through the dark toward the small, loud-playing band. It was real, I knew, and I stopped in the path and looked back, seeing the black outlines of the shack and the thin moon above. Behind the shack the hill arose with the shadowy woods and I knew the lake was still hidden there, reflecting the moon. All was real.

And for a moment I felt much older, as though I had lived swiftly long years into the future and had been as swiftly pushed back again. I tried to remember how it had been when I kissed her, but on my lips my tongue found only the faintest trace of wine. But for that it was gone, and I thought forever, except the memory of the scraggly hairs on her chin. Then I was again aware of the imperious calling of the horns and moved again toward the carnival. Where was that other scalped Indian; where had Buster gone?

KEEP TO THE RHYTHM

First published in 1969 as "Juneteenth," a section from Ellison's forthcoming novel (part of which has appeared as the novel also called Juneteenth*), this selection features the evangelical preachers Bliss (who will later transform himself into Senator Sunraider of "Cadillac Flambé") and Hickman (blues trombonist who has become Bliss's adoptive parent and a man of God), who deliver a dialogue sermon commemorating Emancipation Day. Reverend Hickman laments the death of blacks on America's shores as he affirms the miracle that they danced their way back to life. "And if they ask you in the city why we praise the Lord with bass drums and brass trombones," cries Hickman, "tell them we were rebirthed dancing, we were rebirthed crying affirmation of the Word, quickening our transcended flesh. . . . Oh, Rev. Bliss, we stamped our feet at the trumpet's sound and we clapped our hands, ah, in joy! And we moved, yes, together in a dance, amen! Because we had received a new song in a new land and been resurrected by the Word and Will of God!" In this story, black sufferings have induced the discipline, resiliency, and will to remember that prepare blacks for their turn at national leadership: "Time will swing and turn back around," says Reverend Hickman, whose toughness and patience recall the strategies of the civil-rights movement. "I tell you, time shall swing and spiral back around." If*

jazz may be defined as a rhythmical blues narrative of call and re-
sponse dialogue where the underlying ritual is one of continuity and
hope—perhaps this tent-meeting sermon may be called a blues or
jazz sermon. Certainly it is fiction meant to be performed. Ellison
liked to test his writing by reading aloud into a tape recorder and
playing it back. The recording of his reading and testing of part of
this story (done for a television show in 1965), laughing as he hears
himself performing, is worth its weight in diamonds. (Quarterly
Review of Literature, *1969)*

————

No, the wounded man thought, Oh no! Get back to that;
back to a bunch of old-fashioned Negroes celebrating an illusion of emancipation, and getting it mixed up with the
Resurrection, minstrel shows and vaudeville routines? Back
to that tent in the clearing surrounded by trees, that bowl-
shaped impression in the earth beneath the pines? . . . Lord,
it hurts. Lordless and without loyalty, it hurts. Wordless, it
hurts. Here and especially here. Still I see it after all the rov-
ing years and flickering scenes: Twin lecterns on opposite
ends of the platform, behind one of which I stood on a wide
box, leaning forward to grasp the lectern's edge. Back.
Daddy Hickman at the other. Back to the first day of that
week of celebration. Juneteenth. Hot, dusty. Hot with faces
shining with sweat and the hair of the young dudes metallic
with grease and straightening irons. Back to that? He was
not so heavy then, but big with the quick energy of a fighting bull and still kept the battered silver trombone on top of
the piano, where at the climax of a sermon he could reach
for it and stand blowing tones that sounded like his own
voice amplified; persuading, denouncing, rejoicing—moving
beyond words back to the undifferentiated cry. In strange
towns and cities the jazz musicians were always around him.
Jazz. What was jazz and what religion back there? Ah yes,
yes, I loved him. Everyone did, deep down. Like a great,
kindly, daddy bear along the streets, my hand lost in his
huge paw. Carrying me on his shoulder so that I could touch

the leaves of the trees as we passed. The true father, but black, black. Was he a charlatan—am I—or simply as re-sourceful in my fashion. Did he know himself, or care? Back to the problem of all that. Must I go back to the beginning when only he knows the start . . . ?

Juneteenth and him leaning across the lectern, resting there looking into their faces with a great smile, and then looking over to me to make sure that I had not forgotten my part, winking his big red-rimmed eye at me. And the women looking back and forth from him to me with that bright, birdlike adoration in their faces; their heads cocked to one side. And him beginning:

On this God-given day, brothers and sisters, when we have come together to praise God and celebrate our one-ness, our slipping off the chains, let's us begin this week of worship by taking a look at the ledger. Let us, on this day of deliverance, take a look at the figures writ on our bodies and on the living tablet of our heart. The Hebrew children have their Passover so that they can keep their history alive in their memories—so let us take one more page from their book and, on this great day of deliverance, on this day of emancipation, let's us tell ourselves our story. . . .

Pausing, grinning down. . . . Nobody else is interested in it anyway, so let us enjoy it ourselves, yes, and learn from it.

And thank God for it. Now let's not be too solemn about it either, because this here's a happy occasion. Rev. Bliss over there is going to take the part of the younger generation, and I'll try to tell it as it's been told to me. Just look at him over there, he's ready and raring to go—because he knows that a true preacher is a kind of educator, and that we have got to know our story before we can truly understand God's blessings and how far we have still got to go. Now you've heard him, so you know that he can preach.

Amen! They all responded and I looked preacher-faced

into their shining eyes, preparing my piccolo voice to support his baritone sound.

Amen is right, he said. So here we are, five thousand strong, come together on this day of celebration. Why? We just didn't happen. We're here and that is an undeniable fact—but how come we're here? How and why here in these woods that used to be such a long way from town? What about it, Rev. Bliss, is that a suitable question on which to start?

God, bless you, Rev. Hickman, I think that's just the place we have to start. We of the younger generation are still ignorant about these things. So please, sir, tell us just how we came to be here in our present condition and in this land. . . .

Not back to that me, not to that six-seven year old ventriloquist's dummy dressed in a white evening suit. Not to that charlatan born— must I have no charity for me? . . .

Was it an act of God, Rev. Hickman, or an act of man. . . . Not to that puppet with a memory like a piece of flypaper. . . .

We came, amen, Rev. Bliss, sisters and brothers, as an act of God, but through—I said through, an act of cruel, ungodly man.

An act of almighty God, *my treble echo sounded,* but through the hands of cruel man.

Amen, Rev. Bliss, that's how it happened. It was, as I understand it, a cruel calamity laced up with a blessing—or maybe a blessing laced up with a calamity. . . .

Laced up with a blessing, Rev. Hickman? We understand you partially because you have taught us that God's sword is a two-edged sword. But would you please tell us of the younger generation just why it was a blessing?

It was a blessing, brothers and sisters, because out of all the pain and the suffering, out of the night of storm, we found the Word of God.

So here we found the Word. Amen, so now we are here. But where did we come from, Daddy Hickman?

We come here out of Africa, son; out of Africa.

Africa? Way over across the ocean? The black land? Where the elephants and monkeys and the lions and tigers are?

Yes, Rev. Bliss, the jungle land. Some of us have fair skins like you, but out of Africa too.

Out of Africa truly, sir?

Out of the ravaged mama of the black man, son.

Lord, thou hast taken us out of Africa . . .

Amen, out of our familar darkness. Africa. They brought us here from all over Africa, Rev. Bliss. And some were the sons and daughters of heathen kings . . .

Some were kings, Daddy Hickman? Have we of the younger generation heard you correctly? Some were kin to kings? Real kings?

Amen! I'm told that some were the sons and the daughters of kings . . .

. . . Of Kings! . . .

And some were the sons and daughters of warriors . . .

. . . Of warriors . . .

Of fierce warriors. And some were the sons and the daughters of farmers . . .

Of African farmers . . .

. . . And some of musicians . . .

. . . Musicians . . .

And some were the sons and daughters of weapon makers and of smelters of brass and iron . . .

But didn't they have judges, Rev. Hickman? And weren't there any preachers of the word of God?

Some were judges but none were preachers of the word of God, Rev. Bliss. For we come out of heathen Africa . . .

Heathen Africa?

Out of heathen Africa. Let's tell this thing true; because the truth is the light.

And they brought us here in chains . . .

In chains, son; in iron chains . . .

From half-a-world away, they brought us . . .

In chains and in boats that the history tells us weren't fit for pigs—because pigs cost too much money to be allowed to waste and die as we did. But they stole us and brought us in boats which I'm told could move like the swiftest birds of prey, and which filled the great trade winds with the stench of our dying and their crime . . .

What a crime! Tell us why, Rev. Hickman . . .

It was a crime, Rev. Bliss, brothers and sisters, like the fall of proud Lucifer from Paradise.

But why, Daddy Hickman? You have taught us of the progressive younger generation to ask why. So we want to know how come it was a crime?

Because, Rev. Bliss, this was a country dedicated to the principles of almighty God. That Mayflower boat that you hear so much about Thanksgiving Day was a *Christian* ship—Amen! Yes, and those many-named floating coffins we came here in were Christian too. They had turned traitor to the God who set them free from Europe's tyrant kings. Because, God have mercy on them, no sooner than they got free enough to breathe themselves, they set out to bow us down . . .

They made our Lord shed tears!

Amen! Rev. Bliss, amen. God must have wept like Jesus. Poor Jonah went down into the belly of the whale, but compared to our journey his was like a trip to paradise on a silvery cloud.

Worse than old Jonah, Rev. Hickman?

Worse than Jonah slicked all over with whale puke and gasping on the shore. We went down into hell on those floating coffins and don't you youngsters forget it! Mothers and babies, men and women, the living and the dead and the dying—all chained together. And yet, praise God, most of us arrived here in this land. The strongest came through. Thank God, and we arrived and that's why we're here today. Does that answer the question, Rev. Bliss?

Amen, Daddy Hickman, amen. But now the younger

generation would like to know what they did to us when they got us here. What happened then?

They brought us up onto this land in chains . . .

. . . In chains . . .

. . . And they marched us into the swamps . . .

. . . Into the fever swamps, they marched us . . .

And they set us to work draining the swampland and toiling in the sun . . .

. . . They set us to toiling . . .

They took the white fleece of the cotton and the sweetness of the sugar cane and made them bitter and bloody with our toil . . . And they treated us like one great unhuman animal without any face . . .

Without a *face*, Rev. Hickman?

Without personality, without names, Rev. Bliss, we were made into nobody and not even *mister* nobody either, just nobody. They left us without names. Without choice. Without the right to do or not to do, to be or not to be . . .

You mean without faces and without eyes? We were eyeless like Samson in Gaza? Is that the way, Rev. Hickman?

Amen, Rev. Bliss, like baldheaded Samson before that nameless little lad like you came as the Good Book tells us and led him to the pillars whereupon the big house stood— Oh, you little black boys, and oh, you little brown girls, you're going to shake the building down! And then, Oh, how you will build in the name of the Lord!

Yes Reverend Bliss, we were eyeless like unhappy Samson among the Philistines—and worse . . .

And WORSE?

Worse, Rev. Bliss, because they chopped us up into little bitty pieces like a farmer when he cuts up a potato. And they scattered us around the land. All the way from Kentucky to Florida; from Louisiana to Texas; from Missouri all the way down the great Mississippi to the Gulf. They scattered us around this land.

How now, Daddy Hickman? You speak in parables which

we of the younger generation don't clearly understand. How do you mean, they scattered us?

Like seed, Rev. Bliss; they scattered us just like a dope-fiend farmer planting a field with dragon teeth!

Tell us about it, Daddy Hickman.

They cut out our tongues . . .

. . . They left us speechless . . .

. . . They cut out our tongues . . .

. . . Lord, they left us without words . . .

. . . Amen! They scattered our tongues in this land like seed . . .

. . . And left us without language . . .

. . . They took away our talking drums . . .

. . . Drums that talked, Daddy Hickman? Tell us about those talking drums . . .

Drums that talked like a telegraph. Drums that could reach across the country like a church bell sound. Drums that told the news almost before it happened! Drums that spoke with big voices like big men! Drums like a conscience and a deep heart-beat that knew right from wrong. Drums that told glad tidings! Drums that sent the news of trouble speeding home! Drums that told us *our* time and told us where we were . . .

Those were some drums, Rev. Hickman . . .

. . . Yes and they took those drums away . . .

Away, Amen! Away! And they took away our heathen dances . . .

. . . They left us drumless and they left us danceless . . .

Ah yes, they burnt up our talking drums and our dancing drums . . .

. . . Drums . . .

. . . And they scattered the ashes . . .

. . . Ah, Aaaaaah! Eyeless, tongueless, drumless, danceless, ashes . . .

And a worst devastation was yet to come, Lord God!

Tell us, Reveren Hickman. Blow on your righteous horn!

Ah, but Rev. Bliss, in those days we didn't have any horns . . .

No *horns?* Hear him!

And we had no songs . . .

. . . No songs . . .

. . . And we had no . . .

. . . Count it on your fingers, see what cruel man has done . . .

Amen, Rev. Bliss, lead them . . .

We were eyeless, tongueless, drumless, danceless, hornless, songless!

All true, Rev. Bliss. No eyes to see. No tongue to speak or taste. No drums to raise the spirits and wake up our memories. No dance to stir the rhythm that makes life move. No songs to give praise and prayers to God!

We were truly in the dark, my young brothern and sisteren. Eyeless, earless, tongueless, drumless, danceless, songless, hornless, soundless . . .

And worse to come!

. . . And worse to come . . .

Tell us, Rev. Hickman. But not too fast so that we of the younger generation can gather up our strength to face it. So that we may listen and not become discouraged!

I said, Rev. Bliss, brothers and sisters, that they snatched us out of the loins of Africa. I said that they took us from our mammys and pappys and from our sisters and brothers. I said that they scattered us around this land . . .

. . . And we, let's count it again, brothers and sisters; let's add it up. Eyeless, tongueless, drumless, danceless, songless, hornless, soundless, sightless, dayless, nightless, wrongless, rightless, motherless, fatherless—scattered.

Yes, Rev. Bliss, they scattered us around like seed . . .

. . . Like seed . . .

. . . Like seed, that's been flung broadcast on unplowed ground . . .

Ho, chant it with me, my young brothers and sisters! Eyeless, tongueless, drumless, danceless, songless, hornless, soundless, sightless, wrongless, rightless, motherless, fatherless, brotherless, sisterless, powerless . . .

Amen! But though they took us like a great black giant that had been chopped up into little pieces and the pieces buried; though they deprived us of our heritage among strange scenes in strange weather; divided and divided and divided us again like a gambler shuffling and cutting a deck of cards. Although we were ground down, smashed into little pieces; spat upon, stamped upon, cursed and buried, and our memory of Africa ground down into powder and blown on the winds of foggy forgetfulness . . .

. . . Amen, Daddy Hickman! Abused and without shoes, pounded down and ground like grains of sand on the shores of the sea . . .

. . . Amen! And God—Count it, Rev. Bliss . . .

. . . Left eyeless, earless, noseless, throatless, teethless, tongueless, handless, feetless, armless, wrongless, rightless, harmless, drumless, danceless, songless, hornless, soundless, sightless, wrongless, rightless, motherless, fatherless, sisterless, brotherless, plowless, muleless, foodless, mindless— and Godless, Rev. Hickman, did you say Godless?

. . . At first, Rev. Bliss, he said, his trombone entering his voice, broad, somber and noble. At first. Ah, but though divided and scattered, ground down and battered into the earth like a spike being pounded by a ten pound sledge, we were on the ground and in the earth and the earth was red and black like the earth of Africa. And as we moldered underground we were mixed with this land. We liked it. It fitted us fine. It was in us and we were in it. And then—praise God—deep in the ground, deep in the womb of this land, we began to stir!

Praise God!

At last, Lord, at last.

Amen!

Oh the truth, Lord, it tastes so sweet!

What was it like then, Rev. Bliss? You read the scriptures, so tell us. Give us a word.

WE WERE LIKE THE VALLEY OF DRY BONES!

Amen. Like the Valley of Dry Bones in Ezekiel's dream. Hoooh! We lay scattered in the ground for a long dry season. And the winds blew and the sun blazed down and the rains came and went and we were dead. Lord, we were dead! Except . . . Except . . .

. . . Except what, Rev. Hickman?

Except for one nerve left from our ear . . .

Listen to him!

And one nerve in the soles of our feet . . .

. . . Just watch me point it out, brothers and sisters . . .

Amen, Bliss, you point it out . . . and one nerve left from the throat . . .

. . . From our throat—right *here!*

. . . Teeth . . .

. . . From our teeth, one from all thirty-two of them . . .

. . . Tongue . . .

. . . Tongueless . . .

. . . And another nerve left from our heart . . .

. . . Yes, from our heart . . .

. . . And another left from our eyes and one from our hands and arms and legs and another from our stones . . .

Amen, Hold it right there, Rev. Bliss . . .

. . . All stirring in the ground . . .

. . . Amen, stirring, and right there in the midst of all our death and buriedness, the voice of God spoke down the Word . . .

. . . Crying Do! I said, Do! Crying Doooo—

These dry bones live?

He said, Son of Man . . . under the ground, Ha! Heatless beneath the roots of plants and trees . . . Son of man, do . . .

I said, Do . . .

. . . I said Do, Son of Man, Doooooo!—

These dry bones live?

Amen! And we heard and rose up. Because in all their blasting they could not blast away one solitary vibration of God's true word . . . We heard it down among the roots and among the rocks. We heard it in the sand and in the clay. We heard it in the falling rain and in the rising sun. On the high ground and in the gullies. We heard it lying moldering and corrupted in the earth. We heard it sounding like a bugle call to wake up the dead. Crying, Doooooo! Ay, do these dry bones live!

And did our dry bones live, Daddy Hickman?

Ah, we sprang together and walked around. All clacking together and clicking into place. All moving in time! Do! I said, Dooooo—these dry bones live!

And now strutting in my white tails, across the platform, filled with the power almost to dancing.

Shouting, Amen, Daddy Hickman, is this the way we walked?

Oh we walked through Jerusalem, just like John—That's it, Rev. Bliss, walk! Show them how we walked!

Was this the way?

That's the way. Now walk on back. Lift your knees! Swing your arms! Make your coattails fly! Walk! And him strutting me three times around the pulpit across the platform and back. Ah, yes! And then his voice deep and exultant: And if they ask you in the city why we praise the Lord with bass drums and brass trombones tell them we were rebirthed dancing, we were rebirthed crying affirmation of the Word, quickening our transcended flesh.

Amen!

Oh, Rev. Bliss, we stamped our feet at the trumpet's sound and we clapped our hands, ah, in joy! And we moved, yes, together in a dance, amen! Because we had received a new song in a new land and been resurrected by the Word and Will of God!

Amen! . . .

. . . —We were rebirthed from the earth of this land and revivified by the Word. So now we had a new language and a brand new song to put flesh on our bones . . .

New teeth, new tongue, new word, new song!

We had a new name and a new blood, and we had a new task . . .

Tell us about it, Reveren Hickman . . .

We had to take the Word for bread and meat. We had to take the Word for food and shelter. We had to use the Word as a rock to build up a whole new nation, cause to tell it true, we were born again in chains of steel. Yes, and chains of ignorance. And all we knew was the spirit of the word. We had no schools. We owned no tools; no cabins, no churches, not even our own bodies.

We were chained, young brothers, in steel. We were chained, young sisters, in ignorance. We were schoolless, toolless, cabinless—owned . . .

Amen, Reveren Bliss. We were owned and faced with the awe-inspiring labor of transforming God's word into a lantern so that in the darkness we'd know where we were. Oh God hasn't been easy with us because He always plans for the loooong haul. He's looking far ahead and this time He wants a well-tested people to work his will. He wants some sharp-eyed, quick-minded, generous-hearted people to give names to the things of this world and to its values. He's tired of untempered tools and half-blind masons! Therefore, He's going to keep on testing us against the rocks and in the fires. He's going to heat us till we almost melt and then He's going to plunge us into the ice-cold water. And each time we come out we'll be blue and as tough as cold-blue steel! Ah yes! He means for us to be a new kind of human. Maybe we won't be that people but we'll be a part of that people, we'll be an element in them, Amen! He wants us limber as willow switches and he wants us tough as whit leather, so that when we have to bend, we can bend and snap back into place. He's going to throw bolts of lightning to blast us so that we'll have good foot work and lightning-fast minds. He'll drive us hither and yon around this land and make us run the gauntlet of hard times and tribulations, misunderstanding and abuse. And some will pity you and some will despise you. And some will try to use you and change you. And some will deny you and try to deal you out of the game. And sometimes you'll feel so bad that you'll wish you could die. But it's all the pressure of God. He's giving you a will and He wants you to use it. He's giving you brains and he wants you to train them lean and hard so that you can overcome all the obstacles. Educate your minds! Make do with what you have so as to get what you need! Learn to look at what *you* see and not what somebody tells you is true. Pay lip-service to Caesar if you have to, but put your trust in God. Because nobody has a patent on truth or a copyright on the best way to live and serve almighty God. Learn from what we've lived. Remember that when the labor's back-breaking and the boss man's mean our singing can lift us up. That it can strengthen us and make his meanness but the flyspeck irritation of an empty man. Roll with the blow like ole Jack Johnson. Dance on out of his way like Williams and Walker. Keep to the rhythm and you'll keep to life. God's time is long; and all short-haul horses shall be like horses on a merry-go-round. Keep, keep, keep to the rhythm and you won't get weary. Keep to the rhythm and you won't get lost. We're handicapped, amen! Because the Lord wants us strong! We started out with nothing but the Word—just like the others but they've forgot it . . . We worked and stood up under hard times and tribulations. We learned patience and to understand Job. Of all the animals, man's the only one not born knowing almost everything he'll ever know. It takes him longer than an elephant to grow up because God didn't mean him to leap to any conclusions, for God himself is in the very process of things. We learned that all blessings come mixed with sorrow and all hardships have a streak of laughter. Life is a streak-a-lean—a—streak-a-fat. Ha, yes! We learned to bounce back and to disregard the prizes of fools. And we must keep on learning. Let them have their fun. Even let them eat hummingbird's wings and tell you it's too good for you.—Grits and greens don't turn to ashes in anybody's mouth—How about it, Rev. Eatmore? Amen? Amen! Let everybody say amen. Grits and greens are humble but they make you strong and when the right folks get together to share them they can taste like ambrosia. So draw, so let us draw on our own wells of strength.

Ah yes, so we were reborn, Rev. Bliss. They still had us harnessed, we were still laboring in the fields, but we had a secret and we had a new rhythm . . .

So tell us about this rhythm, Reveren Hickman.

They had us bound but we had our kind of time, Rev. Bliss. They were on a merry-go-round that they couldn't control but we learned to beat time from the seasons. We learned to make this land and this light and darkness and this weather and their labor fit us like a suit of new underwear. With our new rhythm, amen, but we weren't free and they still kept dividing us. There's many a thousand gone down the river. Mama sold from papa and chillun sold from both. Beaten and abused and without shoes. But we had the Word, now, Rev. Bliss, along with the rhythm. They couldn't divide us now. Because anywhere they dragged us we throbbed in time together. If we got a chance to sing, we sang the same song. If we got a chance to dance, we beat back hard times and tribulations with a clap of our hands and the beat of our feet, and it was the same dance. Oh they come out here sometimes to laugh at our way of praising God. They can laugh but they can't deny us. They can curse and kill us but they can't destroy us all. This land is ours because we come out of it, we bled in it, our tears watered it, we fertilized it with our dead. So the more of us they destroy the more it becomes filled with the spirit of our redemption. They laugh but we know who we are and where we are, but they keep on coming in their millions and they don't know and can't get together.

But tell us, how do we know who we are, Daddy Hickman?

We know where we are by the way we walk. We know where we are by the way we talk. We know where we are by the way we sing. We know where we are by the way we dance. We know where we are by the way we praise the Lord on high. We know where we are because we hear a different tune in our minds and in our hearts. We know who we are because when we make the beat of our rhythm to shape our day the whole land says, Amen! It smiles, Rev. Bliss, and it moves to our time! Don't be ashamed, my brothern! Don't be cowed. Don't throw what you have away! Continue! Remember! Believe! Trust the inner beat that tells us who we are. Trust God and trust life and trust this land that is you! Never mind the laughers, the scoffers, they come around because they can't help themselves. They can deny you but not your sense of life. They hate you because whenever they look into a mirror they fill up with bitter gall. So forget them and most of all don't deny yourselves. They're tied by the short hair to a runaway merry-go-round. They make life a business of struggle and fret, fret and struggle. See who you can hate; see what you can get. But you just keep on inching along like an old inchworm. If you put one and one and one together soon they'll make a million too. There's been a heap of Juneteenths before this one and I tell you there'll be a heap more before we're truly free! Yes! But keep to the rhythm, just keep to the rhythm and keep to the way. Man's plans are but a joke to God. Let those who will despise you, but remember deep down inside yourself that the life we have to lead is but a preparation for other things, it's a discipline, Reveren Bliss, Sisters and Brothers; a discipline through which we may see that which the others are too self-blinded to see. Time will come round when we'll have to be their eyes; time will swing and turn back around. I tell you, time shall swing and spiral back around . . .

CADILLAC FLAMBÉ

Along with eight other rather obscurely published pieces of fiction listed as parts of (or, in the case of "A Coupla Scalped Indians," off-shoots from) Ellison's second novel in progress, "Cadillac Flambé" originally figured as a section of the long-anticipated project. Edited out of Juneteenth, *"Cadillac" is presented from the standpoint of a character named McIntyre, a liberal white reporter who—as we learn from another story that Ellison occasionally read in public—has his own troubles vis-à-vis his Harlem girlfriend and her family. This story is part of the ongoing education of Mr. McIntyre, fumbling with his reporter's tape recorder and camera to get this Negro and the burning Cadillac into some kind of comprehensible perspective. But this story also belongs to Senator Sunraider, an obsessively Negro-baiting politician who is passing for white—who at least* looks *white and claims to be "purely" so (so far neither McIntyre nor the reader can tell). Over these fast undercurrents flows the narrative of LeeWillie Minifees, a black jazz bassist with slick hair who happens to catch Sunraider on the car radio defaming his fancy Caddy as a "Coon Cage Eight." In response, LeeWillie decides to torch the car on the senator's front lawn in Washington, D.C. Is this peculiar "sacrifice" (McIntyre's term) an extension of the race riots of the sixties, which often involved blacks burning their own commu-*

nities? Is it a comic (but serious) plea to be heard above what Minifees terms "the difference between what it is and what it's supposed to be?" Consider the strangely dissonant sounds that echo through the tale: Minifees preaching a stomping sermon with references to pop songs and then bursting into a version of "God Bless America" as the car crackles and sighs in flames, and as some in the waiting crowd roar in protest, others begin to weep. Is a parallel being drawn to certain music of the time, namely the mixed protest, blues, and pop material undercut by the jagged dissonances in the works of the Art Ensemble of Chicago, Eric Dolphy, Ornette Coleman, and Jimi Hendrix (whose act sometimes included the dramatic destruction of his guitar) or of that other explosive player of the "bull fiddle," Charles Mingus? "Cadillac Flambé," with its musical references and secular sermons, its floating and then flaming bird-car, its black jazz celebrant and white witnesses, intrigues as it retains its mystery. (American Review, *February 1973*)

———

It had been a fine spring day made even pleasanter by the lingering of the cherry blossoms and I had gone out before dawn with some married friends and their children on a bird-watching expedition. Afterwards we had sharpened our appetites for brunch with rounds of bloody marys and bullshots. And after the beef bouillon ran out, our host, an ingenious man, had improvised a drink from chicken broth and vodka which he proclaimed the "chicken-shot." This was all very pleasant and after a few drinks my spirits were soaring. I was pleased with my friends, the brunch was excellent and varied—chili con carne, cornbread, and oysters Rockefeller, etc.—and I was pleased with my tally of birds. I had seen a bluebird, five rose-breasted grosbeaks, three painted buntings, seven goldfinches, and a rousing consort of mockingbirds. In fact, I had hated to leave.

Thus it was well into the afternoon when I found myself walking past the senator's estate. I still had my binoculars around my neck, and my tape recorder—which I had along to record bird songs—was slung over my shoulder. As I approached, the boulevard below the senator's estate was heavy with cars, with promenading lovers, dogs on leash, old men on canes, and laughing children, all enjoying the fine weather. I had paused to notice how the senator's lawn rises from the street level with a gradual and imperceptible elevation that makes the mansion, set far at the top, seem to float like a dream castle; an illusion intensified by the chicken-shots, but which the art editor of my paper informs me is the result of a trick copied from the landscape architects who designed the gardens of the Bellevedere Palace in Vienna. But be that as it may, I was about to pass on when a young couple blocked my path, and when I saw the young fellow point up the hill and say to his young blonde of a girl, "I bet you don't know who that is up there," I brought my binoculars into play, and there, on the right-hand terrace of the mansion, I saw the senator.

Dressed in a chef's cap, apron, and huge asbestos gloves, he was armed with a long-tined fork which he flourished broadly as he entertained the notables for whom he was preparing a barbecue. These gentlemen and ladies were lounging in their chairs or standing about in groups sipping the tall iced drinks which two white-jacketed Filipino boys were serving. The senator was dividing his attention between the spareribs cooking in a large chrome grill-cart and displaying his great talent for mimicking his colleagues with such huge success that no one at the party was aware of what was swiftly approaching. And, in fact, neither was I.

I was about to pass on when a gleaming white Cadillac convertible, which had been moving slowly in the heavy traffic from the east, rolled abreast of me and suddenly blocked the path by climbing the curb and then continuing across the walk and onto the senator's lawn. The top was back and the driver, smiling as though in a parade, was a well dressed Negro man of about thirty-five, who sported the gleaming hair affected by their jazz musicians and prize-fighters, and who sat behind the wheel with that engrossed, yet relaxed, almost ceremonial attention to form that was once to be observed only among the finest horsemen. So closely did the car brush past that I could have reached out with no effort and touched the rich ivory leather upholstery. A bull fiddle rested in the back of the car. I watched the man drive smoothly up the lawn until he was some seventy-five yards below the mansion, where he braked the machine and stepped out to stand waving toward the terrace, a gallant salutation grandly given.

At first, in my innocence, I placed the man as a musician, for there was, after all, the bull fiddle; then in swift succession I thought him a chauffeur for one of the guests, a driver for a news or fashion magazine or an advertising agency or television network. For I quickly realized that a musician wouldn't have been asked to perform at the spot where the car was stopped, and that since he was alone, it was unlikely that anyone, not even the senator, would have hired a musician to play serenades on a bull fiddle. So next I decided that the man had either been sent with equipment to be used in covering the festivities taking place on the terrace, or that he had driven the car over to be photographed against the luxurious background. The waving I interpreted as the expression of simple-minded high spirits aroused by the driver's pleasure in piloting such a luxurious automobile, the simple exuberance of a Negro allowed a role in what he considered an important public spectacle. At any rate, by now a small crowd had gathered and had begun to watch bemusedly.

Since it was widely known that the senator is a master of the new political technology, who ignores no medium and wastes no opportunity for keeping his image ever in the public's eye, I wasn't disturbed when I saw the driver walk to the trunk and begin to remove several red objects of a certain size and place them on the grass. I wasn't using my binoculars now and thought these were small equipment cases. Unfortunately, I was mistaken.

For now, having finished unpacking, the driver stepped

back behind the wheel, and suddenly I could see the top rising from its place of concealment to soar into place like the wing of some great, slow, graceful bird. Stepping out again, he picked up one of the cases—now suddenly transformed into the type of can which during the war was sometimes used to transport high-octane gasoline in Liberty ships (a highly dangerous cargo for those round bottoms and the men who shipped in them)—and, leaning carefully forward, began emptying its contents upon the shining chariot.

And thus, I thought, *is gilded an eight-valved, three-hundred-and-fifty-horsepowered air-conditioned lily!*

For so accustomed have we Americans become to the tricks, the shenanigans, and frauds of advertising, so adjusted to the contrived fantasies of commerce—indeed, to pseudo-events of all kinds—that I thought that the car was being drenched with a special liquid which would make it more alluring for a series of commercial photographs.

Indeed, I looked up the crowded boulevard behind me, listening for the horn of a second car or station wagon which would bring the familiar load of pretty models, harassed editors, nervous wardrobe mistresses, and elegant fashion photographers who would convert the car, the clothes, and the senator's elegant home into a photographic rite of spring.

And with the driver there to remind me, I even expected a few ragged colored street urchins to be brought along to form a poignant but realistic contrast to the luxurious costumes and high-fashion surroundings: an echo of the somber iconography in which the crucified Christ is flanked by a repentant and an unrepentant thief, or that in which the three Wise Eastern Kings bear their rich gifts before the humble stable of Bethlehem.

But now reality was moving too fast for the completion of this foray into the metamorphosis of religious symbolism. Using my binoculars for a closer view, I could see the driver take a small spherical object from the trunk of the car and a fuzzy tennis ball popped into focus against the dark smoothness of his fingers. This was joined by a long wooden object which he held like a conductor's baton and began forcing against the ball until it was pierced. This provided the ball with a slender handle which he tested delicately for balance, drenched with liquid, and placed carefully behind the left fin of the car.

Reaching into the back seat now, he came up with a bass fiddle bow upon which he accidently spilled the liquid, and I could see drops of fluid roping from the horsehairs and falling with an iridescent spray into the sunlight. Facing us now, he proceeded to tighten the horsehairs, working methodically, very slowly, with his head gleaming in the sunlight and beads of sweat standing over his brow.

As I watched, I became aware of the swift gathering of a crowd around me, people asking puzzled questions, and a certain tension, as during the start of a concert, was building. And I had just thought, *And now he'll bring out the fiddle,* when he opened the door and hauled it out, carrying it, with the dripping bow swinging from his right hand, up the hill some thirty feet above the car, and placed it lovingly on the grass. A gentle wind started to blow now, and I swept my glasses past his gleaming head to the mansion, and as I screwed the focus to infinity, I could see several figures spring suddenly from the shadows on the shaded terrace of the mansion's far wing. They were looking on like the spectators of a minor disturbance at a dull baseball game. Then a large woman grasped that something was out of order and I could see her mouth come open and her eyes blaze as she called out soundlessly, "Hey, you down there!" Then the driver's head cut into my field of vision and I took down the glasses and watched him moving, broad-shouldered and jaunty, up the hill to where he'd left the fiddle. For a moment he stood with his head back, his white jacket taut across his shoulders, looking toward the terrace. He waved then, and shouted words that escaped me. Then, facing the machine, he took something from his pocket and I saw him touch the

flame of a cigarette lighter to the tennis ball and begin blowing gently upon it; then, waving it about like a child twirling
a Fourth of July sparkler, he watched it sputter into a small
blue ball of flame.

I tried, indeed I anticipated what was coming next, but I
simply could not accept it! The Negro was twirling the ball
on that long, black-tipped wooden needle—the kind used
for knitting heavy sweaters—holding it between his thumb
and fingers in the manner of a fire-eater at a circus, and I
couldn't have been more surprised if he had thrown back his
head and plunged the flame down his throat than by what
came next. Through the glasses now I could see sweat bead-
ing out beneath his scalp line and on the flesh above the stiff
hairs of his moustache as he grinned broadly and took up
the fiddle bow, and before I could move he had shot his
improvised, flame-tipped arrow onto the cloth top of the
convertible.

"Why that black son of the devil!" someone shouted, and
I had the impression of a wall of heat springing up from the
grass before me. Then the flames erupted with a stunning
blue roar that sent the spectators scattering. People were
shouting now, and through the blue flames before me I could
see the senator and his guests running from the terrace to
halt at the top of the lawn, looking down, while behind me
there were screams, the grinding of brakes, the thunder of
foot-falls as the promenaders broke in a great spontaneous
wave up the grassy slope, then sensing the danger of explod-
ing gasoline, receded hurriedly to a safer distance below,
their screams and curses ringing above the roar of the
flames.

How, oh, how, I wished for a cinema camera to synchro-
nize with my tape recorder!—which automatically I now
brought into play as heavy fumes of alcohol and gasoline,
those defining spirits of our age, filled the air. There before
me unfolding in *tableau vivant* was surely the most unexpected picture in the year: in the foreground at the bottom

of the slope, a rough semicircle of outraged faces; in the mid-foreground, up the gentle rise of the lawn, the white convertible shooting into the springtime air a radiance of intense blue flame, a flame like that of a welder's torch or perhaps of a huge fowl being flambéed in choice cognac; then on the rise above, distorted by heat and flame, the dark-skinned, white-suited driver, standing with his gleaming face expressive of high excitement as he watched the effect of his deed. Then, rising high in the background atop the grassy hill, the white-capped senator surrounded by his notable guests—all caught in postures eloquent of surprise, shock, or indignation.

The air was filled with an overpowering smell of wood alcohol, which, as the leaping red and blue flames took firm hold, mingled with the odor of burning paint and leather. I became aware of the fact that the screaming had suddenly faded now, and I could hear the swoosh-pop-crackle-and-hiss of the fire. And with the gaily dressed crowd become silent, it was as though I were alone, isolated, observing a conflagration produced by a stroke of lightning flashed out of a clear blue springtime sky. We watched with that sense of awe similar to that with which medieval crowds must have observed the burning of a great cathedral. We were stunned by the sacrificial act and, indeed, it was as though we had become the unwilling participants in a primitive ceremony requiring the sacrifice of a beautiful object in appeasement of some terrifying and long-dormant spirit, which the black man in the white suit was summoning from a long, black sleep. And as we watched, our faces strained as though in anticipation of the spirit's materialization from the fiery metamorphosis of the white machine, a spirit that I was afraid, whatever the form in which it appeared, would be powerfully good or powerfully evil, and absolutely out of place here and now in Washington. It was, as I say, uncanny. The whole afternoon seemed to float, and when I looked again to the top of the hill the people there appeared to move in slow motion through watery waves of heat. Then I saw the senator, with chef cap awry, raising his asbestos gloves above his head and beginning to shout. And it was then that the driver, the firebrand, went into action.

Till now, looking like the chief celebrant of an outlandish rite, he had held firmly to his middle-ground; too dangerously near the flaming convertible for anyone not protected by asbestos suiting to risk laying hands upon him, yet far enough away to highlight his human vulnerability to fire. But now as I watched him move to the left of the flames to a point allowing him an uncluttered view of the crowd, his white suit reflecting the flames, he was briefly obscured by a sudden swirl of smoke, and it was during this brief interval that I heard the voice.

Strong and hoarse and typically Negro in quality, it seemed to issue with eerie clarity from the fire itself. Then I was struggling within myself for the reporter's dedicated objectivity and holding my microphone forward as he raised both arms above his head, his long, limber fingers widespread as he waved toward us.

"Ladies and gentlemen," he said, "please don't be disturbed! I don't mean you any harm, and if you'll just cool it a minute I'll tell you what this is all about . . ."

He paused and the senator's voice could be heard angrily in the background.

"Never mind that joker up there on top of the hill," the driver said. "You can listen to him when I get through. He's had too much free speech anyway. Now it's *my* turn."

And at this a man at the other end of the crowd shouted angrily and tried to break up the hill. He was grabbed by two men and an hysterical, dark-haired woman wearing a well-filled chemise-style dress, who slipped to the ground holding a leg, shouting, "No, Fleetwood. No! That crazy nigger will kill you!"

The arsonist watched with blank-faced calm as the man was dragged protesting back into the crowd. Then a shift in the breeze whipped smoke down upon us and gave rise to a flurry of coughing.

"Now believe me," the arsonist continued, "I know that it's very, very hard for you folks to look at what I'm doing and not be disturbed, because for you it's a crime and a sin."

He laughed, swinging his fiddle bow in a shining arc as the crowd watched him fixedly.

"That's because you know that most folks can't afford to own one of these Caddies. Not even good, hard-working folks, no matter what the pictures in the papers and magazines say. So deep down it makes you feel some larceny. You feel that it's unfair that everybody who's willing to work hard can't have one for himself. That's right! And you feel that in order to get one it's OK for a man to lie and cheat and steal—yeah, even swindle his own mother *if* she's got the cash. That's the difference between what you *say* you believe and the way you *act* if you get the chance. Oh yes, because words is words, but life is hard and earnest and these here Caddies is way, way out of this world!"

Pausing, he loosened the knot in his blue and white tie so that it hung down the front of his jacket in a large loop, then wiped his brow with a blue silk handkerchief.

"I don't mean to insult you," he said, bending toward us now, the fiddle bow resting across his knee, "I'm just reminding you of the facts. Because I can see in your eyes that it's going to cost me more to get *rid* of this Caddy the way I have to do it than it cost me to get it. I don't rightly know what the price will be, but I know that when you people get scaird and shook up, you get violent.—No, wait a minute . . ." He shook his head. "That's not how I meant to say it. I'm sorry. I apologize.

"Listen, here it is: This *morning*," he shouted now, stabbing his bow toward the mansion with angry emphasis. "This morning that fellow Senator *Sunraider* up there, *he* started it when he shot off his mouth over the *radio*. That's what this is all about! I realized that things had gotten out of *control.* I realized all of a sudden that the man was *messing . . .* with . . . my *Cadillac,* and ladies and gentlemen, that's serious as all *hell . . .*

"Listen to me, y'all: A little while ago I was romping past *Richmond,* feeling fine. I had played myself three hundred and seventy-five dollars and thirty-three cents worth of gigs down in Chattanooga, and I was headed home to *Harlem* as straight as I could go. I wasn't bothering any*body.* I didn't even mean to stop by here, because this town has a way of making a man feel like he's living in a fool's *paradise.* When I'm *here* I never stop thinking about the difference between what it *is* and what it's *supposed* to be. In fact, I have the feeling that somebody put the *Indian* sign on this town a long, long time ago, and I don't want to be around when it takes effect. So, like I say, I wasn't even thinking about this town. I was rolling past Richmond and those whitewalls were slapping those concrete slabs and I was rolling and the wind was feeling fine on my face—and that's when I made my sad mistake. Ladies and gentlemen, I turned on the radio. I had nothing against anybody. I was just hoping to hear some Dinah, or Duke, or Hawk so that I could study their phrasing and improve my style and enjoy myself.—But what do I get? I'll tell you what I got—"

He dropped his shoulders with a sudden violent twist as his index finger jabbed toward the terrace behind him, bellowing, "I GOT THAT NO GOOD, NOWHERE SENATOR SUNRAIDER! THAT'S WHAT I GOT! AND WHAT WAS HE DOING? HE WAS TRYING TO GET THE UNITED STATES GOVERNMENT TO MESS WITH MY CADILLAC! AND WHAT'S MORE, HE WAS CALLING MY CADDY A 'COON CAGE.'

"Ladies and gentlemen, I couldn't believe my *ears.* I don't know that senator and I know he doesn't know me from old *Bodiddly.* But just the same, there he is, talking straight to me and there was no use of my trying to dodge. Because I do live in Harlem and I lo-mo-sho do drive a Cadillac. So I had to sit there and take it like a little man. There he was, a United States SENATOR, coming through my own radio telling me what I ought to be driving, and recommending to the United States Senate and the whole country that the name of my car be changed simply because *I*, me, LeeWillie Minifees, was driving it!

"It made me feel faint. It upset my mind like a midnight telegram!

"I said to myself, 'LeeWillie, what on earth is this man *talking* about? Here you been thinking you had it *made*. You been thinking you were as free as a bird—even though a black bird. That good-rolling Jersey Turnpike is up ahead to get you home.—And now here comes this senator putting you in a cage! What in the world is going on?'

"I got so nervous that all at once my foot weighed ninety-nine pounds, and before I knew it I was doing *seventy-five*. I was breaking the law! I guess I was really trying to get away from that voice and what the man had said. But I was rolling and I was listening. I couldn't *help* myself. What I was hearing was going against my whole heart and soul, but I was listening *anyway*. And what I heard was beginning to make me see things in a new light. Yes, and that new light was making my eyeballs ache. And all the time Senator Sunraider up in the Senate was calling my car a 'coon cage.'

"So I looked around and I saw all that fine ivory leather there. I looked at the steel and at the chrome. I looked through the windshield and saw the road unfolding and the houses and the trees was flashing by. I looked up at the top and I touched the button and let it go back to see if that awful feeling would leave me. But it wouldn't leave. The *air* was hitting my face and the *sun* was on my head and I was feeling that good old familiar feeling of *flying*—but ladies and gentlemen, it was no longer the same! Oh, no—because I could still hear that Senator playing the *dozens* with my Cadillac!

"And just then, ladies and gentlemen, I found myself rolling toward an old man who reminded me of my grand-daddy by the way he was walking beside the highway behind a plow hitched to an old, white-muzzled Missouri mule. And when that old man looked up and saw me he waved. And I looked back through the mirror as I shot past him and I could see him open his mouth and say something like, 'Go on, fool!' Then him and that mule was gone even from the mirror and I was rolling on.

"And then, ladies and gentlemen, in a twinkling of an eye it struck me. A voice said to me, 'LeeWillie, that old man is right: you are a fool. And that doggone Senator Sunraider is right, LeeWillie, you are a fool in a coon cage!'

"I tell you, ladies and gentlemen, that old man and his mule both were talking to me. I said, 'What do you mean about his being right?' And they said, 'LeeWillie, look who he *is*,' and I said, 'I *know* who he is,' and they said, 'Well, LeeWillie, if a man like that, in the position he's in, can think the way he doin, then LeeWillie, you have GOT to be wrong!'

"So I said, 'Thinking like that is why you've still got that mule in your lap,' man. 'I worked hard to get the money to buy this Caddy,' and he said, '*Money?* LeeWillie, can't you see that it ain't no longer a matter of money? Can't you see it's done gone way past the question of money? Now it's a question of whether you can afford it in terms *other than money.*'

"And I said, 'Man, what are you talking about, "terms other than money," ' and he said, 'LeeWillie, even this damn mule knows that if a man like that feels the way he's talking and can say it right out over the radio and the T.V., and from the place where he's saying it—there's got to be something drastically wrong with you for even wanting one. Son, the man's done made it mean something different. All you wanted was to have a pretty automobile, but fool, he done changed the Rules on you!'

"So against myself, ladies and gentlemen, I was forced to *agree* with the old man and the mule. That senator up there wasn't simply degrading my Caddy. That wasn't the *point*. It's that he would low-rate a thing so truly fine as a *Cadillac* just in order to degrade *me* and my *people*. He was accusing *me* of lowering the value of the auto, when all I ever wanted was the very best!

"Oh, it hurt me to the quick, and right then and there I had me a rolling revelation. The *scales* dropped from my eyes. I had been BLIND, but the Senator up there on that hill was making me SEE. He was making me see some things I didn't *want* to see! I'd thought I was dressed real FINE, but I was as naked as a jaybird sitting on a limb in the drifting snow. I THOUGHT I was rolling past *Richmond,* but I was really trapped in a COON CAGE, running on one of those little TREADMILLS like a SQUIRREL or a HAMSTER. So now my EYEBALLS were aching. My head was in such a whirl that I shot the car up to ninety, and all I could see up ahead was the road getting NARROW. It was getting as narrow as the eye of a NEEDLE, and that needle looked like the Washington MONUMENT lying down. Yes, and I was trying to thread that Caddy straight through that eye and I didn't care if I made it or not. But while I managed to get that Caddy through I just couldn't thread that COON CAGE because it was like a two-ton knot tied in a piece of fine silk thread. The sweat was pouring off me now, ladies and gentlemen, and my brain was on fire, so I pulled off the highway and asked myself some questions, and I got myself some answers. It went this way:

" 'LeeWillie, who put you in this cage?'

" 'You put your own self in there,' a voice inside me said.

" 'But I paid for it, it's mine. I own it . . .' I said.

" 'Oh, no, LeeWillie,' the voice said, 'what you mean is that it owns *you,* that's why you're *in* the cage. *Admit* it, daddy; you have been NAMED. Senator Sunraider has put the bad-mouth, the NASTY mouth on you and now your Cadillac ain't no Caddy anymore! Let's face it, LeeWillie, from now on everytime you sit behind this wheel you're going to feel those RINGS shooting round and round your TAIL and one of those little black COON'S masks is going to settle down over your FACE, and folks standing on the streets and hanging out the windows will sing out, "HEY! THERE GOES MISTER COON AND HIS COON CAGE!" That's right, LeeWillie! And all those little husky-voiced colored CHILDREN playing in the gutters will point at you and say, "THERE GOES MISTAH GOON AND HIS GOON GAGE"—and that will be right in Harlem!'

"And that did it, ladies and gentlemen; that was the capper, and THAT'S why I'm here!

"Right then and there, beside the *highway,* I made my decision. I rolled that Caddy, I made a U-turn and I stopped only long enough to get me some of that good white wood *alcohol* and good *white* gasoline, and then I headed straight here. So while some of you are upset, you can see that you don't have to be afraid because LeeWillie means nobody any harm.

"I am here, ladies and gentlemen, to make the senator a present. Yes, sir and yes, mam, and it's Sunday and I'm told that *confession* is good for the *soul.*—So Mister Senator," he said, turning toward the terrace above, "this is my public testimony to my coming over to your way of thinking. This is my surrender of the Coon Cage Eight! You have unconverted me from the convertible. In fact, I'm giving it to you, Senator Sunraider, and it is truly mine to give. I hope all my people will do likewise. Because after your speech they ought to run whenever they even *look* at one of these. They ought to make for the bomb shelters whenever one comes close to the curb. So I, me, LeeWillie Minifees, am setting an example and here it is. You can HAVE it, Mister Senator. I don't WANT it. Thank you KINDLY and MUCH obliged . . ."

He paused, looking toward the terrace, and at this point I

saw a great burst of flame which sent the crowd scurrying backward down the hill, and the white-suited firebrand went into an ecstatic chant, waving his violin bow, shaking his gleaming head and stamping his foot:

"Listen to me, Senator: I don't want no JET! (stamp!) But thank you kindly.

"I don't want no FORD! (stamp!)

"Neither do I want a RAMBLER! (stamp!)

"I don't want no NINETY-EIGHT! (stamp!)

"Ditto the THUNDERBIRD! (stamp-stamp!)

"Yes, and keep those CHEVYS and CHRYSLERS away from me—do you (stamp!) *hear* me, Senator?

"YOU HAVE TAKEN THE BEST," he boomed, "SO, DAMMIT, TAKE ALL THE REST! Take ALL the rest!

"In fact, now I don't want anything you think is too good for me and my people. Because, just as that old man and the mule said, if a man in your position is against our having them, then there must be something WRONG in our *wanting* them. So to keep you happy, I, me, LeeWillie Minifees, am prepared to WALK. I'm ordering me some club-footed, pigeon-toed SPACE SHOES. I'd rather crawl or FLY. I'd rather save my money and wait until the A-RABS make a car. The Zulus even. Even the ESKIMOS! Oh, I'll walk and wait. I'll grab me a GREYHOUND or a FREIGHT! So you can have my coon cage, fare thee well!

"Take the TAIL FINS and the WHITEWALLS. Help yourself to the poor raped RADIO. ENJOY the automatic dimmer and the power brakes. ROLL, Mister Senator, with that fluid DRIVE. Breathe that air-conditioned AIR. There's never been a Caddy like this one and I want you to HAVE IT. Take my scientific dreamboat and enjoy that good ole GRACIOUS LIVING! The key's in the ignition and the REGISTRATION'S in the GLOVE compartment! And thank you KINDLY for freeing me from the Coon Cage. Because before I'd be in a CAGE, I'll be buried in my GRAVE—Oh! Oh!"

He broke off, listening; and I became aware of the shrilling of approaching sirens. Then he was addressing the crowd again.

"I knew," he called down with a grin, "that THOSE would be coming soon. Because they ALWAYS come when you don't NEED them. Therefore, I only hope that the senator will beat it on down here and accept his gift before they arrive. And in the meantime, I want ALL you ladies and gentlemen to join LeeWillie in singing 'God Bless America' so that all this won't be in vain.

"I want you to understand that that was a damned GOOD Caddy and I loved her DEARLY. That's why you don't have to worry about me. I'm doing fine. Everything is copacetic. Because, remember, nothing makes a man feel better than giving AWAY something, than SACRIFICING something, that he dearly LOVES!"

And then, most outrageous of all, he threw back his head and actually sang a few bars before the noise of the short-circuited horn set the flaming car to wailing like some great prehistoric animal heard in the throes of its dying.

Behind him now, high on the terrace, the senator and his guests were shouting, but on the arsonist sang, and the effect on the crowd was maddening. Perhaps because from the pleasurable anticipation of watching the beginning of a clever advertising stunt, they had been thrown into a panic by the deliberate burning, the bizarre immolation of the automobile. And now with a dawning of awareness they perceived that they had been forced to witness (and who could turn away?) a crude and most portentous political gesture.

So suddenly they broke past me, dashing up the hill in moblike fury, and it was most fortunate for Minifees that his duet with the expiring Cadillac was interrupted by members of the police and fire departments, who, arriving at this moment, threw a flying wedge between the flaming machine and the mob. Through the noisy action I could see him there, looming prominently in his white suit, a mocking smile flickering on his sweaty face, as the action whirled toward where he imperturbably stood his ground, still singing against the doleful wailing of the car.

He was still singing, his wrists coolly extended now in anticipation of handcuffs—when struck by a veritable football squad of asbestos-garbed policemen and swept, tumbling, in a wild tangle of arms and legs, down the slope to where I stood. It was then I noted that he wore expensive black alligator shoes.

And now, while the crowd roared its approval, I watched as LeeWillie Minifees was pinned down, lashed into a straitjacket and led toward a police car. Up the hill two policemen were running laboredly toward where the senator stood, silently observing. About me there was much shouting and shoving as some of the crowd attempted to follow the trussed-up and still grinning arsonist but were beaten back by the police.

It was unbelievably wild. Some continued to shout threats in their outrage and frustration, while others, both men and women, filled the air with a strangely brokenhearted and forlorn sound of weeping, and the officers found it difficult to disperse them. In fact, they continued to mill angrily about even as firemen in asbestos suits broke through, dragging hoses from a roaring pumper truck and sprayed the flaming car with a foamy chemical, which left it looking like the offspring of some strange animal brought so traumatically and precipitantly to life that it wailed and sputtered in protest, both against the circumstance of its debut into the world and the foaming presence of its still-clinging afterbirth . . .

And what had triggered it? How had the senator sparked this weird conflagration? Why, with a joke! The day before, while demanding larger appropriations for certain scientific research projects that would be of great benefit to our electronics and communications industries, and of great importance to the nation as a whole, the senator had aroused the opposition of a liberal senator from New York who had complained, in passing, of what he termed the extreme vapidness of our recent automobile designs, their lack of adequate safety devices, and of the slackness of our quality-control standards and procedures. Well, it was in defending the automobile industry that the senator passed the remark that triggered LeeWillie Minifees's bizarre reply.

In his rebuttal—the committee session was televised and aired over radio networks—the Senator insisted that not only were our cars the best in the world, the most beautiful and efficiently designed, but that, in fact, his opponent's remarks were a gratuitous slander. Because, he asserted, the only ground which he could see for complaint lay in the circumstance that a certain make of luxury automobile had become so outrageously popular in the nation's Harlems—the archetype of which is included in his opponent's district—that he found it embarrassing to own one. And then with a face most serious in its composure he went on to state:

"We have reached a sad state of affairs, gentlemen, wherein this fine product of American skill and initiative has become so common in Harlem that much of its initial value has been sorely compromised. Indeed, I am led to suggest, and quite seriously, that legislation be drawn up to rename it the 'Coon Cage Eight.' And not at all because of its eight, super-efficient cylinders, nor because of the lean, springing strength and beauty of its general outlines. Not at all, but because it has now become such a common sight to see eight or more of our darker brethren crowded together enjoying its power, its beauty, its neo-pagan comfort, while weaving recklessly through the streets of our great cities and along our super highways. In fact, gentlemen, I was run off the road, forced into a ditch by such a power-drunk group just the other day. It is enough to make a citizen feel alienated from his own times, from the abiding values and recent developments within his own beloved nation.

"And yet, we continue to hear complaints to the effect that these constituents of our worthy colleague are ill-housed, ill-clothed, ill-equipped and under-*treaded!* But, gentlemen, I say to you in all sincerity: Look into the streets! Look at the statistics for automobile sales! And I don't mean the economy cars, but our most expensive luxury machines. Look and see who is purchasing them! Give your attention to who it is that is creating the scarcity and removing these superb machines from the reach of those for whom they were intended! With so many of these good things, what, pray, do those people desire—is it a jet plane on every Harlem rooftop?"

Now for Senator Sunraider this had been mild and far short of his usual maliciousness. And while it aroused some slight amusement and brought replies of false indignation from some of his opponents, it was edited out, as is frequently the case, when the speech appeared in the *Congressional Record* and in the press. But who could have predicted that Senator Sunraider would have brought on Lee Willie Minifees's wild gesture? Perhaps he had been putting on an act, creating a happening, as they say, though I doubted it. There was something more personal behind it. Without question, the senator's remarks were in extremely bad taste, but to cap the joke by burning an expensive car seemed so extreme a reply as to be almost metaphysical.

And yet, I reminded myself, it might simply be a case of overreacting expressed in true Negro abandon, an extreme gesture springing from the frustration of having no adequate means of replying, or making himself heard above the majestic roar of a senator. There was, of course, the recent incident involving a black man suffering from an impacted wisdom tooth who had been so maddened by the blaring of a moisture-shorted automobile horn which had blasted his sleep about three o'clock of an icy morning, that he ran out into the street clothed only in an old-fashioned nightshirt and blasted the hood of the offending automobile with both barrels of a twelve-gauge over-and-under shotgun.

But while toothaches often lead to such extreme acts—

and once in a while to suicide—LeeWillie Minifees had apparently been in no pain—or at least not in *physical* pain. And on the surface at least his speech had been projected clearly enough (allowing for the necessity to shout) and he had been smiling when they led him away. What would be his fate? I wondered; and where had they taken him? I would have to find him and question him, for his action had begun to sound in my mind with disturbing overtones which had hardly been meaningful. Rather they had been like the brief interruption one sometimes hears while listening to an F.M. broadcast of the musical *Oklahoma!*, say, with original cast, when the signal fades and a program of quite different mood from a different wavelength breaks through. It had happened but then a blast of laughter had restored us automatically to our chosen frequency.

LETTERS

Ellison wrote zestfully full letters, illuminated by the publication of Trading Twelves, *his exchanges from 1950 to 1960 with Albert Murray. Here we meet Ellison the rough and ready writer, pulling no punches, suffering fools ungladly. As in the essays, he serves well-shaped, insightful commentary on heroes and friends, including favorite "fools" like the drummer Jo Jones; but his deflations (even sometimes, of heroes like Ellington) and his outright excoriations (of the beboppers in particular) bubble with acerbic eloquence. Offstage, as it were, chatting with like-minded friends, Ellison casually reveals aspects of his life as an intellectual with a voracious hunger for artistic and intellectual stimulation, and who saw himself operating in the spheres of Hemingway, Faulkner, Joyce, Ellington, Armstrong, the Italian Renaissance (and his own Oklahoma-bred ideal of Renaissance manhood, perhaps connected with the New Negro Renaissance), black vernacular culture, professional-level cameras and audio equipment, and—of course—the blues. There are commentaries on music along with frank accounts of pieces in progress and various professional encounters. After the 1958 Newport Jazz Festival, for which Ellison was a board member, he reports a heated exchange with a fellow panelist. "One of the critic-composers inter-*

rupted some remark I made concerning the relationship between Negro dance audiences and jazz bands, to say that he didn't believe that Jazz was connected with the life of any racial group in this country." Ellison lets him have it: "I really don't have much patience anymore, Albert, and I didn't bite my tongue in telling this guy where he came from and who his daddy was—who his black daddy was. I don't fight the race problem in matters of culture but anyone should know the source of their tradition before they start shooting off their mouth about where jazz comes from." There can be no doubt that Ellison believed in the American melting pot and the universality of the arts. Still, jazz comes first from the black side of the tracks, and whites or other nonblacks who want to play the music must pay their dues to their black artistic parents just as surely as Ellison the novelist must pay his to Melville, Hemingway, Joyce, and the rest. The sparkling letter to Ellison's longtime friend Charles Davidson, owner of the Andover Shop in Cambridge, Massachusetts, is a praise-song to Bobby Short the midwesterner, and Short the "black and white" Negro of style despite all obstacles that Patrick Moynihan or James Baldwin, villains of this letter, might detail or "complain about." The letters to Albert Murray are from Trading Twelves, 2000. *The Davidson letter has not been published before.*

———

AMERICAN ACADEMY IN ROME
Via Angelo Masina V
Rome 28, Italy
Oct. 22, 1955

Dear Albert:

I started this letter a few days before we left, but didn't have time to finish it so I'll pick up where I left off before going into the trip, etc. So as I was saying: I went into a store on Madison Avenue the other day and saw a slightly built, balding mose in there stepping around like he had springs in his legs and a bunch of frantic jumping beans in his butt (pronounced ass), and who was using his voice in a precise, clipped way that sounded as though he had worked on its original down home sound with great attention for a long, long time—a true work of art. I dug this stud and was amazed. I was sitting across the store waiting to be served when he got up and came across to the desk to pay for his purchase and leave his address—when the salesman made the mistake of asking him if he wasn't *the* Joe (pardon me, Jo) Jones.

Well man, that definite article triggered him! His eyes flashed, his jaw unlimbered and in a second I thought ole Jo was going to break into a dance. His voice opened up like a drill going through thin metal and before you could say Jackie Robinson he had recalled every time he had been in this store, the style of shoes he bought and why he'd bought them and was going into a tap dancing description of his drumming school, politics, poon-tang in Pogo Pogo and atomic fission—when I remembered what you had told me of his opinion of Alton Davenport and uttered the name. Man, his voice skidded like a jet banking up there where the air ain't air and he started stuttering. "Did you say Davenport?" he said. "And Birmingham, Tuskegee, and points south," I said. And he was off again. In fact, he damn near exploded and the fallout must have swamped the fat-ass Alton way the hell down Birmingham way. I thought I'd better get him out of there to cool him off, so we moved out on the street with him still blowing. I finally managed to tell him that I knew you and he calmed down. He gave me his address to pass along to you so here it is: Jo Jones, 123 W. 44th Street, NYC Room 903. Judson 2-2300. What a character! I'm afraid that he's not only a great drummer, he is—in the colored sense—also a fool. When we separated I followed him at a distance just to see him bouncing and looking as he headed over to 5th Ave., and it was like watching a couple of hopped-up Japanese playing ping pong on a hot floor. Man, they tell a lot of wild stories about boppers but this stud is truly apt to take off like a jet anytime he takes the notion. He probably has to play his bass drum with a twenty pound weight on his trap foot. In fact as I moved behind him I expected any minute to see him re-react to the outrage of Davenport's teaching music and run a hundred yard dash straight up the façade of a building. Drop him a few calming words, man; he needs them.

As you can see, we are here. It took us eleven days on the Constitution, what with one day stops in Algeciras (Spain), Cannes, and Genoa. The food was lousy and the trip was a bore and [we] were damn glad to get off at Naples, where we drove by car to Rome. We're about settled now, here on the Janiculine Hill, in a huge villa where all the Rome Fellows and some Fulbrighters live and work. We have a bedroom and a living room and I have a study located in a one room cottage built against the old Aurelian Wall, which surrounds part of the estate. My windows face the garden which supplies our vegetables and flowers and I'm fairly remote from interruption and most workaday sounds. The only writing I've done however has consisted of an article on music and some letters. For at the end of our first week [we] were carried on a tour of northern Italy. We went by car and saw the art of Orvieto, Perrugia, Urbino, Pisa, Assisi, Todi, Rimini, Ravenna, Florence, Sansepolcro, Sienna and many places in between. We were gone nine days and if we never see anymore we've certainly seen some of the greatest. My eyes are still whirling and we simply must go back to some of the places to isolate and study those works which most moved us. If I had about one choice it would be Florence and the Uffizi Gallerie. I'm aching for a car now, just to get around at will. The Renaissance has sent my imagination on a jag ever since I was shooting snipes in Oklahoma, but here its around you everywhere you turn, the same sky, earth, water, roads, houses, art. And not only that, it's all mingled with the Romans, the Greeks, the Greco-Christians. At a table I hear the Classicists talking the stuff, who did what, when and why and where, and I feel lost in a world that I've got to get with or die of frustration. We've got one of the keys, though, for here is where the myth and ritual business operates in a context not of primitive culture but beneath the foundations of the West. Some of the classical people here are snobbish about this mess but it belongs to anyone who can dig it—and I don't mean picking around in ruins, as important as that is. I've just read a novel titled *Hadrian's Memoirs*[1] which is interesting in its reconstruction of the times, warfare, politics, philosophy, religion and the homosexual love life of the Emperor. It's really more of a scholarly synthesis than a novel [. . .] but it's worth reading. As soon as I can discover who knows what around here I plan to get a reading list so that I can orient myself in relation to the classical background.

Man, I wish I could get over there with a tape recorder and copy some of your records. I bought that French set and it took up a good number of the reels I had so that I need a hell of a lot more jazz tapes to keep me on my proper ration. A man has, after all, to keep his feet on his home ground. As it is I have the Academy ringing with Duke and Count and Jimmy Rushing. I could just use a hell of a lot more. Books are a problem too; I'm only the fifth fellow in literature and they haven't built up much of a library. I guess I have to load up on my Penguins as soon as I can get down into the city. That Fanny is more like you, she's down there every day seeing all the sights. I've been only three times, and then on business. I'll catch up though. She's also speaking some Italian while I've had only one lesson . . .

No important news from home. We have friends living in the apartment and since I couldn't sell the car I stored it. Which bothers me now, for I have been told that I could stay here two years if I wish, and perhaps three. Right now I'd trade it for a Volkswagen and a gallon of gas! Have a letter

[1] *Memoirs of Hadrian,* by Marguerite Yourcenar.

from Foster requesting ideas of what program of Tuskegee should be, I haven't yet written that self-liquidation is the trick.

How are things going with you, Moke and Mique? All three of you stay the hell out of the way of those bloody French. In fact, I suggest that you fly Old Glory everywhere you go. And by no means go around in anything white, 'cause it's better to be shot for a mose than an A-rab any damn day (as you can see I'm still learning how to operate this Italian typewriter). By the way, write me the price of those Moroccan scatter rugs; we have tile floors and we could use a couple in our living room. If they are cheap enough I'd be willing to pay the duty to have them here. Those I remember are white with brown, black, yellow etc. designs. Got to feather this nest, man. Now if I could just find me some chitterlings . . . Allen Tate's wife, Caroline Gordon, is here and as soon as I know her better I'm going to ask her. Cause sure as hell she's going to come up one day wishing for some turnip greens cooked with a ham bone and I have a notion that all the southerners in Rome have a joint which they keep secret. I met Snowden, the Negro cultural attaché at a party and he was operating semi-officially so I didn't bother him at the time. Incidentally, I'm still cutting my own hair; he has less than I have so I didn't ask him about an initiated barber. Nevertheless, I suspect old Snowden can speak the idiom and I'll bet my money that he's an operator. If not I'll find me somebody down around Bricktop's place. Some seamen from the Constitution promised to introduce us to that part of Rome when they came in next trip, so by the time you get over we'll have situation well in hand. Till then if there's anything I can do for you here or through friends in New York, just let me know. Kiss the girls for me and tell 'em love us loves yall.

As ever,
Ralph

Rome,
June 2, 1957.

Dear Albert,

Tapes received and everybody knocked out. With both Duke and Basie I couldn't hope for better word from home; and if they weren't enough, that character who calls himself King Pleasure is about to drive me crazy. The idea of him breaking off the story at that point. Did Moody blow everybody out of the place or did it go limp on him, or did everybody blast everybody else? Well, however it came out that King Pleasure sings more bop rhythm than anyone since Anna Randolph, who was singing it and improvising her lyrics during the days when Dizzy and Monk were confined to Minton's Playhouse. Here's a fool who doesn't know you aren't supposed to sing prose, so he gets away with it. . . . As for the bit from *Drum,* I like, but suspect that here again Duke fails to make the transition from the refinement of his music over to drama—or even over to words; so that what in music would be vital ideas comes over with a slickness and hipster elegance that makes you want to go and tell the man how really good he is and that he should do anything with that Broadway-hipster-Mose decadence but get it mixed up with his music. He should leave that element to Billy Strayhorn. Well, if we have to have that in order to get those diamonds, very well.

As for that Sugar Ray, I won on him against Bobo, would have lost on him when he lost to that meat-headed Fulmer, only the guy who bet me wouldn't bet, and I would have won on him this time if the guy hadn't gone back to the states. Somebody will have to whip Sugar Ray some day but I'll go along with him because he is an artist and I'll bet on grace and art when its coupled with strength before I'd ever bet on simple youth sans these. And you never said a truer word about Jack, he is indeed both hare and bear, and he's bound to get you one way or the other.

Which reminds me that that heart thing worries me, I hope it's nothing serious. As for the weight, you can lick that by walking. I'm down to 181 with my clothes on, which means I'm lean and mean. I think I'll have a physical soon myself just to keep in touch with myself for this spring hasn't been too easy on me. I wish you were stopping here for a day so that I could talk about it. Fanny and I are in a state of crisis at the moment and I might just be acting like a fool in his forties. That's as much as I can say now except that it's painful and confusing. . . . I don't know what our plans are at the moment. Fanny has to go home at the end of next month and I'm still waiting to hear if I'm staying here another year. A. MacLeish is doing something about it and I've been asked if I want to go to Tokyo & Kyoto in Sept. for P.E.N. I think I'll say yes but I don't know where I'll end up but it'll either be to Trieste, Milan, Turin, Genoa, Florence, Naples, and Bari—which promises to be the extent of my travel this summer. I go through the ordeal of a lecture here in Rome on Friday and that'll be the end of that mess. It's worse than playing one-night stands and there is nothing amusing about it, because these people won't blow back at you.

I suppose you've gotten the check by now, Fanny had sent it along with a letter to Mokie which was returned but we used the last address you gave me, thanks for the bag, and as for the books, I have an extra copy of Faulkner's THE TOWN and one of Steegmuller's translation of *Madame Bovary*. If you haven't picked them up yet, just let me know where to mail them. Faulkner has some amusing things, mostly reworked from some of the Snopes stories, but I haven't gotten around to the translation. I've really been too busy battling with myself and with this novel-of-mine-to-be to get much reading done. I'm going to whip the dam thing but it [is] giving me a tough fight; it just looks as though every possible emotional disturbance has to happen to me before I can finish a book. . . . By the way, Hyman sent me a lecture he gave on Negro writing and the folk tradition, in which he writes about the blues, but it was a very disappointing piece. He's so busy looking for African myth in the U.S. that he can't see what's before his eyes, even when he points out that African and Greek myths finally merge in that similar figures appear in both. He sees what he terms the "darky entertainer" i.e. characters like Stepin Fetchit—intelligent men hiding behind the stereotype—as the archetypal figure to writing by Negroes—including mine. This figure, who he also terms a "smart-man-playing-dumb," he sees everywhere in Negro writing and I pointed out to him that that wasn't African, but American. That's Hemingway when he pretends to be a sportsman, or *only* a sportsman; Faulkner when he pretends to be a farmer; Benjamin Franklin when he pretended to be a "child of nature," instead of the hipped operator that he was; even Lincoln when he pretended to be a simple country lawyer. But Stanley, being Jewish and brought up to wear his intellect like a crown of jewels can't see this at all; he thinks mose had to get this mess from Africa when all he had to do was breathe the American air and he was ready to teach other Americans how it was done. But even as sheer method Stanley's approach is weak because he tries to discuss the novelist and folk tradition without discussing the novel, the form which is itself a depository of folk and other traditions reduced to formal order. I knew mose lore yes, but I didn't really know it until I knew something about literature and specifically the novel, then I looked at Negro folklore with a shock of true recognition. I was trying to write novels in the great tradition of the novel, not folk stories. The trick is to get mose lore *into* the novel so that it becomes a part of that tradition. Hell, Hyman don't know that Ulysses is both Jack the rabbit (when that cyclops gets after his ass) and Jack the Bear, Big Smith the Chef, John Henry and everybody else when he starts pumping arrows into those cats who've been after his old lady. Or if he does recognize this, it's only with his mind, not his heart. I was especially disappointed with his treatment of the blues, for while he lists a few themes he restricts their meaning to a few environmental circumstances: Mose can't rise vertically so he's restless; he can't get a good job here so he goes there—missing the fact that there is a metaphysical restlessness built into the American and mose is just another form of it, expressed basically, with a near tragic debunking of the self which is our own particular American style. I really thought I'd raised that boy better than that. But hell, I keep telling you that you're the one who has to write about those blues. The world's getting bluesier all the time, as Joe Williams and Count well know, and even though those Africans have Ghana they still haven't developed to the point where the blues start. Well, what bothers me about Stanley's piece is that after all his work and insight it seems to reveal a basic failure to understand the nature of metaphor, thus he can't really see that Bessie Smith singing a good blues may deal with experience as profoundly as Eliot, with the eloquence of the Eliotic poetry being expressed in her voice and phrasing. Human anguish is human anguish, love love; the difference between Shakespeare and lesser artists is eloquence but when Beethoven writes it it's still the same anguish, only expressed in a different medium by an artist of comparable eloquence. Which reminds me that here, way late, I've discovered Louis singing "Mack the Knife." Shakespeare invented Caliban, or changed himself into him—Who the hell dreamed up Louie? Some of the bop boys consider him Caliban but if he is he's a mask for a lyric poet who is much greater than most now writing. That's a mask for Hyman to study, me too; only I know enough not to miss my train by messing around over looking over in Africa or even down in the West Indies. Hare *and* bear [are] the ticket; man and mask, sophistication and taste hiding behind clowning and crude manners—the American joke, man. Europeans dream of purity—*any* American who's achieved his American consciousness knows that it's a dream so he ain't never been innocent, he's been too busy figuring out his next move. It's just that the only time he ever comes out from behind that mask is when he's cornered— *that's* when you have to watch him. Unless, of course, he's Mose, who has learned to deal with a hell of a lot more pressure. Write about those blues, and love to the girls from me and Fanny.

> Ralph
> Watch that heart!

> Bard College
> Annandale-on-Hudson, NY
> Sept. 28, 1958.

Dear Albert,

The Ellisons are shookup like everyone else, I suppose, but otherwise we're about the same. I've been intending to write but ran into a busy summer of writing and fighting, of all things I don't need, the hayfever. I finished a long piece on Minton's Playhouse for *Esquire*'s special Jazz issue, which is due in Jan. and that took quite a lot of time running around and trying to talk to those screwedup musicians, drinking beer so that I could listen to their miserable hard-bopping noise (defiance with both hands protecting their heads) and finally realizing that I could write the piece without their help; for after all most of them simply know that they're dissatisfied and that they want fame and glory and to be themselves (or Charlie Parker—which would be even better because most have only that which they've copied from him as miserable, beat and lost as *he* sounded most of the time—but hell, they believe in the witchdoctor's warning: If Bird shits on you, wear it). And anyway they suspect, and rightly, that they *ain't* nobody. Man, I wished for you during the Newport festival. I was asked up to participate in the critics symposium and went up there and put the bad mouth on a lot of the characters. I wouldn't be a jazz critic for love or money, but I discovered that I have quite a number of fans who think that's what I've been doing for the *SRL*. So I had my say the first two days and spent the rest of the time looking and listening and a hell of a lot of it was simply pathetic. I finally saw that Chico Hamilton with his mannerisms and that poor, evil, lost little Miles Davis, who on this occasion sounded like he just couldn't get it together. Nor did Coltrane help with his badly executed velocity exercises. These cats have gotten lost, man. They're trying to get hold to something by fucking up the blues, but some of them don't even know the difference between a blues and a spiritual—as was the case of Horace Silver who went wanging away like a slightly drunken gospel group after announcing a blues. Monk, who is supposed to be nuts, got up on stage and outplayed most of the modern boys and was gracious and pleasant while doing so. But Bird had crapped on most of the saxophonists, who try to see how many notes they can play in a phrase and how many "changes," as they like to call their chord progressions, they can cram into even the most banal melodic idea. There was even a cat there trying to play Bird on a Tuba. He was spitting like a couple of tom cats fighting over a piece of tail and that poor ole tuba was wobbling like an elephant with a mouse doing a Lindy-hop up and down inside his long nose hole. Taste was an item conspicuously missing from most of the performances, and once again I could see that there's simply nothing worse than a half-educated Mose unless it's a Mose jazz-modernist who's convinced himself that he's a genius, maybe the next Beethoven, or at least Bartók, and who's certain that he's the only Mose jazzman who has heard the classics or attended a conservatory. Duke didn't do much up there but it was easy to see why. These little fellows are scrambling around trying to get something new; Duke is *the* master of a bunch of masters and when the little boys hear him come on they know that they'll never be more than a bunch of little masturbators and they don't want to think about it. I was at a party given by Columbia Records at the Plaza recently, where they presented Duke, Miles Davis, Jimmy Rushing and Billie Holiday and it was murder. Duke signified on Davis all through his numbers and his trumpeters and saxophonists went after him like a bunch of hustlers in a Georgia skin game fighting with razors. Only Cannonball Adderley sounded as though he might have some of the human quality which sounds unmistakably in the Ellington band. And no question of numbers was involved. They simply had more to say and a hundred more ways in which to say it. I told Jimmy that I'd hoped to hear him sing with Duke but was afraid it would never happen. It was one of those occasions when the whole band was feeling like playing and they took off behind him and it was like the old Basie band playing the Juneteenth ramble at Forest Park in Okla. City. Duke left for Europe Mon. for the first time in about ten years and invited us to join the mob of fans, writers, and friends who were there to see them off. They served champagne, which helped offset the rainy morning but it didn't stop Duke from talking that gooie bullshit which he feels forced to spread. Great man until he opens his mouth. They did the number he wrote for the Great South Bay festival at the Plaza and it sounded well constructed and generally interesting. Watch out for it. . . . This business of writing on jazz is quite interesting. Quite a lot of fan mail goes with it and while some of the younger "critics" are friendly, some of the others react as though I'm moving into their special preserve. Old John Wilson of the *Times* won't even acknowledge my presence at the various publicity gatherings—which amuses me to no end, since we aren't playing the same game anyway. At

Newport, one of the critic-composers interrupted some remark I made concerning the relationship between Negro dance audiences and jazz bands, to say that he didn't believe that Jazz was connected with the life of any racial group in this country—but when one of his numbers was played by the International Youth band, a Swedish boy stood up and tried to play Bubber Miley on a trumpet and the voicing was something copied from Duke. I really don't have much patience anymore, Albert, and I didn't bite my tongue in telling this guy where he came from and who his daddy was—who his *black* daddy was. I don't fight the race problem in matters of culture but anyone should know the source of their tradition before they start shooting off their mouth about where jazz comes from.

It looks as though I'll have enough pieces before long to form part of a book and in the meantime it gives me a chance to earn a buck. *Esquire* is interested in anything I do, article or story. If you have anything you should send it to Harold Hayes and mention my name. There is a young crowd there these days who are trying to raise its standard and I think they should be encouraged—especially since they're paying dam well. On the ninth they're running a symposium on fiction along with Columbia University and I'm being paid fifty bucks just to be there just in case someone doesn't show—in which case I'll get five hundred and I'm not even bothering to prepare notes. . . . And what am I doing up here? I'm living in Bellow's house while they are away at Minn. and when I'm not struggling with my novel, I'm working on my notes for that single class in the American novel which I'm teaching at Bard College: I go to campus only once a week, and though it doesn't pay me much it does make it possible for me to stay up here most of the time. It's only two hours away from the city so that I can go down there or Fanny can come up here fairly easily. I'm a little desperate about the book so took this as a way to have the peace to get it over with. . . . Man, you'll soon have property all over the place, which seems like a good idea at that. Which reminds me that while I'm not yet in the position to send you all your dough outright, I *could* start paying you off at a hundred books a throw. In fact, I've been asked to let *Esquire* see some of the novel which I shall do as soon as I can solve a few problems connected with a certain section, and if they take it I should be able to send you the whole sum. . . . Had a call from Gwen Mitchell the other morning, she's up there at City College and Juilliard (This was down in New York) and tells me that Mitch is building at Tuskegee. I guess every fox has got a hole but me . . . What you tell me of L.A. is depressing but the next time you're there I'd appreciate it if you would drop over to 1917 Jefferson and see my brother Herbert and let me know your impressions. He works from 4:30 in the afternoon until late at night so you could reach him during the day. I'll tell him to watch out for you. . . . I know how depressing it is to see Negroes getting lost in the American junk pile and being satisfied with so little after all the effort to break out of the South. It makes you want to kick their behinds and then go after Roy Wilkins and that crowd who still don't see that Civil rights are only the beginning. Or maybe I should go after myself for not being more productive and for not having more influence upon how we think of ourselves and our relationship to what is truly valuable in the country. I'm trying in this damn book but even if I'm lucky one book can do very little. And wouldn't a damn nutty woman pick King to kill instead of some southern politician? I'm surprised that she wasn't torn to shreds right there on the spot.[1] The New York papers are reporting the

---

[1] On September 20, 1958, Dr. Martin Luther King, Jr., was stabbed in the side by a mentally ill woman while in New York for a book signing. The injury was nearly fatal, but King recovered in the hospital and at the Brooklyn home of a friend.

gifts of money and letters of well wishers which the crack-
ers are sending this bitch, a further indication of how de-
praved this southern thing can become. And they think
we're fighting to become integrated into that insanity! I almost cracked my sides when I heard that baleful voiced
hypocrite [Arkansas Senator] John McClellan lecturing
Jimmy Hoffa with such high moral tone. Those sons-
abitches don't even have a sense of humor. He doesn't see
that with his attacks on the Supreme Court he's doing more
to undermine the country than Hoffa is or could even if he
were stealing a million a day and bribing every so-called
respectable official with an itching palm—of which there
must be thousands—that he could find in Washington. It
would delight me no end if some reporter got to digging
into McClellan's background and told the story of how he
became such a moral leader, *that* would make interesting
reading, because being a southern politician is by definition
one of the most corrupt careers to be found anywhere.
Everything about this mess breeds sickness, the bastard's
lost his sons one right after the other and it's human to feel
sorry for such misfortunes and indeed, it's the kind of thing
which is apt to touch me most poignantly, since we have no
children at all but hell, how can I sympathize with his loss
when he's trying to deprive my kids of a chance to realize
themselves? No, I hate him and his kind and I believe the
world will be a better place when the last of them is put
away forever. Certainly this country will have a bit more
self-respect. . . . I saw something of Norman Mailer during
the summer and have been discussing Kerouac and that
crowd with Bernie Wolfe[2] and I understand something of
how far you got underneath that Greenwich Village poet's
skin that summer in Paris. These characters are all trying to
reduce the world to sex, man, they have strange problems

---

[2] Bernard Wolfe, novelist and coauthor of *Really the Blues*, the autobiography of jazzman Mezz Mezzrow.

in bed; they keep score à la Reich on the orgasm and try to verbalize what has to be basically warmth, motion, rhythm, timing, affection and technique. I've also talked to Bellow about this and it would seem that puritan restraints are more operative among the bohemians than elsewhere. That's what's behind Mailer's belief in the hipster and the "white Negro" as the new culture hero—he thinks all hipsters are cocksmen possessed of great euphoric orgasms and are out to fuck the world into peace, prosperity and creativity. The same old primitivism crap in a new package. It makes you hesitant to say more than the slightest greetings to their wives lest they think you're out to give them a hot fat injection. What a bore.

Let me know what's happening with you. Are you still shooting? I've been too busy to do much but plan to carry a camera with me when I start hunting the countryside here abouts. How's your health? Mine is weakened more than you'd expect by this damn hayfever but I look fairly well, am a bit more bald and taken to smoking a type of mild Conn. cigar which I discovered in New Milford this summer. Otherwise I haven't slowed much. Got drunk at a party recently and danced a young chick bowlegged, but hell, a rounder never changes. Love to them gals and let me hear what's cooking.

Ralph

730 Riverside Drive
New York, N.Y. 10031
July 10, 1971

Dear Charlie:

Last Friday evening after spending a pleasant hour listening to Bobby Short performing and being interviewed over the radio, it occurred to me that despite my best intentions I hadn't thanked you for sending me his autobiography. Last month I tried to reach you by telephone but you and Terry were away and I simply left my name with one of the girls. It made the fourth time I've missed you although the other calls were to the store and though disappointed I figured that you were probably looking after Porkchopper. Despite my tardiness in thanking you for the book I found it thoroughly enjoyable. Indeed, I was disappointed that it hadn't continued for another hundred pages or so. For not only does it offer insights into what makes Bobby Short tick, it is highly entertaining and an important contribution to American cultural history. With popular entertainment being a mixture of high culture, low culture, family and neighborhood culture and personal talent, how nice it is to learn something of how a highly successful product of that mixture came to be!

Listening to Short on the radio caused me to think, What a gifted, charming and insufferable little rascal of a man and what a gifted artist! He's good, he knows he's good and he means to see to it that neither the interviewer nor anyone else misses the fact that he knows his own high value . . . Which is as it should be. He could probably charm a steak out of the jaws of a hungry dog and then have the poor animal dancing to his piano. In short, Short is long on class, the kind of class that causes George Frazier to flip his typewriting lid. And as for those sociologists and half-assed politicos who've been filling the bookstores with vapid, dehumanized nonsense about what they term "*The* black experience," Short's account of the background of an individual Negro American of Mid-Western origins gives a richer sense of the general Negro experience than all their pronouncements. It restores some of the sense of complexity, wonder and diversity which I recognize as part of my own life. Against the dreary, reductive, paper-thin images of Negro American life-style and personality that are now so fashionable it was a pleasure to recall many of the details of my own life in Oklahoma. The aspirations, folkways, manners, hard-and-good times of his mother and her friends were a duplication with variations of those of the people I grew up among. It makes for a strange and volatile mixture and if you try to class angle it you're dead. Short is younger than I am and I grew up in a completely segregated state while his was deceptively unsegregated, but the sense of promise that his people shared despite the racism and other disadvantages (and others that were merely *apparent*) kept them fighting and trying to move ahead. So it's good to read a man who appreciates the human and cultural *richness* of what was, more often than not, an economically under-privileged background. And I'm sure that had Short failed to respond to and against that human and cultural richness (including the goddam phonograph and radio!), he wouldn't have been prepared for the same economic good-times that lay ahead. In this country one thing leads to another—no matter what the "other" turns out to be. And if we stop living to give ourselves over to complaint the best we can expect is more frustration. His sister's "Social Aristocrats" club might strike some readers as quaint, but those chicks were teaching themselves the felicities of social conduct, and I'll bet you that the food they served was as good as their dancing. One such girl I knew back in Oklahoma has been operating on high levels in Washington for years and her style comes from just such clubs.

So I consider the photographs of his family and friends precious documents. They capture the pathos, the aspiration, sense of style, age and youth of a given moment of our under-valued history. I've seen photographs of my father's sister dressed very much as his mother did when young—hat, suit and mutton sleeves. Yes, but all I can say about his father is that the cat was damn elegant in the hat! Should

Bobby Short publish another volume of his autobiography (and I hope he does) I hope his publisher will send it to me early for possible comment. In the meantime you can believe that I am recommending *Black and White Baby* to all my reading friends. Especially to those literary intellectuals who take their ideas of black Americans from such as Pat-of-the-monkey-hand* and Jimmy Baldwin. I want the bastards to contemplate, if they can, the wonderful mystery of American experience made manifest in the phenomena of such an elegant and sophisticated artist as Short emerging from Black Danville. Recently, in the June issue of *Vogue,* I saw Short photographed with a group that frequents Elaine's restaurant. It was a good photo by Irving Penn, a photographer whom I admire a great deal, and at least three of the fellows are friends of mine. Nevertheless I couldn't help but feel that the magazine might have served its readers to a more instructive effect had it given itself over to an excerpt of Short's book. The magazine operates on the mystification of social hierarchy—Jet Set, 'Beautiful People' and all that—as well as of fashion, but for its readers there's a far more intriguing mystery in the little brown-skinned man with moustache standing near the center of the photograph.

Things go on here as usual, I'm still writing and trying to make life meaningful. I miss seeing you but can't seem to get up to Boston anymore. Plan to do something about that this fall. Meantime give our warmest regards to Terry, and if you get down to this nasty fun city please give us a ring.

Sincerely,
Ralph

---

* Ellison refers to Daniel Patrick Moynihan, author of "The Negro Family: The Case for National Action," 1965 (also called "The Moynihan Report").

P.S. If you don't have a tape of Flip Wilson telling the story about the preacher and the Go-Rilla let me know as I'd like you to hear it.

P.P.S. Charles Graham, the guy doing the book on Hawk, had something to do with the jazz concerts at the Museum of Modern Art and has been an editor and writer for audio electronic magazines. I knew him fifteen years or so ago but haven't run into him recently. I'm sending out scouts and plan to keep an eye on him!

R.W.E.

INTERVIEW WITH WKY-TV,

OKLAHOMA, 1976

On August 22, 1976, a new branch of the Oklahoma City public library, The Ralph Ellison Library, was officially opened for business. On that day, Ellison delivered a speech recalling the first public library opened to black Oklahoma City dwellers: a hastily improvised arrangement of books, with Negro librarian, in a pool hall—all in response to the discovery that the extant library system had not been officially segregated. "In recalling this," Ellison told the crowd on the day of dedication, "it is not my purpose to stir up the fires of resentment. . . . Rather, my purpose is to celebrate the confusion—to celebrate, understand me, to celebrate*—the confusion of motives, which in the loose, relatively unstructured affairs of Oklahoma's young statehood allowed so many of us who are gathered here today our first opportunity to make acquaintance with the wonders of the library." Conducted a few days later in Oklahoma City, the radio interview presented here touches upon The Ralph Ellison Library, its makeshift but remarkably fruitful predecessor, and upon other issues involving music and the work of the artist. An underlying question throughout: What experiences forge a writer of Ellison's brilliance?*

———

WKY-TV Interviewer: *Ralph, I wonder if you can say how you feel about having a library named for you?*

Ralph Ellison: Well, actually, Dan, it sounds like a massive hint that I should write enough books to fill it. [laughter] But beyond that it is such an honor that I think it will be a while before I can really arrive at any stable reaction to it. I do know, however, that as far as I am concerned it is a symbolic gesture. I stand in for a lot of people who have made that library possible. And I think that is pretty much the way it is going to be in my mind.

Interviewer: *In your talk the other day you referred to the library as the "nexus of dreams"?*

Ellison: Well, of course it would go back to my own experience with libraries. As I thought about that material for that talk I gave under all that pressure you put me under on the twenty-first, I recalled that that old library was *not* the first library that I became acquainted with. I lived for a few months in Gary, Indiana, and in Gary I blundered into a building where I watched and followed other children and where eventually I found some books called the "Brownie Books." Well, they fascinated me. And so when I found out that something like this was going to be possible in Oklahoma City, then I went there looking for these little green volumes, because that is what they were. But when I said a "nexus of dreams," I meant that the library is the place where the great dreams of mankind are stored and where you can find them.

Interviewer: *For you as an artist, the oral tradition is related to the written word.*

Ellison: Yes, well, I used to work at Randolph's Drug Store down on Second Street. And on rainy days and days of ice and snow the older men would sit there and drink their Coca-Colas (or maybe they would spike them with something, I don't know). But they would get to telling stories and sometimes I would be told by one of these men: "You know, your daddy told this story years ago." It might have to do with burying money or searching for buried treasure. And it was when I went into the library and began to read Poe that

I realized that these were somewhat the same stories I had been hearing. And here the oral tradition and the literary tradition would come together.

Interviewer: *Did you incorporate this sort of oral work in the writing that you have put on the written page?*

Ellison: Oh, for me it is inescapable; you'll hear people talking as you are in the process of creating a character. And as they speak, I'm listening to the accents and I'm listening for the imagery. It's a sort of feedback process wherein you're not consciously trying to project any known person, but you're using all of your responses to their character as projected by voice, expression, and inflection. You're concerned with the sheer impact of the individual when he speaks of things that are abiding, repetitious in the experience of people in the name of a given character. We have great storytellers here in this city. And since it is part of my background, I use it more or less automatically.

Interviewer: *In your background you were really into music before you were into writing. How did that early musical background influence your writing?*

Ellison: Well, the good thing about music is that not so much mystery is made of the relationship between expression and mastering technique. Speaking of the trumpet, you're taught that, well, you have got to learn how to *blow* that thing. You've got to know many things very consciously about how music is written and expressed. When I blundered into writing, I didn't feel that there was anything unusual going around to find people who had written about writing and usually the best guides were the writers themselves.

Interviewer: *Do you think your musical training gave you a discipline or an understanding of a need for discipline in order to approach a new artistic craft?*

Ellison: Yes, you didn't expect to be able to play because you felt something. You were taught very quickly that there were ways in which the body had to be taught to react, to project itself, to relate to the instrument and to the score. So you began to discipline yourself that way. At Tuskegee I had to get up at five o'clock in the morning and stand in an open window and blow sustained tones on the trumpet for an hour before breakfast. So when I got to writing I said, "Well, if I worked for music it must work the same way for writing." And therefore I wrote many short stories, and in fact I attempted a novel six months after I decided I was going to try to write. But I put these things aside because I looked upon them as what they were: just exercises which would allow me to learn something of the nature of the craft. You see, with writing people get the feeling that a writer is someone that *feels* things passionately; that all you have to do is go to a typewriter or pick up a pen and pencil and put your feelings down. And of course nothing is done that way.

Interviewer: *You're also into teaching. Can people be taught to appreciate literature?*

Ellison: I think so. I was taught. We had a teacher over at Douglass, Mrs. MacFarlane, who was very much interested in the Negro Renaissance of the twenties. And she would bring to class the writings, the poetry, and the short stories of Langston Hughes, of Countee Cullen, of Claude McKay; and so we felt like we knew these people. It was a mysterious craft, but hearing narrative gave me great pleasure. And all of us had plenty of prior conditioning: after all, there are nursery rhymes, bedtime stories, biblical stories, sermons when projected by a really eloquent minister of which we had quite a number in this city. So it was a matter of transferring all of these oral forms and your love for them, your ardor for them, to the printed word. When you've got a person who read to you and who read with some expressional eloquence, you began to increase and intensify your love of reading.

Interviewer: *I know from your speech that you also had an introduction to libraries that was not necessarily traditional: They hastily erected a library to serve the northeastern side—I believe it was above an old pool hall.*

Ellison: It was *in* an old pool hall.

Interviewer: *You said that they did not arrange the books in a conventional way. Rather you described the arrangement as literary chaos, but out of that came some interesting forays.*

Ellison: Oh yes. Reading Ruskin, reading, as I said the other day, Dr. A. A. Brille's translation of Freud's *Interpretation of Dreams*, which I took home thinking to be an elaborate and more scholarly form of a dream book, which people use to place their bets in playing the Negro policy game. But I read the classical children's stories, English boys' books were there, American boys' books, cowboy stories, detective fiction, just any and everything was available and there hadn't been time to classify them. So there was nobody to say, "You're too young to read that."

Interviewer: *I guess I hope that we don't have libraries overorganized, so that people can experience some of that chaos and some of the benefits.*

Ellison: Well, one of the things that I noticed after the opening, when there was still a great crowd there, was that the children were already in business in the library. And I began to hear a good Bessie Smith blues! I had never heard that in a library before, and I think it's precisely the kind of thing that *should* be in a library. This is classical music, classical vernacular music, and it ties in with that particular part of my background and it relates to literature, too. I found this a very warm welcome—that was almost an *epiphany.*

Interviewer: *What did that part of your exposure to culture in Oklahoma City mean to you? What was the role of jazz, in particular?*

Ellison: Well, the sheer irresistible attraction of jazz came from what Whitney Balliett of *The New Yorker* has called *the sound of surprise:* that marvelous, unexpected virtuosity expressed by people whom you knew very well and upon themes, melodies that were so traditional that even when the player has done something really original, you understood how the originality related to the traditional. That was exciting. In fact, jazz seems somehow to give expression to the times much better than does classical music in the European tradition—though of course I love them both. But you put the Blue Devils Orchestra upstairs at Carnegie Hall together with what you were learning from Mr. Hebestreit. (I used to cut grass for Hebie in exchange for trumpet lessons. My mother worked in service over on Glossen Boulevard and Seventeenth Street, and Hebie lived nearby. And I'd go and cut his grass, but instead of really teaching me trumpet, he'd take a score by Wagner, for instance, and sit at the paper and dissect it and play out parts of it because he knew that's what I was interested in. And by the way he used to invite me as his guest to the local symphony concerts. I supposed I was the only brother of color who got into those concerts in those days.) But you put those things together, and they were part of my total conception, of what made a whole experience. And I didn't think in abstracts, but I remember that I valued one art form just as much as the other.

Interviewer: *You have mentioned this repetition twice now. Are they related, that the storytellers repeat the same stories, and that the jazz musician repeats themes in music and embroiders them? Is that process similar to the novelist's way of writing?*

Ellison: Well, I think so, yes. I think the novelist—we can call him a poet in the larger sense—deals with those abiding patterns of human experience which are associated with man's identity as an animal and as a symbol-using animal: man the animal gifted with speech, the being who cannot feel at home in the world unless he has given names to it, unless he has set up schemes of value related to action and to scenes and to atmosphere, and to any and everything. We ennoble and too often corrupt with our ability to use words. The novelist operates in that area of human life wherein the themes which have given us pause, which have given us wonder, which have given us pleasure. Those dilemmas which are relived again and again by all kinds of people in all kinds of civilizations: this is our area. What we do is to re-duce these experiences to form and of course the novel is a traditional form, but we modify according to our own needs, our own vision. So again you have that unity and diversity, the unity of traditional themes which have been here for ages, plus the diversity of our individual vision, your indi-vidual eloquence as you project your vision of that particu-lar theme.

Interviewer: *When you have projected it, and it's developed in a book, how much do you care what critics have to say about it?*

Ellison: Well, you do care. You appreciate informed readers. And of course some critics are very understanding, they have insight and knowledge of the form. While I don't write for them, one can always appreciate perception, especially from people who can tell other people that the work is pretty good. [laughing]

Interviewer: *Ralph, we were talking about the jazzmen and their relationship to the novelist and the storytellers' role. At one point, you mentioned that there was almost a priestlike aspect to the jazz musi-cian's role. Would you compare this to the role of the storyteller and the novelist?*

Ellison: Well, I think that when I was speaking of those jazzmen of the thirties, and I suppose this is still true: that their motivation wasn't primarily economic. It was a dedica-tion to what was in many ways an outlaw art. (Every time someone tried to make a movie of a murder or some other crime, they'd put in somebody playing jazz music, usually bad jazz.) But the people who devoted themselves to making jazz music were as dedicated as any group of artists I know to perfecting that art, to making it more eloquent. Ulti-mately they were performing a social function: They were bringers of joy. I think jazz artists relate to novelists who have some of the same functions—except that since we do deal with words and ideas, we're supposed to be a little more explicit, in a subtle way, than musicians are supposed to be.

I should mention something here about the relationship between the writer and his craft. I have to say to students all the time that books are not written out of raw emotion, they're written out of other books. I know of no novelist, or poet for that matter, who does not know a great deal of the best of the works in the form in which he works. I could use the metaphor of the physician. You become a surgeon by learning the craft of a surgeon, very consciously so. And the same is true for the writer. The library is the university, it's the grade school of the novelist. He writes out of other books. That's how he learns his craft. That's how he learns what has been done and what he dare not try to repeat.

Interviewer: *Who are some of the writers who have helped you in that way, whom you've admired?*

Ellison: There's Melville, there's Faulkner, there's Emerson, there's Dostoyevsky, there's André Malraux, there's of course Hemingway, all of the better ones I've read at some time. Not only the better ones but the pulp writers. I lived in McAlester for a year, and the baggage man at the hotel where my mother worked used to save all the pulp magazines that the salesmen would drop off, so I'd read all of that.

Interviewer: *We hear so much about the writer's craft referring to discipline. Have you a discipline as a writer? What is it and has it influenced your life, your family life? Do you have to give up something to maintain that discipline?*

Ellison: We, yes, you give up certain pleasures. Hunting, you don't have time to do that. But really the basic discipline is just staying at the machine, at the ideas, even when you're not at the machine. Actually, part of the technique of writing has to do with a mental balance. Sometimes when I'm shaving or walking along the street, I'm writing. Other times I'm not, I'm just shaving or walking down the street. [laughing] It's something to which you dedicate your life, and thus you shape your life, you order your life around that function. And this is very difficult sometimes for my wife, I'm sure. But she is a good wife and she's put up with it. [laughing] But it's like being an athlete. You cannot violate your discipline if you are going to be a winner.

Interviewer: *You mentioned that at Douglass High School you were exposed to the writings of many members of the Negro Renaissance. Then you made your way for a period of time to New York and came to know some of these men directly. Did they have a direct impact on your work as well as through their writings?*

Ellison: Well, yes and no. I was not a writer, I was a musician when I first went to New York. I met Langston Hughes the second day I was in New York. Langston was very helpful, and I had read his stuff for so long. He did not influence me as a writer as much as Richard Wright did. It was Richard Wright who got me into writing by asking me to write a book review. I wrote a book review which he published and then he needed short stories. It never occurred to me to try to write fiction. And he said, "Well, you tell about all these experiences, you've read a lot." I was then reading a lot of critics and writers.

Interviewer: *So you wrote short stories, too?*

Ellison: My first story didn't get into print because the magazine failed. You see, I was trying to find my own way, and I was trying to find insights in some of the complexities of Afro-American life which I didn't get in the writers that I knew. I began to say, "Well, if they don't have the answers, I'll go and look wherever I can." Some of what I think are my own insights into my own group's experience in this country I got out of Dostoyevsky. I began to realize that if you looked at literature at moments of great social chaos you were getting an American experience, if you knew how to apply it. So I found this to be a very liberating discovery. This was based of course on the random reading that I began to do as a kid. And by the way, when I was reading a story, nobody got in the way of me being the hero! This I think kids do naturally. While reading, I lived the experience, I possessed that experience. And maybe when I got out on the street I wouldn't speak to you because you'd bring me down to reality. [laughing]

Interviewer: *As a reader and a library user, do you have a quick suggestion to librarians on how we can get more people into libraries?*

Ellison: I'd say: Get people to bring their children. In so many places, the library is not an accepted institution, it's exotic. Adults and their children have got to be made to understand that it's *their* library. Maybe playing the blues inside is part of the secret.

Interviewer: *Ralph Ellison, thank you very much.*

"MY STRENGTH COMES FROM

LOUIS ARMSTRONG":

INTERVIEW WITH ROBERT G. O'MEALLY, 1976

On a bright Saturday in May 1976, I interviewed Ellison in his apartment on Riverside Drive in Upper Manhattan. He had invited me to come up from Washington, D.C., where I was teaching at Howard University, in response to my request for an interview. Having recently completed my dissertation, I was working hard to turn it into what eventually became The Craft of Ralph Ellison. *For his part, Ellison was eager to correct misconceptions he saw in the manuscript, based mainly on an overvaluation of class as a factor in his upbringing—he made the point very clear that he grew up poor but with solidly sustaining values—and an underappreciation of the difficulty involved in how a writer transforms his experience with "folklore" into fiction. He insisted on a much more complicated picture than sociological formulas could frame—and on the cultural "links" (perhaps another term for "institutions") he believed to be so vital in connecting one generation to another. Ellison smoked a cigar off and on as we talked, for nearly four hours, and was a gracious host. He expressed an urgency to get the record straight not only with me and my manuscript but with my role as a representative of a generation of black scholars with whom he had been at odds for his stances on the black arts and black power movements. This did not mean that he would soften what he had to say about Malcolm X or the*

Left or anybody or anything else. There was a wistfulness about his reminiscences, but as the interview turned toward familiar grounds of controversy, I could feel the heat. In this, one of Ellison's last extended interviews, he fills out the Oklahoma City and Tuskegee pictures, and, perhaps, sends us back through Living with Music *with a coda that calls for repetition after repetition.*

———

Robert G. O'Meally: *Did you play in bands in Oklahoma City?*

Ralph Ellison: Well, I played gigs, you know, in small bands, say like those put together by Edward Christian, Charlie Christian's brother. Charlie was a younger fellow. He was in my brother's class. I liked him, but he hadn't become the Charlie Christian that we know now, the heroic figure. His brother Edward played violin, string bass, tuba, piano, and arranged, and was much more in the heroic mold as far as I was concerned. But I did that kind of thing. I was never a professional jazz musician, but I could play and I read very well, and it was easy enough to go on these jobs.

O'Meally: *Did you play with the Christian family group?*

Ellison: No, in that group the father played guitar and sang, and Edward played violin, and Clarence, a brother who was the second boy, played violin and guitar. They were known for serenading. They would go into white neighborhoods and play and collect whatever money they could playing a range of things, including popular music, blues, light classics, and so on.

O'Meally: *And occasionally you would play a gig with them?*

Ellison: Well, Edward was a professional musician, although he was still in high school when this began. He would get dance dates. Someone would book him and he would get a group of us together. And we played head arrangements and, you know, that kind of thing, the popular music of the time. And very often this was for whites. There were so many professionals around that kids didn't get too much of that to do.

O'Meally: *Were you ever involved in gladiatorial exchanges at Halley Richardson's?*

Ellison: Oh, no, not really. Halley's was a place where musicians hung out, and they received jobs there. People would call in there for orchestras or for musicians. There was some gambling which went on in the back. This was the time of Prohibition, and there would be liquor back there. Now, of course, my mother was not going to allow me to hang around there; and any number of other adults would've told her that I was spending time there—so no, I didn't. I could go in the front part of it sometimes, but it wasn't a place where I was allowed to hang out. And they didn't do most of their jamming there; usually when they jammed there, nowhere else was available at the moment. Rehearsals, yes, I used to attend jazz band rehearsals at Slaughter's Hall all the time.

O'Meally: *So you knew members of these bands personally, Count Basie, for instance . . .*

Ellison: No, I didn't know Count Basie personally. I knew all of the members of the Blue Devils, who preceded Basie. I knew George E. Lee, and members of the Bennie Moten orchestra. I knew Keith Holden, out of Arkansas, but out of Oklahoma City for a long time; from the Clouds of Joy, I knew Andy Kirk and Mrs. Kirk, because they lived in Oklahoma City. They played in territorial bands that were based a good part of the time in Kansas City, which was the big music town, but they were constantly in my town. So I got to know them. I worked in the drug store and was all over the place. I was the delivery boy. But I didn't know Basie. Basie came on the scene after I had gone to Tuskegee. Remember that Basie is from Red Bank, New Jersey. And he went out with Gonzelle White, or some small group which broke up, and he landed in Oklahoma City. And that began a new phase which led to the Basie band.

O'Meally: *When did you meet Jimmy Rushing?*

Ellison: Well, Jimmy Rushing worked for my father before I was born. And Jimmy's father owned a building where they had a luncheonette that sold fruit, and hamburgers, and root beer, and ice cream, that kind of thing. They were right next to the Aldridge Theater. So you stopped by there to get your hamburger and your root beer before you went in to see your Saturday movie. I was only allowed to go to movies on Saturday. That was really when I first became aware of Jimmy, on one of those movie days. I knew Jimmy, his father and his mother and his brothers and certain of his relatives—I knew them all my life. Long before he went with Basie, I remember when he used to play dances, when he would play piano and sing for private parties. Jimmy died here in Jamaica, Queens. They had the funeral in New York City. His lodge has its headquarters up on 155th Street.

O'Meally: *You remained friends through the years?*

Ellison: Yes. Well, the Basie band came here in about '36—about the same time I came to town—and I was always going around them and of course used to visit Jimmy and his wife, Connie. They lived in Manhattan for a long time, and then moved out to Jamaica. And we used to go out there and see them. And, of course, with the musicians they moved back and forth on the road, to Europe and so on. There would be intervals though, and we carried on telephone conversations for an hour at a time.

O'Meally: *Can you say a word about Mrs. Zelia Breaux, from back in Oklahoma City?*

Ellison: Mrs. Breaux was a co-owner of the Aldridge Theater which was the main and sometimes the only Negro-owned movie house. And it was there that Ida Cox and King Oliver and such people came on a regular basis.

O'Meally: *She was also connected with Douglass High School, right?*

Ellison: She was the supervisor of school music for the Negro schools, which meant that although she taught mainly at Douglass, she went around and instructed students and their teachers. But mainly she was supervisor of teachers in the district schools of Oklahoma City, so she was constantly in touch with what was going on. She also administered the music appreciation program, which was very important, and taught harmony. We had four years of harmony, in junior high school and high school, which was very unusual.

O'Meally: *Did you study voice as well?*

Ellison: I didn't have a singing voice, and I don't know now to what extent she instructed individuals in voice culture; but she did have a glee club, a boys' glee club and a girls' glee club, and a school chorus. And each year she put on an operetta. And these operettas were given in the theater, not over at the school; there were no facilities for that there. But all the scenery and props were staged at the Aldridge, which was also the neighborhood movie house. And before the day of sound movies, she had a pit orchestra. So some of the members of the Ideal Orchestra, who later became part of the Blue Devils, would play the scores in the orchestra pit at the Aldridge. She did not teach jazz, but she was encouraging to jazz musicians. She employed them, and once in a while she would bring some fellow in, like Mr. Icky Lawrence, to help with the band. She played trumpet herself, as well as violin and piano.

O'Meally: *Did you play instruments aside from trumpet?*

Ellison: Well, I played the valve instruments—except tuba. I never bothered with tuba. And I picked up a working knowledge of saxophone. She had a soprano saxophone, and she let me take that and I began to play it. But I never did much with it. Trumpet was my instrument.

O'Meally: *You had considered going to Langston University in Oklahoma, right? But instead you went off to Tuskegee. What happened to the idea of attending Langston?*

Ellison: I couldn't get a job; couldn't get a scholarship. And I had no money. I had an older friend, that same friend in whose parents' library I read my first Harvard Classics.

They were from Nashville, Tennessee. He had been a member of the Tuskegee band, and encouraged me to go to Tuskegee because it had a band and a music school. The people at Tuskegee knew about Mrs. Breaux, that they had a band in Oklahoma City and had pretty good musicians. So I was given the scholarship. I really wanted to go to Fisk; but they didn't have a music school. And they did not offer me a scholarship.

O'Meally: *Was there something valuable about Douglass and Tuskegee as all-black schools?*

Ellison: All these things must exist in time, and in terms of historical periods. Some of my teachers were of the first group to be educated after Reconstruction. There were not a lot of teachers around. In a segregated situation, you had to have segregated schools or you had *nothing*. Douglass had the advantage of people like Mrs. Breaux who, because of her interest in music and her passion to educate kids, did things which perhaps would have been overruled in white schools. I don't know any school today—except special ones in music or art—where they give you four years of harmony. You had the advantage of knowing people who lived in your own communities, who knew your parents, and who kept an eye on you, and who set examples which were not befogged by race. I didn't like *all* my teachers—I'm not saying that. And I had some bad ones. But I've been teaching long enough now to know that that happens in white schools, too.

But if you ask me what I think today—I think that integrating these schools without breaking them up on the level of the faculty would have made for a better transition. Because there are certain aspects of Negro life which have to be considered as you teach these children. You should know something about his *possible* attitudes. You should realize their inhibitions, hang-ups, and what-not: then you can help them get over them. This does not mean that our schools should not have white teachers. I'm thinking of a place like

Tuskegee, which has now had white teachers for a number of years. Talladega always had white teachers; and it is not unusual for schools in the South to have had white teachers, because when they were established, most of us did not have the kind of education necessary. What were they doing? They were transmitting *knowledge* from one generation to another. And you're doing this in a concrete historical situation. So finally, when we began to develop teachers, there came the glamour of getting rid of white teachers. And very often what they were replaced with were not as good—not because they were *black*, but because they hadn't had time enough to absorb all the knowledge that they needed. And our schools have suffered from that. There were teachers at Tuskegee who should not have been teaching *anywhere*. And yet there were others who could have *taught* anywhere. Certainly William L. Dawson at Tuskegee could have taught anywhere . . . Dawson really is a *genius.*

O'Meally: *Did you ever play at a public dance in Oklahoma, or did you play then in Alabama? Wouldn't Dawson have disapproved of such playing?*

Ellison: I don't recall playing at Slaughter's Hall in Oklahoma City. I played at smaller places, or for whites. I guess these were private dances or something. I never belonged, say, to the Blue Devils or any of the bigger orchestras. But at Tuskegee, you see, all the dances on campus were played by student musicians—except those where some traveling professional band came in when a dance was given. There were two student orchestras, and I played in one of them—oh, for a year or more, and then sat in from time to time. We played dances in places like Opelika, Alabama, and then Columbus, Georgia, near Fort Benning, and played dances for the white country clubs.

None of this could have been done without the okay of the Tuskegee administration, by the way. The division over jazz as against classics sprang, to a great extent, from a concern with proper teaching, and they wanted to see that you didn't violate the techniques which were being taught. That's important. And it goes beyond any class attitudes or religious attitudes toward jazz, because Tuskegee always had dances—that is, during my time. Teddy Wilson tells me that he remembers when they didn't dance at Tuskegee, but they *marched.* They'd get in this big dining hall which was a pretty tremendous space, and would march and they got a great deal of pleasure out of that. And in my time, we had dances in the gym and we played jazz concerts in auditoriums in the basement of the dining hall. So the matrons kept an eye on what you were doing, but nevertheless you were dancing.

O'Meally: *Then, too, Dawson must have respected vernacular music?*

Ellison: Oh, he did. Dawson had already composed his *Folk Symphony.* Some of the most exciting arrangements and renditions of the spirituals were to be had by the Tuskegee choir, arranged by Dawson. And he had a great respect for other arrangers of spirituals: John W. Work, and there was Henrietta Crawley Meyers at Fisk that used to have the Jubilee Singers. Dawson was very much influenced by her; he had studied with her. Dawson was part of the Tuskegee set-up, and he did not view his job as teaching jazz. But the spirituals were not neglected at all. He could take kids who could not read music, and make them into a choir that could phrase like a symphony orchestra.

O'Meally: *I was told that Dawson had discouraged your interest in jazz.*

Ellison: No, that isn't so. At Tuskegee, the music faculty didn't want you to play jazz because the techniques of jazz, and the use of the instrument, was somewhat different than what you're spending days and days and hours of every day to learn. I used to get up at five o'clock in the morning and play sustained tones out of the window just to learn to control an instrument, to develop tone. Many jazz musicians could not make the horn *sound* that way. They were incorrectly taught. One of the most popular musicians, by the way, to come out of Tuskegee was Shorty Hall, the trumpet player. He taught Dizzy Gillespie later over in North Carolina, where Dizzy studied for a while. But Shorty had been taught by Captain Drye, and he could play very difficult classical solos: themes and variations and so on, of works for organ and saxophone. I guess Tuskegee faculty figured you would pick up jazz on your own. But both Drye and Dawson had played in orchestras. Dawson, when he was the first trombonist in the Chicago Civic Symphony, played with Freddie Keppard; and I think he played in orchestra at the State Theater with Louis Armstrong.

O'Meally: *One of the school bands you traveled with was organized by Captain Drye.*

Ellison: The Tuskegee band was a band that came into existence very early in the history of the Institute when Booker T. Washington had a very famous military bandsman—Walter Loving—to come down and train the bands. Booker Washington brought in military training very early, and the Tuskegee band was a very famous band in those days. Captain Drye did not organize the band, the band was there. But he was director of the band, and during the time of the music school, you had instructors in clarinet and saxophone, and the reeds—oboe and so on—as well as instructors for the orchestra. Sandra Fletcher Rosemond was there, for instance, and Hazel Harrison taught piano, and there was a woman who taught the organ. Abbie Mitchell taught voice. Orrin Suthern, who is now and has for many years been at Lincoln. Mrs. Patterson, one of the matrons, taught piano, and there were a number of people who taught piano. And I took a course on the history of music and conducting and so on from Mrs. Sultan. And so you had that, and teachers of the various band instruments. So that the band was an established institution with a tradition of its own and a large repertory—that is a large library, some of which was absolutely unusable because you didn't have students of the musicianship at a given year, while at other times you had a well-developed bunch and so you could play just about anything.

O'Meally: *What is the story about you and the Duke Ellington band?*

Ellison: Well, I met Ellington at Tuskegee when the band came there, I guess in '35 or so. In the following year, I was taken by his home, and we went up to Ellington's apartment at 555 Edgecomb Avenue, and Ellington remembered that I had been at Tuskegee. He suggested that I come to rehearsal the next day, and then realized that he couldn't do it.

O'Meally: *And you didn't pursue it any more?*

Ellison: No, I didn't. It would have been rather frightening to have entered that band, and I didn't want to be presumptuous. If he had made the gesture a second time, then I would have gone.

O'Meally: *Public dances are no more. There's not the same sense of communal exchange at a disco, is there?*

Ellison: Well, it's pretty hard to have that kind of exchange with a phonograph. Well, the times have changed, and I think it's unfortunate, because the interchange between the orchestra and a moving audience was quite exciting and creative. It becomes a communal experience, while I guess after bop entered the picture the dancing went out, to a large extent. There used to be groups of people who made the public dance part of a total experience. They went whenever there was a dance, and they knew the musicians, and they knew, in their own way, the various music styles. And they reacted to them. I haven't encountered that in a long time. I guess the last dance that I can remember where there was that kind of excitement was when some rather wealthy people gave a dance in a downtown hotel with the Ellington orchestra. And that was quite wonderful.

O'Meally: *I wonder if we've lost something important without that institution of the jazz dance.*

Ellison: I would think we've lost something important. And I think it came out of a kind of misunderstanding of the institution—some of this on the part of the musicians who began to take themselves too seriously, I guess, in a kind of political way, wanting people simply to sit still and listen to them when they aren't always that exciting, *at best.* And all of the politicizing of jazz, which came with bebop, sort of turned people off. They couldn't follow the beat, and it was no longer as pleasant. Of course, there were economic reasons for the demise of the big bands: the exploiting of musicians by the entertainment industry, the breaking up of bands to promote smaller units, combos, and so on. And playing upon the egos of sidemen who sometimes were good leaders but very often were not. That helped break up the dancing community. It's rather regrettable, I think, that this is a country that puts a lot of stock in novelty. Suddenly something which you think is very permanent is no longer to be found.

O'Meally: *Don't you feel that when it comes to live, danceable music, there's a general feeling that we need to get back something precious that we've lost?*

Ellison: Well, I suppose so, and I rather hope so. I know a couple of the people who were behind "Bubbling Brown Sugar." One of them is the same person who is behind the Kennedy Center, Roger Stevens, who does have an appreciation for the quality of the music, and so does the producer himself. I would think that so much of what happens is up to people of our background; but very often they're so full of ideology—something they call *blackness*—that they don't quite know what to do about it, except sometimes to boast about it. The people who worked in the jazz tradition, the jazz dance tradition, were not ideologists; they were, well, they were *artists.* And their canons of excellence came out of the tradition itself. Now it would seem that we'll have to go back and regain it, but we can only regain it as a conscious effort. When you think of how many men in the Ellington band died off within a decade, or *less* than a decade, you re-alize that the end of something very precious had been reached, with too few people to carry on.

The rock phenomenon sort of engaged the attention of the audience which has always been the audience for jazz— that's young people. That young audience has dispersed. So now if the jazz audience comes back, then it will have to come back in some form which will fit in with the changes. I don't know whether it is possible to have big public dances anymore; whether it's possible to have battles of music which made for so much vitality—certainly in Southwest-ern jazz and here in New York, too, because they used to have battles over at the Savoy Ballroom. One of the worst cultural disasters to hit New York was when they tore down the Savoy Ballroom. And our Harlem people, I mean the *leaders,* didn't consider the Savoy important enough as a cul-tural institution. They don't think of jazz as a *cultural* phe-nomenon, but as "entertainment," which is a narrower term. And so while a library was saved, as it should have been, and churches—I guess we could do without some of them— they tore down one of America's most important cultural institutions, because that's where bands really were pitted against one another, and where the dance styles were devel-oped and brought to a high point of finesse, and where all kinds of artists, black and white, came to learn and to test themselves.

O'Meally: *Haven't these Afro-American dance styles remained vital? What about shows like* Soul Train?

Ellison: They're *awful,* but they're dancing. We watch it from time to time, and some of the things they do are *unbelievable,* but the choreographic skill, the dancing skill is still there, I agree. How to *use* that in a broader way, I don't know. With so many of the *Soul Train* kids, I can see that they're just *liv-ing* to get in front of that camera; they can hardly keep their eyes off it. Of course, that brings up another part of the phenomenon. When they dance together, they don't succeed in being very skillful or very graceful. It's the *acrobatics,* the personal expression that has been the main focus. I'm just hoping that people can get back to dancing face to face again—not to show how funky they are.

O'Meally: *You feel that a style, a grace has just gone out of it.*

Ellison: I think there's a grace that's gone out of it. And I think that a feeling of community, starting with the basic unit of a man and woman, sort of adds to the general communal sense of the dance. And I think it puts the sexual aspect into a proper perspective. It doesn't become sterile. So much of what the kids do is so extreme that it becomes sterile. Now this is no longer a mating dance, and there's always that aspect of dancing. Even ballet is always, in some form, concerned with the sexual. Now with this *Soul Train* kind of thing, the unhealthiness is in its vulgarity. And I'm not talking about clowning; I'm talking about an extreme concentration on the pelvis. And I don't think I'm being prudish about that; I was a belly rubber. But that had a proper *place.* You had to do more than that or no one wanted to dance with you.

O'Meally: *Did your mother encourage your interest in classical music?*

Ellison: She didn't press me on that. I was studying the classics, she knew; and she knew I liked to go to dances and that I liked dance music. She didn't bother about that. It wasn't that kind of pressure at all.

O'Meally: *What was church like at Avery Chapel? Was it a shouting church?*

Ellison: Well, it was not quite a "shouting church," though some people did shout in it. It was an African Methodist Episcopalian church. It was more on the formal side and was considered among the more formal of Oklahoma City's black churches. But it had a choir, it had an organ. The director of the choir did not prefer the spirituals. There was a lot of European music sung—the *Messiah* and such things. It was a rather warm church; you knew everybody, they knew you. The kindergarten that I attended was in the basement of the church. There were college graduates and professional people who were members of the church, members of the board of trustees. It was not the largest church in town; but it owned its own building, it was that kind of thing.

O'Meally: *Did it ever occur to you to be a preacher?*

Ellison: No, no. Hell, I used to sit and just wait 'til I could get out. And I used to have to be punished to make me attend church. We had a youth program—the Sunday evening service for kids. And I didn't like to go at all, but I went because my mother insisted. And she was a stewardess in the church, and very devoted to it. Some days, the Sunday school would serve luncheons on Wednesdays and sometimes on other days, too.

O'Meally: *Did you go through a traumatic conversion experience?*

Ellison: Like Jimmy Baldwin? No, I was baptized in the church, and was quite religious, even until I got to Tuskegee. But I also read a lot. I was a Shavian. So arguments about religion and so on, controversies, I was quite aware of. And thanks to my being a delivery boy, I also saw all *levels* of life; went into all kinds of places. So I developed a sort of skepticism. I was learning the difference between an ideal assertion of religiosity and the many, many ways in which these ideals were violated. I don't know that it led to a loss of respect for the religious leaders, but I realized that they were human beings. It was that kind of experience. But as far as the emotional attachment to religion, I liked some of the sermons, when they were good, when I didn't have anything else to do.

O'Meally: *I recall Buster's line in one of your stories: "Amazing grace, how sweet the sound / A bullfrog slapped my grandma down."*

Ellison: Well, yes, the irreverence toward religious ceremonies—this is an escape valve, of which there's a large body of lore; that is, part of the folklore is given over to telling stories in which the minister is seen in a ridiculous light. But this lore functions to release doubt, and to give it some sort of social expression. And doubt *strengthens.* So we thought these stories, these songs, and jokes very funny. I guess it allowed us to express our dissatisfaction at having to sit still all that time.

O'Meally: *Sometimes I wonder about my students' indifference toward the church.*

Ellison: Well, the church still remains an important institution in most of the United States, as far as Negro Americans are concerned. And if you're not in touch with it, you're in trouble. Fanny and I went to Pittsburgh a few weeks ago. The *Pittsburgh Courier* gave a group of us what are called "top hat" awards. I saw a group of black people, mainly Pittsburghers, and many of them were attached to churches. And this man, Fauntroy of Washington—he was there, and he talked. And I was thinking, "Now, here's a world that I used to see, and be in contact with at least once a week." I'm not anymore. But it still exists, with all of the fancy clothes and so on, it's there. This morning the Seventh Day Adventists are allowed to park their cars down here on the wrong side of the street on Saturday, because their church is up above Broadway and 150th. And when I go up to get the *Times,* I see the styles of the women and the men, the familiar gestures, the decorum and so on. And tomorrow you can go all over Harlem at a certain hour, and you'll see these ladies with their little mink shawls and what-not will be footing it up the hill. And you know they're involved in an institution which has been there for a long time. Fabulous as they are, some of those buildings have been owned by them for years and years. And a great part of these people's attitude toward society depends on what goes on in those churches. And if the kids have no contact with it, then that's certainly a loss of continuity. I wonder what they think of the fact that politicians, millionaires, all kinds of people maintain a connection with churches. In Washington, those churches aren't empty on Sunday. And there you have all those other institutions. And what of the fact that at least one of the few American heroes out of the sixties was a minister—overlooking Adam Powell—who was a very influential man. I was here. I was walking the picket lines back during the thirties and forties when we went down to Washington. This should tell us something. And Malcolm X had to get certain speech patterns from religion, before he became a spokesman.

O'Meally: *Malcolm spoke in the style of a preacher.*

Ellison: That plus the barbershop.

O'Meally: *The barbershop?*

Ellison: Well, much of his rhetoric was just barbershop rhetoric. You know, you could blow it *down* if you wanted to, if you wanted to engage in it on that level. People were just bamboozled into thinking that the stuff he said was being said for the first time. And you could hear the same kind of shooting off of the mouth in pool halls and barbershops all over the country. What was new about it was the place where he said it, which was on television. Which is fine; I wouldn't take anything away from it; but as a student of culture, I would be remiss if I didn't recognize that this is a barbershop kind of rhetoric. The slaves used to call it "barking at the big gate," with the implication that like a dog barking at the big gate, if someone came in you would *cut out.*

Seriously, I did find the sort of deification of Malcolm X rather strange and uncritical: giving him credit for a certain kind of effectiveness. I *don't* think that he was the intellectual leader that so many people want to take him for. He was a kind of *exhorter.* And that was all to the good; he raised a certain kind of consciousness, but he also stressed a sort of narrowness of vision which, taken literally, got a lot of people into trouble; and maybe a few *dead.* The Panthers, these militants who spoke of the gun every time you came around, didn't realize how vulnerable they were. They were taken in by kinds of techniques which the slaves learned years and years ago to deal with. And I think that's *deplorable,* and one reason that they were vulnerable is that they talked so much about things that they could have *done* more effectively if they hadn't been yakking so much. You cannot challenge a great nation on that level. And you certainly can't challenge the United States that way, because there are too many violent people who want to do *nothing but kill blacks!* There's a *tradition* for that. Our parents knew it. They weren't *afraid.* They were afraid of getting the white folks afraid! And that's a wisdom that was lost during the sixties, and it caused a lot of death.

O'Meally: *What has become of your Federal Writers Project work?*
Ellison: I don't know what happened to that material. Roi Ottley used some of it. I never did any finished writing. But I did do a lot of research, and tried to offer interpretation, which more likely than not he would reject. He didn't see what I saw or what I thought I saw. He was the supervisor of the project, and did most of the rewriting, but he very often lost the point as far as I was concerned.

O'Meally: *Do you remember working on "Chase the White Horse"?*
Ellison: Yes, I worked on the folklore project. And I do know some edition of the *Journal of the American Folklore Society* published some of the rhymes that I had collected. But I had collected a lot of other stuff. I went to, I would say, hundreds of apartments, talking to people, adults as well as children. The concentration was on play-rhymes, games, and songs, and things. I exchanged stories with people, and so on. I was working for myself as well as for the Project, to see what I could pick up. But I carried out the assignments: I gave them all the folklore and the games, and rhymes that I could find.

O'Meally: *Were you able to use that, consciously, in your work?*
Ellison: Oh, not necessarily. I worked out of a *sense* of this folk material and what it means. No, there was very little *direct* use. For instance, High John the Conqueror was a mythical figure. High John the Conqueror is the name for *lodestone,* which people wore in little bags, and so on—people

wore it as a charm. But someone else mentioned Peter Wheatstraw as the man who took the name of a blues singer; but Peter Wheatstraw is a *mythological* figure that any number of people are *named* because they possess certain qualities. There's been a lot of confusion about this, which is so interesting, because there again you find a discontinuity. People of a generation ago would have known that these were just figures like Jack-the-Bear—a folk figure, whose name and exploits got to be credited to some living person.

O'Meally: *Was the Communist Party for you a "god that failed"?*

Ellison: Well, for me the party was not by any means a god. I didn't have that involvement that Wright had, I didn't have that stake in it. I had seen other things. This was a matter of difference in background as well as of personality. But at the time the party promised me the availability of association which was important not only to me but to any number of young intellectuals, black and white—that part can't be denied. I knew all kinds of people and I got the chance to find out how they thought and to compare my own experience with theirs. And very often I found that their reactions came out of an experience which was far simpler than mine, and that their view of the United States and of culture was simplistic. I first questioned whether I wasn't wrong, and if there was something wrong with me, but finally I had to fall back on my own experience: "Well now, this isn't it. You're leaving out too much."

But see, I never had the feeling that I couldn't make it in the world as it existed then, whether as a musician—and I was thinking of myself as a musician during that period—or as a writer. (Well, I hadn't started writing. I really started writing after 1938. Then I was on the Project, and that made becoming a writer a possibility. I was doing their work during the day and my own work at night. I was writing stories and essays and I began to publish. I published my first stuff right at the beginning in 1937 with Wright, and then I published in *New Masses* and a number of other places.) But before I finished high school I had been offered a job directing a band at the reformatory for Negro boys at Foley. So that gave me enough confidence to know that I could teach. I had already been giving trumpet lessons to one younger boy. But I had no sense of being backed up so firmly against the wall as Wright seems to have had or chose to have had. The people that I worked around and I grew up around were relatively successful people. They owned their own homes. They were professional people or they were jazz musicians who were famous in their own *section* if not nationally.

O'Meally: *Why didn't Wright draw upon the richness in his black folk background?*

Ellison: Maybe he didn't have the same kind of experience. It's a mystery to me, because he always had an ideological explanation for his life. Maybe my approach was ideological, too, but it certainly wasn't Communist ideology. I really don't know, but perhaps Wright's having been a Seventh Day Adventist in a place where most people were Baptist and Methodist may have been a factor. Maybe a very strict grandmother or something. But for all of his having come from Mississippi, he didn't know a lot of the folklore. And although he tried to write a blues, he knew nothing about that or jazz. He didn't dance. It was not part of his experience.

O'Meally: *Uncle Tom's Children is full of folklore, though. Why did he choose not to use folklore later?*

Ellison: It's a real question for criticism. Certain attitudes were stated—even in *Black Boy*—certain attitudes where what he called the "bleakness of life" was stressed. And this negative assessment of black folk life simply isn't *true.* He seems to have stylized his attitudes toward the folklore of that time. Maybe he'd made certain decisions about it, and decided that the folk stuff did not work, I don't know. We read a lot of Gorki. He was reading Gorki, I was reading Gorki, and a lot of the other Russians and so on. And certainly in none of that writing do you get the failure to stress the vitality of peasant background. So it's a mystery.

O'Meally: *Do I overstress your use of folklore in* Invisible Man?

Ellison: You might well have overstressed it in terms of *conscious* use. When you're trying to create characters you're not really thinking of the raw materials. Any raw material that I consider folklore and such would come into focus and would be drawn into the characters themselves. I wouldn't just say, "Well, I'm going to use folklore." The folklore would come out of certain types of people or certain situations wherein I could dramatize the meaning of folklore in terms of a specific situation. In the hospital scene, Invisible Man was working back to his memory, and folk identities would be important. When he runs into the man on the street—the ragman or whatever—the challenge of the past in terms of folk material seems to be meaningful.

O'Meally: *Someone has told me that Dupree is a folk character.*

Ellison: Well, Dupree has turned up in folk narratives: there's the "Dupree Blues" and so on. Sometimes you use a name because it *sounds* right. But what this guy does—I don't know of any folk character who's gone and organized a building burning.

O'Meally: *Have you considered making* Invisible Man *into a movie?*

Ellison: That's just a rumor. People have approached me about doing a movie. But no one has come up with enough money. I'm not particularly interested in making *Invisible Man* into a movie. But I've talked with people over the years who've been interested . . . John Lewis of the Modern Jazz Quartet has been interested in doing an opera. But I don't know what's happened. I don't know if he did anything about it. As far as a movie is concerned, no one yet has satisfied me that they really have what it takes to do it.

O'Meally: *How have you felt about the reaction to* Invisible Man *by people like LeRoi Jones/Baraka?*

Ellison: Well, they can yak at *Invisible Man* all they want to;

it's still *here*. Oh, god. No, you know, you get annoyed, because you feel that some of the attacks made on the novel are made by people who've never read the book. I arrived a long time ago at the place they now claim they want to reach! And as far as using what comes out of our particular experience and treating it with what I thought was dignity, and certainly with love, I did that. So that all the howling— first it annoyed me and then I ceased to pay any attention. And Baraka—in one case, out of Harlem, was calling on me, trying to see if I couldn't get him some *money* to operate on. I never had any quarrel with these people. But they found me the convenient whipping boy; so I figured, well, I guess every group has to have one.

O'Meally: *Why the violent reactions? For instance, how do you explain the reaction of John Killens, who has called* Invisible Man *a betrayal of the black community? He told me that* Invisible Man *wants to be white.*

Ellison: He never read the book if he thinks that. And as far as the other statement, the narrator proclaims that he doesn't want to be forced to be white. Keep up with this conformity business and everybody will turn out to be gray. And, well, what do you do? Why do these people keep arguing about a book? I don't see the point. Go on and write other books! They don't realize that part of the irony of the book is that certain things were bad for us because we were of *high* visibility. That's one of the basic ironies in the damn title. But I don't know what to do about it. They want to stay in a certain groove, and that's their privilege. They come up with all kinds of exotic aesthetics, and then you read their work, and they've been influenced by all kinds of people— not particularly black people.

O'Meally: *What have you thought of Addison Gayle's "new black aesthetic critics"?*

Ellison: Oh, *god!* What kind of . . . you know, I can't take that *seriously*! He has to block out too much, to blind himself to too much in order to take that position. I'll say this: if they come up with good books, good poems, good dramas, and so on—fine. Let them do it. What I want to see is great art, or at least good art in the name of whatever ideology. But to keep beating on that particular note doesn't say anything to me. It wouldn't help me get *my* work done.

O'Meally: *How have you felt about Africa as an influence on modern writers?*

Ellison: It's fine for them. If that's what it is—good. Now, this house is full of African art. I've been collecting African art for years, buying the best that I could. That little Bioly figure over there on the left of that cabinet I've had—oh, I don't know *how* long—twenty-five, maybe thirty years. And I've had an interest in African art. But as far as identifying with Africa, I've *never* identified with Africa. Now, I'm not denying my Afro-blood at *all*. But there's a complex mass of cultures over there. I can hardly remember the tribes these figures represent and I live with these things every day. So I wouldn't get any strength from that. My strength comes from Louis Armstrong and Jimmy Rushing, Hot Lips Page and people on that level, Duke Ellington, Mrs. Breaux, Mark Twain—all kinds of American figures who have been influenced by and contributed to that complex interaction of background and cultures which is specifically *American*.

O'Meally: *Is it important to stress* Afro-*American? Is it contradictory?*

Ellison: It's not contradictory. Much of what's called white American culture wouldn't be what it is without us. And we don't know where we sound and where we stand and where we are visible in the best of American culture. We've been more segregated than the white folks actually intended us to be! If I can't read the best of American literature and recognize where it's been influenced by our presence, and our forms of expression, then I shouldn't call myself a critic. I shouldn't call myself a writer.

O'Meally: *Let's go back to Tuskegee for a moment: Were you regarded as kind of a renegade there?*

Ellison: No, look, any attitude of resentment that I aroused came from manner and a certain strangeness about me, not because I was considered a renegade. And the attitudes about me were very mixed. There were some people who were part of the old Booker Washington background who thought very highly of me, people who liked to talk to me and invited me to their homes. It shouldn't be overlooked that I was student director of the band, and that I played in the jazz orchestra. So I had that mixed thing where some people didn't care for me and others found me a threat for various reasons. But I had my own admirers. And if I was unhappy it had much to do with my expecting much more than the school could offer, and my having to work so damn hard to stay there. I had no run-ins with Dr. Moton or Dr. Patterson.

O'Meally: *None with Dean Neely or Dawson?*

Ellison: Neely—I had run-ins with Neely, but no lines or anything from my exchanges with Neely, and there were very few, are in *Invisible Man*. They steered you wrong on that.

O'Meally: *Was the clash because you were a Southwesterner?*

Ellison: I think that had something to do with it, and also my being more of an obvious intellectual as against the great stress upon "the trades" as they were called. Neely didn't care for the intellectual type at all. He thought that students should be *farmers,* and he said as much to me, "You should be out on the ag-side learning something!" Well, I just didn't have that interest and I certainly wasn't going to let Neely or anybody else push me from the goal that I'd set for myself.

And as far as Dawson was concerned, my conflict had to do with his feeling that you should come to him as if you had no background in music. And I had had nothing *but* music, and that made for conflict during that first week. But when Dawson wanted special things done with that chapel orchestra, he would pull me out of my trumpet chair, and give me the job. I played cymbals in the percussion section in one big program that he had, because he felt that I was the person who knew how to give him the effect that he needed at a certain time. I've had Dawson call me down for carrying so many books around and reading so many other things; but then turn right around and cuss the other members of the class out because they *didn't* do so. So it's a complex thing—part of it being a clash in, shall we say, cultural styles. But looking back, it was no more unpleasant a college experience than you would get anywhere else.

O'Meally: *I hesitate to ask about the new novel.*

Ellison: No, I won't talk about it. I'm still working on it.

List of Permissions

About the Author

RALPH ELLISON was born in Oklahoma City in 1914. He was educated at the Frederick Douglass School and at Tuskegee Institute, where he studied the trumpet and music composition. Ellison moved to New York City in 1936 and lived in Harlem until his death in 1994. His novel *Invisible Man* (1952) was the winner of the National Book Award and one of the most important and influential American novels of the twentieth century. Ellison was elected to the American Academy of Arts and Letters in 1975 and was awarded the National Medal of Arts in 1985.

About the Editor

Robert G. O'Meally is the Zora Neale Hurston Professor of Comparative Literature at Columbia University and the founder and director of the Center for Jazz Studies. He is a leading interpreter of the dynamics of jazz in American culture. O'Meally is the author of several books, including *Lady Day: The Many Faces of Billie Holiday* and *The Craft of Ralph Ellison*. He edited *The Jazz Cadence of American Culture*, which won an ASCAP–Deems Taylor Award. In 1999, he received a Grammy nomination for his work as coproducer of the five-CD set *The Jazz Singers*. He lives in New York.

A Note on the Type

The principal text of this Modern Library edition was set in a
digitized version of Janson, a typeface that dates from about
1690 and was cut by Nicholas Kis, a Hungarian working in
Amsterdam. The original matrices have survived and are held
by the Stempel foundry in Germany. Hermann Zapf
redesigned some of the weights and sizes for Stempel, basing
his revisions on the original design.

MODERN LIBRARY IS ONLINE AT
WWW.MODERNLIBRARY.COM

MODERN LIBRARY ONLINE IS YOUR GUIDE
TO CLASSIC LITERATURE ON THE WEB

THE MODERN LIBRARY E-NEWSLETTER

Our free e-mail newsletter is sent to subscribers, and features sample chapters, interviews with and essays by our authors, upcoming books, special promotions, announcements, and news.

To subscribe to the Modern Library e-newsletter, send a blank e-mail to: **sub_modernlibrary@info.randomhouse.com** or visit **www.modernlibrary.com**

THE MODERN LIBRARY WEBSITE

Check out the Modern Library website at
www.modernlibrary.com for:

- The Modern Library e-newsletter
- A list of our current and upcoming titles and series
- Reading Group Guides and exclusive author spotlights
- Special features with information on the classics and other paperback series
- Excerpts from new releases and other titles
- A list of our e-books and information on where to buy them
- The Modern Library Editorial Board's 100 Best Novels and 100 Best Nonfiction Books of the Twentieth Century written in the English language
- News and announcements

Questions? E-mail us at **modernlibrary@randomhouse.com**.
For questions about examination or desk copies, please visit
the Random House Academic Resources site at
www.randomhouse.com/academic

Printed in the United States
by Baker & Taylor Publisher Services